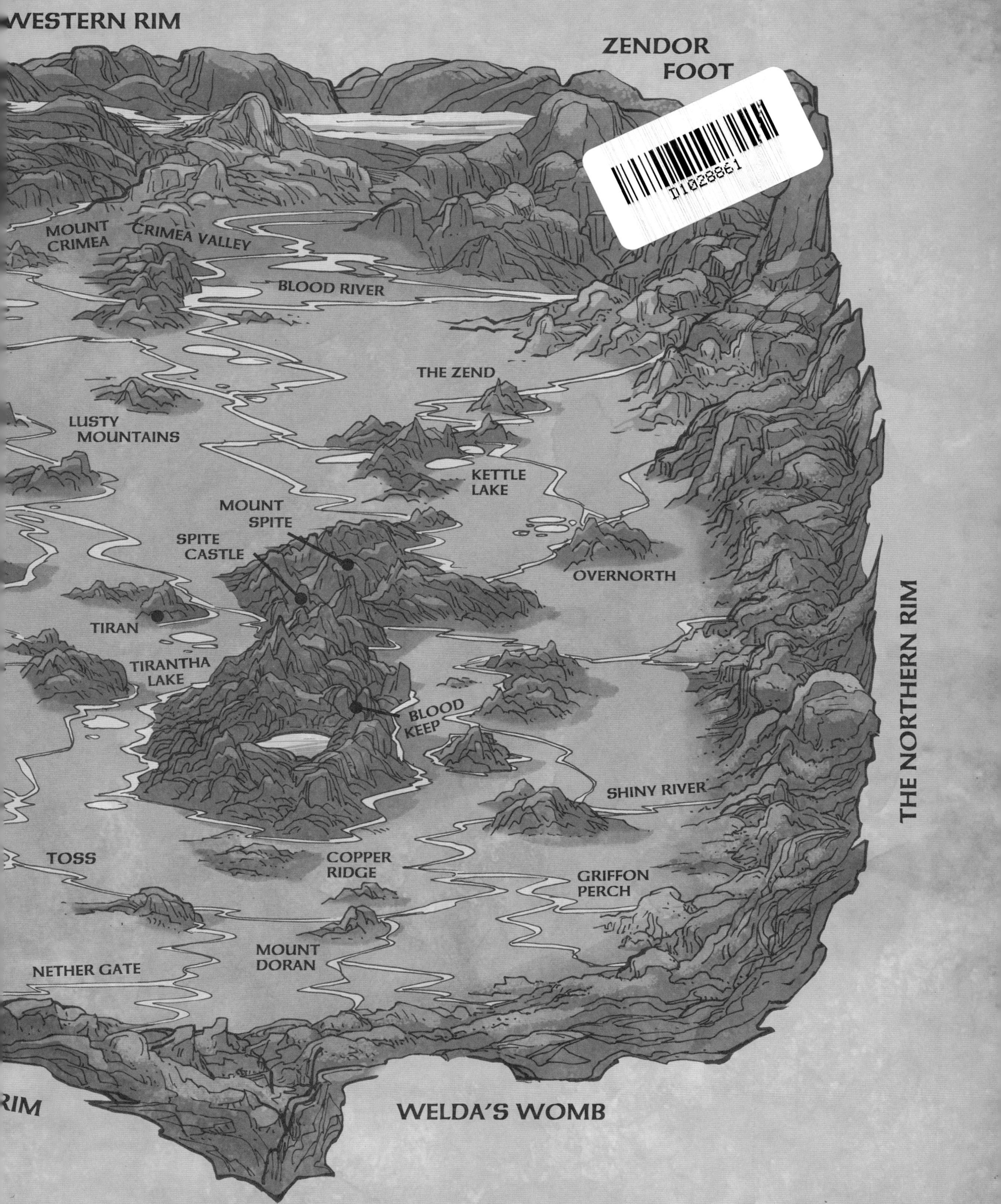

WESTERN RIM
ZENDOR
FOOT
MOUNT
CRIMEA
CRIMEA VALLEY
BLOOD RIVER
THE ZEND
LUSTY
MOUNTAINS
KETTLE
LAKE
MOUNT
SPITE
SPITE
CASTLE
OVERNORTH
TIRAN
TIRANTHA
LAKE
BLOOD
KEEP
THE NORTHERN RIM
SHINY RIVER
TOSS
COPPER
RIDGE
GRIFFON
PERCH
MOUNT
DORAN
NETHER GATE
RIM
WELDA'S WOMB

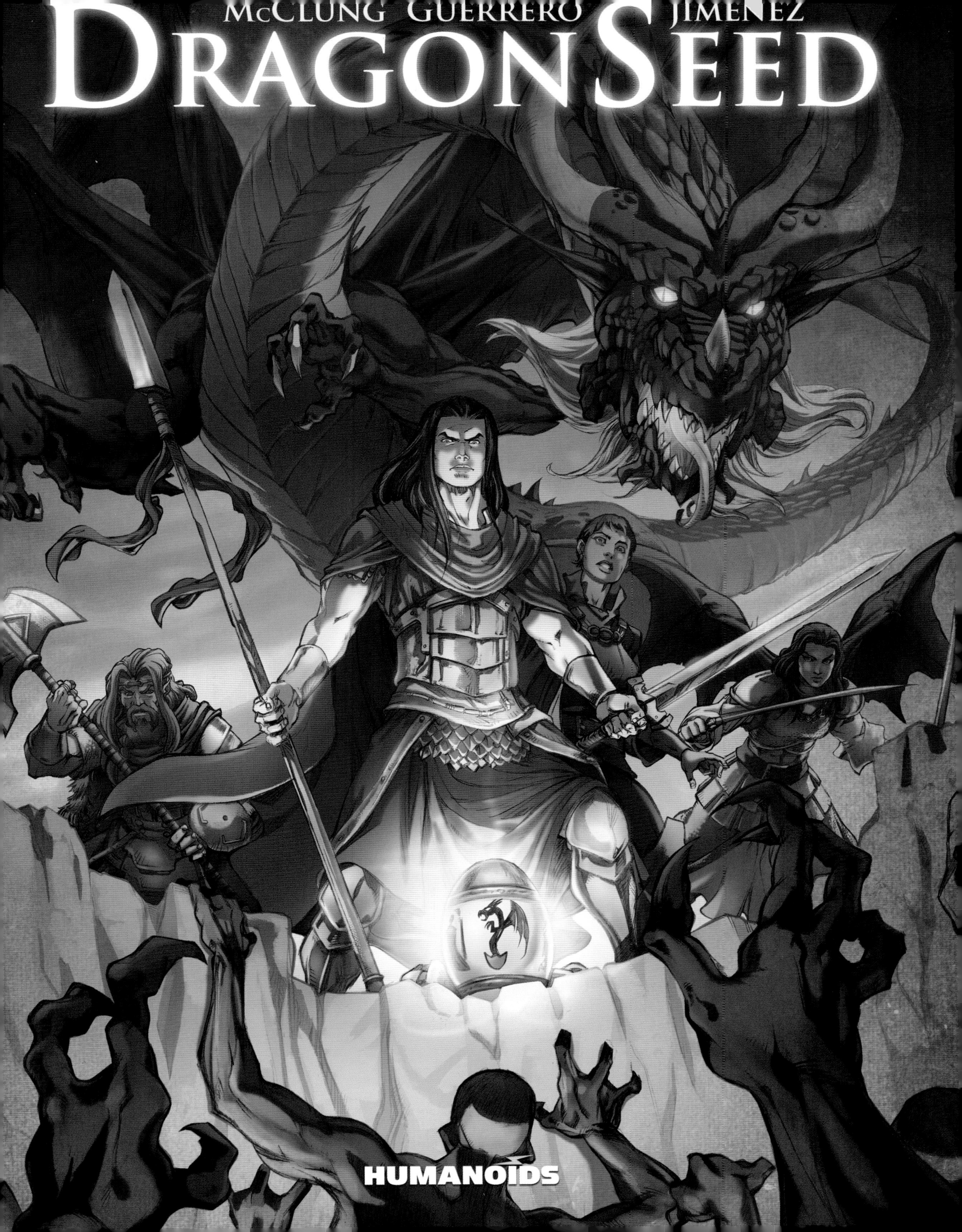
McCLUNG GUERRERO JIMENEZ
DRAGONSEED
HUMANOIDS

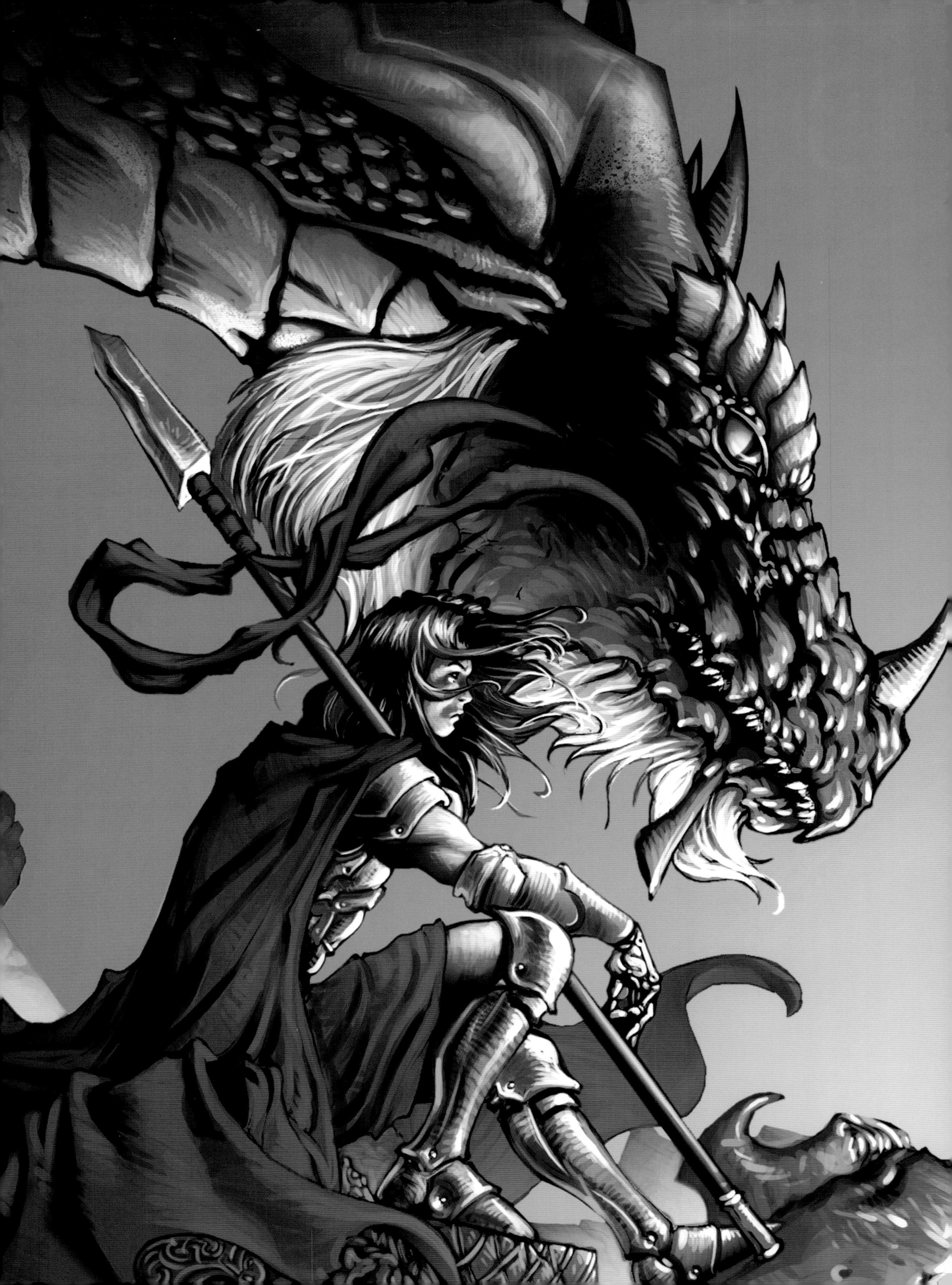

KURT McCLUNG
Writer

MATEO GUERRERO
Artist

AURE JIMENEZ
Inker (pages 5 to 112)

JOSE MARIA REYES PARRA
(pages 5 to 58)
STUDIO KM ZÉRO: COSIMO LORENZO PANCINI,
LINDA CAVALLINI, SAMANTHA ALGATI,
& NAOMI MALLEGNI
(Pages 59 to 112)
JOËLLE COMTOIS
assisted by **VALÉRIE MARTINEAU**
(Pages 113 to 166, cover and title page)
JAVIER MARTIN
(Backcover)
Colorists

JERRY FRISSEN
Senior Art Director

TIM PILCHER &
ALEX DONOGHUE
U.S. Edition Editors

FABRICE GIGER
Publisher

Rights & Licensing - licensing@humanoids.com
Press and Social Media - pr@humanoids.com

DRAGONSEED. This title is a publication of Humanoids, Inc. 8033 Sunset Blvd. #628, Los Angeles, CA 90046.

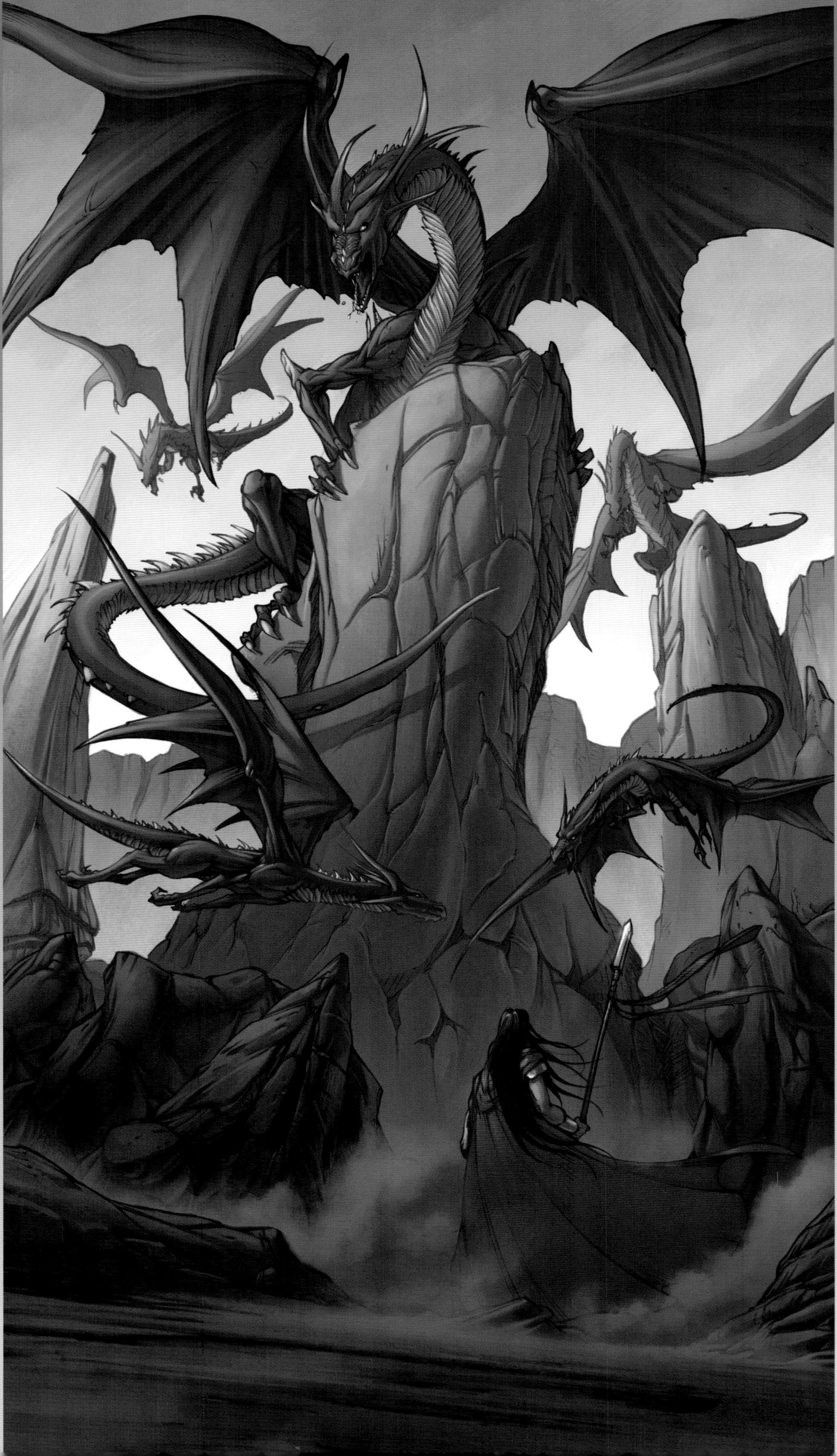

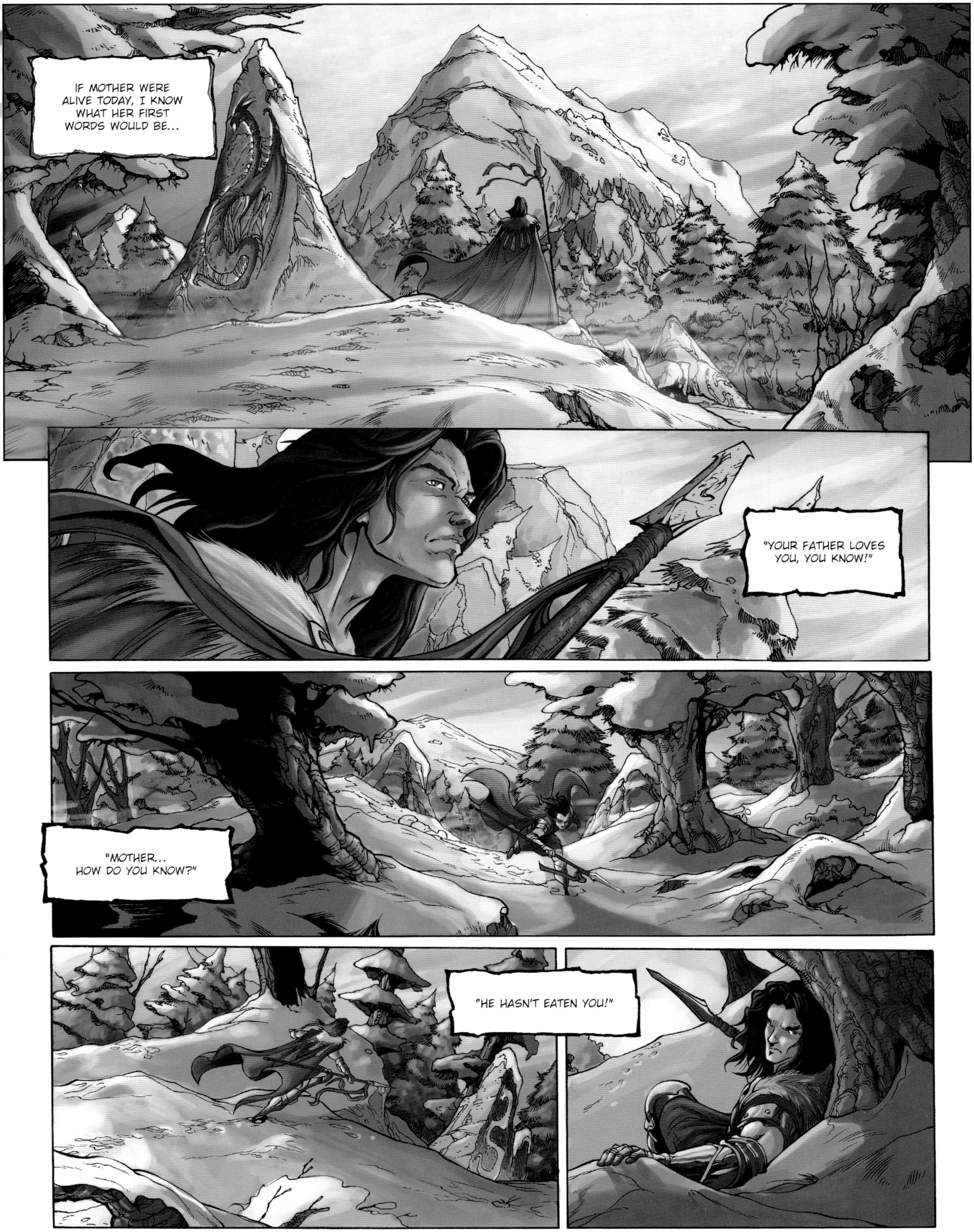
IF MOTHER WERE ALIVE TODAY, I KNOW WHAT HER FIRST WORDS WOULD BE...
"YOUR FATHER LOVES YOU, YOU KNOW!"
"MOTHER... HOW DO YOU KNOW?"
"HE HASN'T EATEN YOU!"

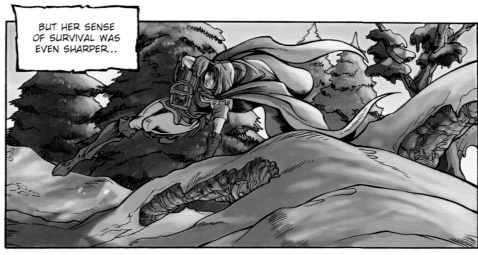

BUT HER SENSE OF SURVIVAL WAS EVEN SHARPER...

MY MOTHER HAD QUITE THE SENSE OF HUMOR.

...ESPECIALLY IN MATTERS CONCERNING THE HEART. FATHER HADN'T EATEN HER EITHER.

WHAT HAVE WE HERE...?

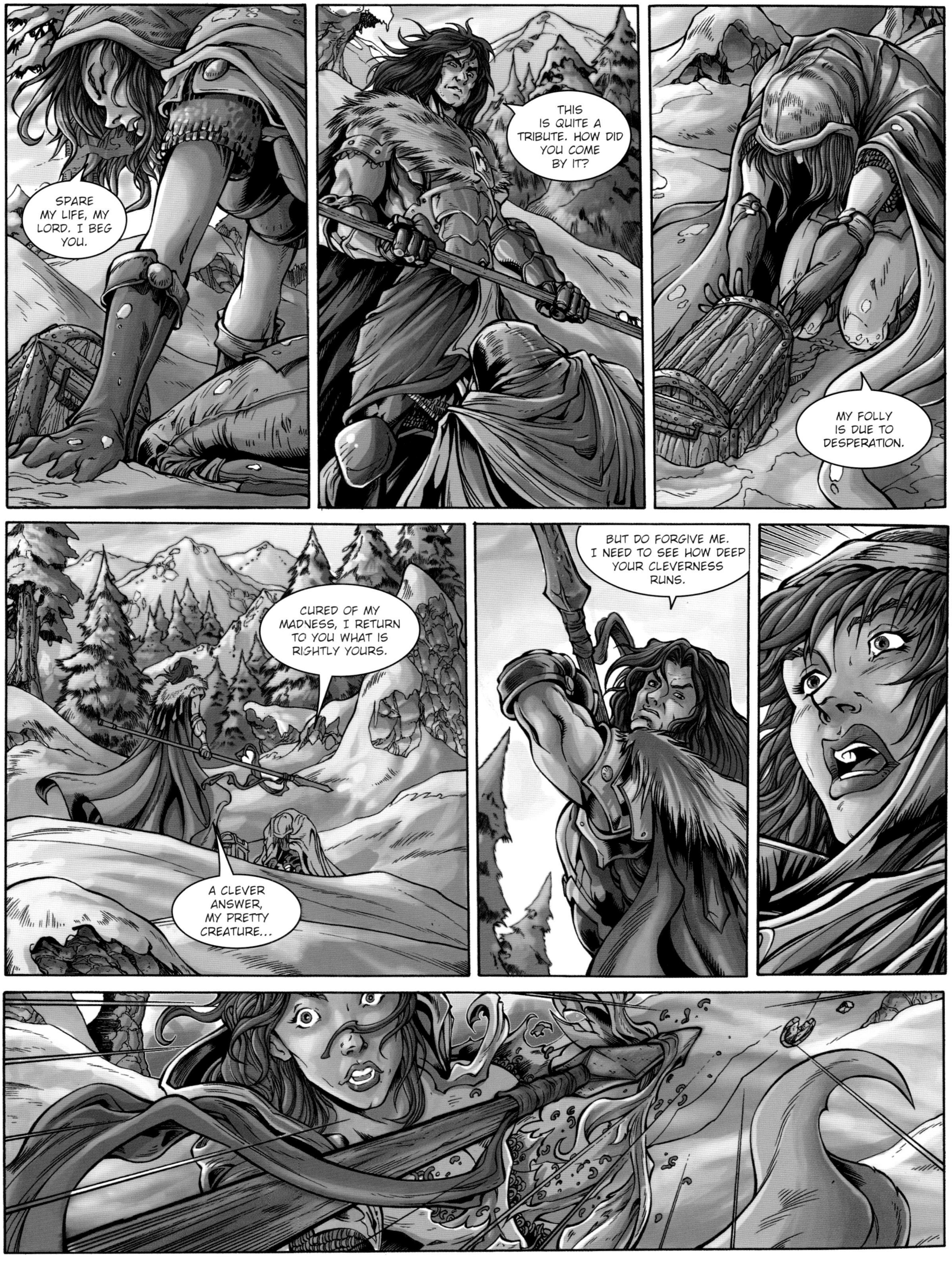
SPARE MY LIFE, MY LORD. I BEG YOU.
THIS IS QUITE A TRIBUTE. HOW DID YOU COME BY IT?
MY FOLLY IS DUE TO DESPERATION.
CURED OF MY MADNESS, I RETURN TO YOU WHAT IS RIGHTLY YOURS.
A CLEVER ANSWER, MY PRETTY CREATURE...
BUT DO FORGIVE ME. I NEED TO SEE HOW DEEP YOUR CLEVERNESS RUNS.

MERCY... PLEASE...

RULE FOR THE WISE...

THE HONOR CODE OF THIEVES WAS INVENTED TO BETTER LINE THEIR POCKETS.

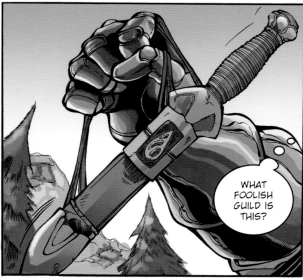

WHAT FOOLISH GUILD IS THIS?

BUT YOU ARE NOT THE FIRST THIEF I'VE... REVEALED.

POCKETS ARE LIKE SECRETS.

TO KNOW TRULY WHAT THEY HIDE YOU MUST TURN THEM OUTSIDE IN.

8

THE NEXT TIME I SEE YOU ON MY MOUNTAIN, MY SWEET...

...I'LL BE INCLINED TO CHECK WITH DEEPER SCRUTINY.

LOVE IS A COMPLEX POWER.

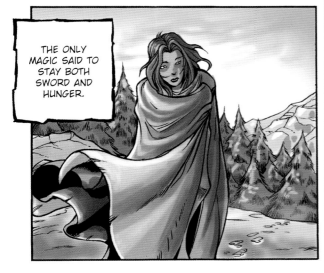

THE ONLY MAGIC SAID TO STAY BOTH SWORD AND HUNGER.

IT CAN INSPIRE YOU TO SHOW MERCY...

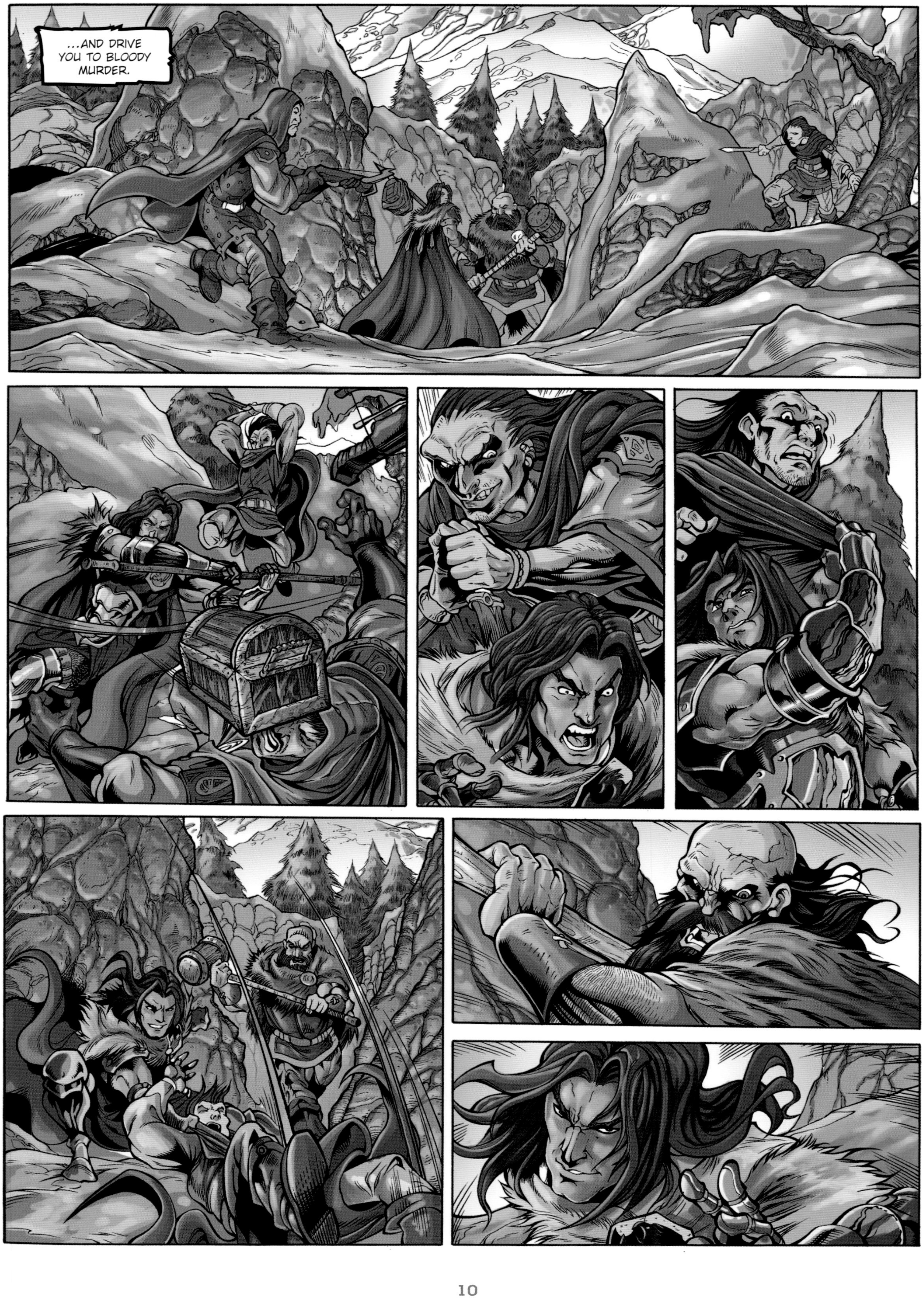
...AND DRIVE YOU TO BLOODY MURDER.

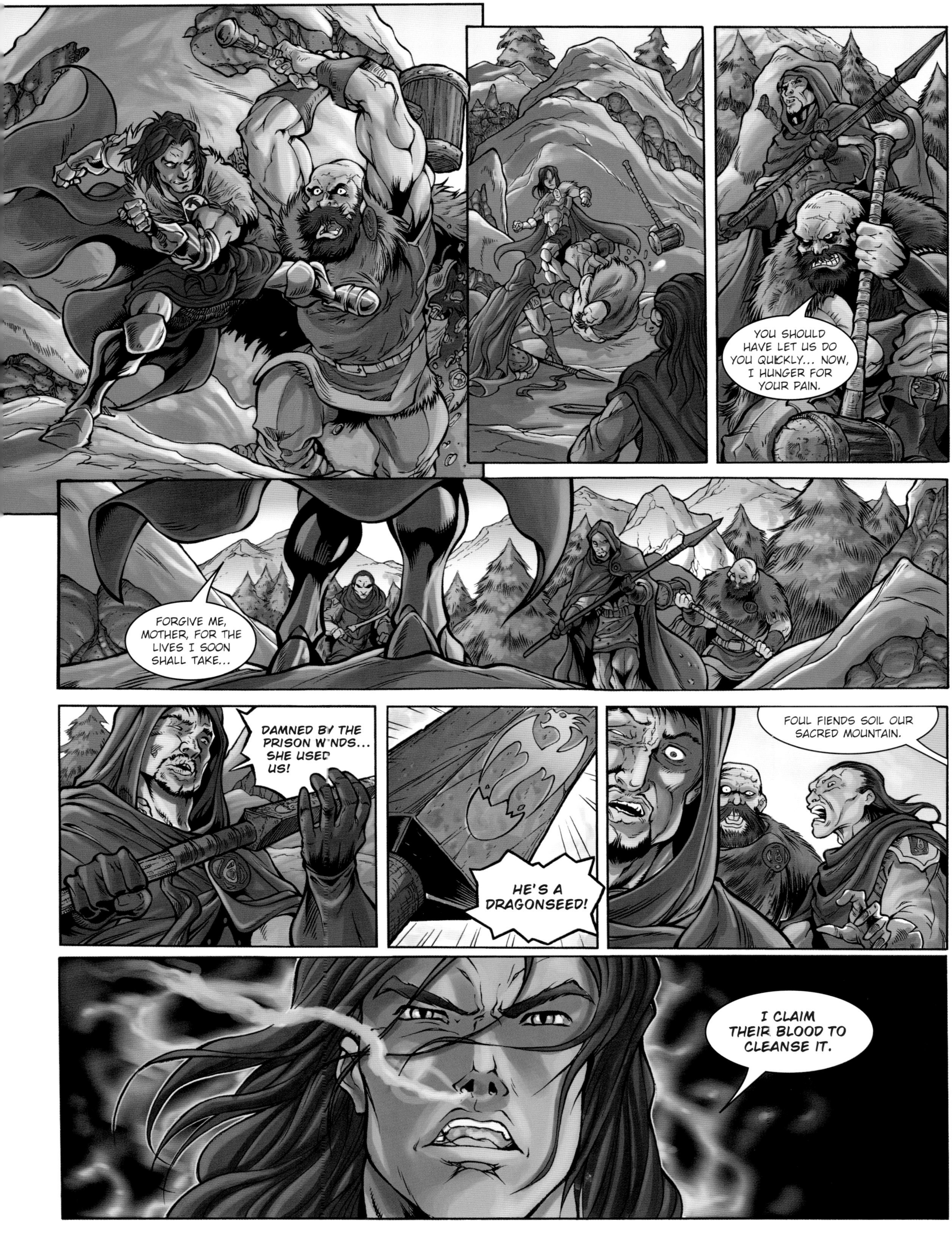
YOU SHOULD HAVE LET US DO YOU QUICKLY... NOW, I HUNGER FOR YOUR PAIN.
FORGIVE ME, MOTHER, FOR THE LIVES I SOON SHALL TAKE...
DAMNED BY THE PRISON WINDS... SHE USED US!
HE'S A DRAGONSEED!
FOUL FIENDS SOIL OUR SACRED MOUNTAIN.
I CLAIM THEIR BLOOD TO CLEANSE IT.

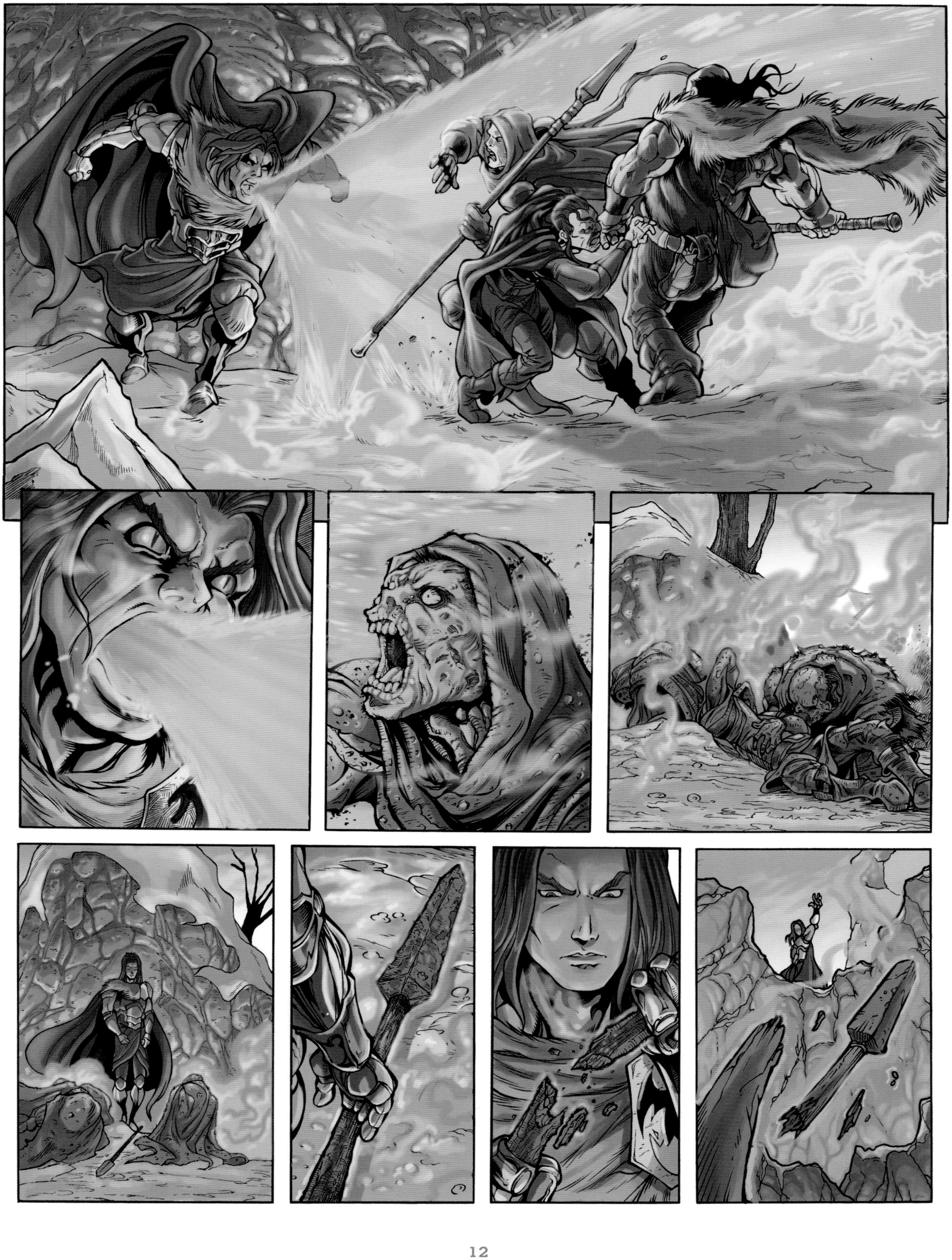

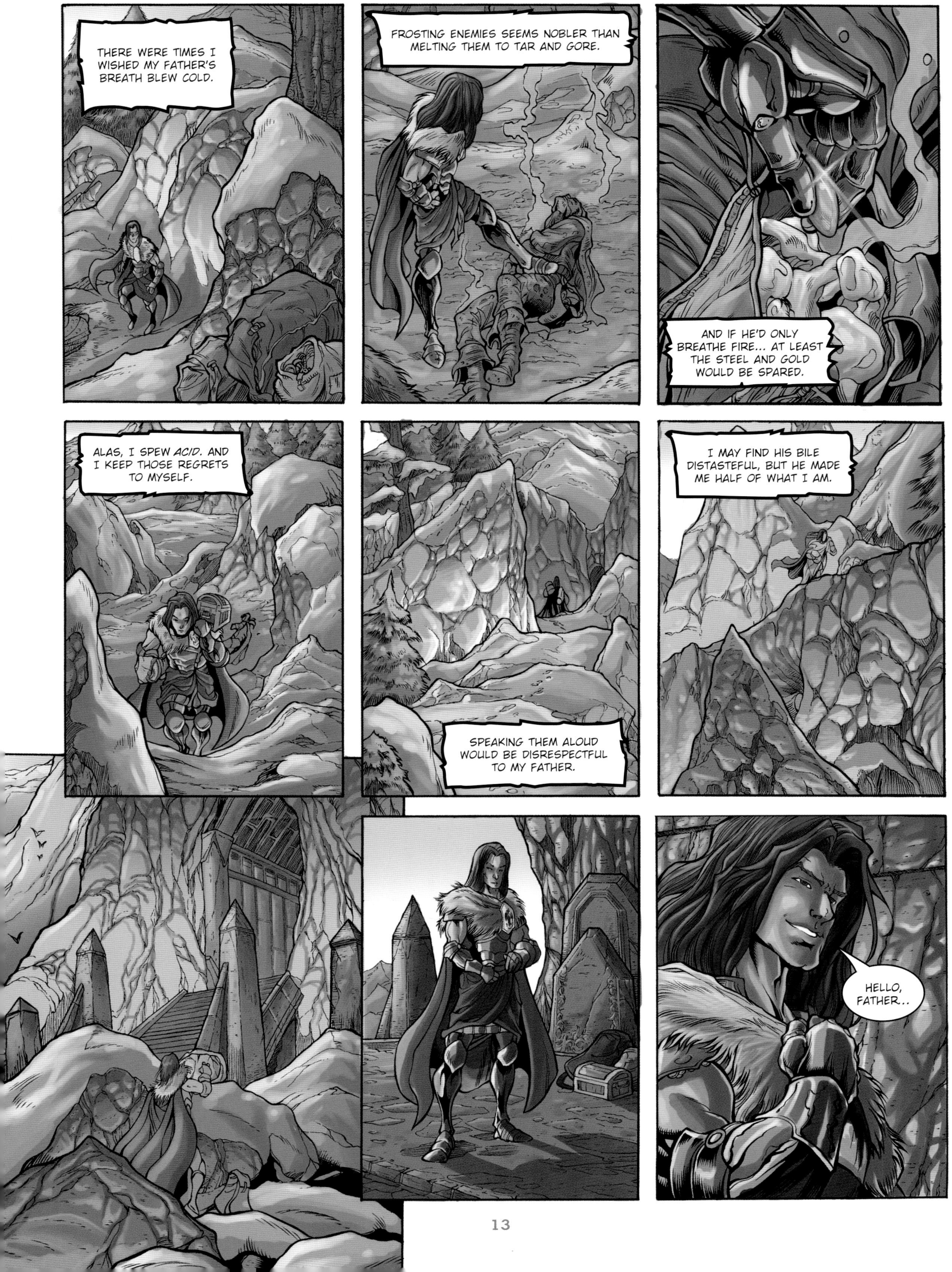

THERE WERE TIMES I WISHED MY FATHER'S BREATH BLEW COLD.
FROSTING ENEMIES SEEMS NOBLER THAN MELTING THEM TO TAR AND GORE.
AND IF HE'D ONLY BREATHE FIRE... AT LEAST THE STEEL AND GOLD WOULD BE SPARED.
ALAS, I SPEW *ACID*. AND I KEEP THOSE REGRETS TO MYSELF.
SPEAKING THEM ALOUD WOULD BE DISRESPECTFUL TO MY FATHER.
I MAY FIND HIS BILE DISTASTEFUL, BUT HE MADE ME HALF OF WHAT I AM.
HELLO, FATHER...

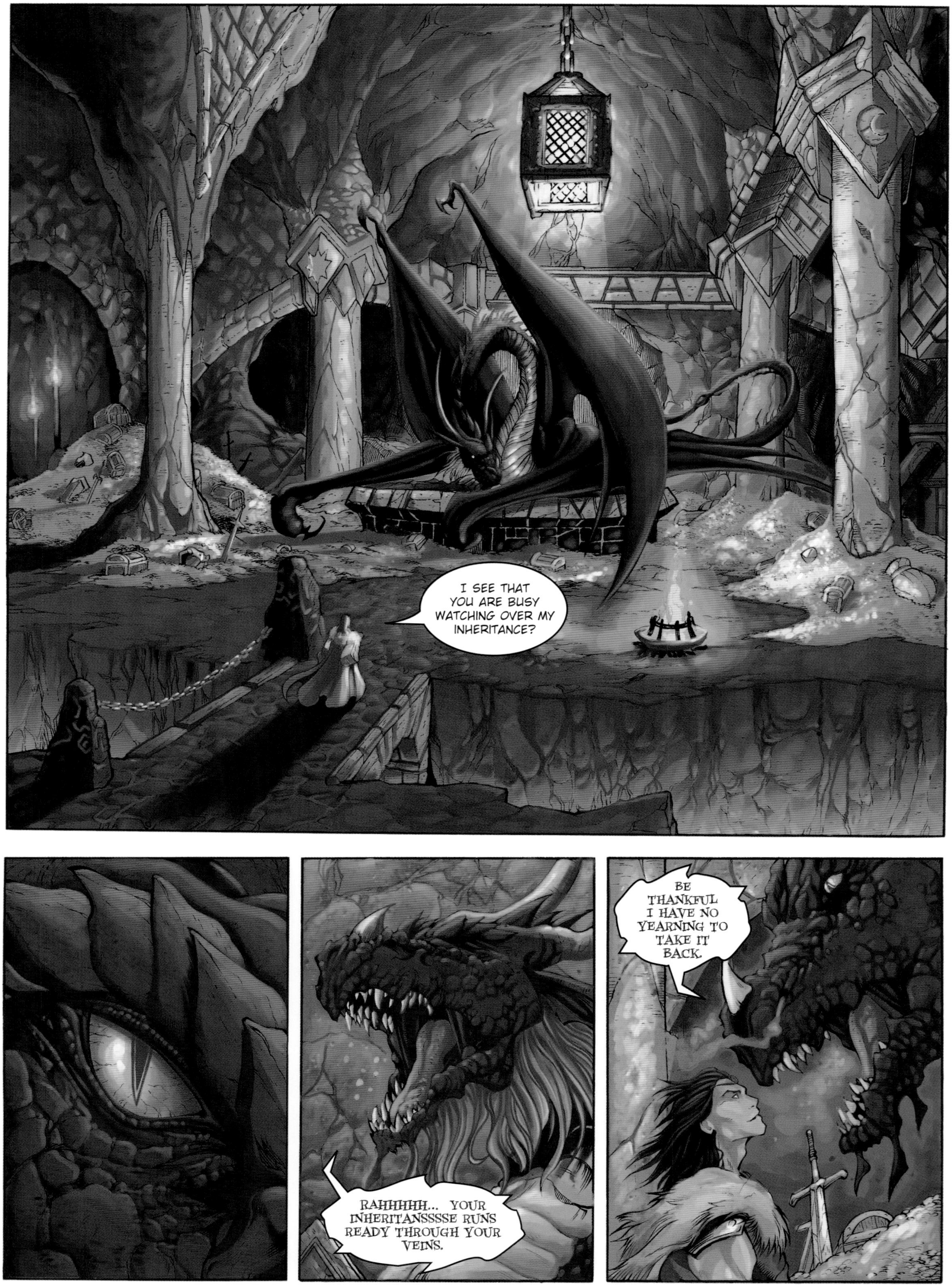
I SEE THAT YOU ARE BUSY WATCHING OVER MY INHERITANCE?
RAHHHHH... YOUR INHERITANSSSSE RUNS READY THROUGH YOUR VEINS.
BE THANKFUL I HAVE NO YEARNING TO TAKE IT BACK.

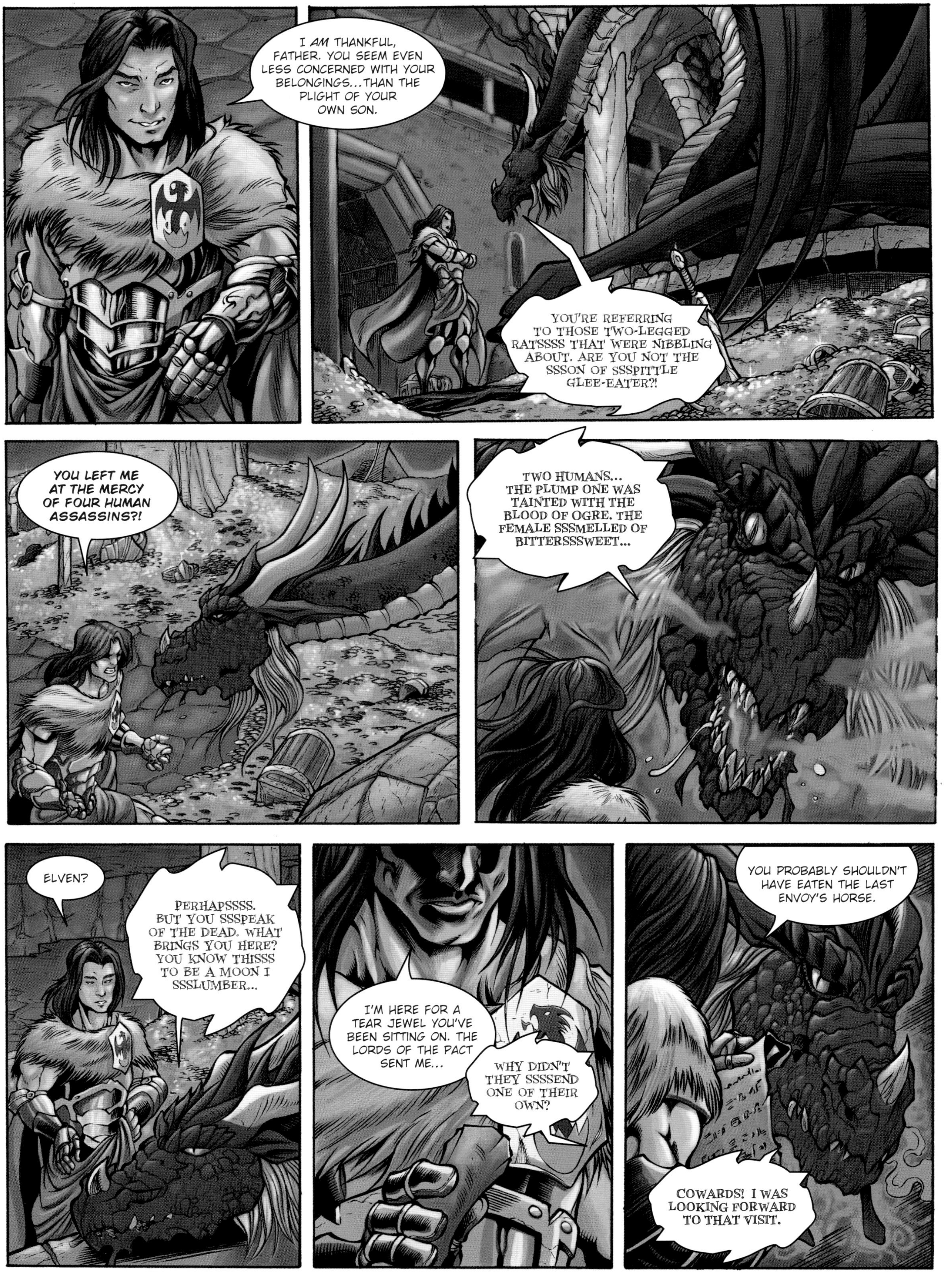
I *AM* THANKFUL, FATHER. YOU SEEM EVEN LESS CONCERNED WITH YOUR BELONGINGS...THAN THE PLIGHT OF YOUR OWN SON.
YOU'RE REFERRING TO THOSE TWO-LEGGED RATSSSS THAT WERE NIBBLING ABOUT. ARE YOU NOT THE SSSON OF SSSPITTLE GLEE-EATER?!
YOU LEFT ME AT THE MERCY OF FOUR HUMAN ASSASSINS?!
TWO HUMANS... THE PLUMP ONE WAS TAINTED WITH THE BLOOD OF OGRE. THE FEMALE SSSMELLED OF BITTERSSSWEET...
ELVEN?
PERHAPSSSS. BUT YOU SSSPEAK OF THE DEAD. WHAT BRINGS YOU HERE? YOU KNOW THISSS TO BE A MOON I SSSLUMBER...
I'M HERE FOR A TEAR JEWEL YOU'VE BEEN SITTING ON. THE LORDS OF THE PACT SENT ME...
WHY DIDN'T THEY SSSSEND ONE OF THEIR OWN?
YOU PROBABLY SHOULDN'T HAVE EATEN THE LAST ENVOY'S HORSE.
COWARDS! I WAS LOOKING FORWARD TO THAT VISIT.

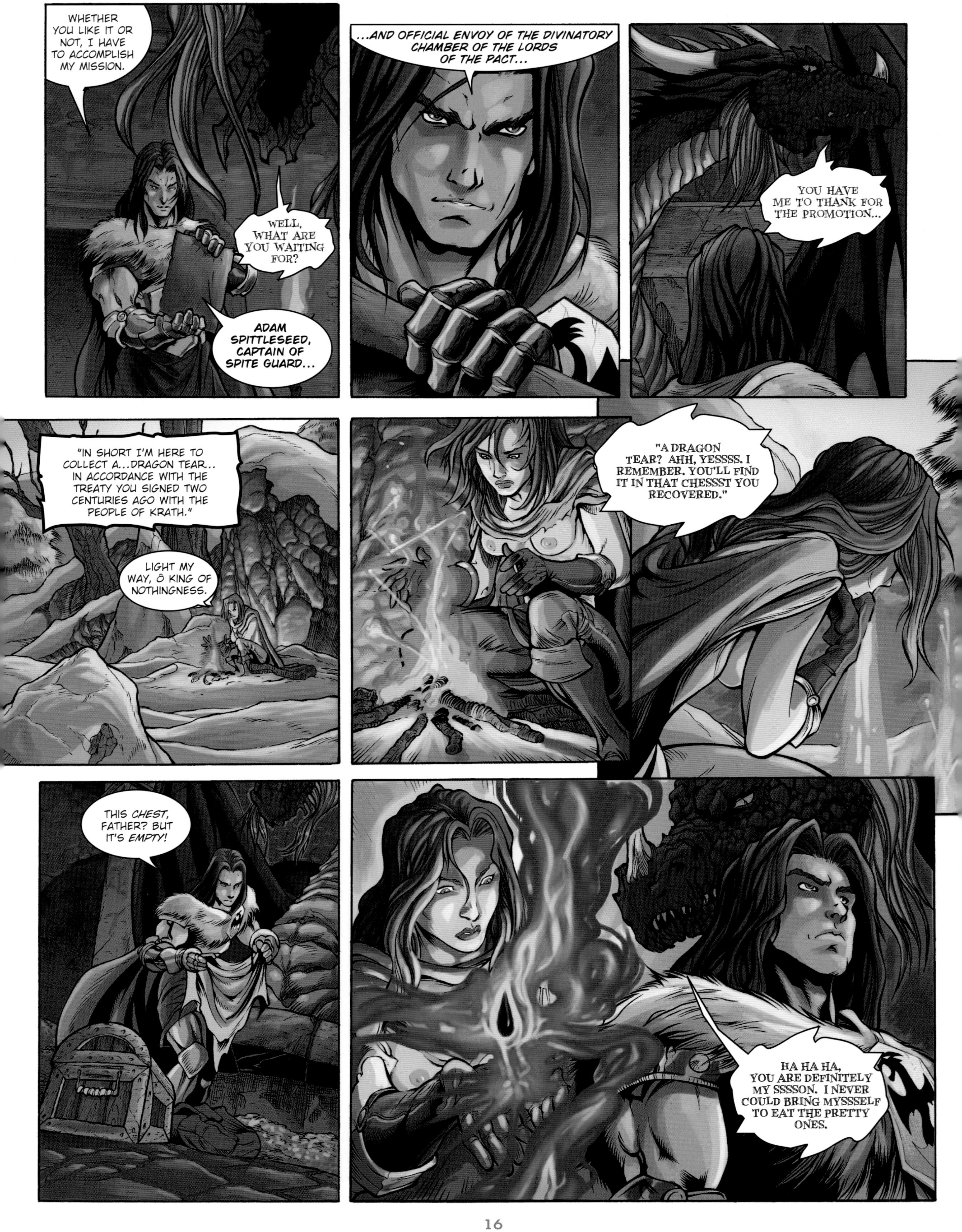

WHETHER YOU LIKE IT OR NOT, I HAVE TO ACCOMPLISH MY MISSION.
WELL, WHAT ARE YOU WAITING FOR?
ADAM SPITTLESEED, CAPTAIN OF SPITE GUARD...
...AND OFFICIAL ENVOY OF THE DIVINATORY CHAMBER OF THE LORDS OF THE PACT...
YOU HAVE ME TO THANK FOR THE PROMOTION...
"IN SHORT I'M HERE TO COLLECT A...DRAGON TEAR... IN ACCORDANCE WITH THE TREATY YOU SIGNED TWO CENTURIES AGO WITH THE PEOPLE OF KRATH."
LIGHT MY WAY, Ô KING OF NOTHINGNESS.
"A DRAGON TEAR? AHH, YESSSS. I REMEMBER. YOU'LL FIND IT IN THAT CHESSST YOU RECOVERED."
THIS *CHEST*, FATHER? BUT IT'S *EMPTY*!
HA HA HA, YOU ARE DEFINITELY MY SSSSON. I NEVER COULD BRING MYSSSELF TO EAT THE PRETTY ONES.

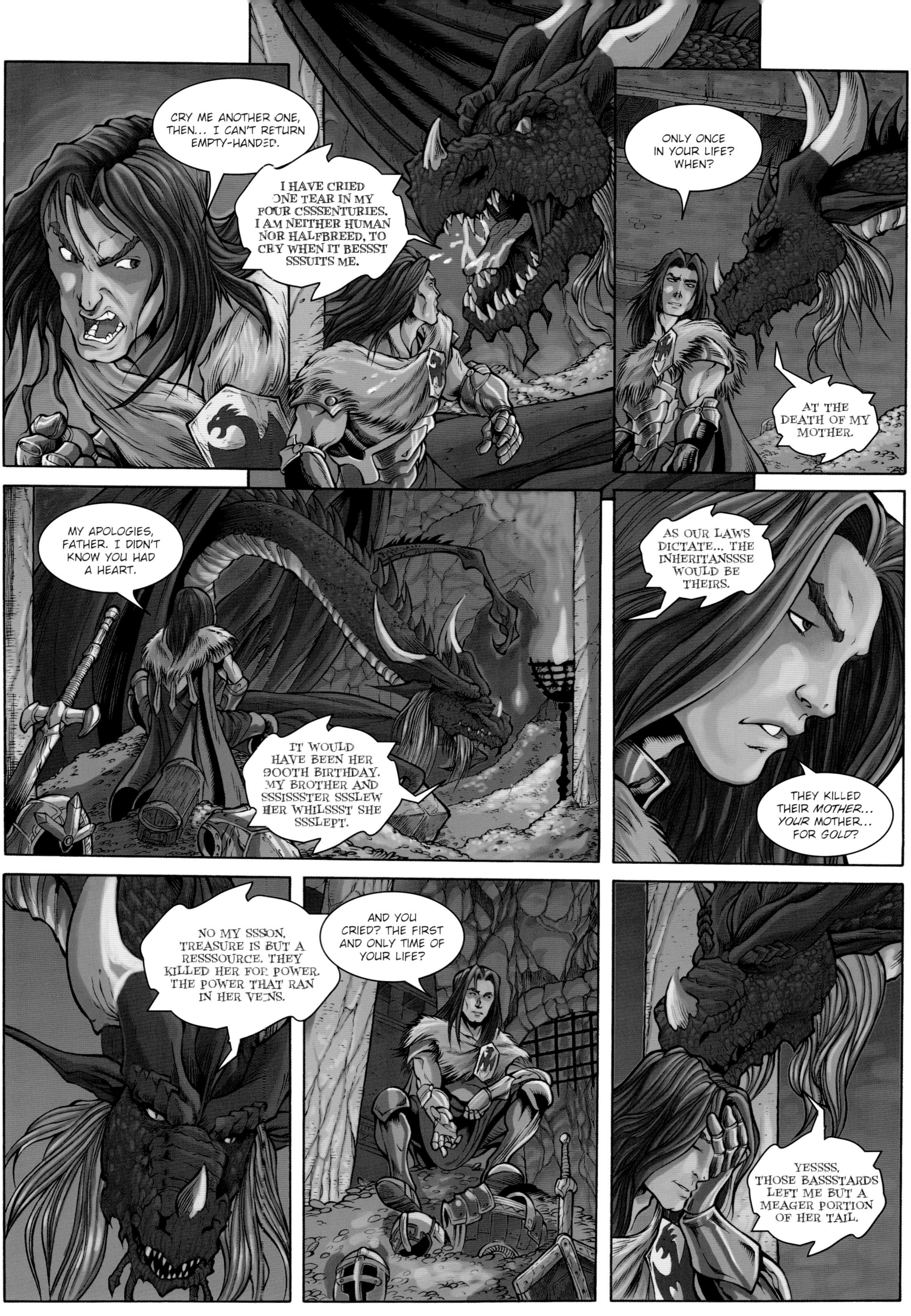
CRY ME ANOTHER ONE, THEN... I CAN'T RETURN EMPTY-HANDED.
I HAVE CRIED ONE TEAR IN MY FOUR CSSSENTURIES. I AM NEITHER HUMAN NOR HALFBREED, TO CRY WHEN IT BESSST SSSUITS ME.
ONLY ONCE IN YOUR LIFE? WHEN?
AT THE DEATH OF MY MOTHER.
MY APOLOGIES, FATHER. I DIDN'T KNOW YOU HAD A HEART.
IT WOULD HAVE BEEN HER 900TH BIRTHDAY. MY BROTHER AND SSSISSSTER SSSLEW HER WHILSSST SHE SSSLEPT.
AS OUR LAWS DICTATE... THE INHERITANSSSE WOULD BE THEIRS.
THEY KILLED THEIR *MOTHER*... *YOUR MOTHER*... FOR GOLD?
NO MY SSSON, TREASURE IS BUT A RESSSOURCE. THEY KILLED HER FOR POWER. THE POWER THAT RAN IN HER VEINS.
AND YOU CRIED? THE FIRST AND ONLY TIME OF YOUR LIFE?
YESSSS, THOSE BASSSTARDS LEFT ME BUT A MEAGER PORTION OF HER TAIL.

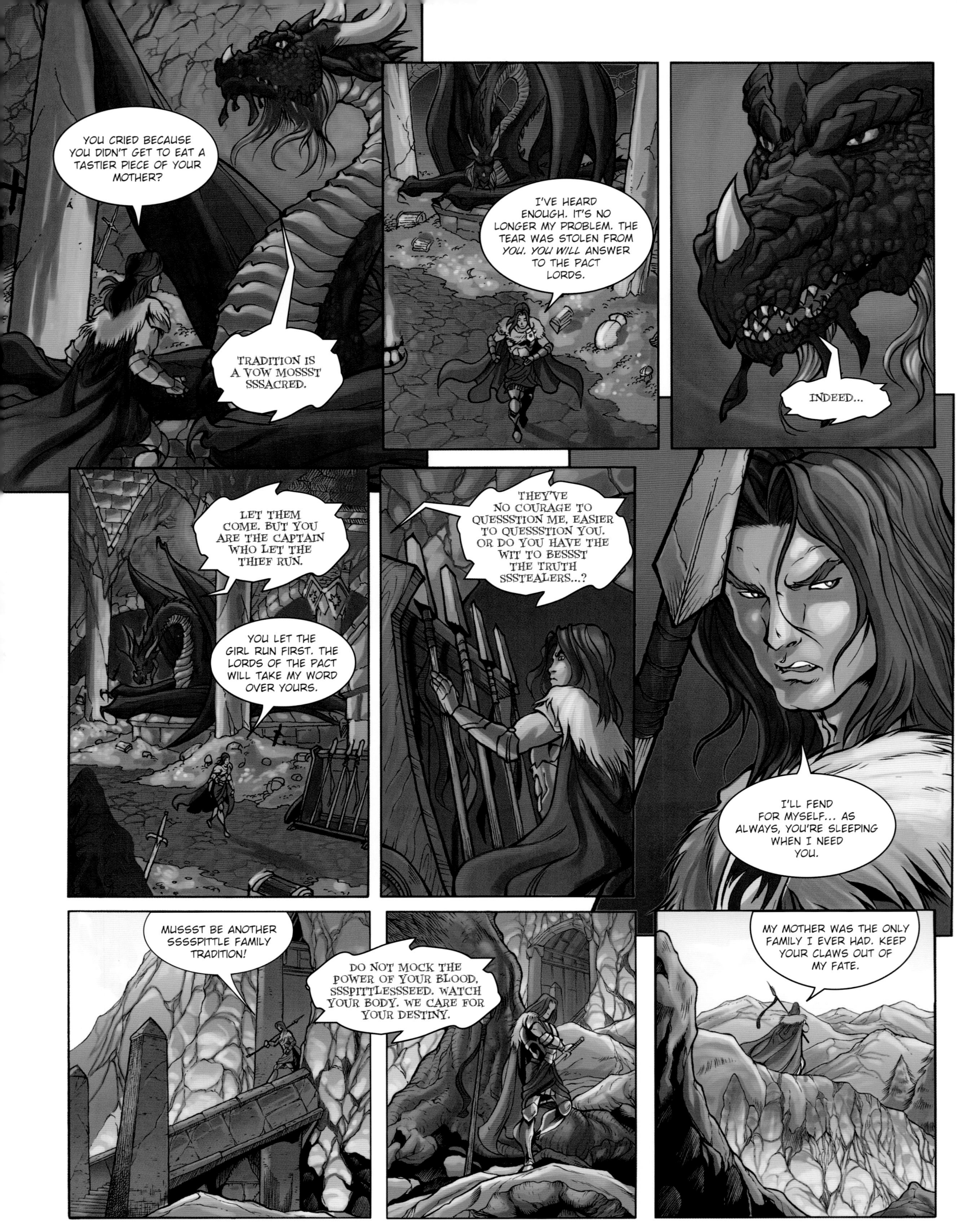
YOU CRIED BECAUSE YOU DIDN'T GET TO EAT A TASTIER PIECE OF YOUR MOTHER?
TRADITION IS A VOW MOSSST SSSACRED.
I'VE HEARD ENOUGH. IT'S NO LONGER MY PROBLEM. THE TEAR WAS STOLEN FROM *YOU*. *YOU WILL* ANSWER TO THE PACT LORDS.
INDEED...
LET THEM COME. BUT YOU ARE THE CAPTAIN WHO LET THE THIEF RUN.
YOU LET THE GIRL RUN FIRST. THE LORDS OF THE PACT WILL TAKE MY WORD OVER YOURS.
THEY'VE NO COURAGE TO QUESSSTION ME, EASIER TO QUESSSTION YOU. OR DO YOU HAVE THE WIT TO BESSST THE TRUTH SSSTEALERS...?
I'LL FEND FOR MYSELF... AS ALWAYS, YOU'RE SLEEPING WHEN I NEED YOU.
MUSSST BE ANOTHER SSSSPITTLE FAMILY TRADITION!
DO NOT MOCK THE POWER OF YOUR BLOOD, SSSPITTLESSSEED. WATCH YOUR BODY. WE CARE FOR YOUR DESTINY.
MY MOTHER WAS THE ONLY FAMILY I EVER HAD. KEEP YOUR CLAWS OUT OF MY FATE.

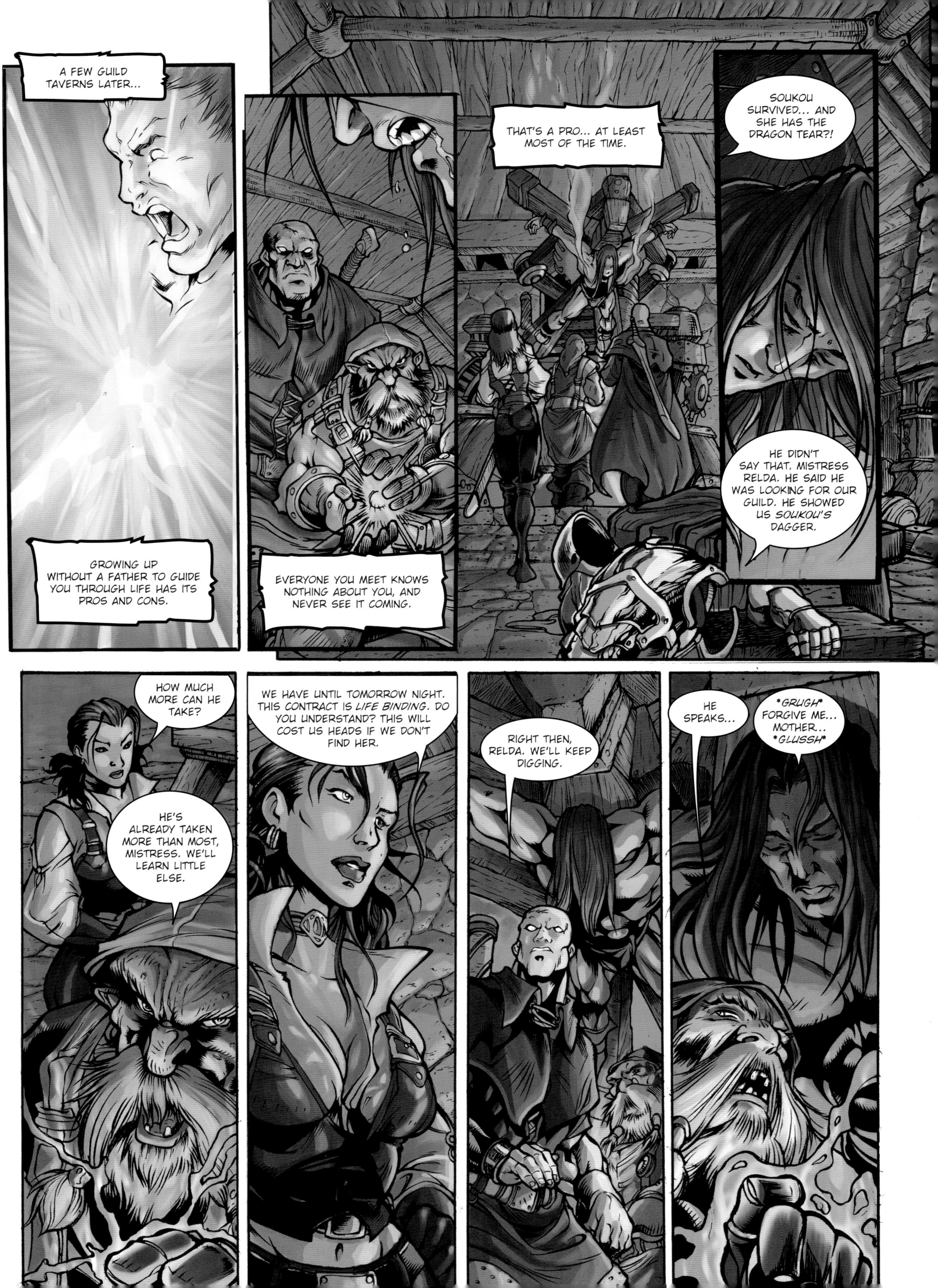
A FEW GUILD TAVERNS LATER...
GROWING UP WITHOUT A FATHER TO GUIDE YOU THROUGH LIFE HAS ITS PROS AND CONS.
EVERYONE YOU MEET KNOWS NOTHING ABOUT YOU, AND NEVER SEE IT COMING.
THAT'S A PRO... AT LEAST MOST OF THE TIME.
SOUKOU SURVIVED... AND SHE HAS THE DRAGON TEAR?!
HE DIDN'T SAY THAT, MISTRESS RELDA. HE SAID HE WAS LOOKING FOR OUR GUILD. HE SHOWED US *SOUKOU'S* DAGGER.
HOW MUCH MORE CAN HE TAKE?
HE'S ALREADY TAKEN MORE THAN MOST, MISTRESS. WE'LL LEARN LITTLE ELSE.
WE HAVE UNTIL TOMORROW NIGHT. THIS CONTRACT IS *LIFE BINDING*. DO YOU UNDERSTAND? THIS WILL COST US HEADS IF WE DON'T FIND HER.
RIGHT THEN, RELDA. WE'LL KEEP DIGGING.
HE SPEAKS...
GRUGH FORGIVE ME... MOTHER... *GLUSSH*

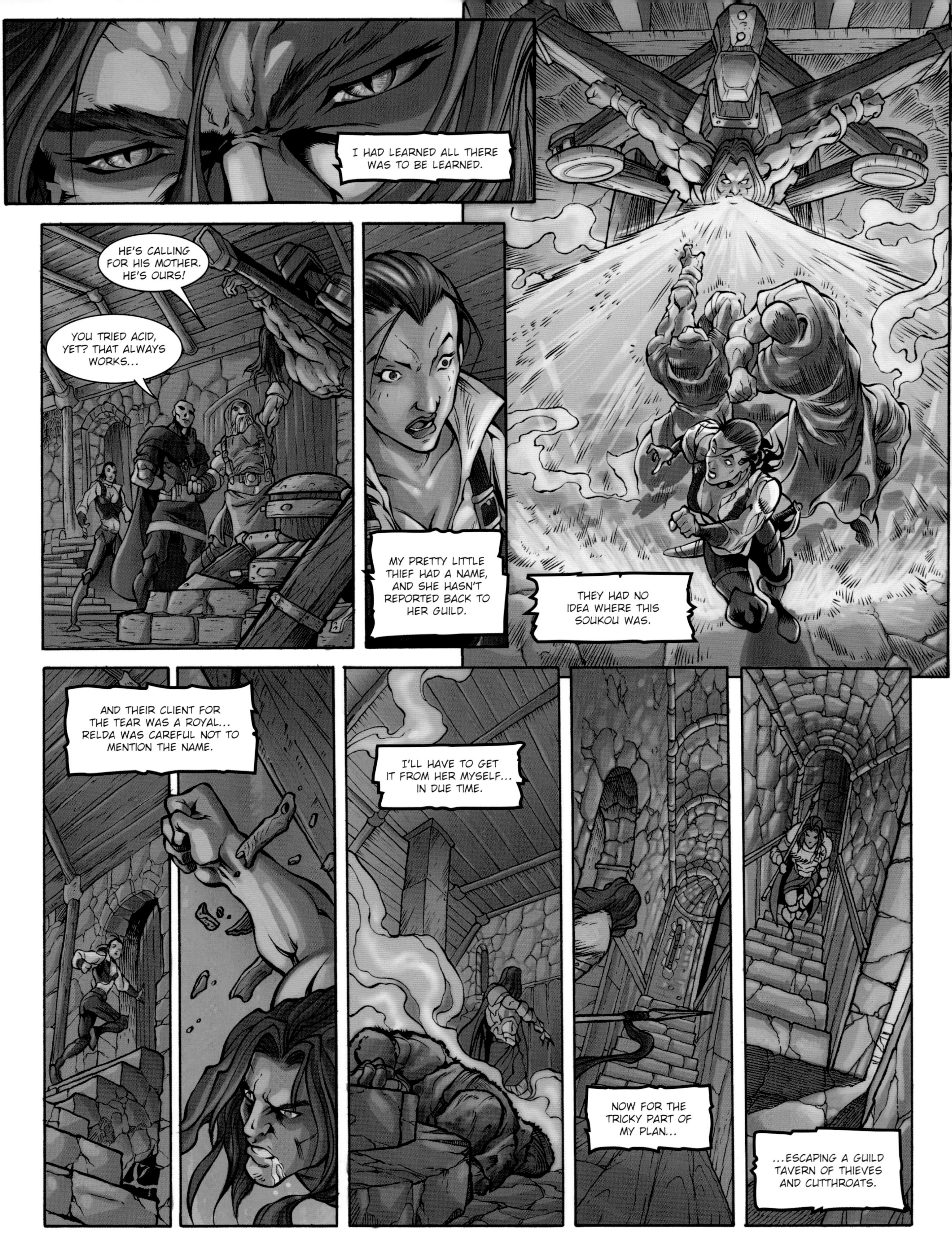
I HAD LEARNED ALL THERE WAS TO BE LEARNED.
HE'S CALLING FOR HIS MOTHER. HE'S OURS!
YOU TRIED ACID, YET? THAT ALWAYS WORKS...
MY PRETTY LITTLE THIEF HAD A NAME, AND SHE HASN'T REPORTED BACK TO HER GUILD.
THEY HAD NO IDEA WHERE THIS SOUKOU WAS.
AND THEIR CLIENT FOR THE TEAR WAS A ROYAL... RELDA WAS CAREFUL NOT TO MENTION THE NAME.
I'LL HAVE TO GET IT FROM HER MYSELF... IN DUE TIME.
NOW FOR THE TRICKY PART OF MY PLAN...
...ESCAPING A GUILD TAVERN OF THIEVES AND CUTTHROATS.

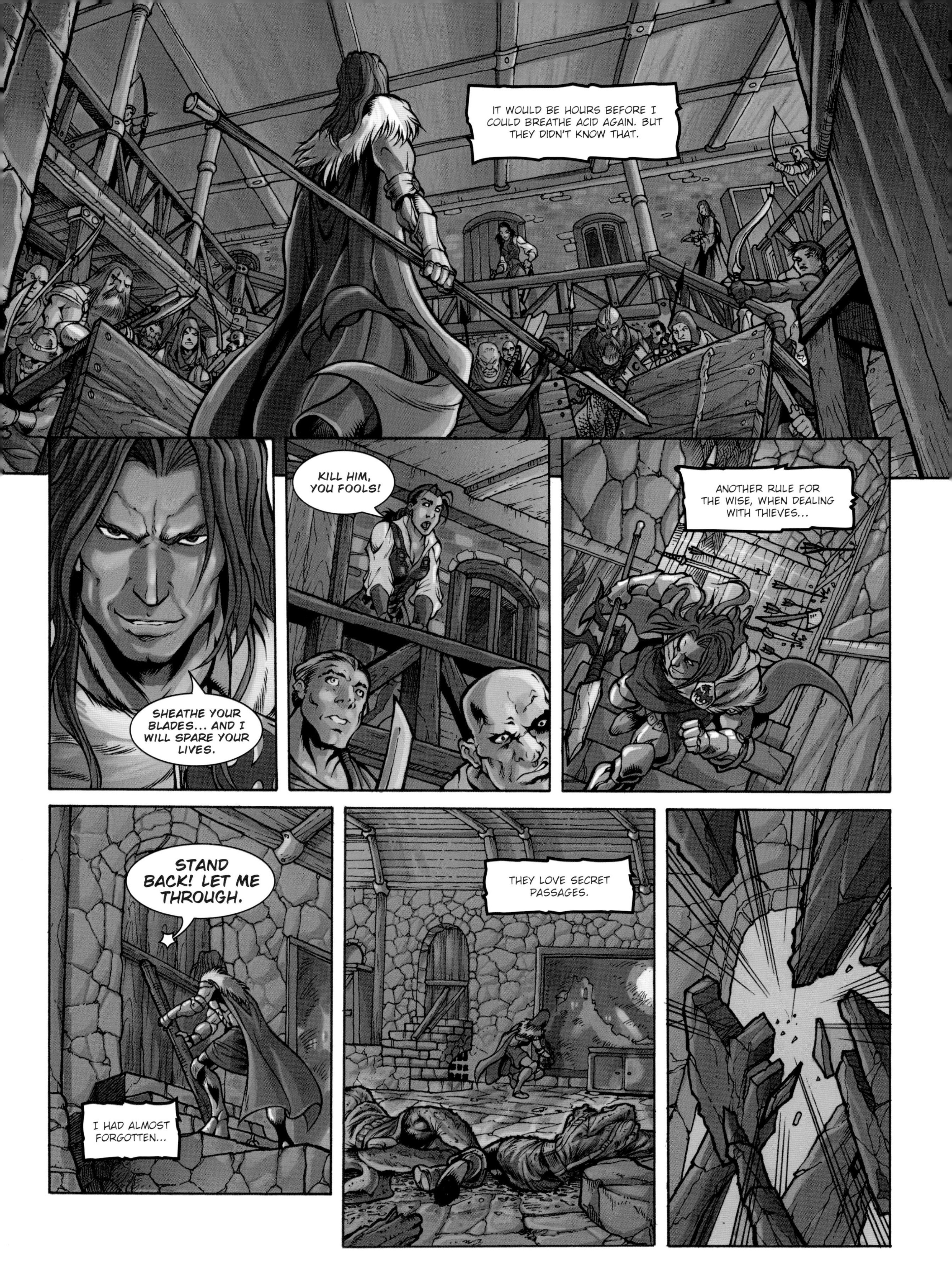
IT WOULD BE HOURS BEFORE I COULD BREATHE ACID AGAIN. BUT THEY DIDN'T KNOW THAT.
SHEATHE YOUR BLADES... AND I WILL SPARE YOUR LIVES.
KILL HIM, YOU FOOLS!
ANOTHER RULE FOR THE WISE, WHEN DEALING WITH THIEVES...
STAND BACK! LET ME THROUGH.
I HAD ALMOST FORGOTTEN...
THEY LOVE SECRET PASSAGES.

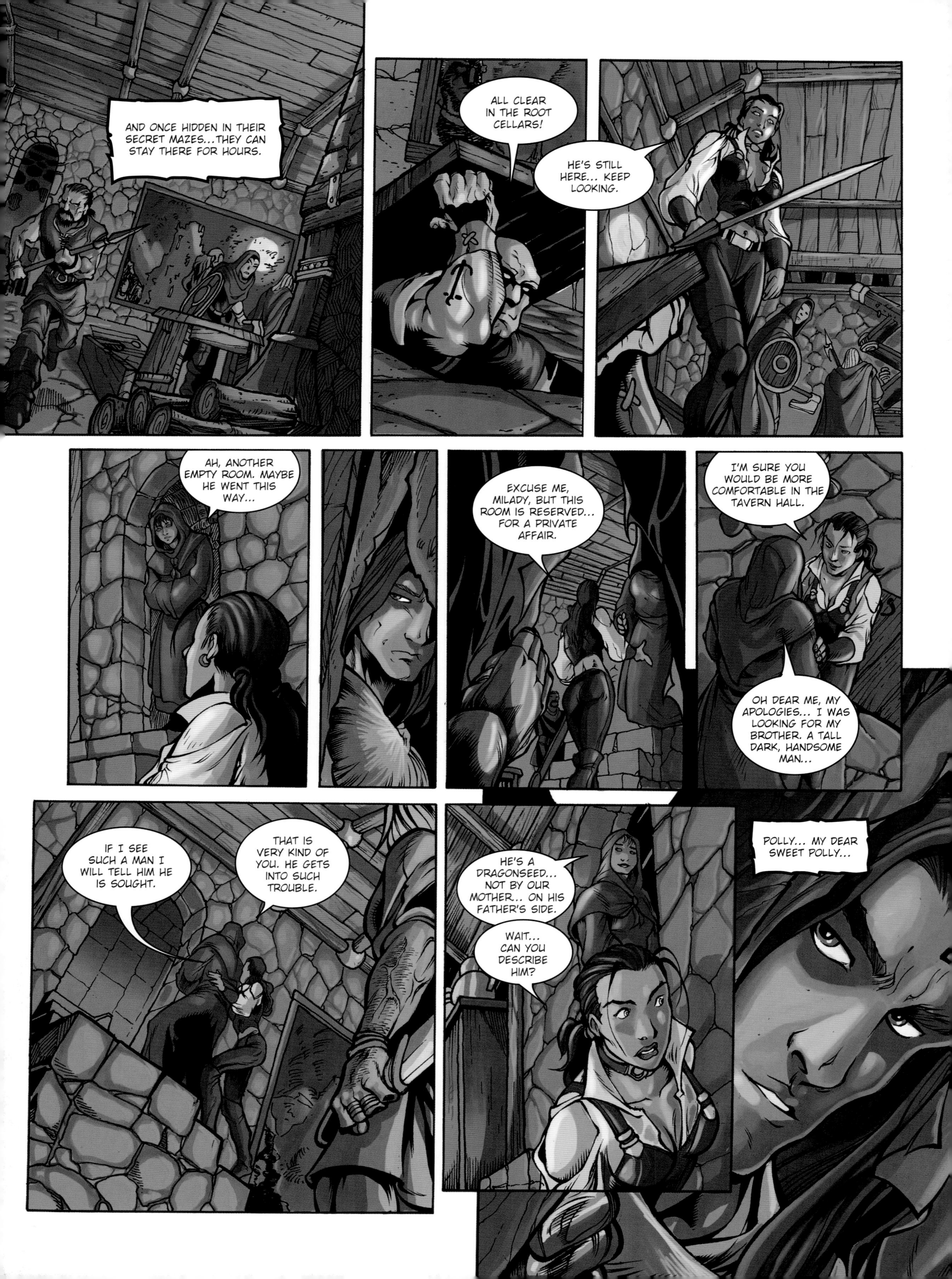
AND ONCE HIDDEN IN THEIR SECRET MAZES...THEY CAN STAY THERE FOR HOURS.
ALL CLEAR IN THE ROOT CELLARS!
HE'S STILL HERE... KEEP LOOKING.
AH, ANOTHER EMPTY ROOM. MAYBE HE WENT THIS WAY...
EXCUSE ME, MILADY, BUT THIS ROOM IS RESERVED... FOR A PRIVATE AFFAIR.
I'M SURE YOU WOULD BE MORE COMFORTABLE IN THE TAVERN HALL.
OH DEAR ME, MY APOLOGIES... I WAS LOOKING FOR MY BROTHER. A TALL DARK, HANDSOME MAN...
IF I SEE SUCH A MAN I WILL TELL HIM HE IS SOUGHT.
THAT IS VERY KIND OF YOU. HE GETS INTO SUCH TROUBLE.
HE'S A DRAGONSEED... NOT BY OUR MOTHER... ON HIS FATHER'S SIDE.
WAIT... CAN YOU DESCRIBE HIM?
POLLY... MY DEAR SWEET POLLY...

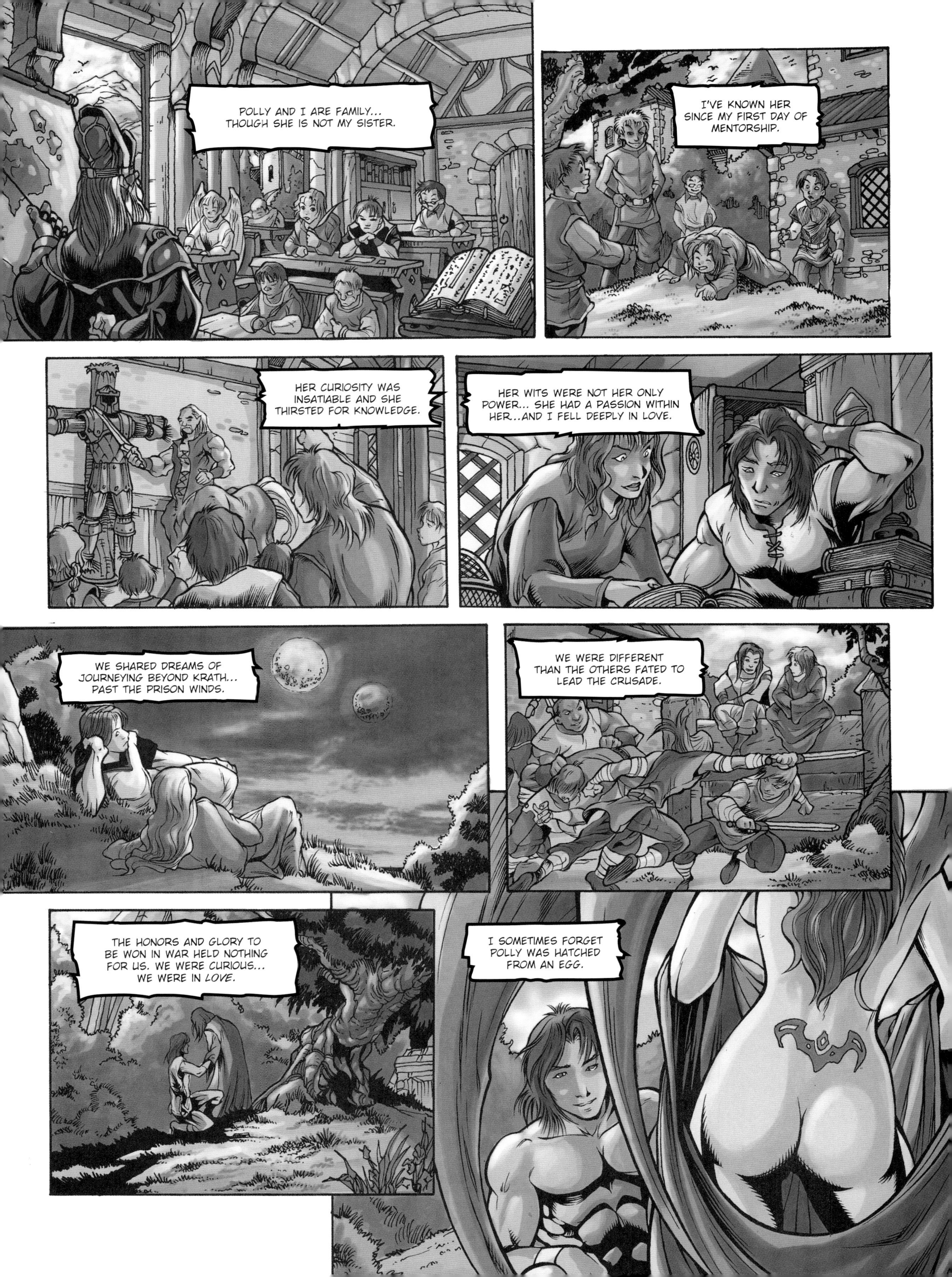
POLLY AND I ARE FAMILY... THOUGH SHE IS NOT MY SISTER.
I'VE KNOWN HER SINCE MY FIRST DAY OF MENTORSHIP.
HER CURIOSITY WAS INSATIABLE AND SHE THIRSTED FOR KNOWLEDGE.
HER WITS WERE NOT HER ONLY POWER... SHE HAD A PASSION WITHIN HER...AND I FELL DEEPLY IN LOVE.
WE SHARED DREAMS OF JOURNEYING BEYOND KRATH... PAST THE PRISON WINDS.
WE WERE DIFFERENT THAN THE OTHERS FATED TO LEAD THE CRUSADE.
THE HONORS AND GLORY TO BE WON IN WAR HELD NOTHING FOR US. WE WERE CURIOUS... WE WERE IN *LOVE*.
I SOMETIMES FORGET POLLY WAS HATCHED FROM AN EGG.

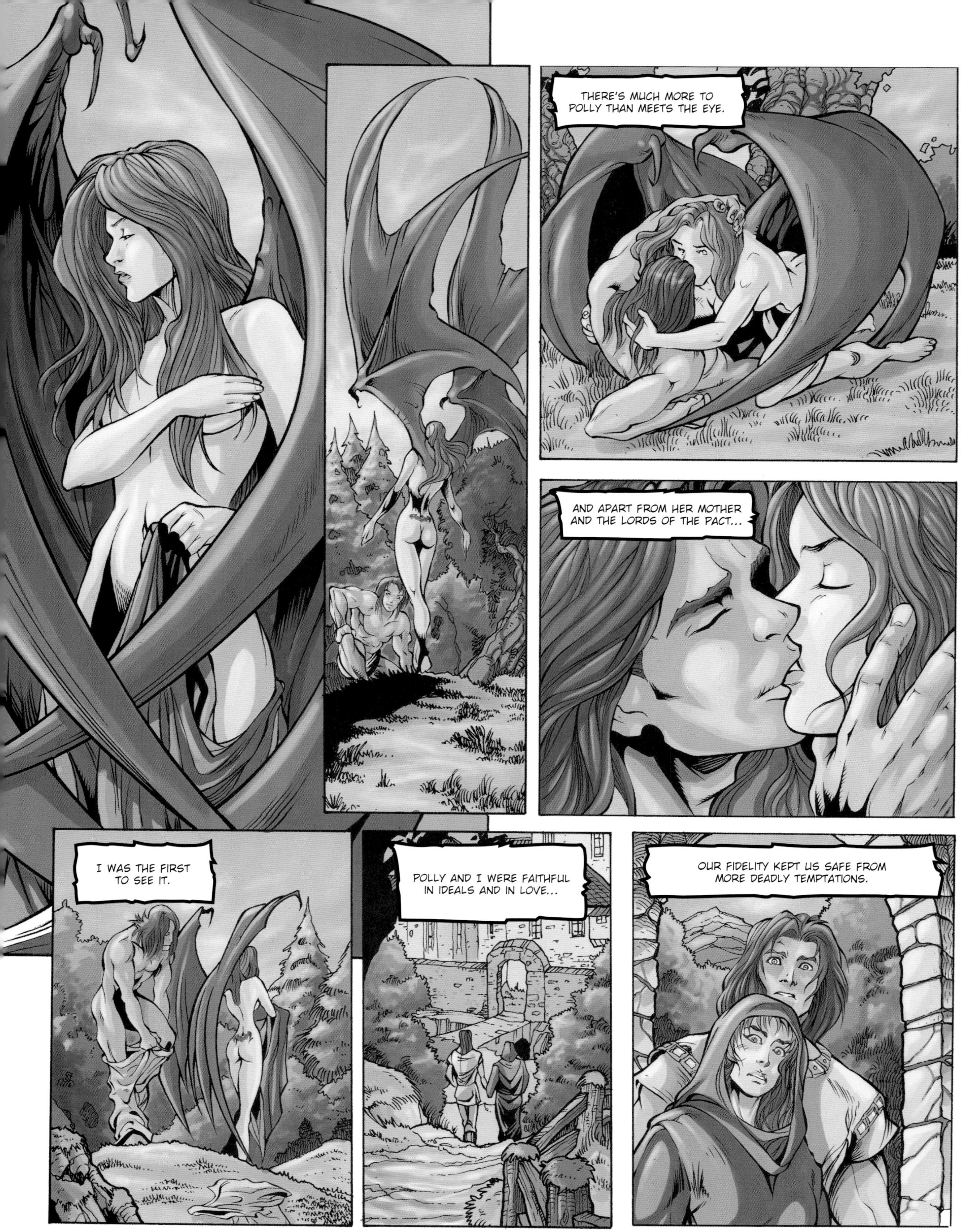
THERE'S MUCH MORE TO POLLY THAN MEETS THE EYE.
AND APART FROM HER MOTHER AND THE LORDS OF THE PACT...
I WAS THE FIRST TO SEE IT.
POLLY AND I WERE FAITHFUL IN IDEALS AND IN LOVE...
OUR FIDELITY KEPT US SAFE FROM MORE DEADLY TEMPTATIONS.

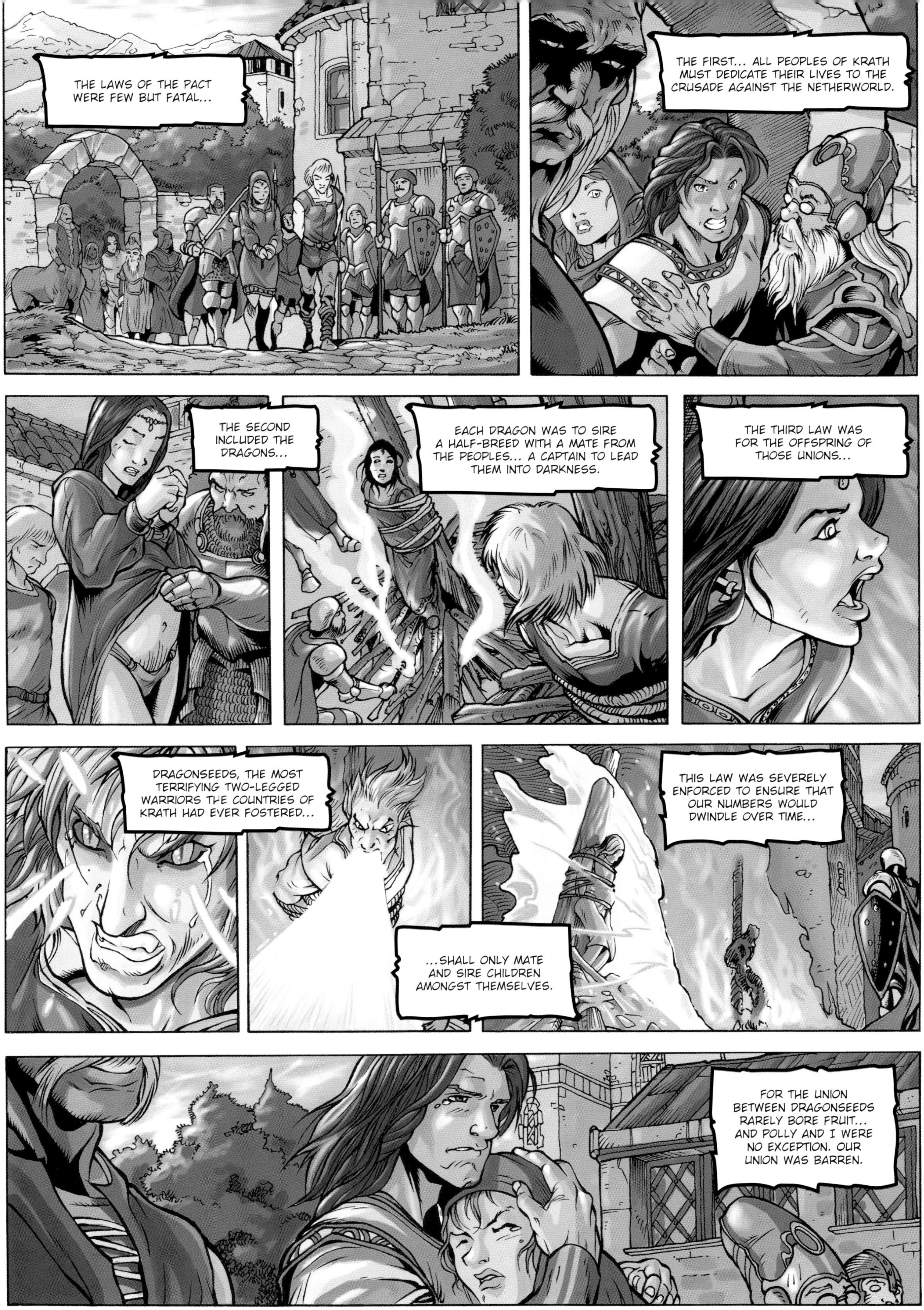
THE LAWS OF THE PACT WERE FEW BUT FATAL...
THE FIRST... ALL PEOPLES OF KRATH MUST DEDICATE THEIR LIVES TO THE CRUSADE AGAINST THE NETHERWORLD.
THE SECOND INCLUDED THE DRAGONS...
EACH DRAGON WAS TO SIRE A HALF-BREED WITH A MATE FROM THE PEOPLES... A CAPTAIN TO LEAD THEM INTO DARKNESS.
THE THIRD LAW WAS FOR THE OFFSPRING OF THOSE UNIONS...
DRAGONSEEDS, THE MOST TERRIFYING TWO-LEGGED WARRIORS THE COUNTRIES OF KRATH HAD EVER FOSTERED...
...SHALL ONLY MATE AND SIRE CHILDREN AMONGST THEMSELVES.
THIS LAW WAS SEVERELY ENFORCED TO ENSURE THAT OUR NUMBERS WOULD DWINDLE OVER TIME...
FOR THE UNION BETWEEN DRAGONSEEDS RARELY BORE FRUIT... AND POLLY AND I WERE NO EXCEPTION. OUR UNION WAS BARREN.

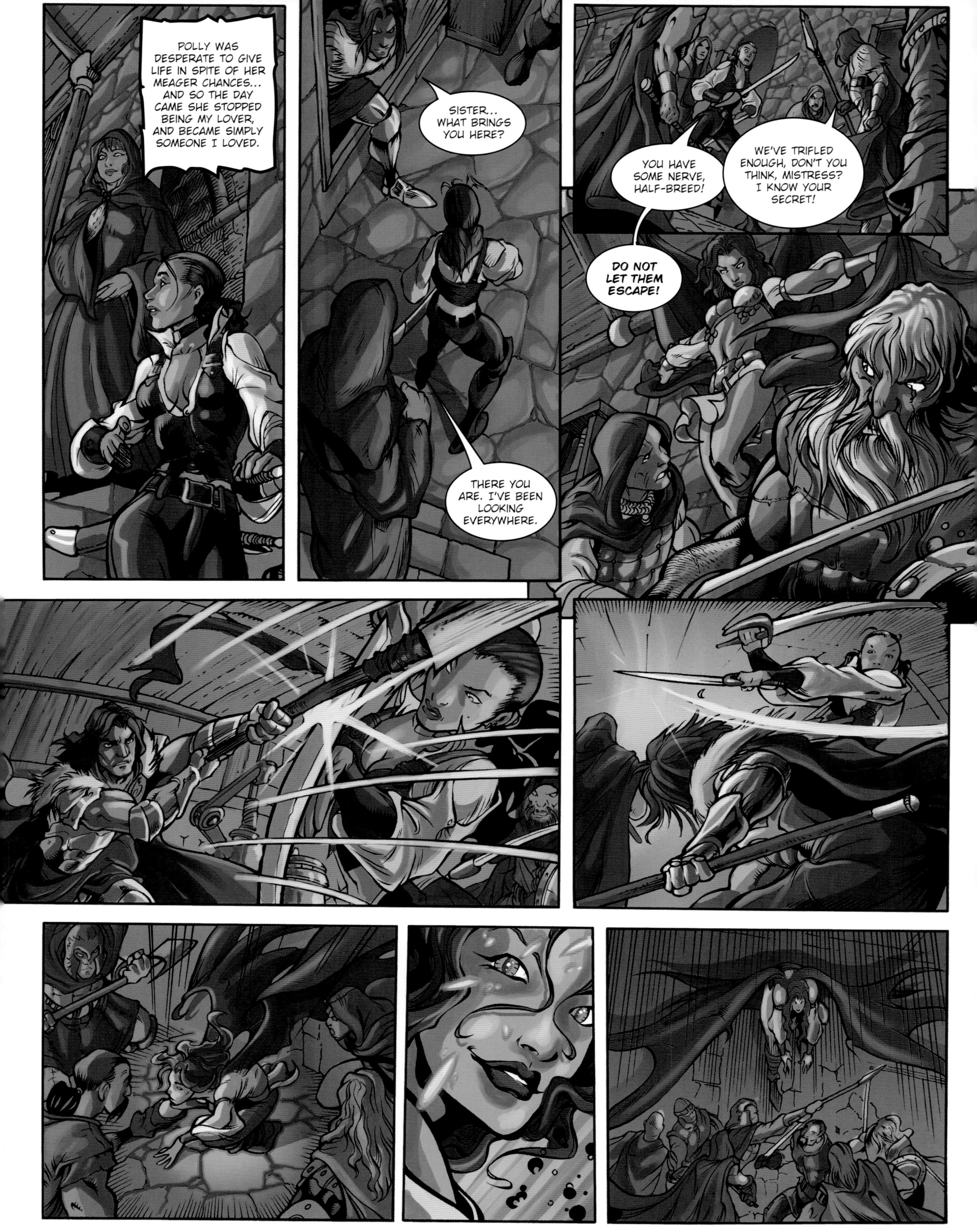
POLLY WAS DESPERATE TO GIVE LIFE IN SPITE OF HER MEAGER CHANCES... AND SO THE DAY CAME SHE STOPPED BEING MY LOVER, AND BECAME SIMPLY SOMEONE I LOVED.
SISTER... WHAT BRINGS YOU HERE?
THERE YOU ARE. I'VE BEEN LOOKING EVERYWHERE.
YOU HAVE SOME NERVE, HALF-BREED!
WE'VE TRIFLED ENOUGH, DON'T YOU THINK, MISTRESS? I KNOW YOUR SECRET!
DO NOT LET THEM ESCAPE!

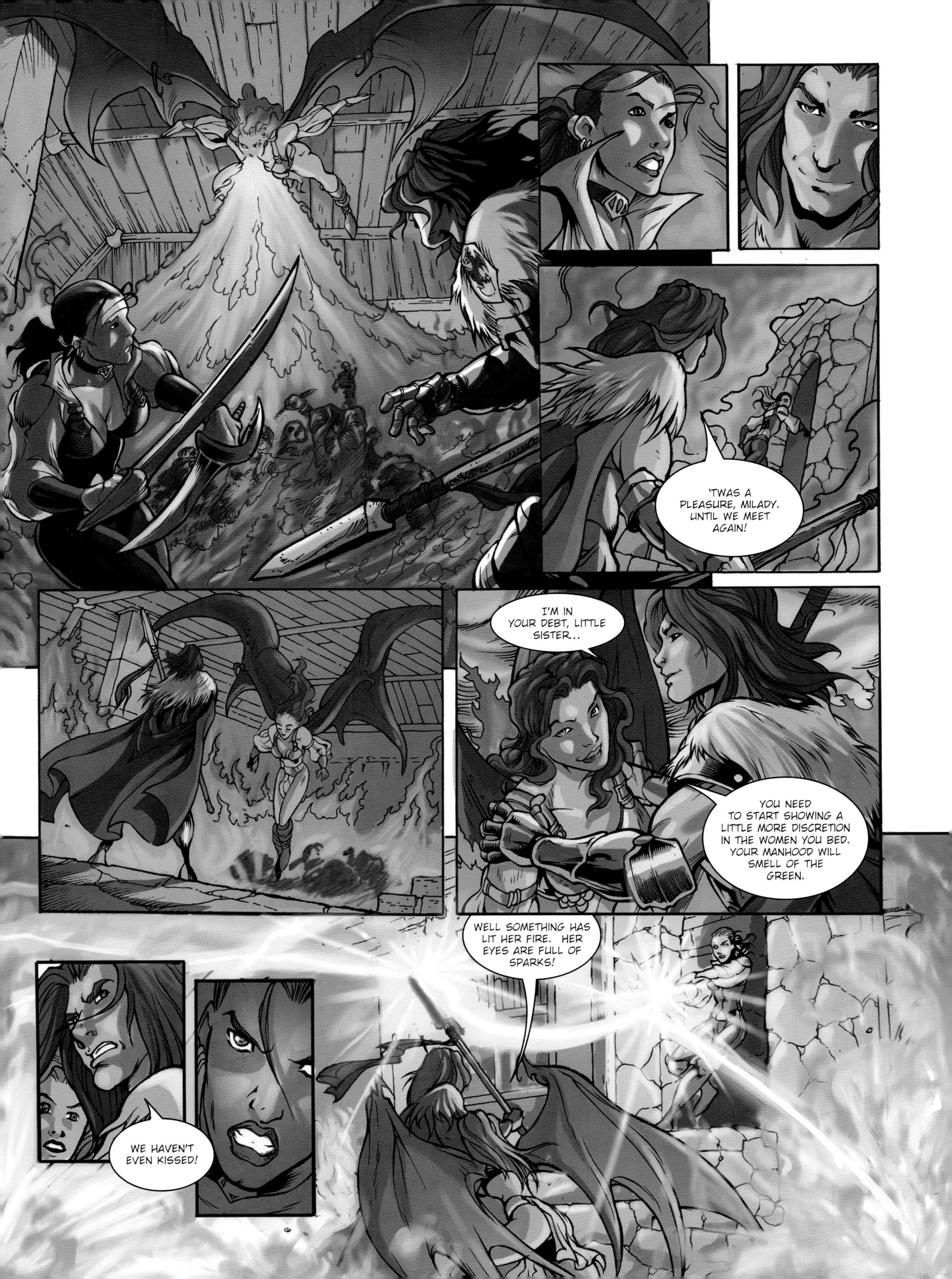
'TWAS A PLEASURE, MILADY. UNTIL WE MEET AGAIN!
I'M IN YOUR DEBT, LITTLE SISTER..
YOU NEED TO START SHOWING A LITTLE MORE DISCRETION IN THE WOMEN YOU BED. YOUR MANHOOD WILL SMELL OF THE GREEN.
WE HAVEN'T EVEN KISSED!
WELL SOMETHING HAS LIT HER FIRE. HER EYES ARE FULL OF SPARKS!

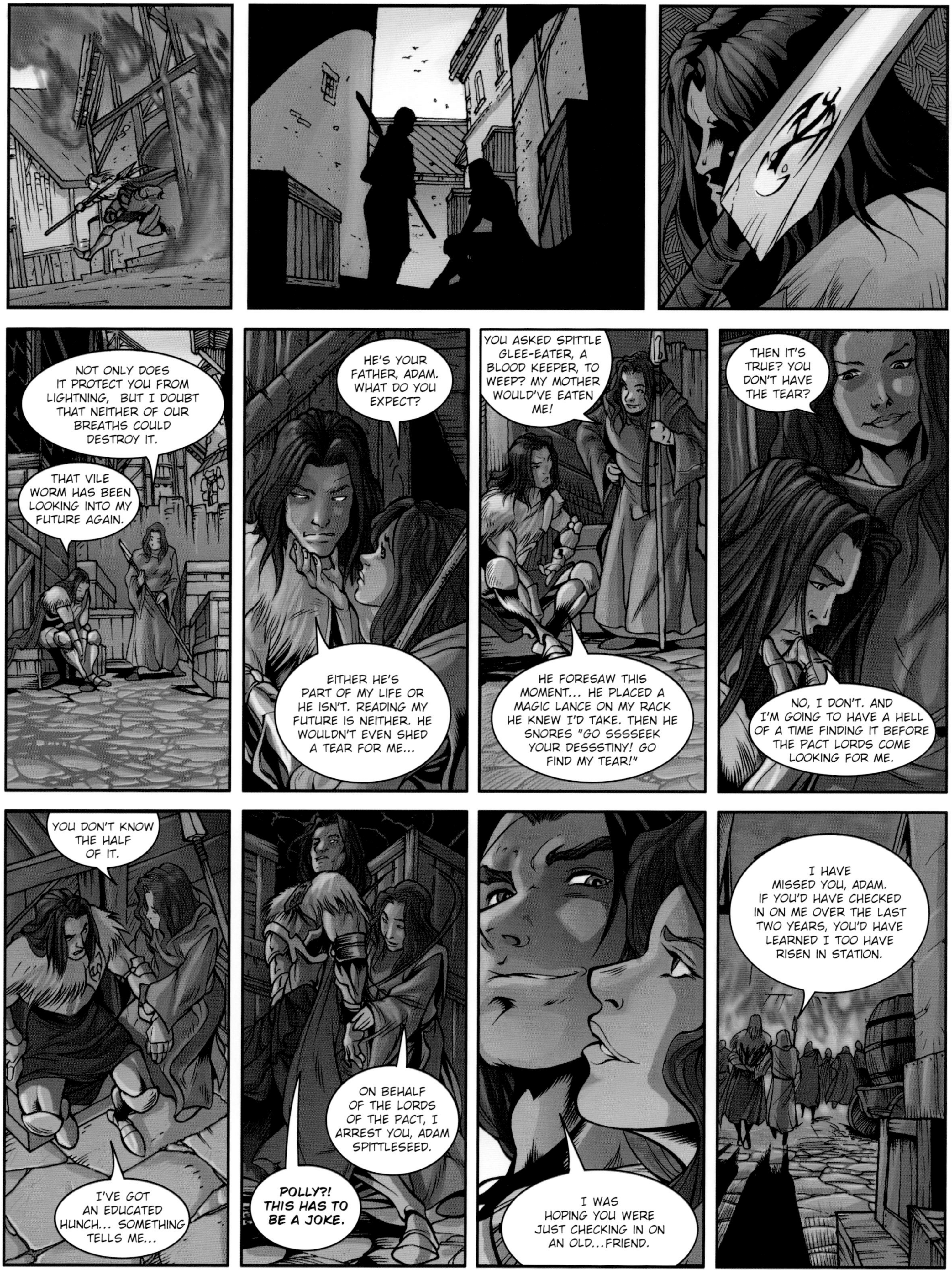
NOT ONLY DOES IT PROTECT YOU FROM LIGHTNING, BUT I DOUBT THAT NEITHER OF OUR BREATHS COULD DESTROY IT.
THAT VILE WORM HAS BEEN LOOKING INTO MY FUTURE AGAIN.
HE'S YOUR FATHER, ADAM. WHAT DO YOU EXPECT?
EITHER HE'S PART OF MY LIFE OR HE ISN'T. READING MY FUTURE IS NEITHER. HE WOULDN'T EVEN SHED A TEAR FOR ME...
YOU ASKED SPITTLE GLEE-EATER, A BLOOD KEEPER, TO WEEP? MY MOTHER WOULD'VE EATEN ME!
HE FORESAW THIS MOMENT... HE PLACED A MAGIC LANCE ON MY RACK HE KNEW I'D TAKE. THEN HE SNORES "GO SSSSEEK YOUR DESSSTINY! GO FIND MY TEAR!"
THEN IT'S TRUE? YOU DON'T HAVE THE TEAR?
NO, I DON'T. AND I'M GOING TO HAVE A HELL OF A TIME FINDING IT BEFORE THE PACT LORDS COME LOOKING FOR ME.
YOU DON'T KNOW THE HALF OF IT.
I'VE GOT AN EDUCATED HUNCH... SOMETHING TELLS ME...
ON BEHALF OF THE LORDS OF THE PACT, I ARREST YOU, ADAM SPITTLESEED.
POLLY?! THIS HAS TO BE A JOKE.
I WAS HOPING YOU WERE JUST CHECKING IN ON AN OLD...FRIEND.
I HAVE MISSED YOU, ADAM. IF YOU'D HAVE CHECKED IN ON ME OVER THE LAST TWO YEARS, YOU'D HAVE LEARNED I TOO HAVE RISEN IN STATION.

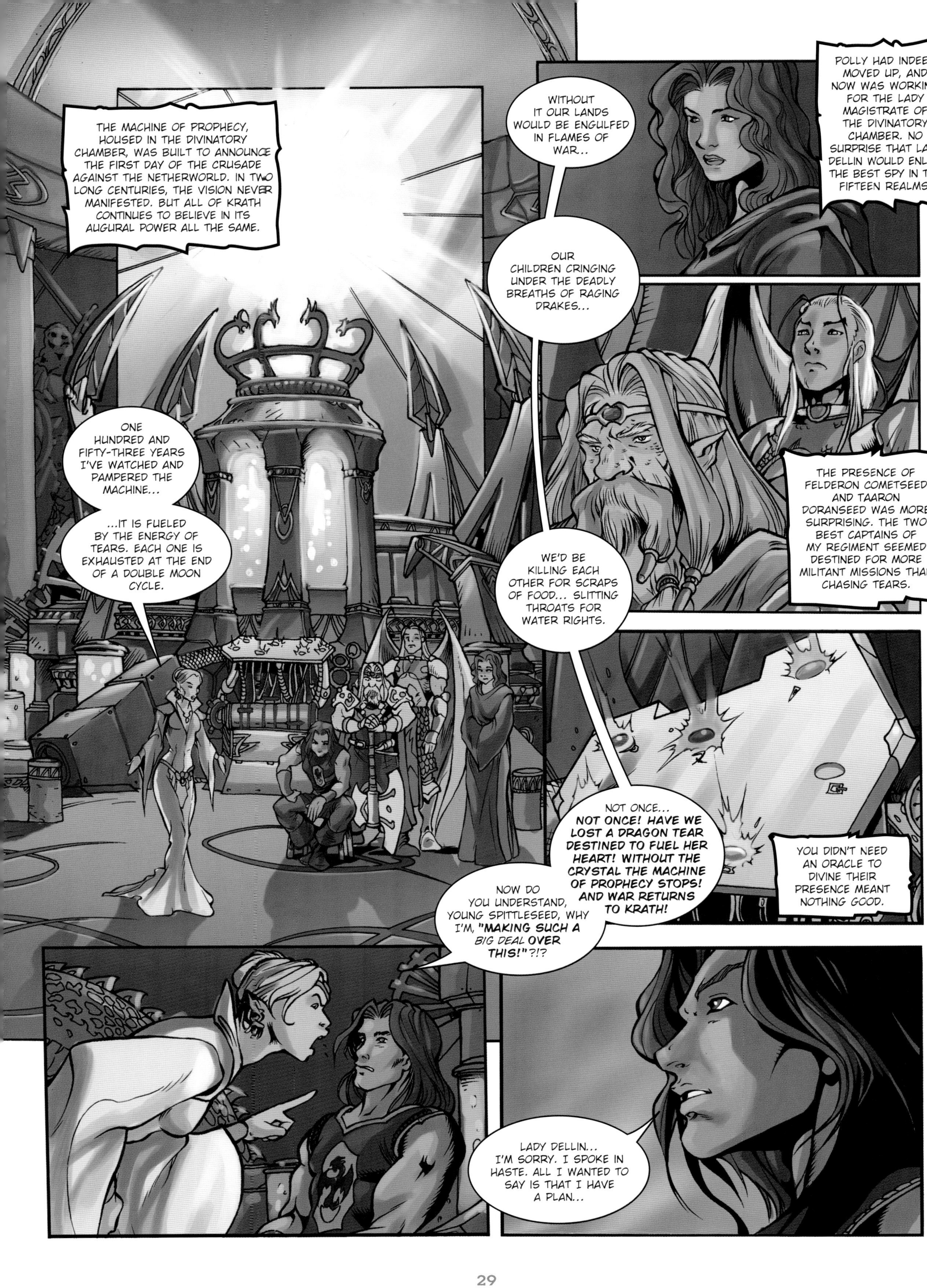

THE MACHINE OF PROPHECY, HOUSED IN THE DIVINATORY CHAMBER, WAS BUILT TO ANNOUNCE THE FIRST DAY OF THE CRUSADE AGAINST THE NETHERWORLD. IN TWO LONG CENTURIES, THE VISION NEVER MANIFESTED. BUT ALL OF KRATH CONTINUES TO BELIEVE IN ITS AUGURAL POWER ALL THE SAME.
ONE HUNDRED AND FIFTY-THREE YEARS I'VE WATCHED AND PAMPERED THE MACHINE...
...IT IS FUELED BY THE ENERGY OF TEARS. EACH ONE IS EXHAUSTED AT THE END OF A DOUBLE MOON CYCLE.
WITHOUT IT OUR LANDS WOULD BE ENGULFED IN FLAMES OF WAR...
POLLY HAD INDEED MOVED UP, AND NOW WAS WORKING FOR THE LADY MAGISTRATE OF THE DIVINATORY CHAMBER. NO SURPRISE THAT LADY DELLIN WOULD ENLIST THE BEST SPY IN THE FIFTEEN REALMS.
OUR CHILDREN CRINGING UNDER THE DEADLY BREATHS OF RAGING DRAKES...
THE PRESENCE OF FELDERON COMETSEED AND TAARON DORANSEED WAS MORE SURPRISING. THE TWO BEST CAPTAINS OF MY REGIMENT SEEMED DESTINED FOR MORE MILITANT MISSIONS THAN CHASING TEARS.
WE'D BE KILLING EACH OTHER FOR SCRAPS OF FOOD... SLITTING THROATS FOR WATER RIGHTS.
NOT ONCE... **NOT ONCE! HAVE WE LOST A DRAGON TEAR DESTINED TO FUEL HER HEART! WITHOUT THE CRYSTAL THE MACHINE OF PROPHECY STOPS! AND WAR RETURNS TO KRATH!**
YOU DIDN'T NEED AN ORACLE TO DIVINE THEIR PRESENCE MEANT NOTHING GOOD.
NOW DO YOU UNDERSTAND, YOUNG SPITTLESEED, WHY I'M, **"MAKING SUCH A *BIG DEAL* OVER THIS!"**?!?
LADY DELLIN... I'M SORRY. I SPOKE IN HASTE. ALL I WANTED TO SAY IS THAT I HAVE A PLAN...

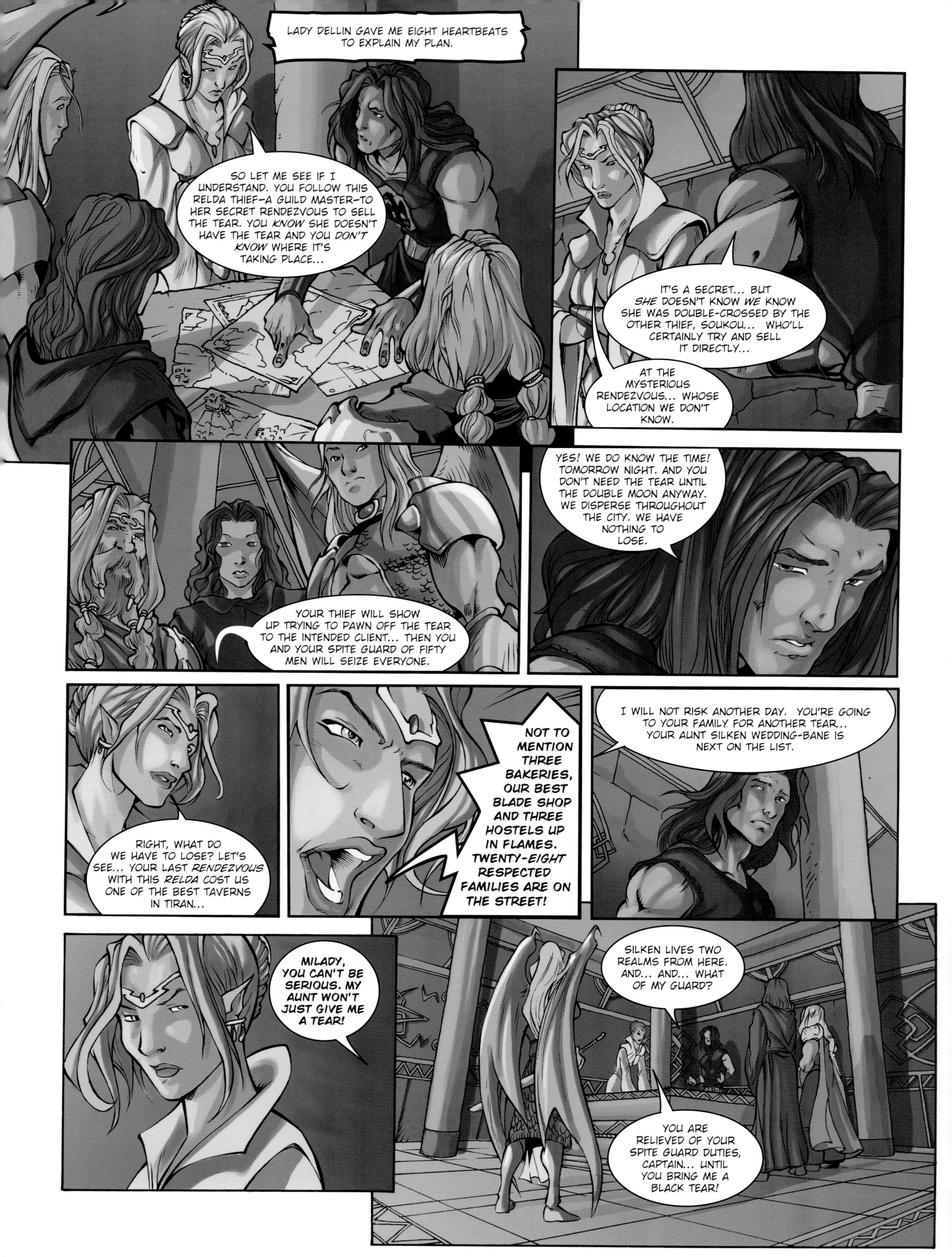
LADY DELLIN GAVE ME EIGHT HEARTBEATS TO EXPLAIN MY PLAN.
SO LET ME SEE IF I UNDERSTAND. YOU FOLLOW THIS RELDA THIEF—A GUILD MASTER—TO HER SECRET RENDEZVOUS TO SELL THE TEAR. YOU *KNOW* SHE DOESN'T HAVE THE TEAR AND YOU *DON'T KNOW* WHERE IT'S TAKING PLACE...
IT'S A SECRET... BUT *SHE* DOESN'T KNOW *WE* KNOW SHE WAS DOUBLE-CROSSED BY THE OTHER THIEF, SOUKOU... WHO'LL CERTAINLY TRY AND SELL IT DIRECTLY...
AT THE MYSTERIOUS RENDEZVOUS... WHOSE LOCATION WE DON'T KNOW.
YOUR THIEF WILL SHOW UP TRYING TO PAWN OFF THE TEAR TO THE INTENDED CLIENT... THEN YOU AND YOUR SPITE GUARD OF FIFTY MEN WILL SEIZE EVERYONE.
YES! WE DO KNOW THE TIME! TOMORROW NIGHT. AND YOU DON'T NEED THE TEAR UNTIL THE DOUBLE MOON ANYWAY. WE DISPERSE THROUGHOUT THE CITY. WE HAVE NOTHING TO LOSE.
RIGHT, WHAT DO WE HAVE TO LOSE? LET'S SEE... YOUR LAST *RENDEZVOUS* WITH THIS *RELDA* COST US ONE OF THE BEST TAVERNS IN TIRAN...
NOT TO MENTION THREE BAKERIES, OUR BEST BLADE SHOP AND THREE HOSTELS UP IN FLAMES. TWENTY-*EIGHT* RESPECTED FAMILIES ARE ON THE STREET!
I WILL NOT RISK ANOTHER DAY. YOU'RE GOING TO YOUR FAMILY FOR ANOTHER TEAR... YOUR AUNT SILKEN WEDDING-BANE IS NEXT ON THE LIST.
MILADY, YOU CAN'T BE SERIOUS. MY AUNT WON'T JUST GIVE ME A TEAR!
SILKEN LIVES TWO REALMS FROM HERE. AND... AND... WHAT OF MY GUARD?
YOU ARE RELIEVED OF YOUR SPITE GUARD DUTIES, CAPTAIN... UNTIL YOU BRING ME A BLACK TEAR!

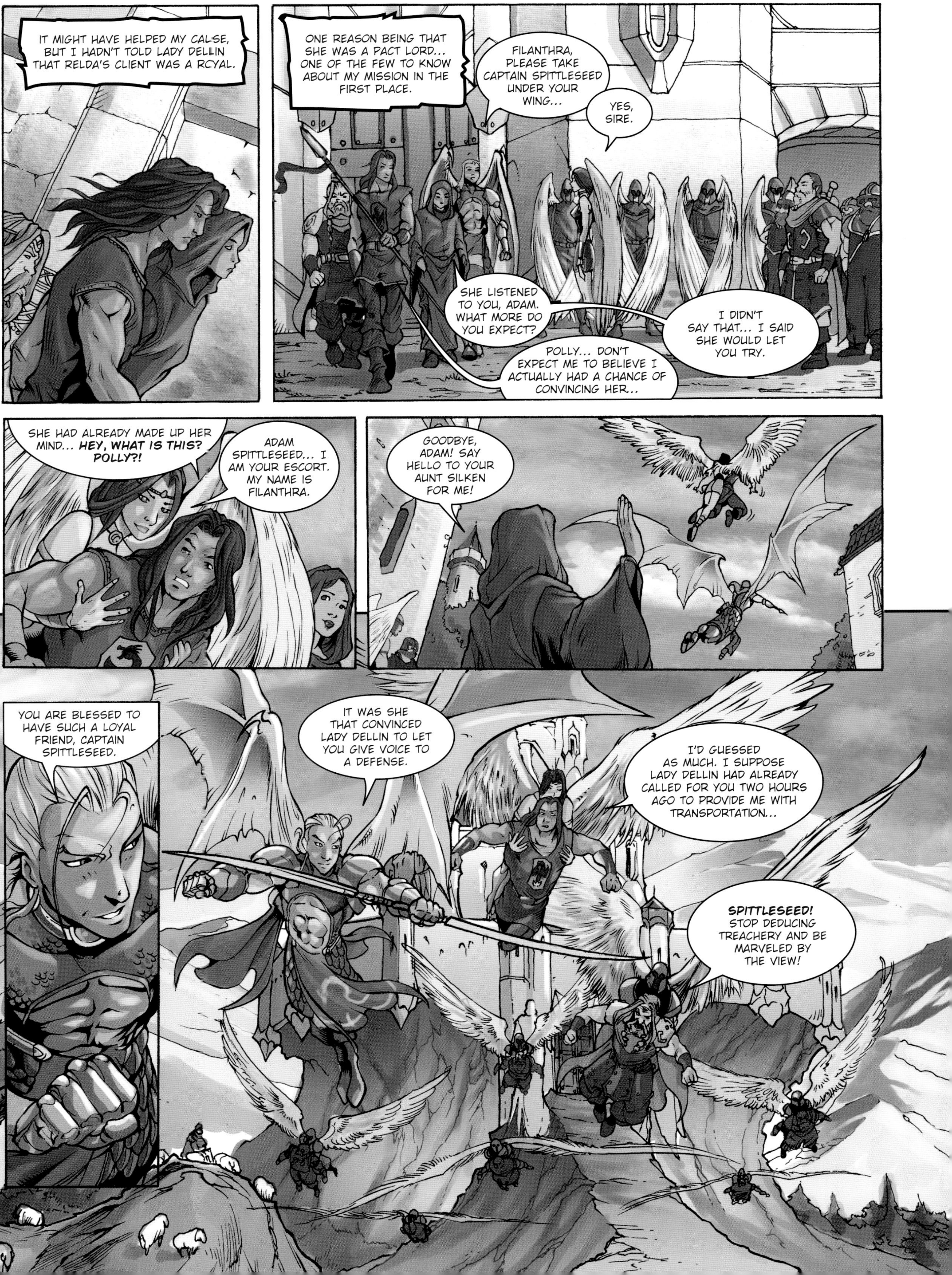
IT MIGHT HAVE HELPED MY CALSE, BUT I HADN'T TOLD LADY DELLIN THAT RELDA'S CLIENT WAS A RCYAL.
ONE REASON BEING THAT SHE WAS A PACT LORD... ONE OF THE FEW TO KNOW ABOUT MY MISSION IN THE FIRST PLACE.
FILANTHRA, PLEASE TAKE CAPTAIN SPITTLESEED UNDER YOUR WING...
YES, SIRE.
SHE LISTENED TO YOU, ADAM. WHAT MORE DO YOU EXPECT?
I DIDN'T SAY THAT... I SAID SHE WOULD LET YOU TRY.
POLLY... DON'T EXPECT ME TO BELIEVE I ACTUALLY HAD A CHANCE OF CONVINCING HER...
SHE HAD ALREADY MADE UP HER MIND... **HEY, WHAT IS THIS? POLLY?!**
ADAM SPITTLESEED... I AM YOUR ESCORT. MY NAME IS FILANTHRA.
GOODBYE, ADAM! SAY HELLO TO YOUR AUNT SILKEN FOR ME!
YOU ARE BLESSED TO HAVE SUCH A LOYAL FRIEND, CAPTAIN SPITTLESEED.
IT WAS SHE THAT CONVINCED LADY DELLIN TO LET YOU GIVE VOICE TO A DEFENSE.
I'D GUESSED AS MUCH. I SUPPOSE LADY DELLIN HAD ALREADY CALLED FOR YOU TWO HOURS AGO TO PROVIDE ME WITH TRANSPORTATION...
SPITTLESEED! STOP DEDUCING TREACHERY AND BE MARVELED BY THE VIEW!

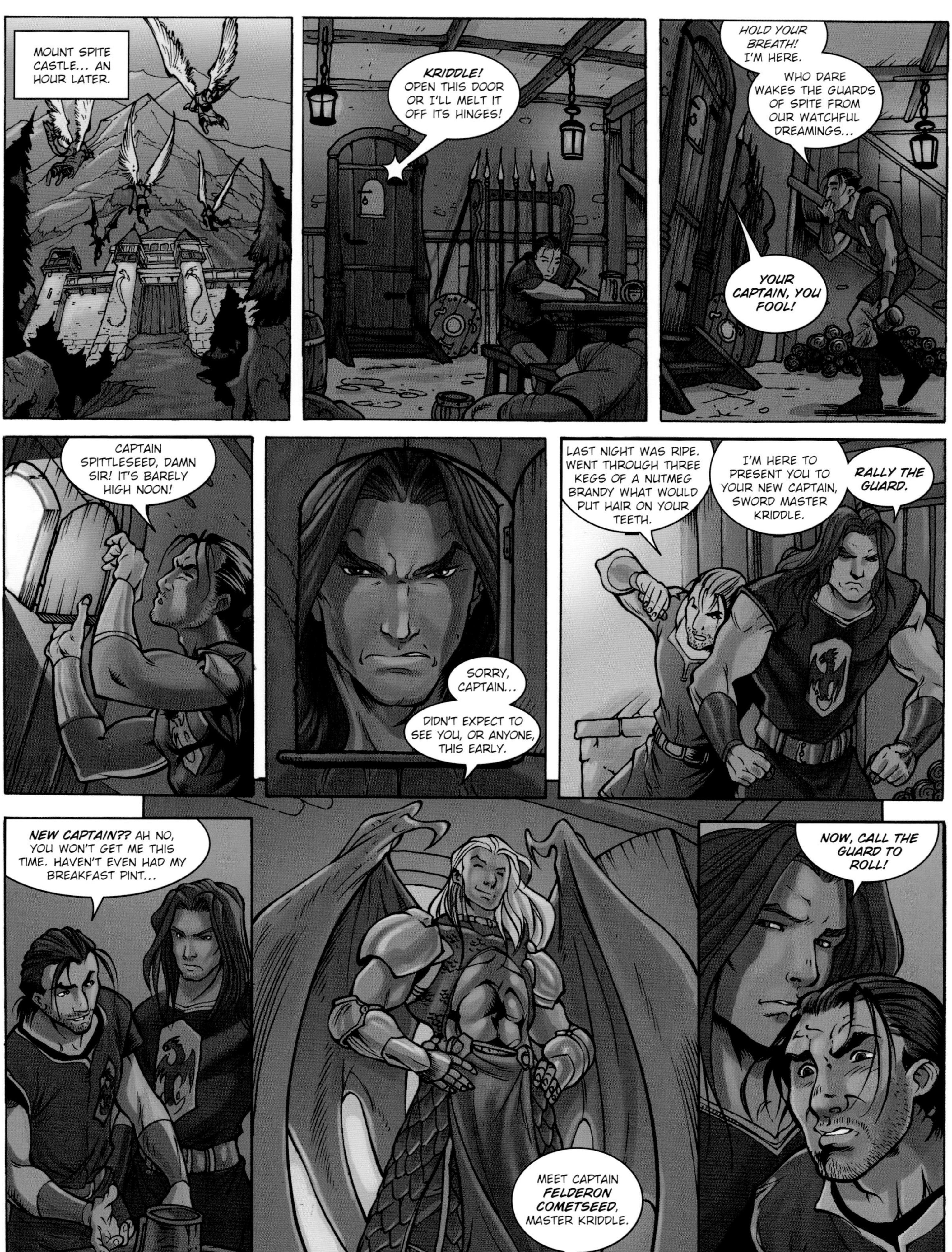
MOUNT SPITE CASTLE... AN HOUR LATER.
KRIDDLE! OPEN THIS DOOR OR I'LL MELT IT OFF ITS HINGES!
HOLD YOUR BREATH! I'M HERE.
WHO DARE WAKES THE GUARDS OF SPITE FROM OUR WATCHFUL DREAMINGS...
YOUR CAPTAIN, YOU FOOL!
CAPTAIN SPITTLESEED, DAMN SIR! IT'S BARELY HIGH NOON!
SORRY, CAPTAIN...
DIDN'T EXPECT TO SEE YOU, OR ANYONE, THIS EARLY.
LAST NIGHT WAS RIPE. WENT THROUGH THREE KEGS OF A NUTMEG BRANDY WHAT WOULD PUT HAIR ON YOUR TEETH.
I'M HERE TO PRESENT YOU TO YOUR NEW CAPTAIN, SWORD MASTER KRIDDLE.
RALLY THE GUARD.
NEW CAPTAIN?? AH NO, YOU WON'T GET ME THIS TIME. HAVEN'T EVEN HAD MY BREAKFAST PINT...
MEET CAPTAIN FELDERON COMETSEED, MASTER KRIDDLE.
NOW, CALL THE GUARD TO ROLL!

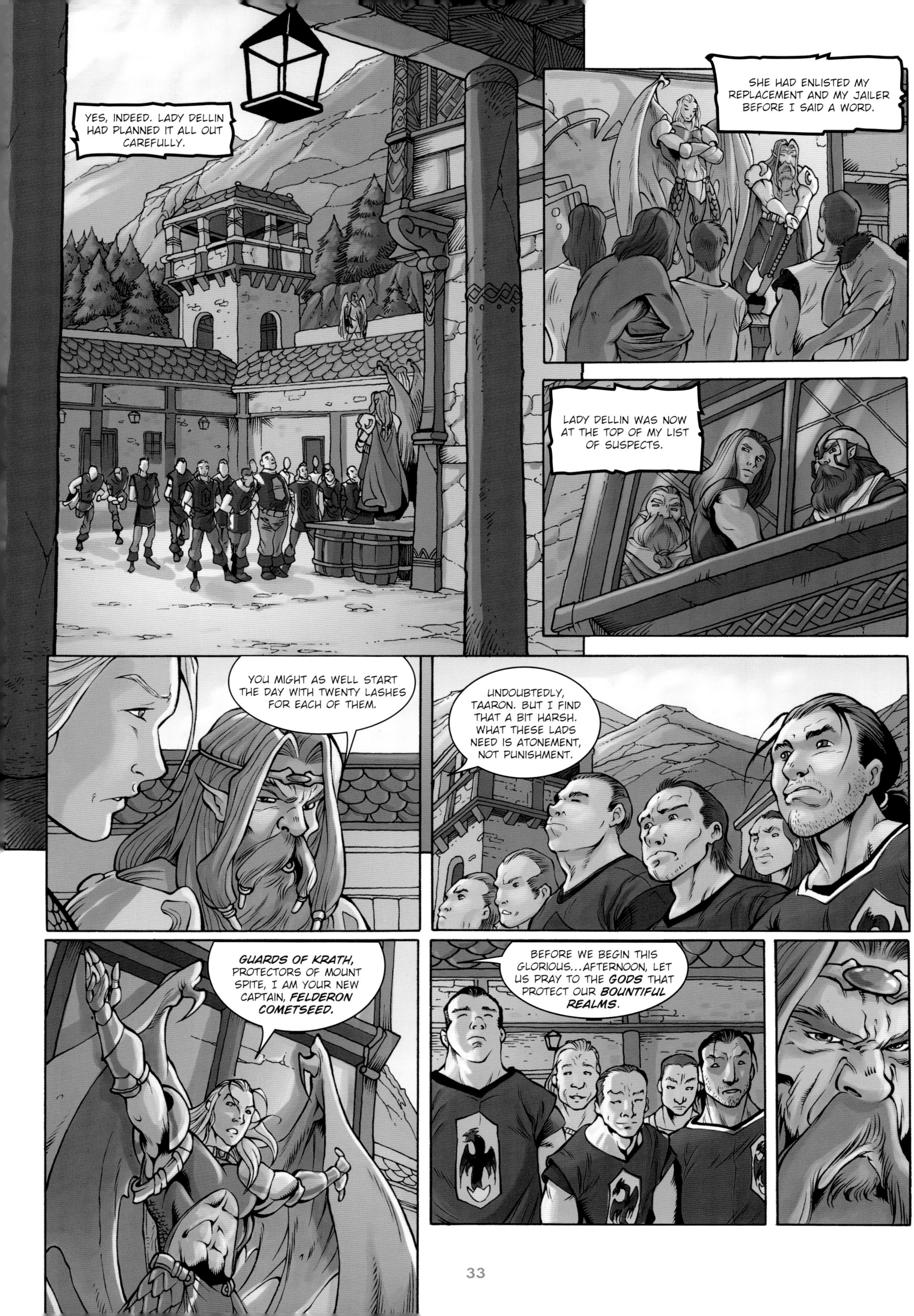
YES, INDEED. LADY DELLIN HAD PLANNED IT ALL OUT CAREFULLY.
SHE HAD ENLISTED MY REPLACEMENT AND MY JAILER BEFORE I SAID A WORD.
LADY DELLIN WAS NOW AT THE TOP OF MY LIST OF SUSPECTS.
YOU MIGHT AS WELL START THE DAY WITH TWENTY LASHES FOR EACH OF THEM.
UNDOUBTEDLY, TAARON. BUT I FIND THAT A BIT HARSH. WHAT THESE LADS NEED IS ATONEMENT, NOT PUNISHMENT.
GUARDS OF KRATH, PROTECTORS OF MOUNT SPITE, I AM YOUR NEW CAPTAIN, *FELDERON COMETSEED.*
BEFORE WE BEGIN THIS GLORIOUS...AFTERNOON, LET US PRAY TO THE *GODS* THAT PROTECT OUR *BOUNTIFUL REALMS*.

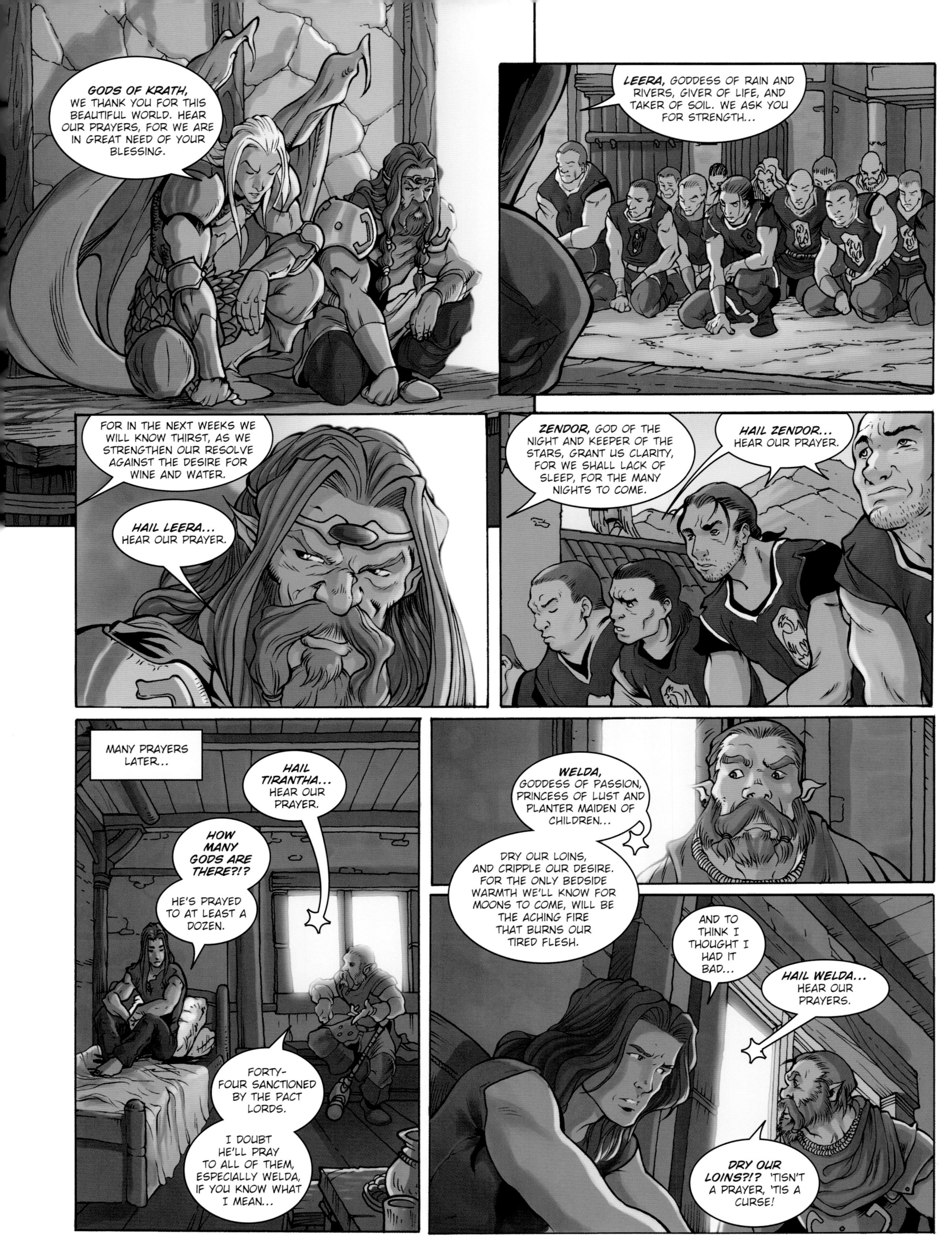
GODS OF KRATH, WE THANK YOU FOR THIS BEAUTIFUL WORLD. HEAR OUR PRAYERS, FOR WE ARE IN GREAT NEED OF YOUR BLESSING.
LEERA, GODDESS OF RAIN AND RIVERS, GIVER OF LIFE, AND TAKER OF SOIL. WE ASK YOU FOR STRENGTH...
FOR IN THE NEXT WEEKS WE WILL KNOW THIRST, AS WE STRENGTHEN OUR RESOLVE AGAINST THE DESIRE FOR WINE AND WATER.
HAIL LEERA... HEAR OUR PRAYER.
ZENDOR, GOD OF THE NIGHT AND KEEPER OF THE STARS, GRANT US CLARITY, FOR WE SHALL LACK OF SLEEP, FOR THE MANY NIGHTS TO COME.
HAIL ZENDOR... HEAR OUR PRAYER.
MANY PRAYERS LATER...
HAIL TIRANTHA... HEAR OUR PRAYER.
HOW MANY GODS ARE THERE?!?
HE'S PRAYED TO AT LEAST A DOZEN.
FORTY-FOUR SANCTIONED BY THE PACT LORDS.
I DOUBT HE'LL PRAY TO ALL OF THEM, ESPECIALLY WELDA, IF YOU KNOW WHAT I MEAN...
WELDA, GODDESS OF PASSION, PRINCESS OF LUST AND PLANTER MAIDEN OF CHILDREN...
DRY OUR LOINS, AND CRIPPLE OUR DESIRE. FOR THE ONLY BEDSIDE WARMTH WE'LL KNOW FOR MOONS TO COME, WILL BE THE ACHING FIRE THAT BURNS OUR TIRED FLESH.
AND TO THINK I THOUGHT I HAD IT BAD...
HAIL WELDA... HEAR OUR PRAYERS.
DRY OUR LOINS?!? 'TISN'T A PRAYER, 'TIS A CURSE!

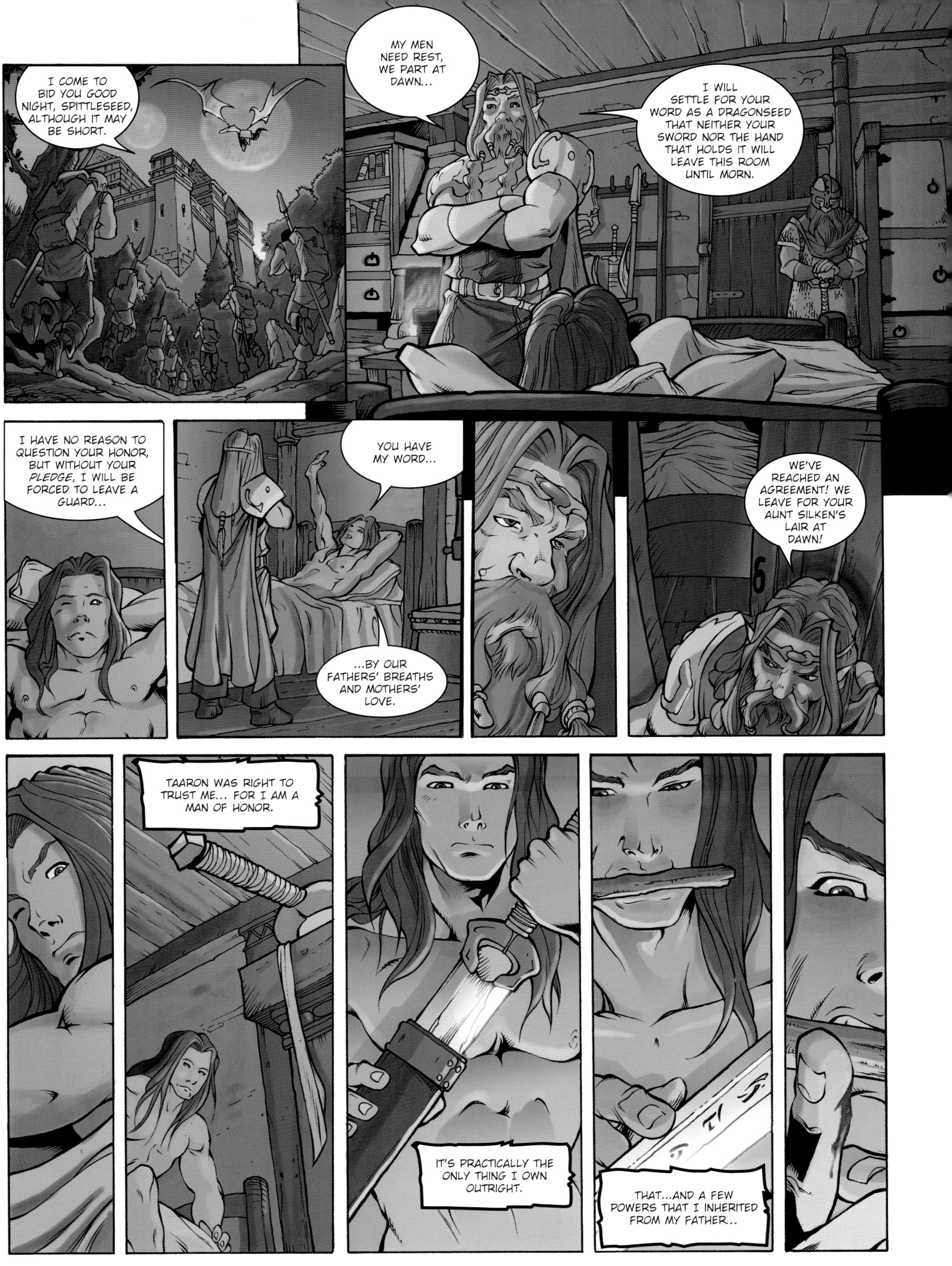
I COME TO BID YOU GOOD NIGHT, SPITTLESEED, ALTHOUGH IT MAY BE SHORT.
MY MEN NEED REST, WE PART AT DAWN...
I WILL SETTLE FOR YOUR WORD AS A DRAGONSEED THAT NEITHER YOUR SWORD NOR THE HAND THAT HOLDS IT WILL LEAVE THIS ROOM UNTIL MORN.
I HAVE NO REASON TO QUESTION YOUR HONOR, BUT WITHOUT YOUR *PLEDGE*, I WILL BE FORCED TO LEAVE A GUARD...
YOU HAVE MY WORD...
...BY OUR FATHERS' BREATHS AND MOTHERS' LOVE.
WE'VE REACHED AN AGREEMENT! WE LEAVE FOR YOUR AUNT SILKEN'S LAIR AT DAWN!
TAARON WAS RIGHT TO TRUST ME... FOR I AM A MAN OF HONOR.
IT'S PRACTICALLY THE ONLY THING I OWN OUTRIGHT.
THAT...AND A FEW POWERS THAT I INHERITED FROM MY FATHER...

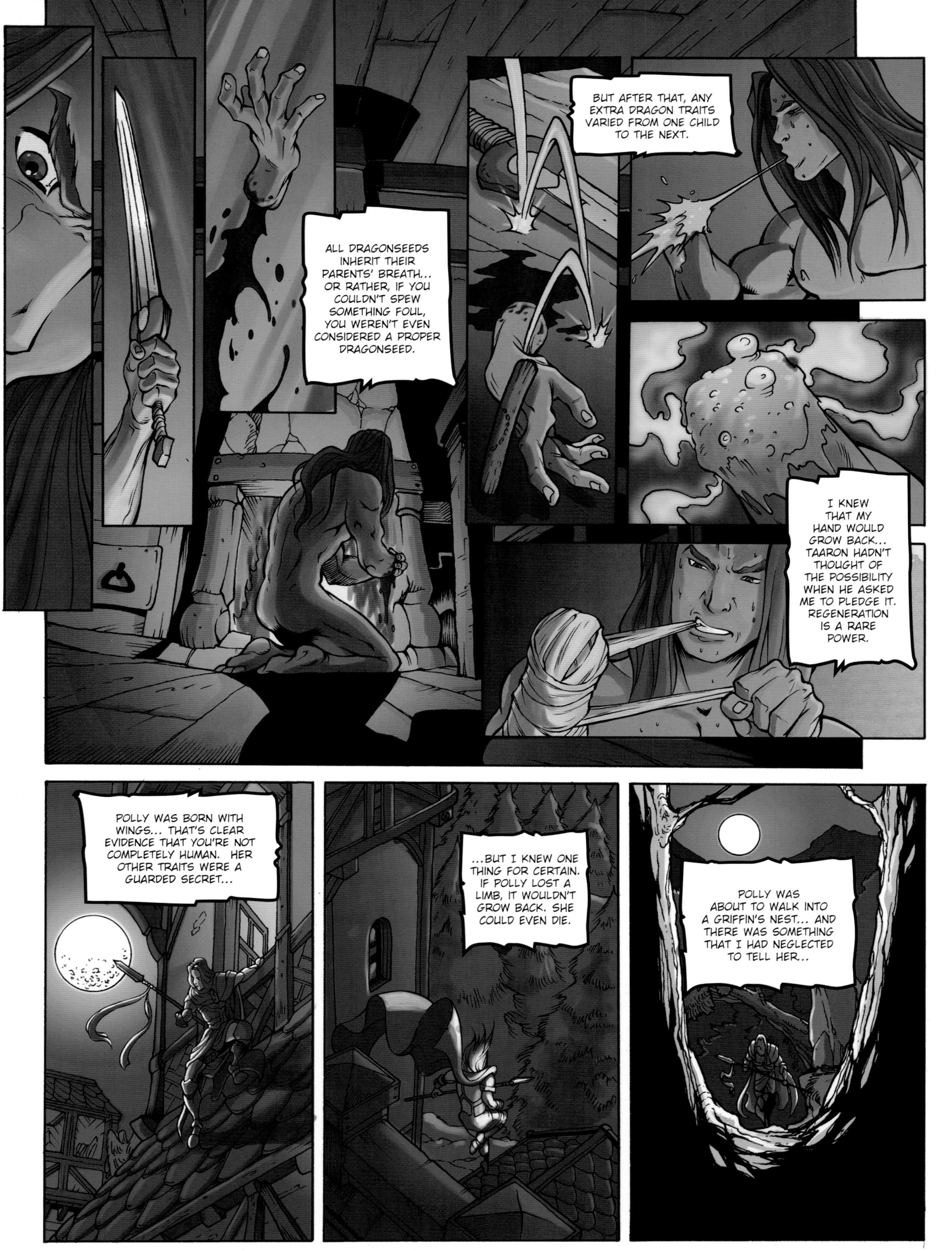
ALL DRAGONSEEDS INHERIT THEIR PARENTS' BREATH... OR RATHER, IF YOU COULDN'T SPEW SOMETHING FOUL, YOU WEREN'T EVEN CONSIDERED A PROPER DRAGONSEED.
BUT AFTER THAT, ANY EXTRA DRAGON TRAITS VARIED FROM ONE CHILD TO THE NEXT.
I KNEW THAT MY HAND WOULD GROW BACK... TAARON HADN'T THOUGHT OF THE POSSIBILITY WHEN HE ASKED ME TO PLEDGE IT. REGENERATION IS A RARE POWER.
POLLY WAS BORN WITH WINGS... THAT'S CLEAR EVIDENCE THAT YOU'RE NOT COMPLETELY HUMAN. HER OTHER TRAITS WERE A GUARDED SECRET...
...BUT I KNEW ONE THING FOR CERTAIN. IF POLLY LOST A LIMB, IT WOULDN'T GROW BACK. SHE COULD EVEN DIE.
POLLY WAS ABOUT TO WALK INTO A GRIFFIN'S NEST... AND THERE WAS SOMETHING THAT I HAD NEGLECTED TO TELL HER..

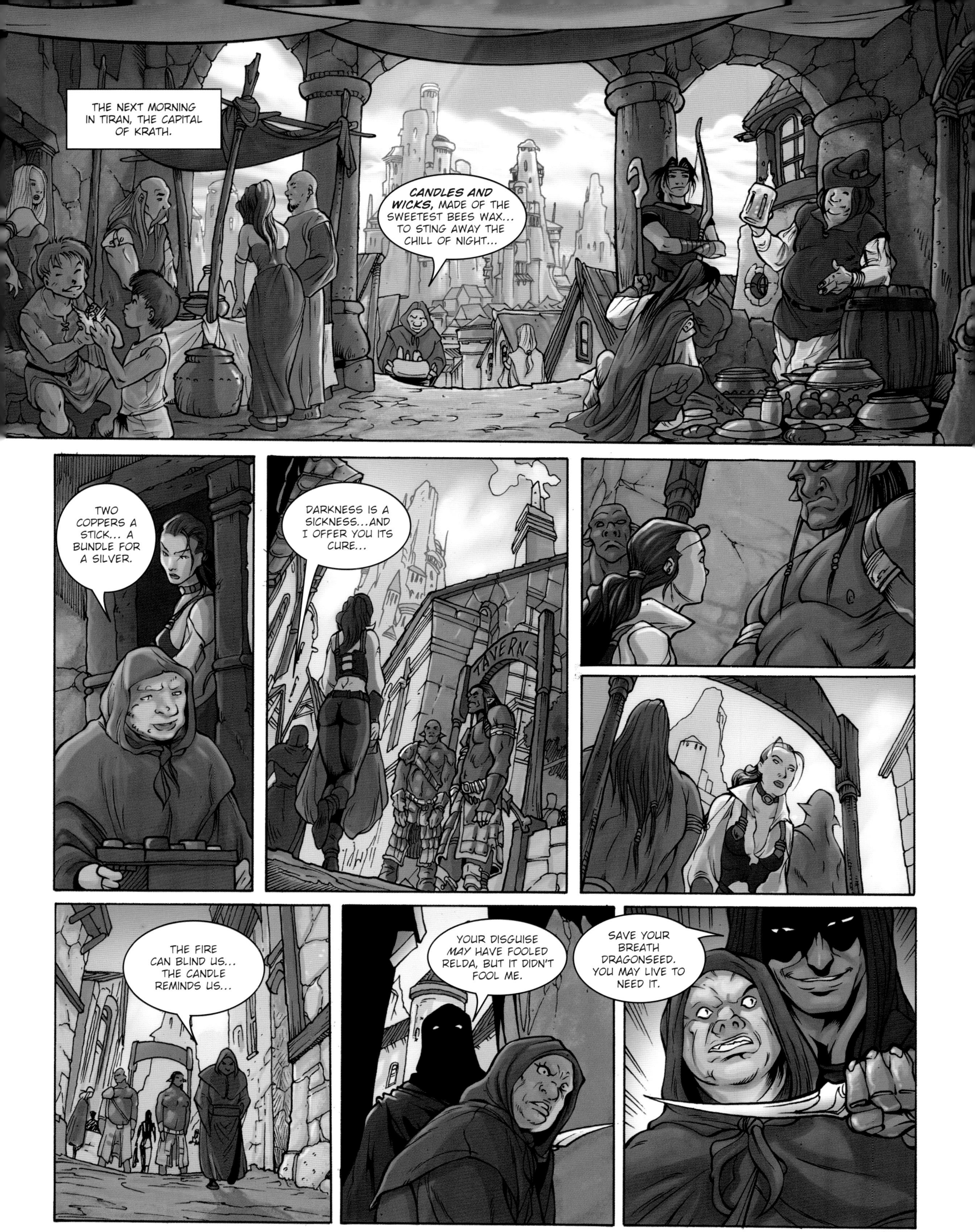
THE NEXT MORNING IN TIRAN, THE CAPITAL OF KRATH.
CANDLES AND WICKS, MADE OF THE SWEETEST BEES WAX... TO STING AWAY THE CHILL OF NIGHT...
TWO COPPERS A STICK... A BUNDLE FOR A SILVER.
DARKNESS IS A SICKNESS...AND I OFFER YOU ITS CURE...
TAVERN
THE FIRE CAN BLIND US... THE CANDLE REMINDS US...
YOUR DISGUISE MAY HAVE FOOLED RELDA, BUT IT DIDN'T FOOL ME.
SAVE YOUR BREATH DRAGONSEED. YOU MAY LIVE TO NEED IT.

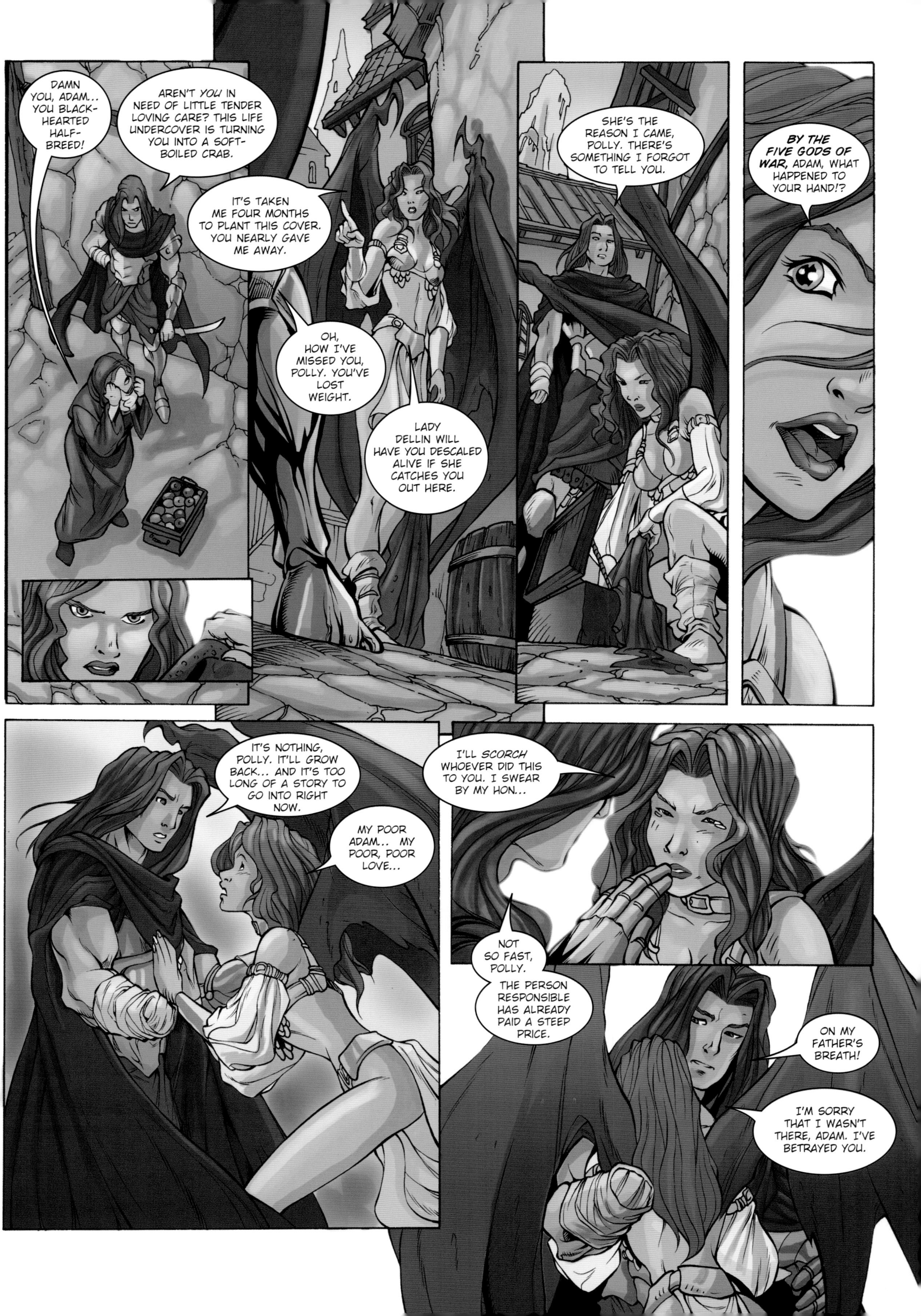
DAMN YOU, ADAM... YOU BLACK-HEARTED HALF-BREED!
AREN'T *YOU* IN NEED OF LITTLE TENDER LOVING CARE? THIS LIFE UNDERCOVER IS TURNING YOU INTO A SOFT-BOILED CRAB.
IT'S TAKEN ME FOUR MONTHS TO PLANT THIS COVER. YOU NEARLY GAVE ME AWAY.
OH, HOW I'VE MISSED YOU, POLLY. YOU'VE LOST WEIGHT.
LADY DELLIN WILL HAVE YOU DESCALED ALIVE IF SHE CATCHES YOU OUT HERE.
SHE'S THE REASON I CAME, POLLY. THERE'S SOMETHING I FORGOT TO TELL YOU.
BY THE FIVE GODS OF WAR, ADAM, WHAT HAPPENED TO YOUR HAND!?
IT'S NOTHING, POLLY. IT'LL GROW BACK... AND IT'S TOO LONG OF A STORY TO GO INTO RIGHT NOW.
MY POOR ADAM... MY POOR, POOR LOVE...
I'LL *SCORCH* WHOEVER DID THIS TO YOU. I SWEAR BY MY HON...
NOT SO FAST, POLLY.
THE PERSON RESPONSIBLE HAS ALREADY PAID A STEEP PRICE.
ON MY FATHER'S BREATH!
I'M SORRY THAT I WASN'T THERE, ADAM. I'VE BETRAYED YOU.

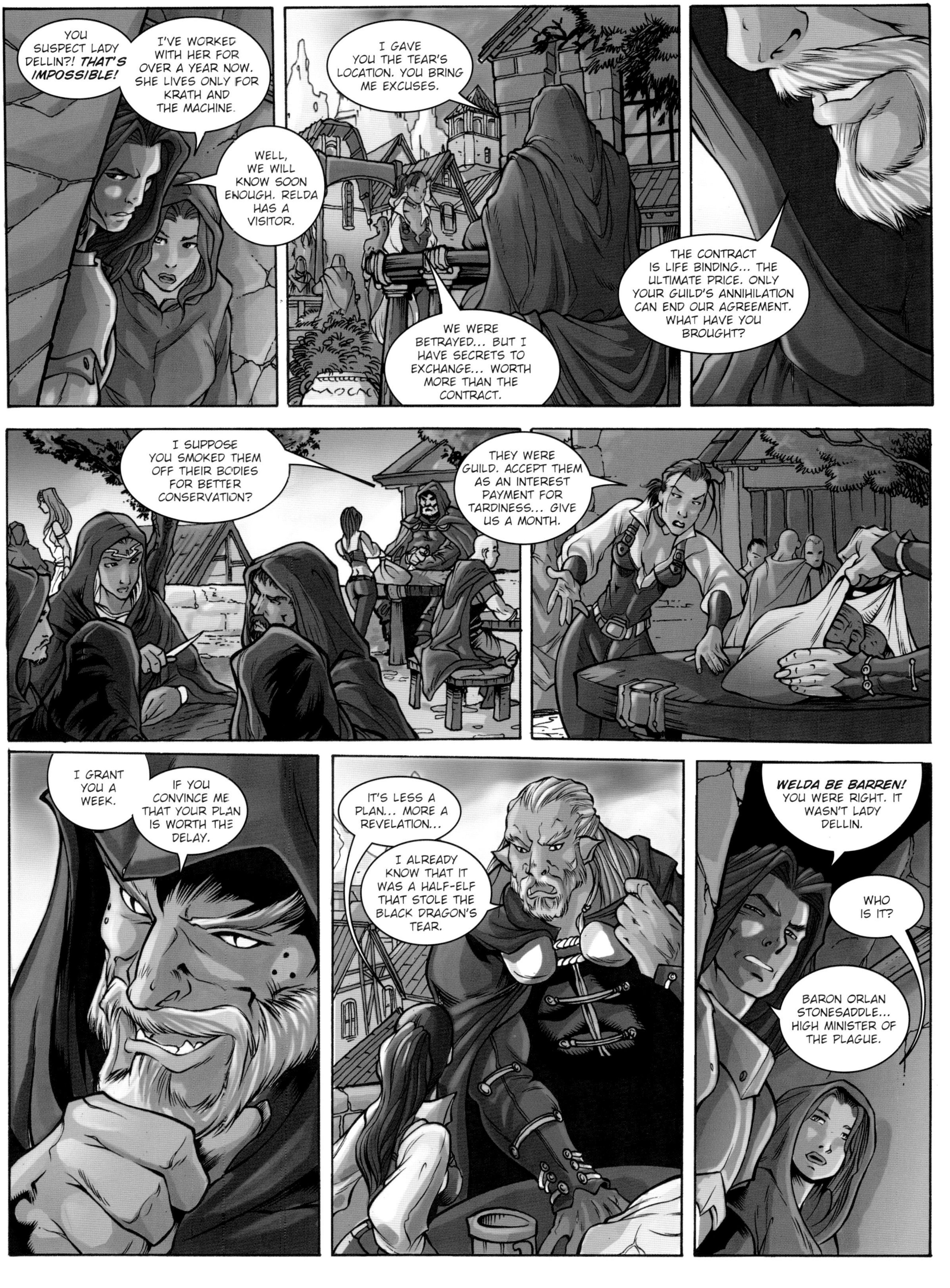
YOU SUSPECT LADY DELLIN?! THAT'S IMPOSSIBLE!
I'VE WORKED WITH HER FOR OVER A YEAR NOW. SHE LIVES ONLY FOR KRATH AND THE MACHINE.
WELL, WE WILL KNOW SOON ENOUGH. RELDA HAS A VISITOR.
I GAVE YOU THE TEAR'S LOCATION. YOU BRING ME EXCUSES.
WE WERE BETRAYED... BUT I HAVE SECRETS TO EXCHANGE... WORTH MORE THAN THE CONTRACT.
THE CONTRACT IS LIFE BINDING... THE ULTIMATE PRICE. ONLY YOUR GUILD'S ANNIHILATION CAN END OUR AGREEMENT. WHAT HAVE YOU BROUGHT?
I SUPPOSE YOU SMOKED THEM OFF THEIR BODIES FOR BETTER CONSERVATION?
THEY WERE GUILD. ACCEPT THEM AS AN INTEREST PAYMENT FOR TARDINESS... GIVE US A MONTH.
I GRANT YOU A WEEK.
IF YOU CONVINCE ME THAT YOUR PLAN IS WORTH THE DELAY.
IT'S LESS A PLAN... MORE A REVELATION...
I ALREADY KNOW THAT IT WAS A HALF-ELF THAT STOLE THE BLACK DRAGON'S TEAR.
WELDA BE BARREN! YOU WERE RIGHT. IT WASN'T LADY DELLIN.
WHO IS IT?
BARON ORLAN STONESADDLE... HIGH MINISTER OF THE PLAGUE.

I ALSO KNOW THAT, *SHE* LIVES, AND HAS NO INTENTION OF SELLING IT TO ME... OR SHE WOULD BE HERE.

BUT THAT IS NOT ALL I KNOW, MY LORD... I KNOW HER NAME... WHERE SHE IS FROM...

I DON'T CARE WHERE SHE RUNS... AS LONG AS IT IS FAR FROM HERE.

BUT SIRE, LET'S BE REASONABLE... I THOUGHT YOU WANTED... I CAN FIND HER...

I'M NOT INTERESTED IN WHAT YOU COULD DISCOVER. IN MY OPINION YOU KNOW *TOO MUCH* ALREADY.

GET HER OUT OF HERE... SHE OWES US HER HEAD... I WANT IT PICKLED!

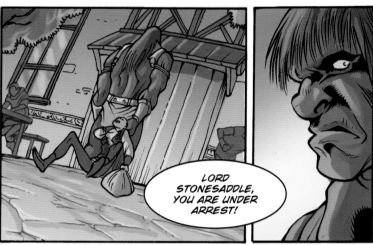

LORD STONESADDLE, YOU ARE UNDER ARREST!

BY THE INVESTED POWERS OF THE LORDS OF THE PACT... I ARREST YOU FOR TREASON TO THE CRUSADE.

LADY DELLIN... WHAT HAVE I DONE? IS IT THE QUALITY OF OUR FOOD?

YOU ARE MY PRISONER. FOLLOW ME FOR QUESTIONING, OR I SHALL BE FORCED TO EMPLOY MAGIC AND BRUTE FORCE.

HERE I WAS DOING MY BEST TO WIN YOU OVER AS A REGULAR CUSTOMER. YOUR MEAL WAS PREPARED WITH SPECIAL CARE.

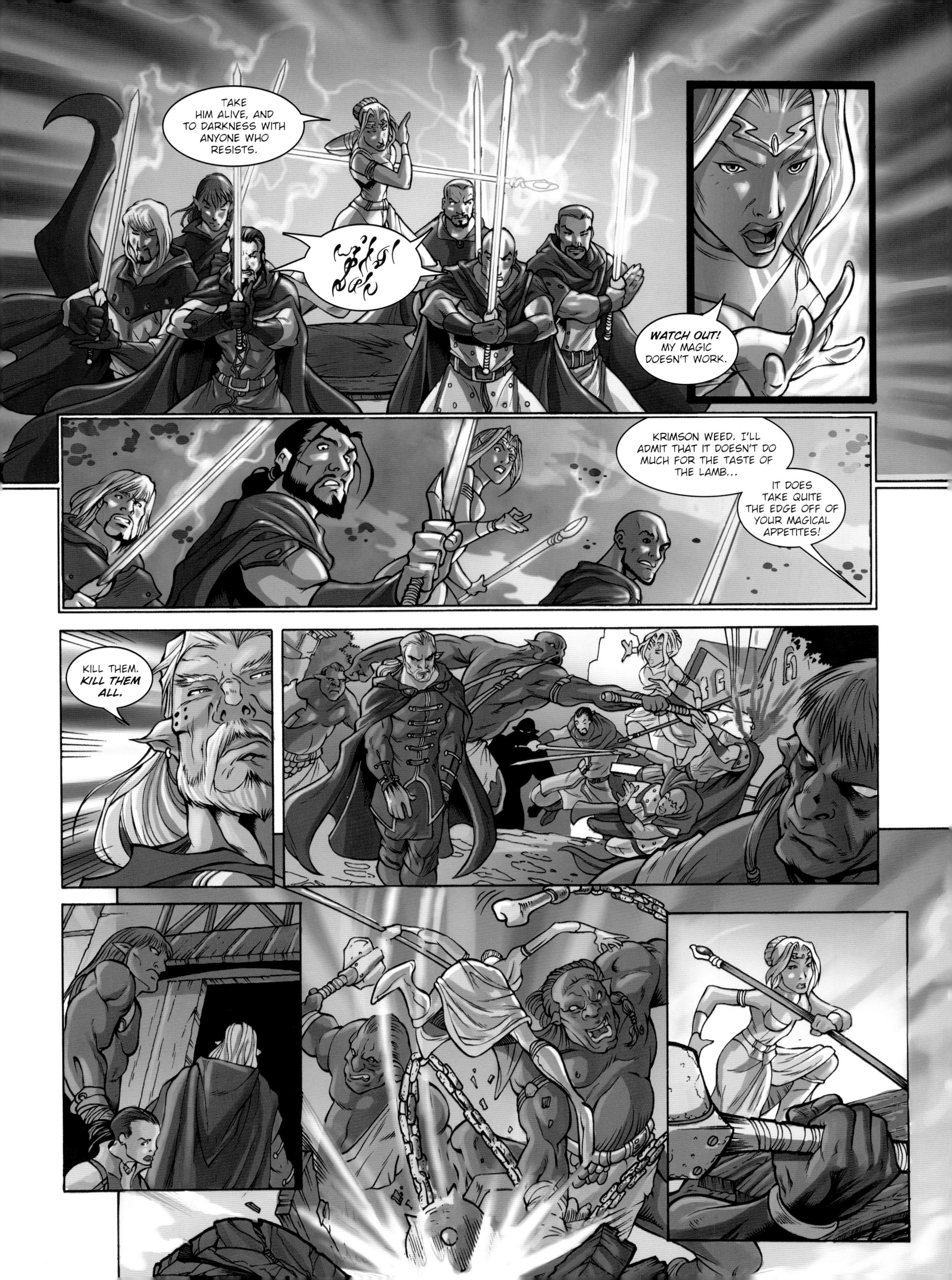
TAKE HIM ALIVE, AND TO DARKNESS WITH ANYONE WHO RESISTS.
WATCH OUT! MY MAGIC DOESN'T WORK.
KRIMSON WEED. I'LL ADMIT THAT IT DOESN'T DO MUCH FOR THE TASTE OF THE LAMB...
IT DOES TAKE QUITE THE EDGE OFF OF YOUR MAGICAL APPETITES!
KILL THEM. KILL THEM ALL.

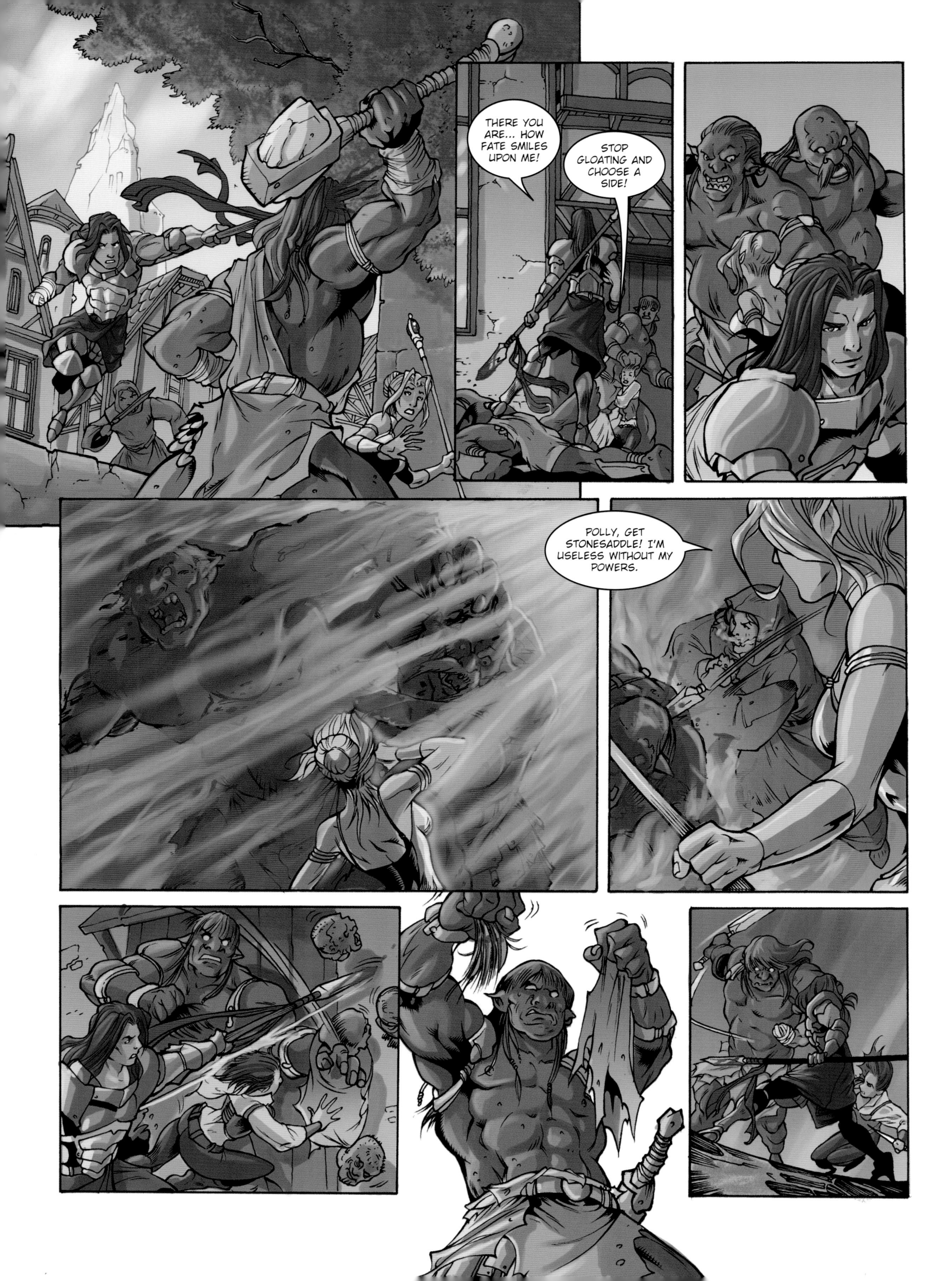
THERE YOU ARE... HOW FATE SMILES UPON ME!
STOP GLOATING AND CHOOSE A SIDE!
POLLY, GET STONESADDLE! I'M USELESS WITHOUT MY POWERS.

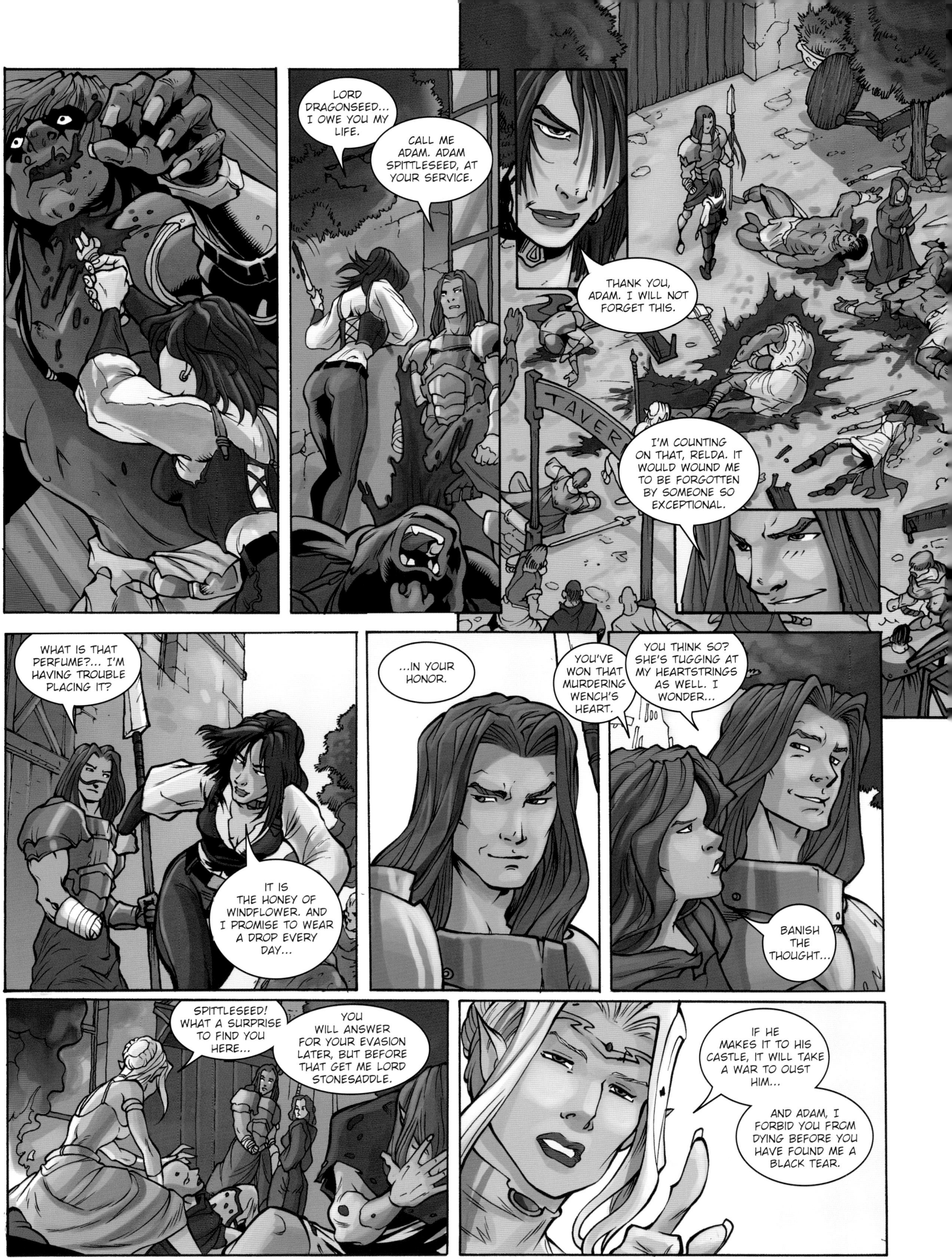
LORD DRAGONSEED... I OWE YOU MY LIFE.
CALL ME ADAM. ADAM SPITTLESEED, AT YOUR SERVICE.
THANK YOU, ADAM. I WILL NOT FORGET THIS.
TAVER
I'M COUNTING ON THAT, RELDA. IT WOULD WOUND ME TO BE FORGOTTEN BY SOMEONE SO EXCEPTIONAL.
WHAT IS THAT PERFUME?... I'M HAVING TROUBLE PLACING IT?
IT IS THE HONEY OF WINDFLOWER. AND I PROMISE TO WEAR A DROP EVERY DAY...
...IN YOUR HONOR.
YOU'VE WON THAT MURDERING WENCH'S HEART.
YOU THINK SO? SHE'S TUGGING AT MY HEARTSTRINGS AS WELL. I WONDER...
BANISH THE THOUGHT...
SPITTLESEED! WHAT A SURPRISE TO FIND YOU HERE...
YOU WILL ANSWER FOR YOUR EVASION LATER, BUT BEFORE THAT GET ME LORD STONESADDLE.
IF HE MAKES IT TO HIS CASTLE, IT WILL TAKE A WAR TO OUST HIM...
AND ADAM, I FORBID YOU FROM DYING BEFORE YOU HAVE FOUND ME A BLACK TEAR.

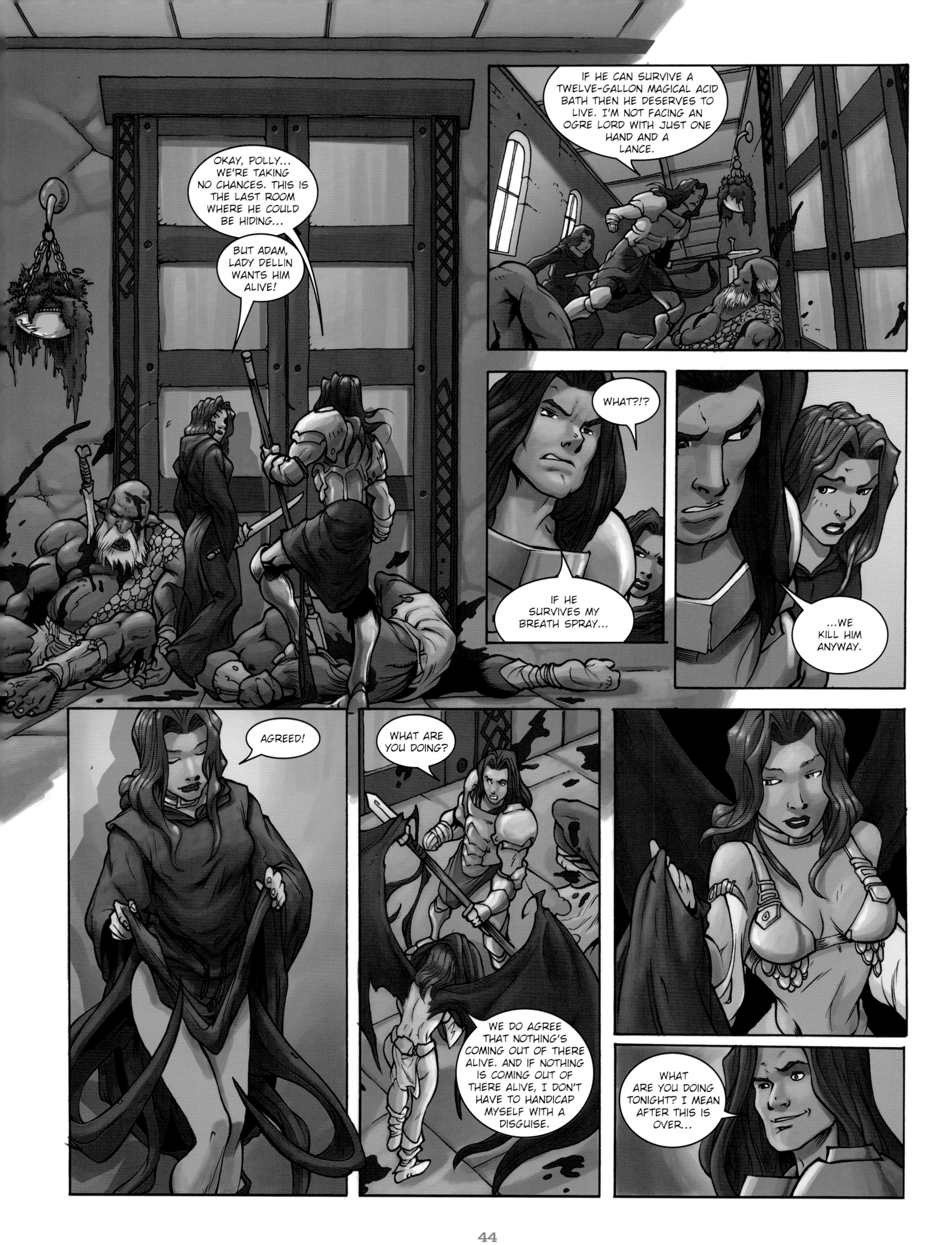
OKAY, POLLY... WE'RE TAKING NO CHANCES. THIS IS THE LAST ROOM WHERE HE COULD BE HIDING...
BUT ADAM, LADY DELLIN WANTS HIM ALIVE!
IF HE CAN SURVIVE A TWELVE-GALLON MAGICAL ACID BATH THEN HE DESERVES TO LIVE. I'M NOT FACING AN OGRE LORD WITH JUST ONE HAND AND A LANCE.
WHAT?!?
IF HE SURVIVES MY BREATH SPRAY...
...WE KILL HIM ANYWAY.
AGREED!
WHAT ARE YOU DOING?
WE DO AGREE THAT NOTHING'S COMING OUT OF THERE ALIVE. AND IF NOTHING IS COMING OUT OF THERE ALIVE, I DON'T HAVE TO HANDICAP MYSELF WITH A DISGUISE.
WHAT ARE YOU DOING TONIGHT? I MEAN AFTER THIS IS OVER...

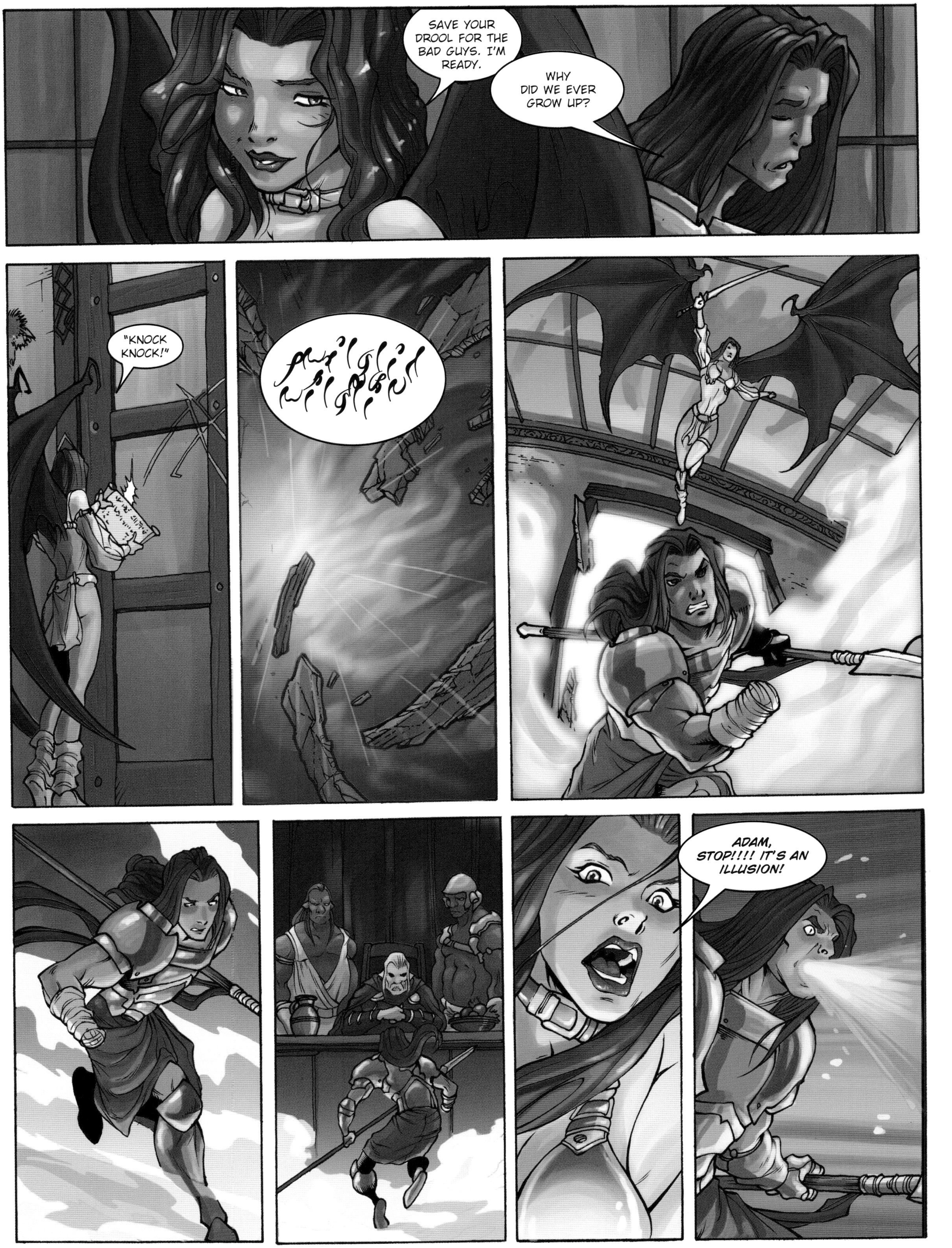
SAVE YOUR DROOL FOR THE BAD GUYS. I'M READY.
WHY DID WE EVER GROW UP?
"KNOCK KNOCK!"
ADAM, STOP!!!! IT'S AN ILLUSION!

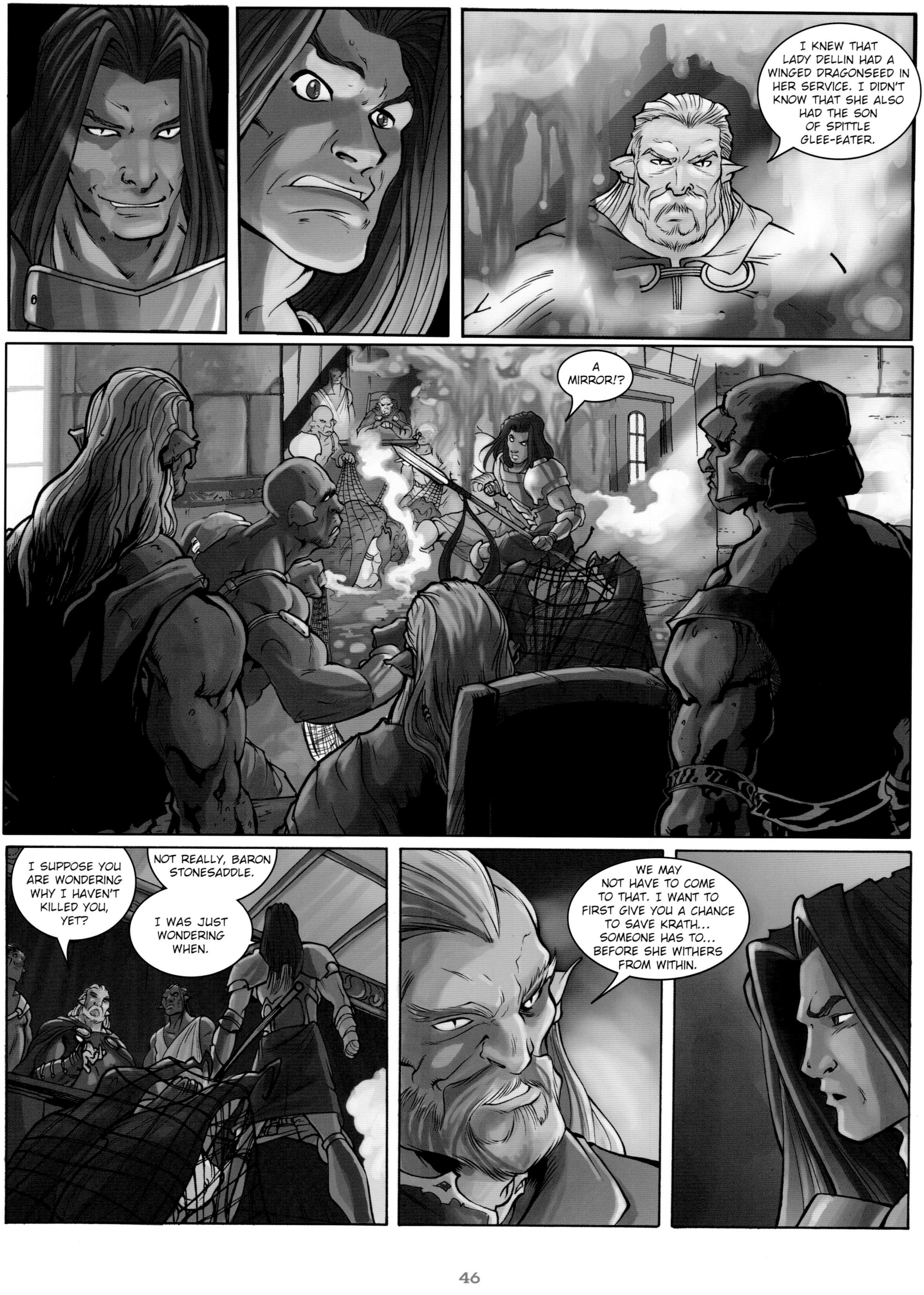
I KNEW THAT LADY DELLIN HAD A WINGED DRAGONSEED IN HER SERVICE. I DIDN'T KNOW THAT SHE ALSO HAD THE SON OF SPITTLE GLEE-EATER.
A MIRROR!?
I SUPPOSE YOU ARE WONDERING WHY I HAVEN'T KILLED YOU, YET?
NOT REALLY, BARON STONESADDLE.
I WAS JUST WONDERING WHEN.
WE MAY NOT HAVE TO COME TO THAT. I WANT TO FIRST GIVE YOU A CHANCE TO SAVE KRATH... SOMEONE HAS TO... BEFORE SHE WITHERS FROM WITHIN.

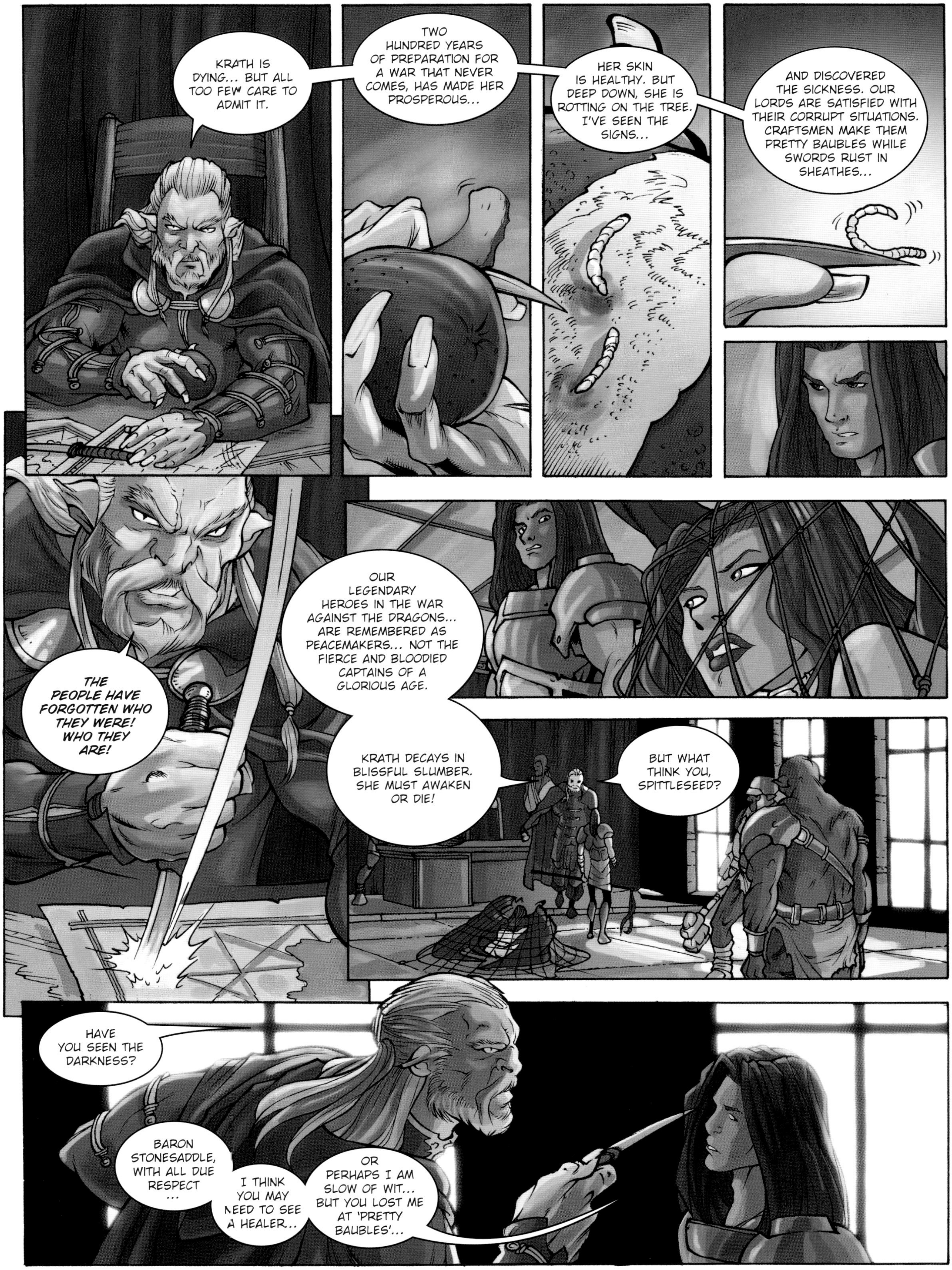
KRATH IS DYING... BUT ALL TOO FEW CARE TO ADMIT IT.
TWO HUNDRED YEARS OF PREPARATION FOR A WAR THAT NEVER COMES, HAS MADE HER PROSPEROUS...
HER SKIN IS HEALTHY. BUT DEEP DOWN, SHE IS ROTTING ON THE TREE. I'VE SEEN THE SIGNS...
AND DISCOVERED THE SICKNESS. OUR LORDS ARE SATISFIED WITH THEIR CORRUPT SITUATIONS. CRAFTSMEN MAKE THEM PRETTY BAUBLES WHILE SWORDS RUST IN SHEATHES...
THE PEOPLE HAVE FORGOTTEN WHO THEY WERE! WHO THEY ARE!
OUR LEGENDARY HEROES IN THE WAR AGAINST THE DRAGONS... ARE REMEMBERED AS PEACEMAKERS... NOT THE FIERCE AND BLOODIED CAPTAINS OF A GLORIOUS AGE.
KRATH DECAYS IN BLISSFUL SLUMBER. SHE MUST AWAKEN OR DIE!
BUT WHAT THINK YOU, SPITTLESEED?
HAVE YOU SEEN THE DARKNESS?
BARON STONESADDLE, WITH ALL DUE RESPECT ...
I THINK YOU MAY NEED TO SEE A HEALER...
OR PERHAPS I AM SLOW OF WIT... BUT YOU LOST ME AT 'PRETTY BAUBLES'...

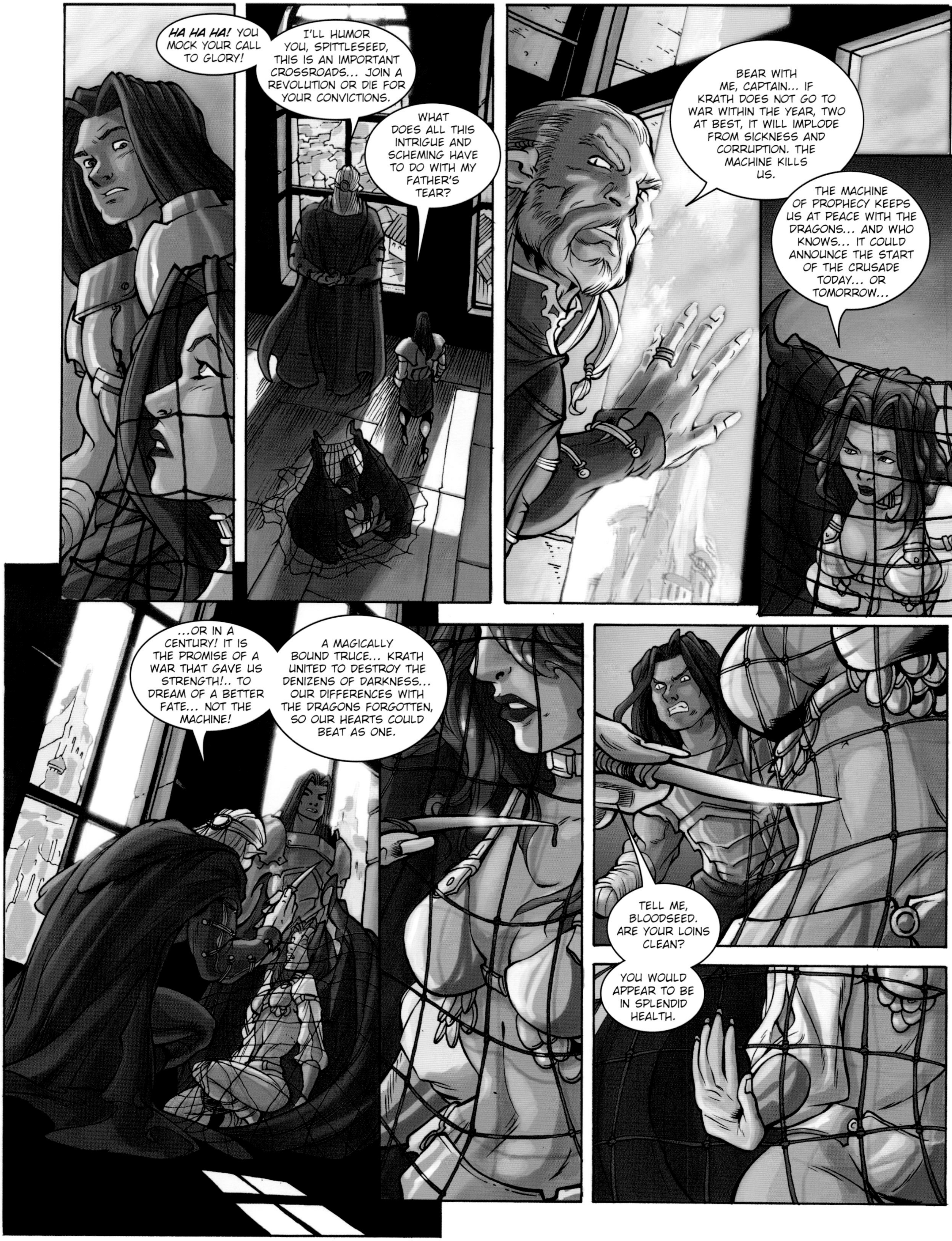
HA HA HA! YOU MOCK YOUR CALL TO GLORY!
I'LL HUMOR YOU, SPITTLESEED, THIS IS AN IMPORTANT CROSSROADS... JOIN A REVOLUTION OR DIE FOR YOUR CONVICTIONS.
WHAT DOES ALL THIS INTRIGUE AND SCHEMING HAVE TO DO WITH MY FATHER'S TEAR?
BEAR WITH ME, CAPTAIN... IF KRATH DOES NOT GO TO WAR WITHIN THE YEAR, TWO AT BEST, IT WILL IMPLODE FROM SICKNESS AND CORRUPTION. THE MACHINE KILLS US.
THE MACHINE OF PROPHECY KEEPS US AT PEACE WITH THE DRAGONS... AND WHO KNOWS... IT COULD ANNOUNCE THE START OF THE CRUSADE TODAY... OR TOMORROW...
...OR IN A CENTURY! IT IS THE PROMISE OF A WAR THAT GAVE US STRENGTH!.. TO DREAM OF A BETTER FATE... NOT THE MACHINE!
A MAGICALLY BOUND TRUCE... KRATH UNITED TO DESTROY THE DENIZENS OF DARKNESS... OUR DIFFERENCES WITH THE DRAGONS FORGOTTEN, SO OUR HEARTS COULD BEAT AS ONE.
TELL ME, BLOODSEED. ARE YOUR LOINS CLEAN?
YOU WOULD APPEAR TO BE IN SPLENDID HEALTH.

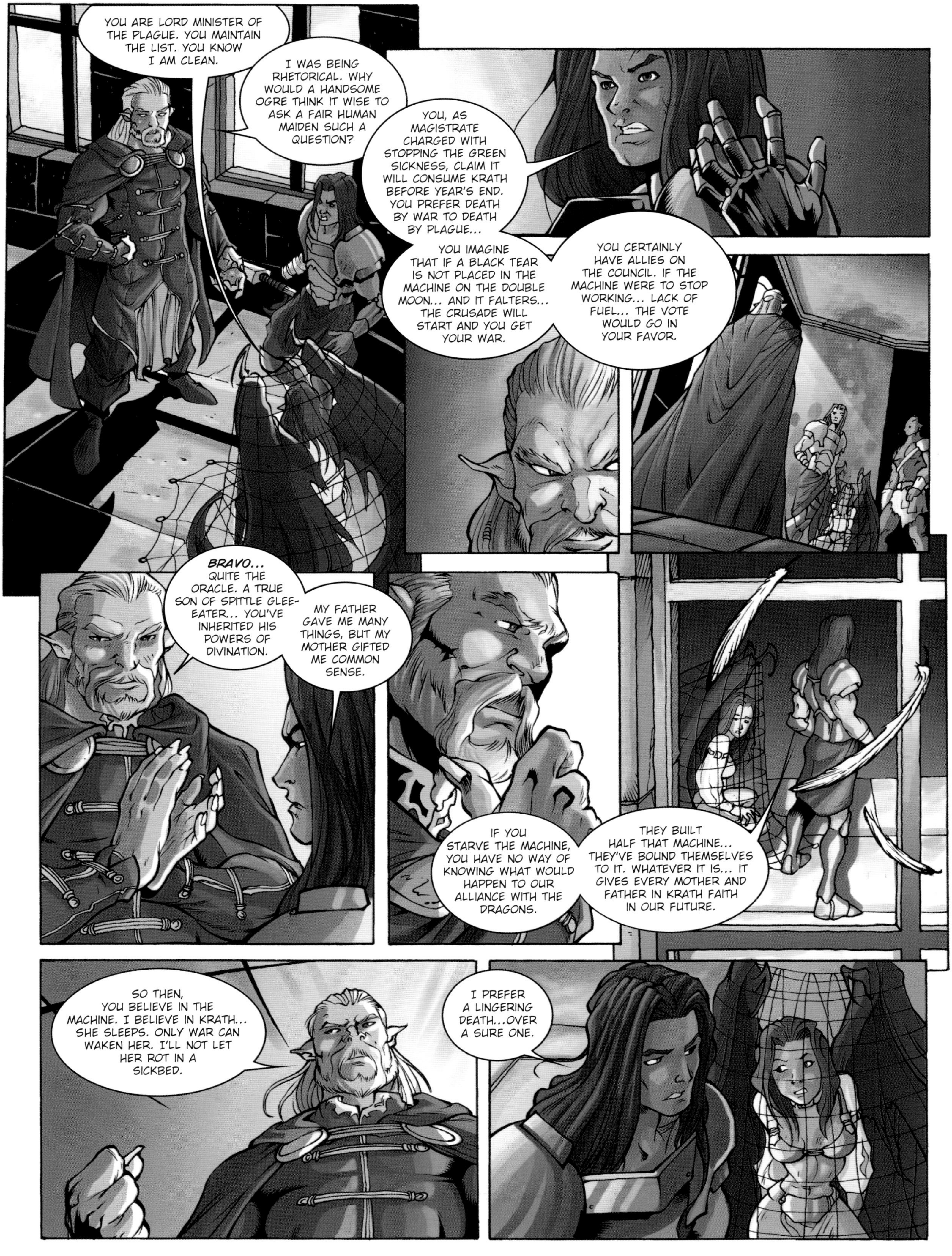
YOU ARE LORD MINISTER OF THE PLAGUE. YOU MAINTAIN THE LIST. YOU KNOW I AM CLEAN.
I WAS BEING RHETORICAL. WHY WOULD A HANDSOME OGRE THINK IT WISE TO ASK A FAIR HUMAN MAIDEN SUCH A QUESTION?
YOU, AS MAGISTRATE CHARGED WITH STOPPING THE GREEN SICKNESS, CLAIM IT WILL CONSUME KRATH BEFORE YEAR'S END. YOU PREFER DEATH BY WAR TO DEATH BY PLAGUE...
YOU IMAGINE THAT IF A BLACK TEAR IS NOT PLACED IN THE MACHINE ON THE DOUBLE MOON... AND IT FALTERS... THE CRUSADE WILL START AND YOU GET YOUR WAR.
YOU CERTAINLY HAVE ALLIES ON THE COUNCIL. IF THE MACHINE WERE TO STOP WORKING... LACK OF FUEL... THE VOTE WOULD GO IN YOUR FAVOR.
BRAVO... QUITE THE ORACLE. A TRUE SON OF SPITTLE GLEE-EATER... YOU'VE INHERITED HIS POWERS OF DIVINATION.
MY FATHER GAVE ME MANY THINGS, BUT MY MOTHER GIFTED ME COMMON SENSE.
IF YOU STARVE THE MACHINE, YOU HAVE NO WAY OF KNOWING WHAT WOULD HAPPEN TO OUR ALLIANCE WITH THE DRAGONS.
THEY BUILT HALF THAT MACHINE... THEY'VE BOUND THEMSELVES TO IT. WHATEVER IT IS... IT GIVES EVERY MOTHER AND FATHER IN KRATH FAITH IN OUR FUTURE.
SO THEN, YOU BELIEVE IN THE MACHINE. I BELIEVE IN KRATH... SHE SLEEPS. ONLY WAR CAN WAKEN HER. I'LL NOT LET HER ROT IN A SICKBED.
I PREFER A LINGERING DEATH...OVER A SURE ONE.

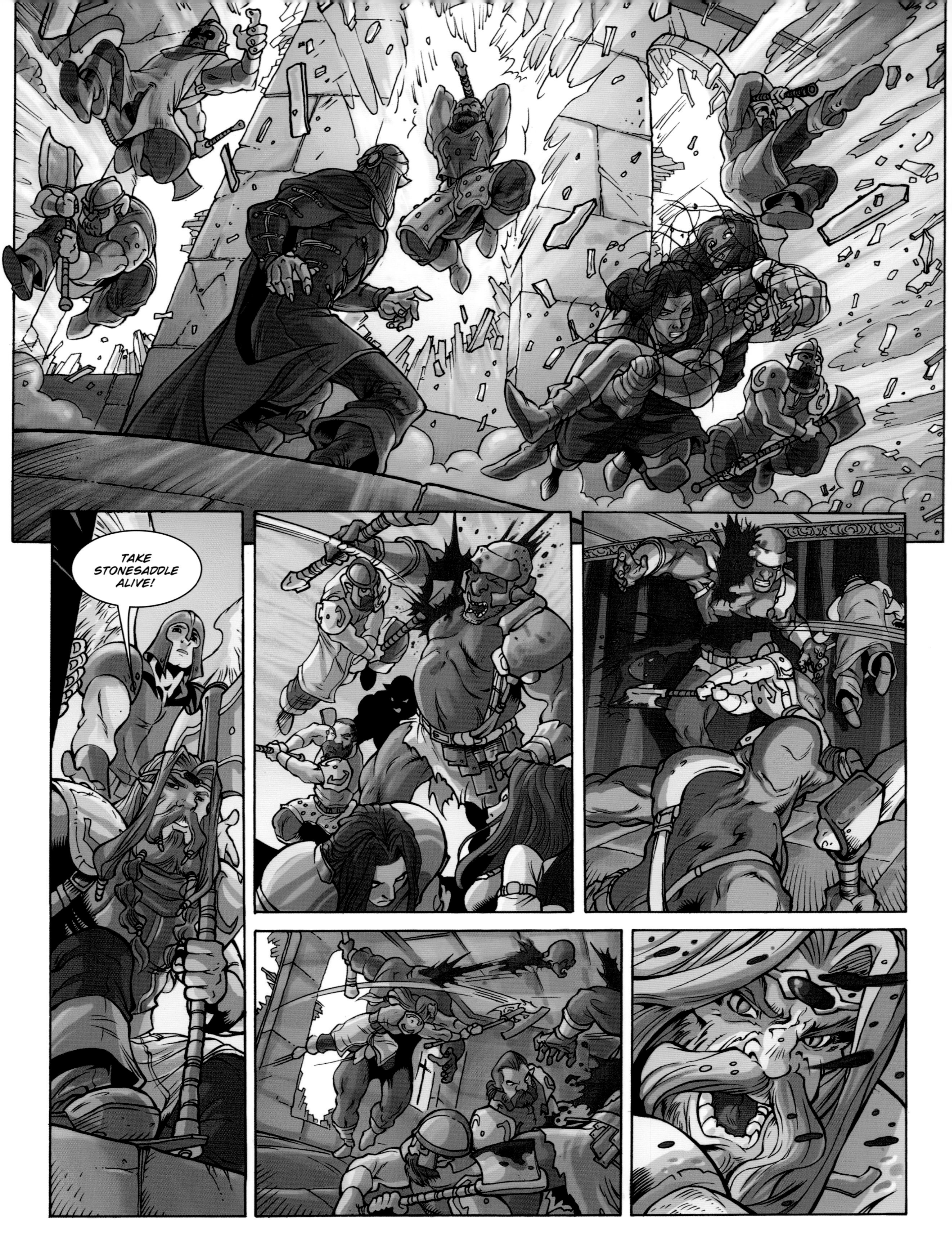
TAKE STONESADDLE ALIVE!

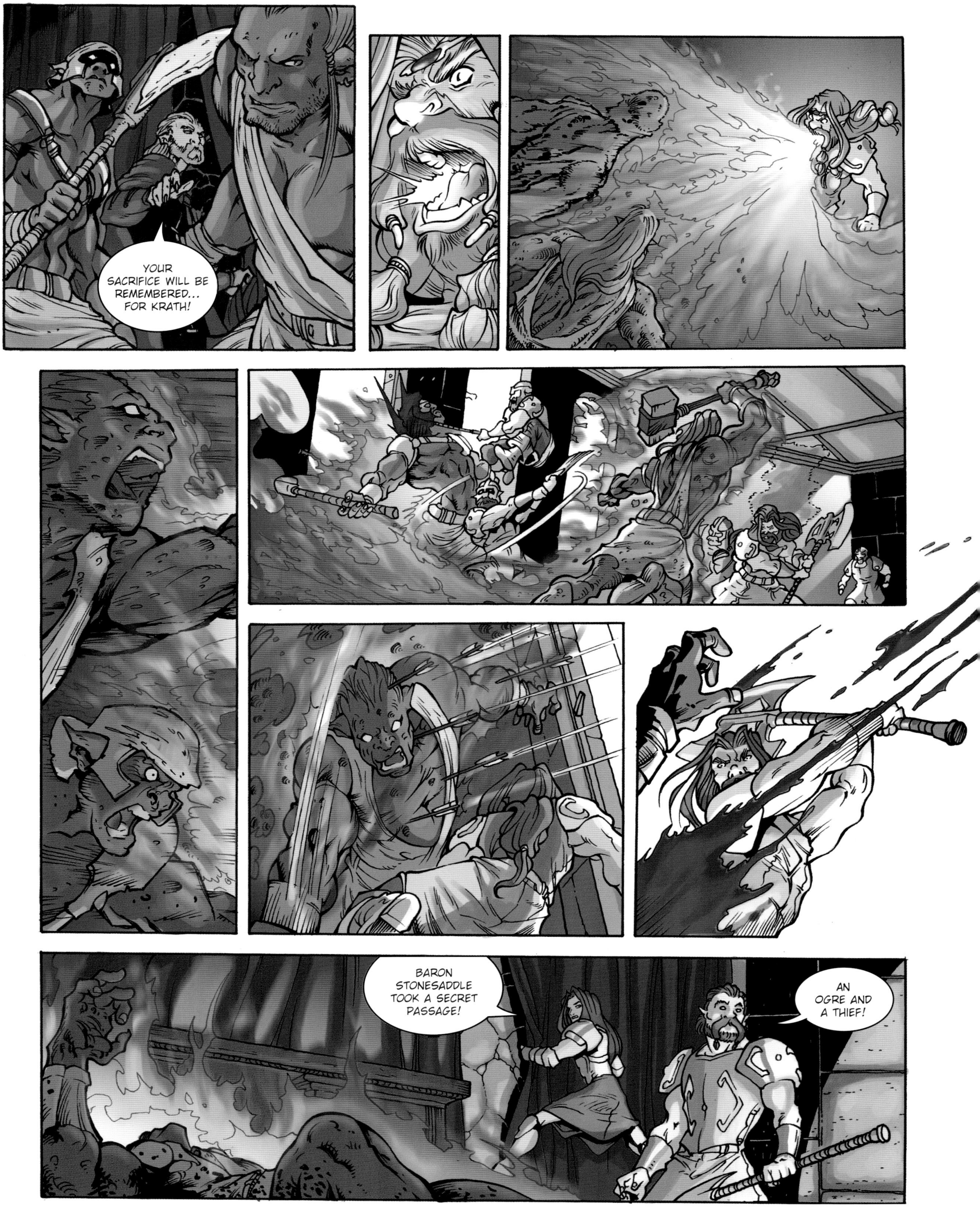
YOUR SACRIFICE WILL BE REMEMBERED... FOR KRATH!
BARON STONESADDLE TOOK A SECRET PASSAGE!
AN OGRE AND A THIEF!

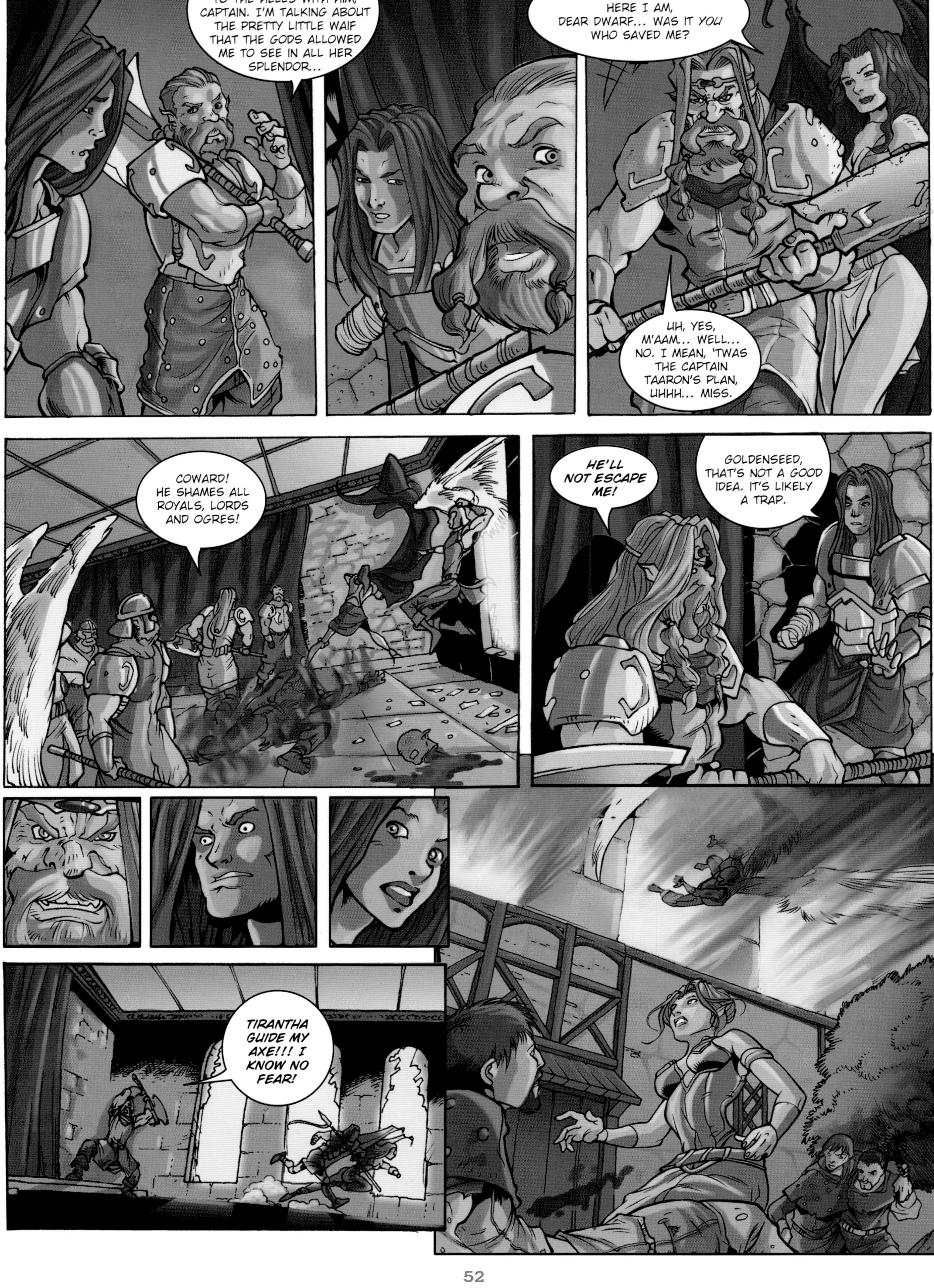
TO THE HELLS WITH HIM, CAPTAIN. I'M TALKING ABOUT THE PRETTY LITTLE WAIF THAT THE GODS ALLOWED ME TO SEE IN ALL HER SPLENDOR...
HERE I AM, DEAR DWARF... WAS IT *YOU* WHO SAVED ME?
UH, YES, M'AAM... WELL... NO. I MEAN, 'TWAS THE CAPTAIN TAARON'S PLAN, UHHH... MISS.
COWARD! HE SHAMES ALL ROYALS, LORDS AND OGRES!
HE'LL NOT ESCAPE ME!
GOLDENSEED, THAT'S NOT A GOOD IDEA. IT'S LIKELY A TRAP.
TIRANTHA GUIDE MY AXE!!! I KNOW NO FEAR!

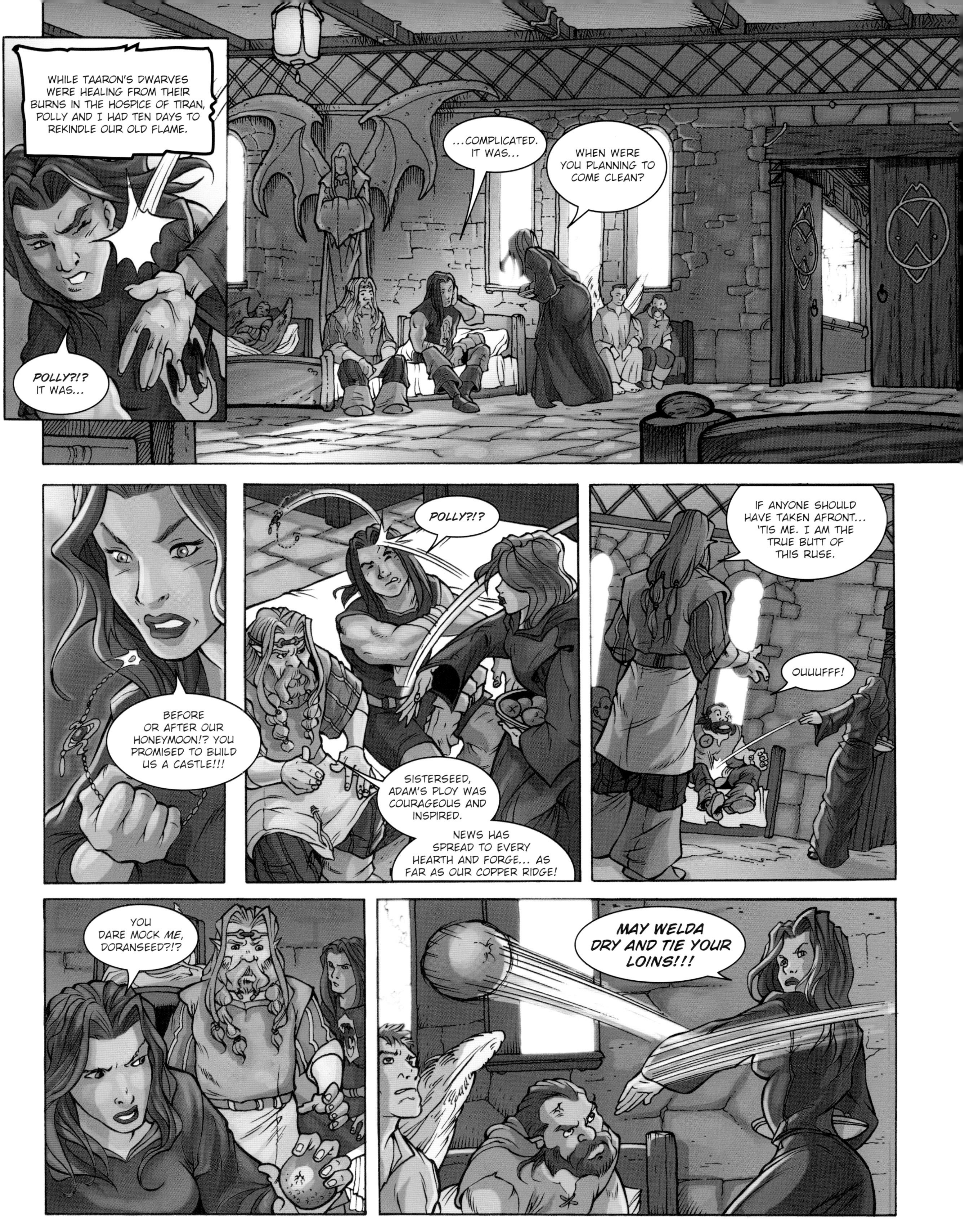
WHILE TAARON'S DWARVES WERE HEALING FROM THEIR BURNS IN THE HOSPICE OF TIRAN, POLLY AND I HAD TEN DAYS TO REKINDLE OUR OLD FLAME.
WHEN WERE YOU PLANNING TO COME CLEAN?
...COMPLICATED. IT WAS...
POLLY?!? IT WAS...
BEFORE OR AFTER OUR HONEYMOON!? YOU PROMISED TO BUILD US A CASTLE!!!
POLLY?!?
SISTERSEED, ADAM'S PLOY WAS COURAGEOUS AND INSPIRED.
NEWS HAS SPREAD TO EVERY HEARTH AND FORGE... AS FAR AS OUR COPPER RIDGE!
IF ANYONE SHOULD HAVE TAKEN AFRONT... 'TIS ME. I AM THE TRUE BUTT OF THIS RUSE.
OUUUFFF!
YOU DARE MOCK ME, DORANSEED?!?
MAY WELDA DRY AND TIE YOUR LOINS!!!

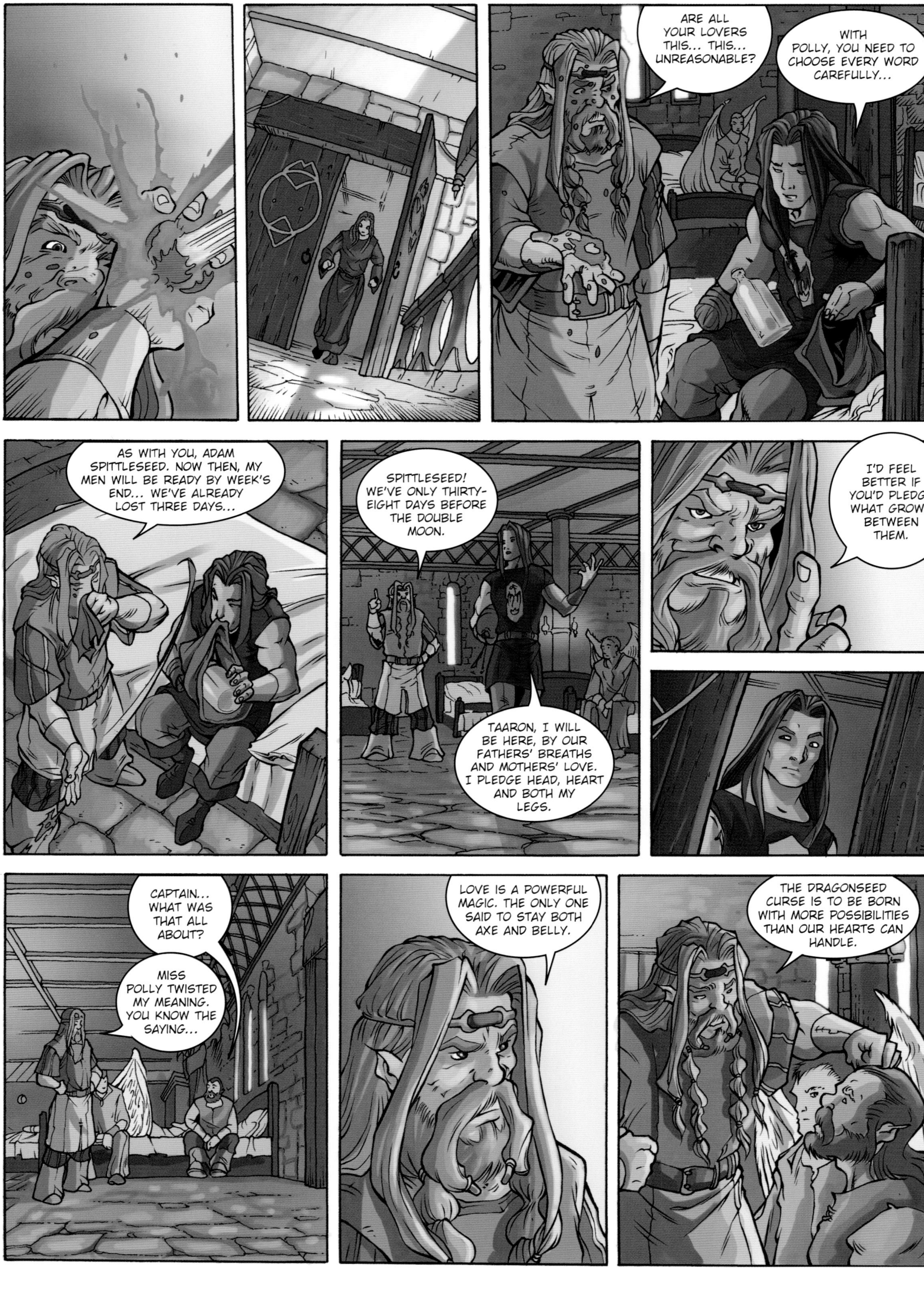
ARE ALL YOUR LOVERS THIS... THIS... UNREASONABLE?
WITH POLLY, YOU NEED TO CHOOSE EVERY WORD CAREFULLY...
AS WITH YOU, ADAM SPITTLESEED. NOW THEN, MY MEN WILL BE READY BY WEEK'S END... WE'VE ALREADY LOST THREE DAYS...
SPITTLESEED! WE'VE ONLY THIRTY-EIGHT DAYS BEFORE THE DOUBLE MOON.
TAARON, I WILL BE HERE, BY OUR FATHERS' BREATHS AND MOTHERS' LOVE. I PLEDGE HEAD, HEART AND BOTH MY LEGS.
I'D FEEL BETTER IF YOU'D PLEDGE WHAT GROWS BETWEEN THEM.
CAPTAIN... WHAT WAS THAT ALL ABOUT?
MISS POLLY TWISTED MY MEANING. YOU KNOW THE SAYING...
LOVE IS A POWERFUL MAGIC. THE ONLY ONE SAID TO STAY BOTH AXE AND BELLY.
THE DRAGONSEED CURSE IS TO BE BORN WITH MORE POSSIBILITIES THAN OUR HEARTS CAN HANDLE.

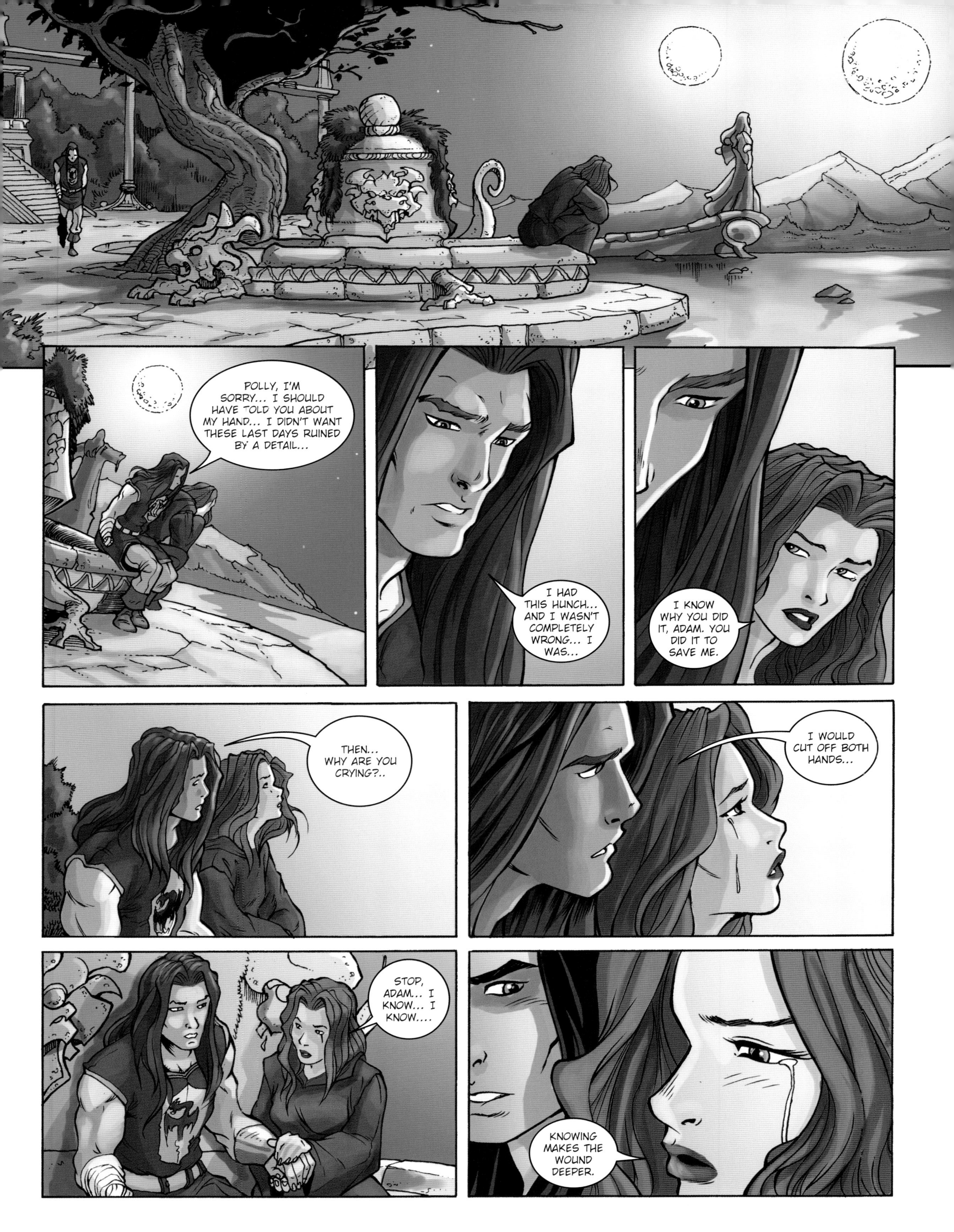
POLLY, I'M SORRY... I SHOULD HAVE TOLD YOU ABOUT MY HAND... I DIDN'T WANT THESE LAST DAYS RUINED BY A DETAIL...
I HAD THIS HUNCH... AND I WASN'T COMPLETELY WRONG... I WAS...
I KNOW WHY YOU DID IT, ADAM. YOU DID IT TO SAVE ME.
THEN... WHY ARE YOU CRYING?..
I WOULD CUT OFF BOTH HANDS...
STOP, ADAM... I KNOW... I KNOW....
KNOWING MAKES THE WOUND DEEPER.

I WANT CHILDREN, ADAM... WE CAN'T... WE'LL NEVER BE...

DON'T CRY POLLY... I UNDERSTAND.

I'M SORRY... I FORGOT... I WANTED TO FORGET.

I'LL ALWAYS LOVE YOU... YOU KNOW THAT.

OH, ADAM...

THERE NOW, MY DEAREST FRIEND...

I'VE HAD ENOUGH DRAGON TEARS FOR A LIFETIME...

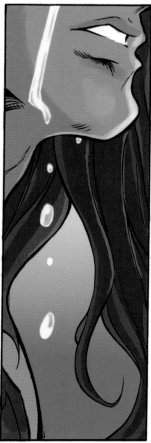

...AND OF ANY COLOR.

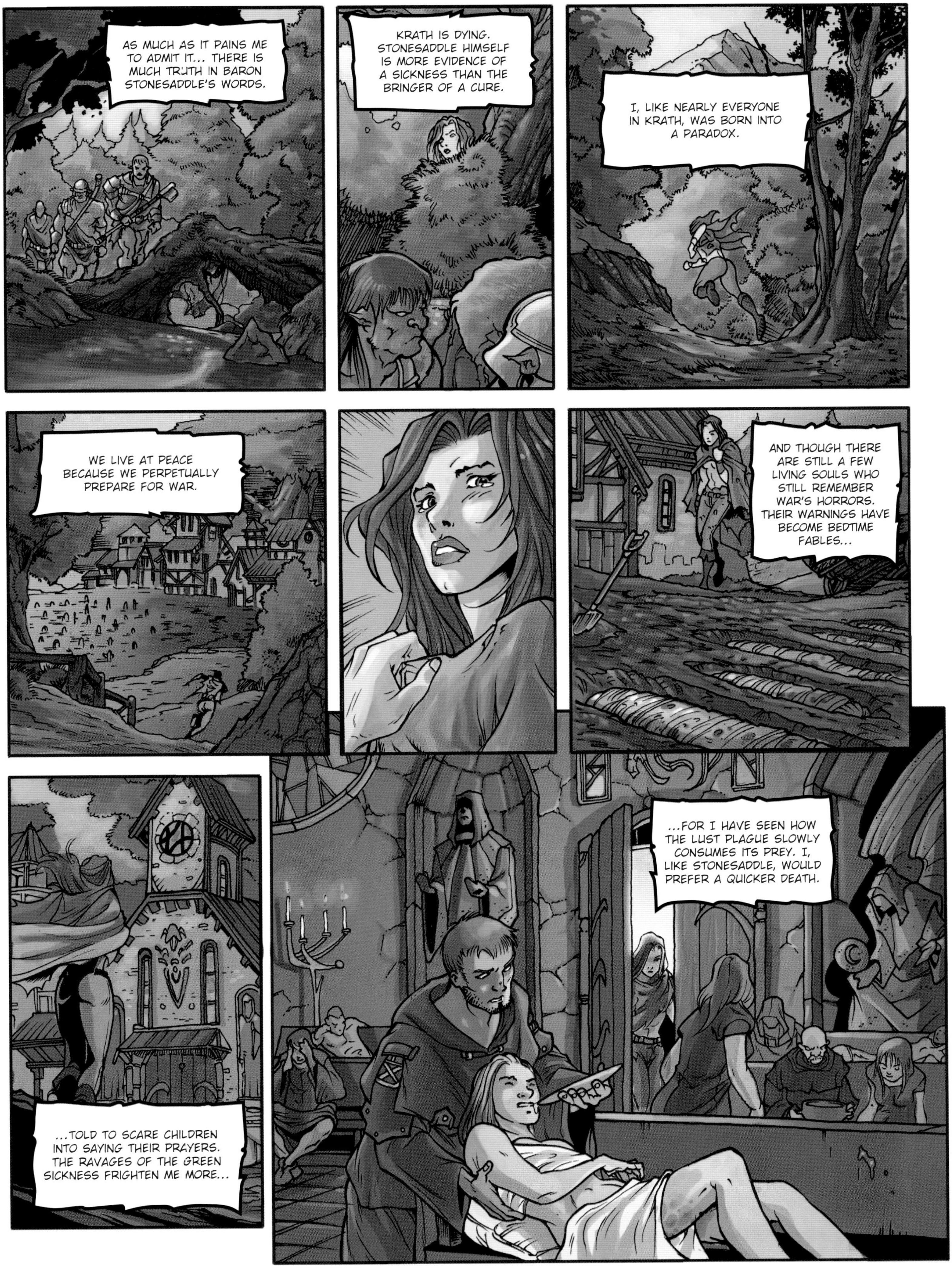
AS MUCH AS IT PAINS ME TO ADMIT IT... THERE IS MUCH TRUTH IN BARON STONESADDLE'S WORDS.
KRATH IS DYING. STONESADDLE HIMSELF IS MORE EVIDENCE OF A SICKNESS THAN THE BRINGER OF A CURE.
I, LIKE NEARLY EVERYONE IN KRATH, WAS BORN INTO A PARADOX.
WE LIVE AT PEACE BECAUSE WE PERPETUALLY PREPARE FOR WAR.
AND THOUGH THERE ARE STILL A FEW LIVING SOULS WHO STILL REMEMBER WAR'S HORRORS. THEIR WARNINGS HAVE BECOME BEDTIME FABLES...
...TOLD TO SCARE CHILDREN INTO SAYING THEIR PRAYERS. THE RAVAGES OF THE GREEN SICKNESS FRIGHTEN ME MORE...
...FOR I HAVE SEEN HOW THE LUST PLAGUE SLOWLY CONSUMES ITS PREY. I, LIKE STONESADDLE, WOULD PREFER A QUICKER DEATH.

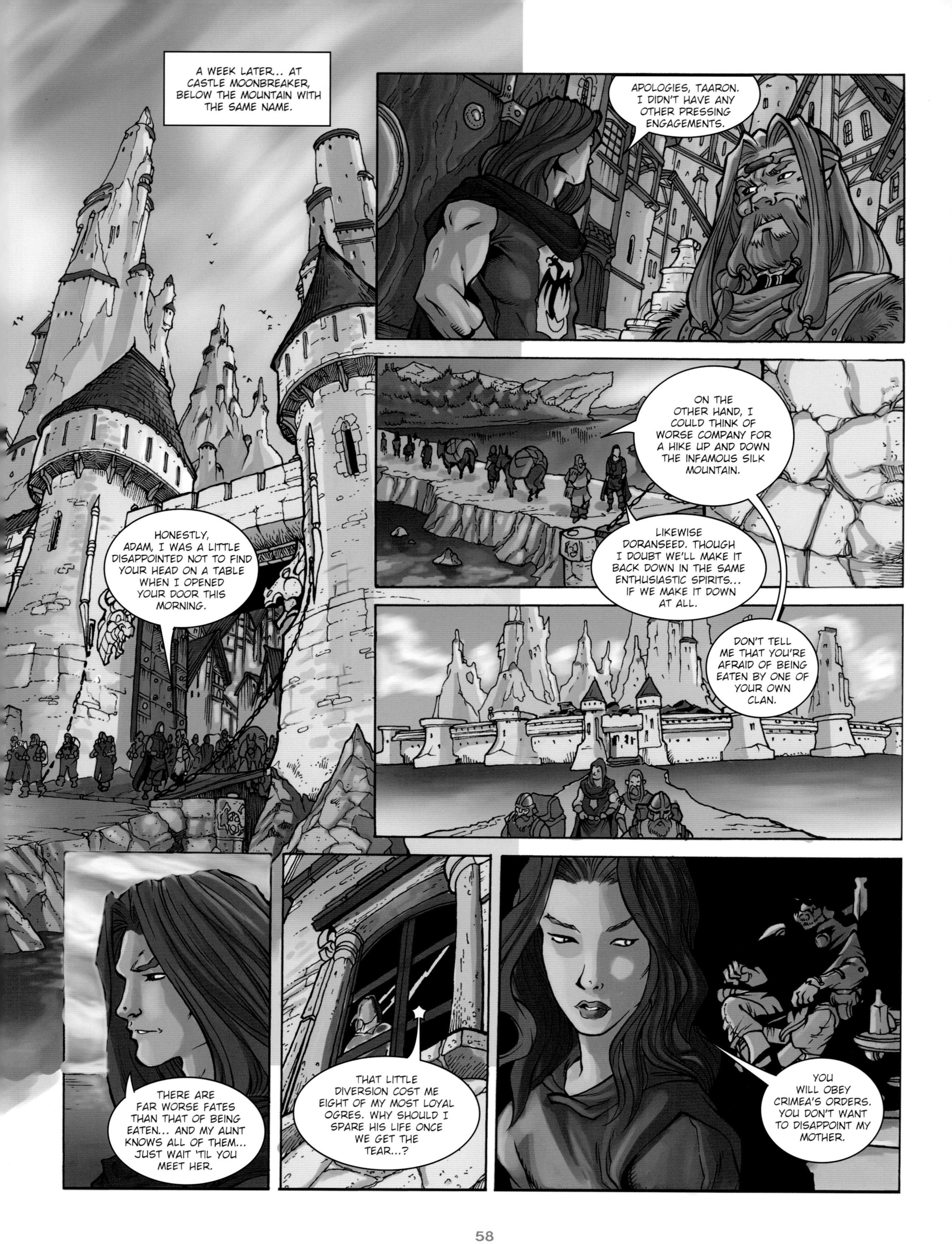
A WEEK LATER... AT CASTLE MOONBREAKER, BELOW THE MOUNTAIN WITH THE SAME NAME.
HONESTLY, ADAM, I WAS A LITTLE DISAPPOINTED NOT TO FIND YOUR HEAD ON A TABLE WHEN I OPENED YOUR DOOR THIS MORNING.
APOLOGIES, TAARON. I DIDN'T HAVE ANY OTHER PRESSING ENGAGEMENTS.
ON THE OTHER HAND, I COULD THINK OF WORSE COMPANY FOR A HIKE UP AND DOWN THE INFAMOUS SILK MOUNTAIN.
LIKEWISE DORANSEED. THOUGH I DOUBT WE'LL MAKE IT BACK DOWN IN THE SAME ENTHUSIASTIC SPIRITS... IF WE MAKE IT DOWN AT ALL.
DON'T TELL ME THAT YOU'RE AFRAID OF BEING EATEN BY ONE OF YOUR OWN CLAN.
THERE ARE FAR WORSE FATES THAN THAT OF BEING EATEN... AND MY AUNT KNOWS ALL OF THEM... JUST WAIT 'TIL YOU MEET HER.
THAT LITTLE DIVERSION COST ME EIGHT OF MY MOST LOYAL OGRES. WHY SHOULD I SPARE HIS LIFE ONCE WE GET THE TEAR...?
YOU WILL OBEY CRIMEA'S ORDERS. YOU DON'T WANT TO DISAPPOINT MY MOTHER.

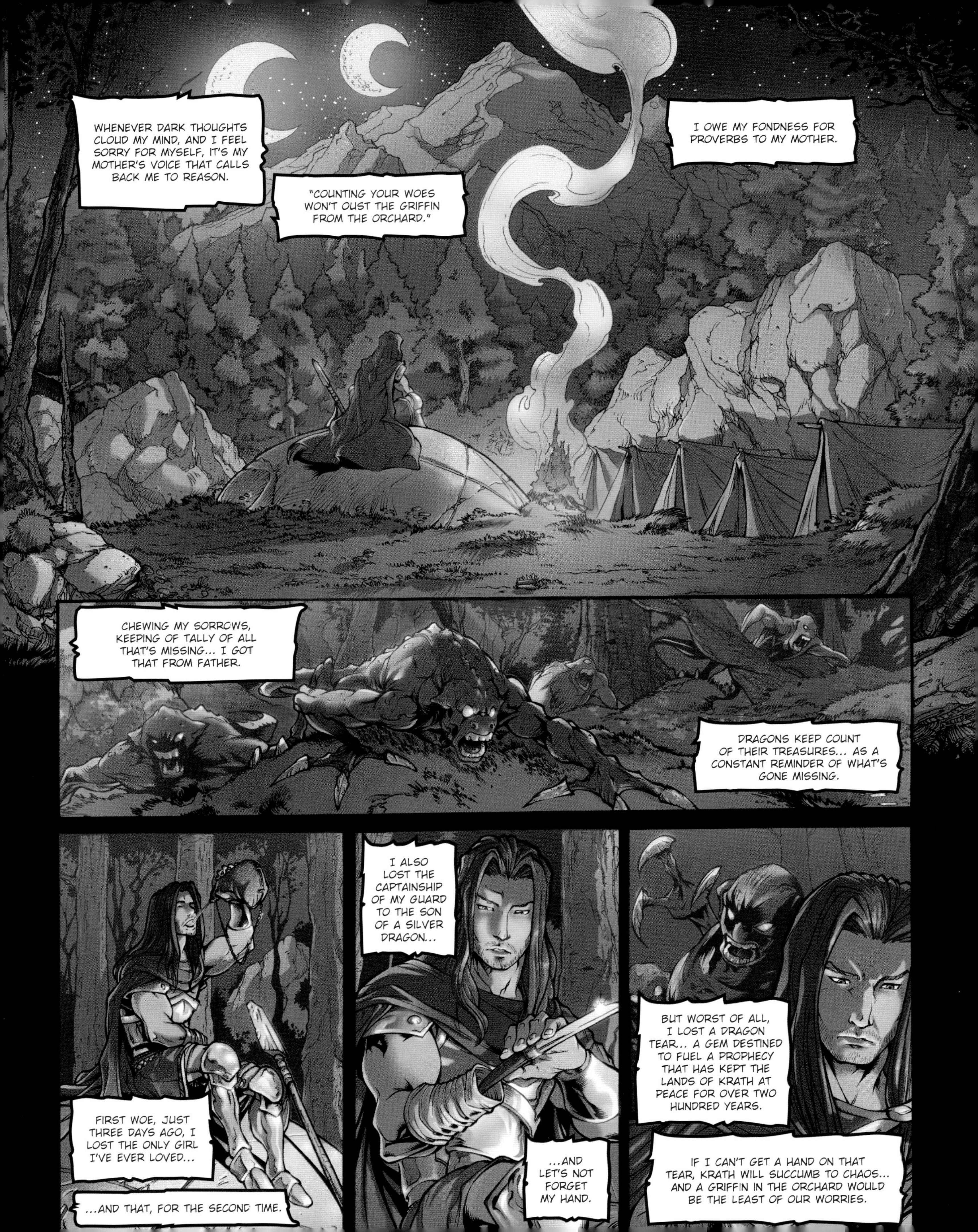
WHENEVER DARK THOUGHTS CLOUD MY MIND, AND I FEEL SORRY FOR MYSELF, IT'S MY MOTHER'S VOICE THAT CALLS BACK ME TO REASON.
"COUNTING YOUR WOES WON'T OUST THE GRIFFIN FROM THE ORCHARD."
I OWE MY FONDNESS FOR PROVERBS TO MY MOTHER.
CHEWING MY SORROWS, KEEPING OF TALLY OF ALL THAT'S MISSING... I GOT THAT FROM FATHER.
DRAGONS KEEP COUNT OF THEIR TREASURES... AS A CONSTANT REMINDER OF WHAT'S GONE MISSING.
FIRST WOE, JUST THREE DAYS AGO, I LOST THE ONLY GIRL I'VE EVER LOVED...
...AND THAT, FOR THE SECOND TIME.
I ALSO LOST THE CAPTAINSHIP OF MY GUARD TO THE SON OF A SILVER DRAGON...
...AND LET'S NOT FORGET MY HAND.
BUT WORST OF ALL, I LOST A DRAGON TEAR... A GEM DESTINED TO FUEL A PROPHECY THAT HAS KEPT THE LANDS OF KRATH AT PEACE FOR OVER TWO HUNDRED YEARS.
IF I CAN'T GET A HAND ON THAT TEAR, KRATH WILL SUCCUMB TO CHAOS... AND A GRIFFIN IN THE ORCHARD WOULD BE THE LEAST OF OUR WORRIES.

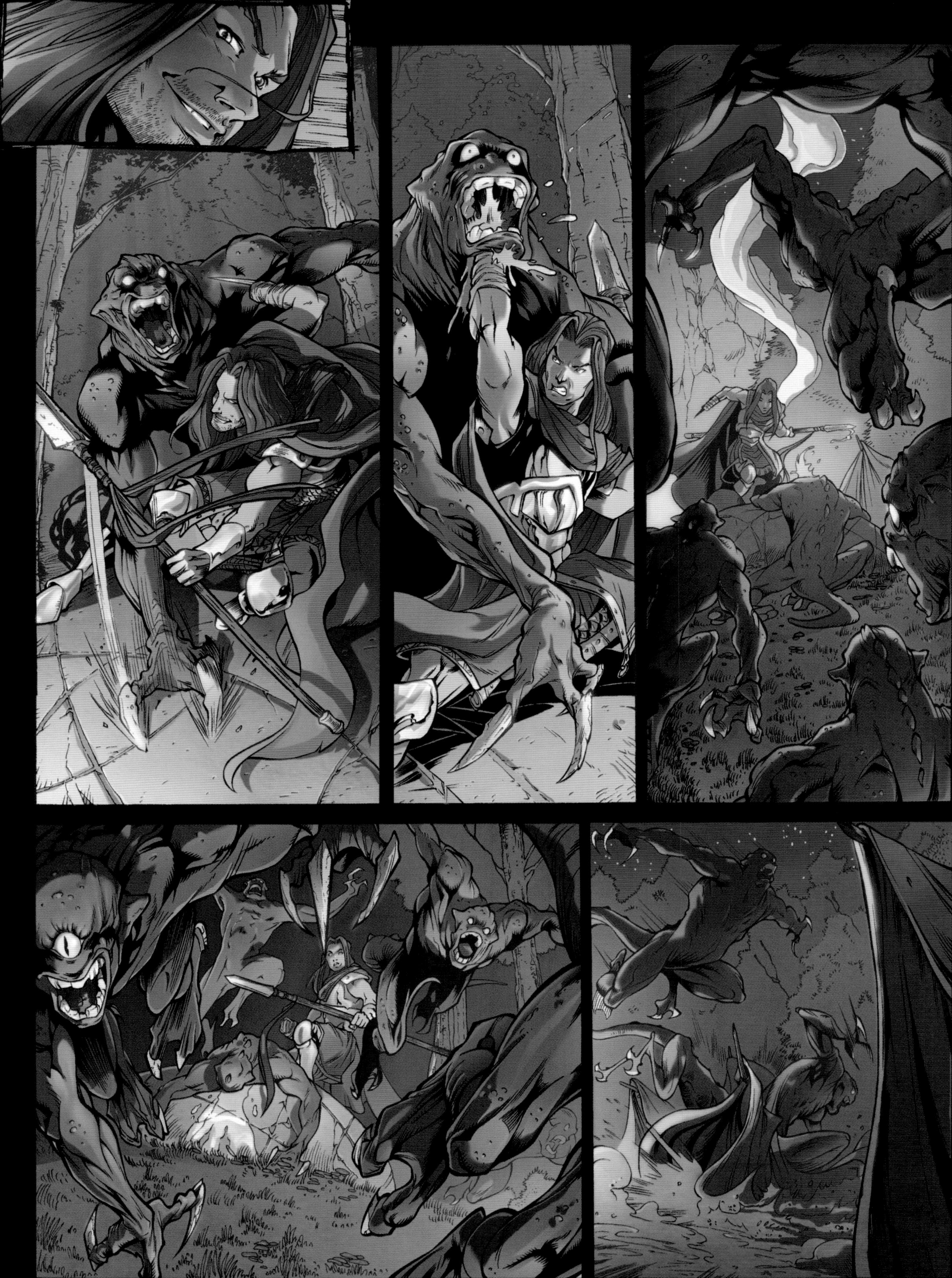

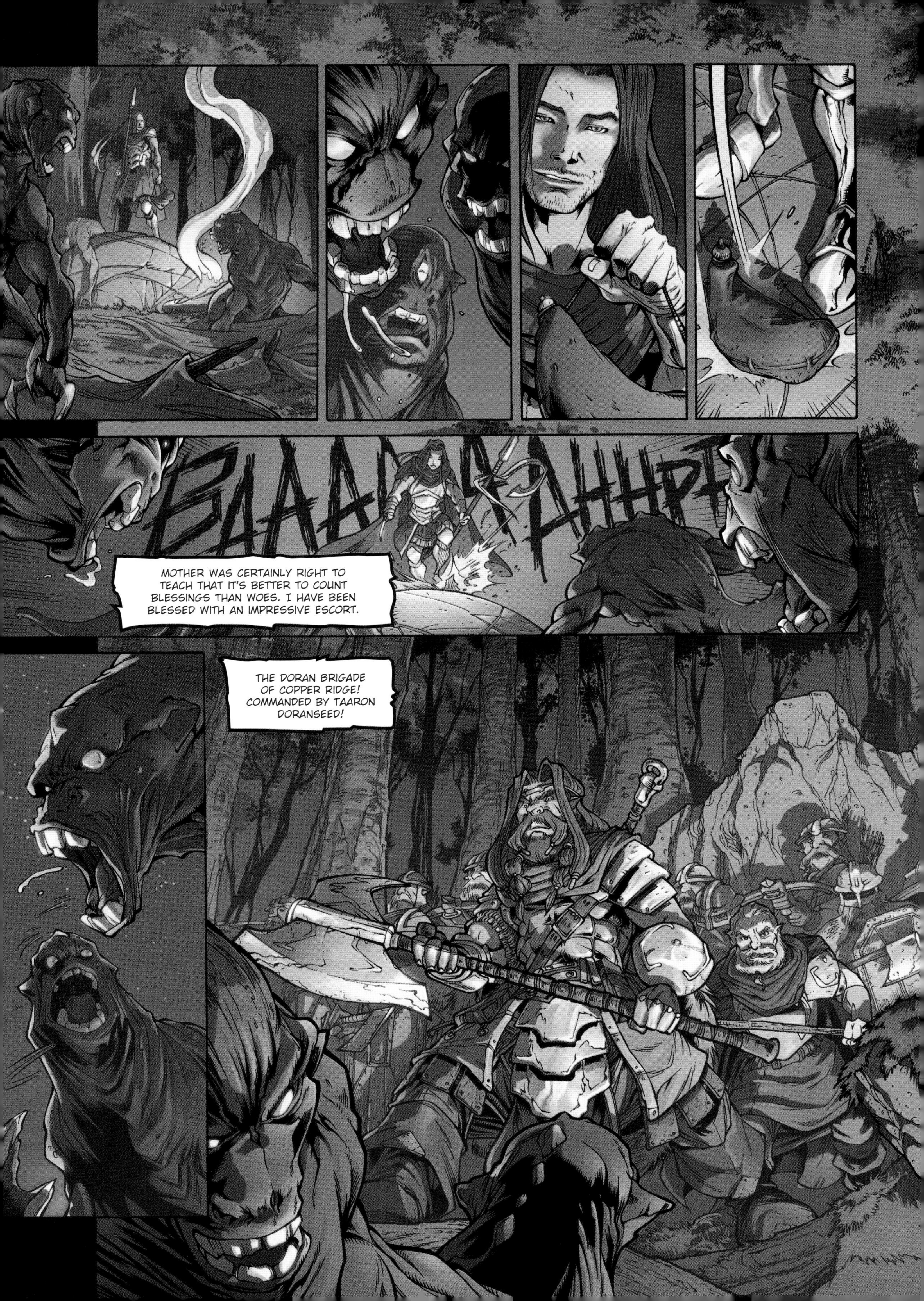
MOTHER WAS CERTAINLY RIGHT TO TEACH THAT IT'S BETTER TO COUNT BLESSINGS THAN WOES. I HAVE BEEN BLESSED WITH AN IMPRESSIVE ESCORT.
THE DORAN BRIGADE OF COPPER RIDGE! COMMANDED BY TAARON DORANSEED!

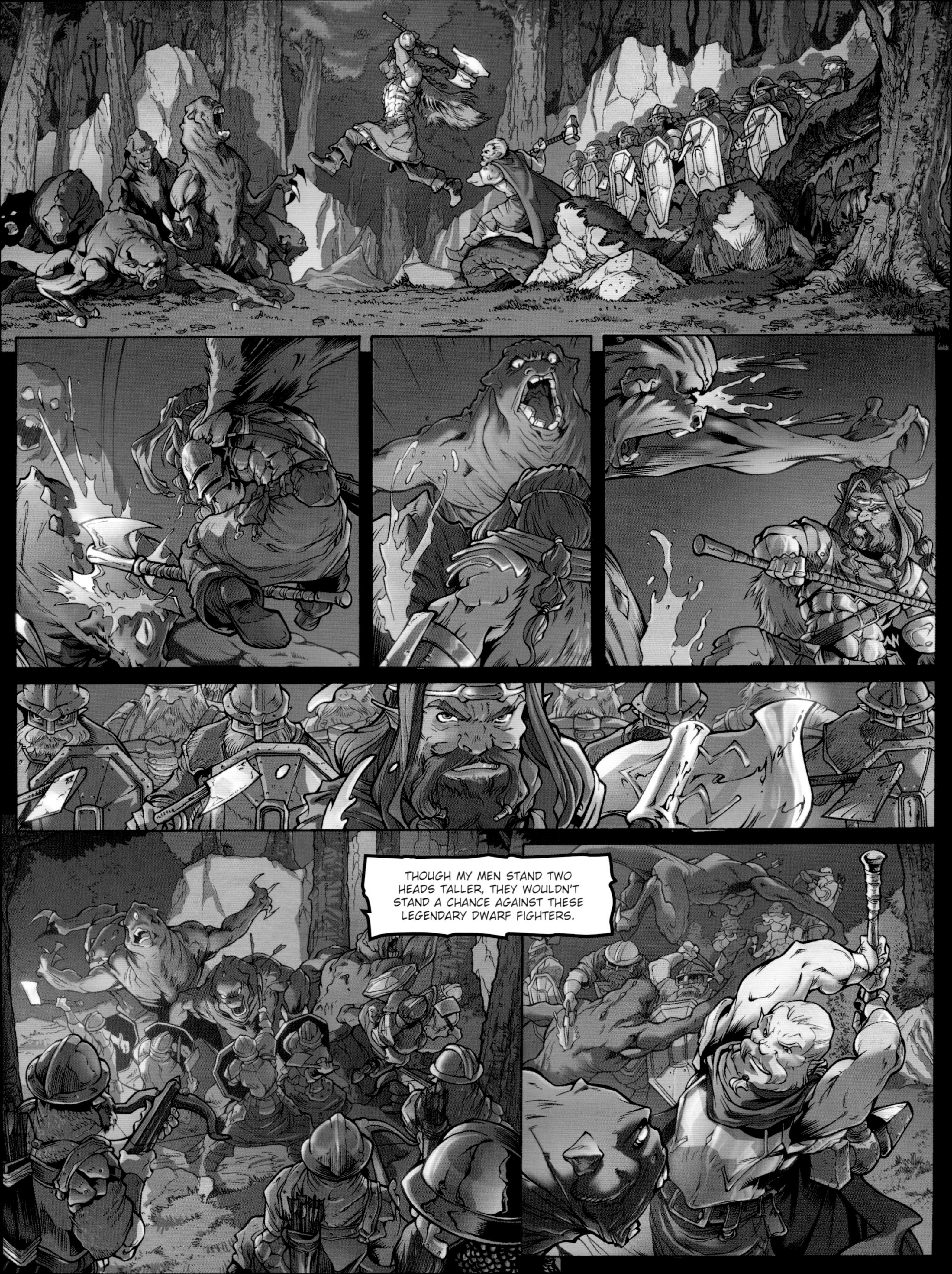
THOUGH MY MEN STAND TWO HEADS TALLER, THEY WOULDN'T STAND A CHANCE AGAINST THESE LEGENDARY DWARF FIGHTERS.

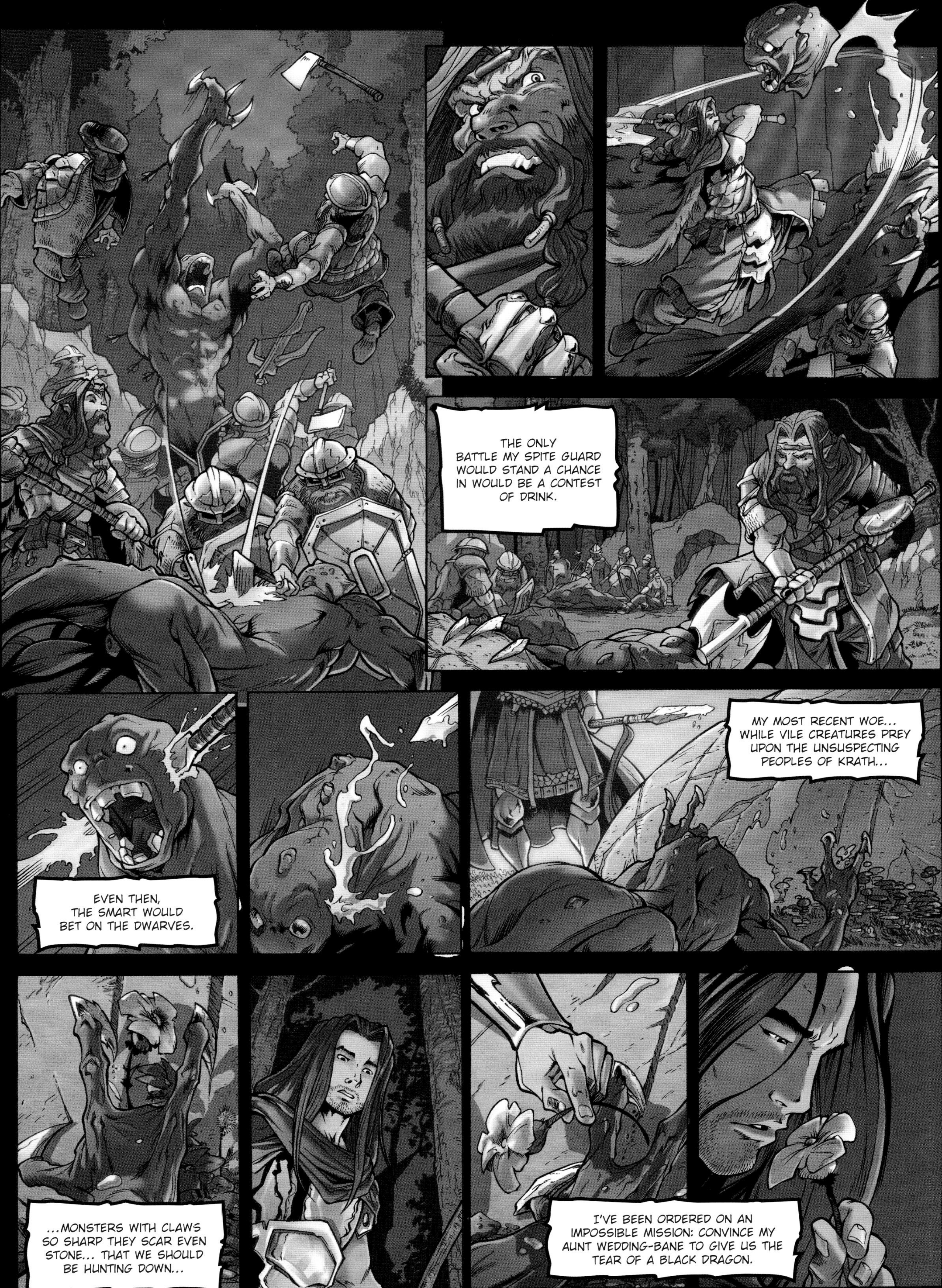
THE ONLY BATTLE MY SPITE GUARD WOULD STAND A CHANCE IN WOULD BE A CONTEST OF DRINK.
EVEN THEN, THE SMART WOULD BET ON THE DWARVES.
MY MOST RECENT WOE... WHILE VILE CREATURES PREY UPON THE UNSUSPECTING PEOPLES OF KRATH...
...MONSTERS WITH CLAWS SO SHARP THEY SCAR EVEN STONE... THAT WE SHOULD BE HUNTING DOWN...
I'VE BEEN ORDERED ON AN IMPOSSIBLE MISSION: CONVINCE MY AUNT WEDDING-BANE TO GIVE US THE TEAR OF A BLACK DRAGON.

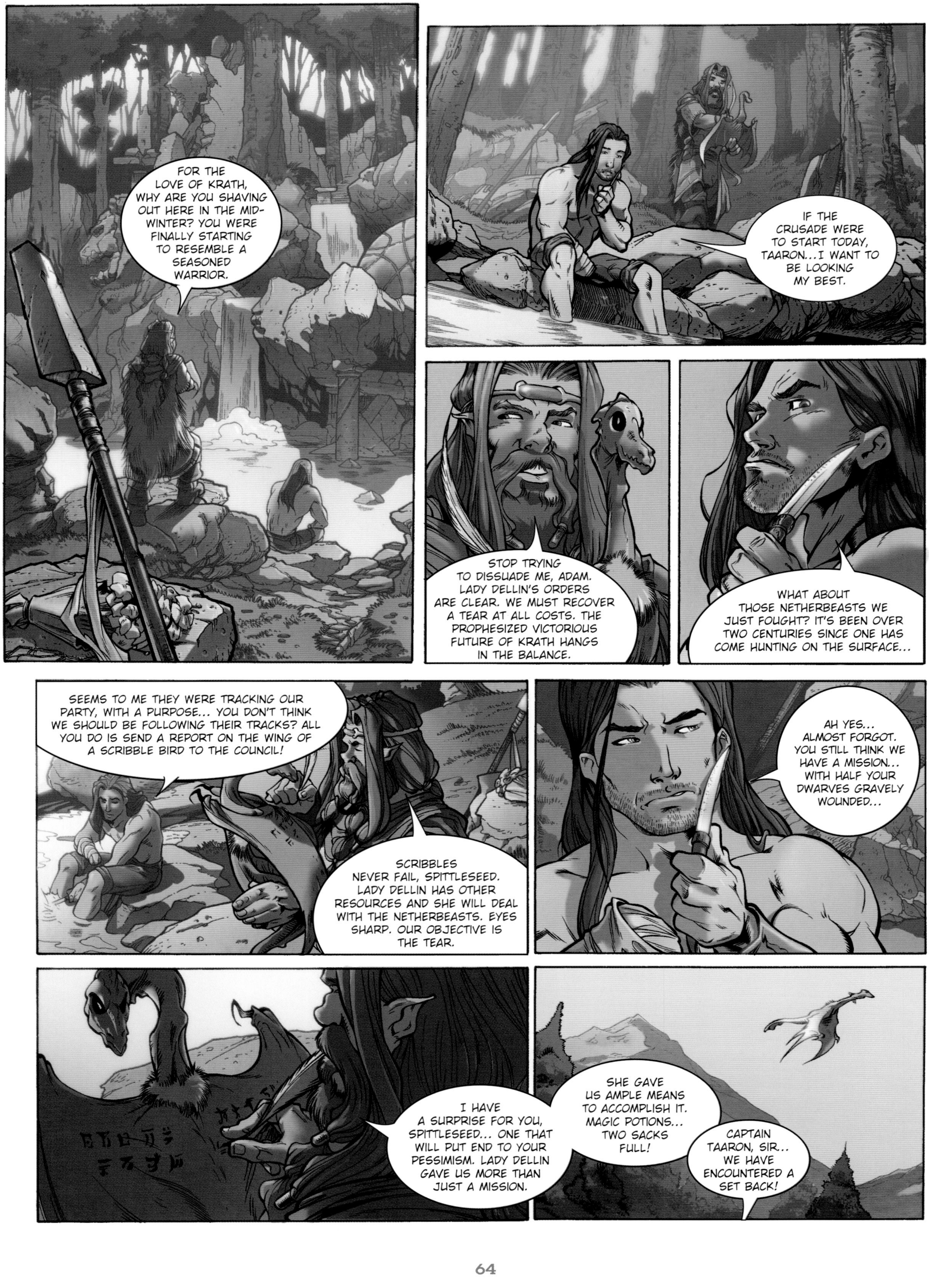
FOR THE LOVE OF KRATH, WHY ARE YOU SHAVING OUT HERE IN THE MID-WINTER? YOU WERE FINALLY STARTING TO RESEMBLE A SEASONED WARRIOR.
IF THE CRUSADE WERE TO START TODAY, TAARON... I WANT TO BE LOOKING MY BEST.
STOP TRYING TO DISSUADE ME, ADAM. LADY DELLIN'S ORDERS ARE CLEAR. WE MUST RECOVER A TEAR AT ALL COSTS. THE PROPHESIZED VICTORIOUS FUTURE OF KRATH HANGS IN THE BALANCE.
WHAT ABOUT THOSE NETHERBEASTS WE JUST FOUGHT? IT'S BEEN OVER TWO CENTURIES SINCE ONE HAS COME HUNTING ON THE SURFACE...
SEEMS TO ME THEY WERE TRACKING OUR PARTY, WITH A PURPOSE... YOU DON'T THINK WE SHOULD BE FOLLOWING THEIR TRACKS? ALL YOU DO IS SEND A REPORT ON THE WING OF A SCRIBBLE BIRD TO THE COUNCIL!
SCRIBBLES NEVER FAIL, SPITTLESEED. LADY DELLIN HAS OTHER RESOURCES AND SHE WILL DEAL WITH THE NETHERBEASTS. EYES SHARP. OUR OBJECTIVE IS THE TEAR.
AH YES... ALMOST FORGOT. YOU STILL THINK WE HAVE A MISSION... WITH HALF YOUR DWARVES GRAVELY WOUNDED...
I HAVE A SURPRISE FOR YOU, SPITTLESEED... ONE THAT WILL PUT END TO YOUR PESSIMISM. LADY DELLIN GAVE US MORE THAN JUST A MISSION.
SHE GAVE US AMPLE MEANS TO ACCOMPLISH IT. MAGIC POTIONS... TWO SACKS FULL!
CAPTAIN TAARON, SIR... WE HAVE ENCOUNTERED A SET BACK!

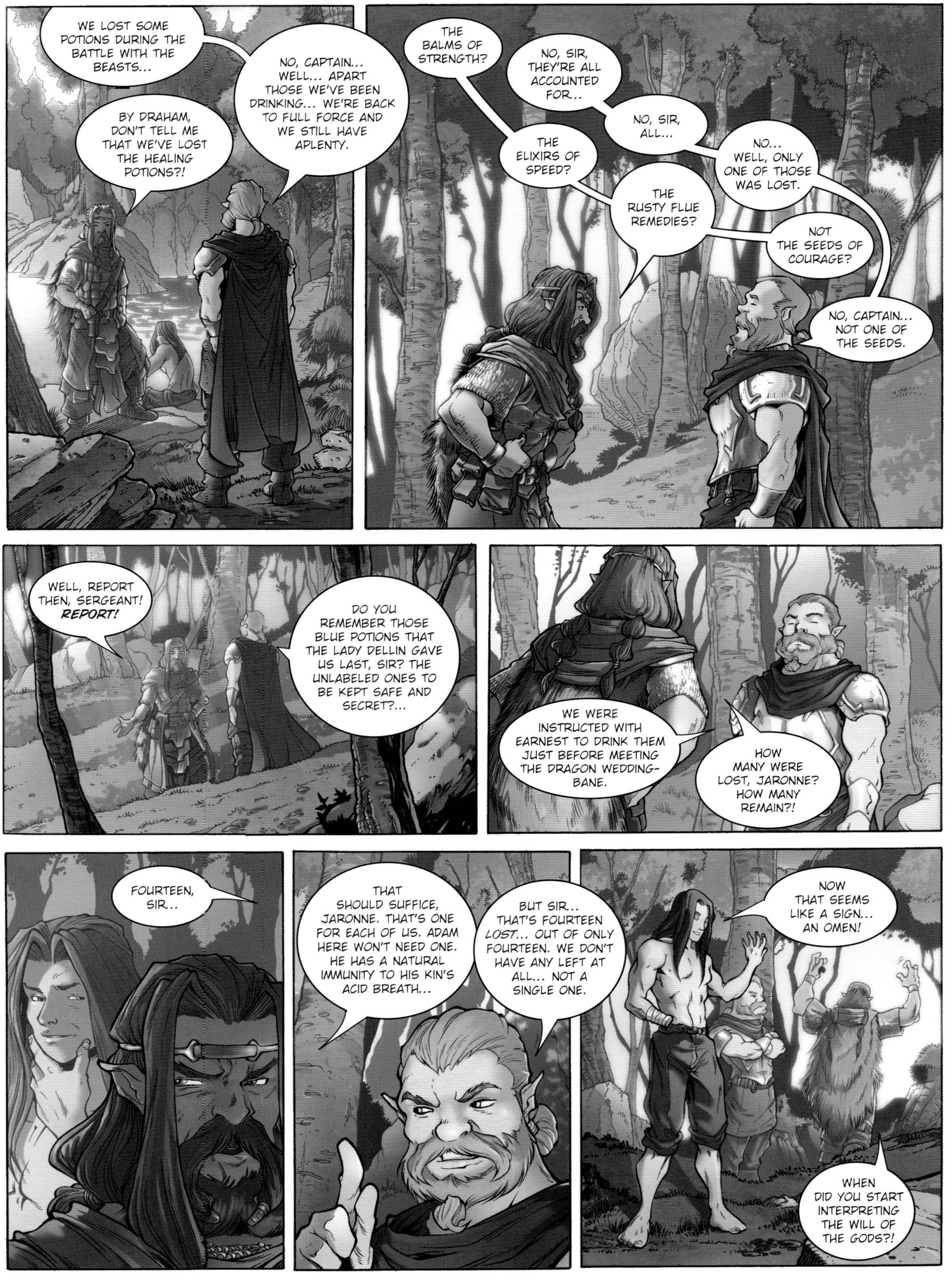
WE LOST SOME POTIONS DURING THE BATTLE WITH THE BEASTS...
BY DRAHAM, DON'T TELL ME THAT WE'VE LOST THE HEALING POTIONS?!
NO, CAPTAIN... WELL... APART THOSE WE'VE BEEN DRINKING... WE'RE BACK TO FULL FORCE AND WE STILL HAVE APLENTY.
THE BALMS OF STRENGTH?
NO, SIR, THEY'RE ALL ACCOUNTED FOR...
THE ELIXIRS OF SPEED?
NO, SIR, ALL...
THE RUSTY FLUE REMEDIES?
NO... WELL, ONLY ONE OF THOSE WAS LOST.
NOT THE SEEDS OF COURAGE?
NO, CAPTAIN... NOT ONE OF THE SEEDS.
WELL, REPORT THEN, SERGEANT! REPORT!
DO YOU REMEMBER THOSE BLUE POTIONS THAT THE LADY DELLIN GAVE US LAST, SIR? THE UNLABELED ONES TO BE KEPT SAFE AND SECRET?...
WE WERE INSTRUCTED WITH EARNEST TO DRINK THEM JUST BEFORE MEETING THE DRAGON WEDDING-BANE.
HOW MANY WERE LOST, JARONNE? HOW MANY REMAIN?!
FOURTEEN, SIR...
THAT SHOULD SUFFICE, JARONNE. THAT'S ONE FOR EACH OF US. ADAM HERE WON'T NEED ONE. HE HAS A NATURAL IMMUNITY TO HIS KIN'S ACID BREATH...
BUT SIR... THAT'S FOURTEEN LOST... OUT OF ONLY FOURTEEN. WE DON'T HAVE ANY LEFT AT ALL... NOT A SINGLE ONE.
NOW THAT SEEMS LIKE A SIGN... AN OMEN!
WHEN DID YOU START INTERPRETING THE WILL OF THE GODS?!

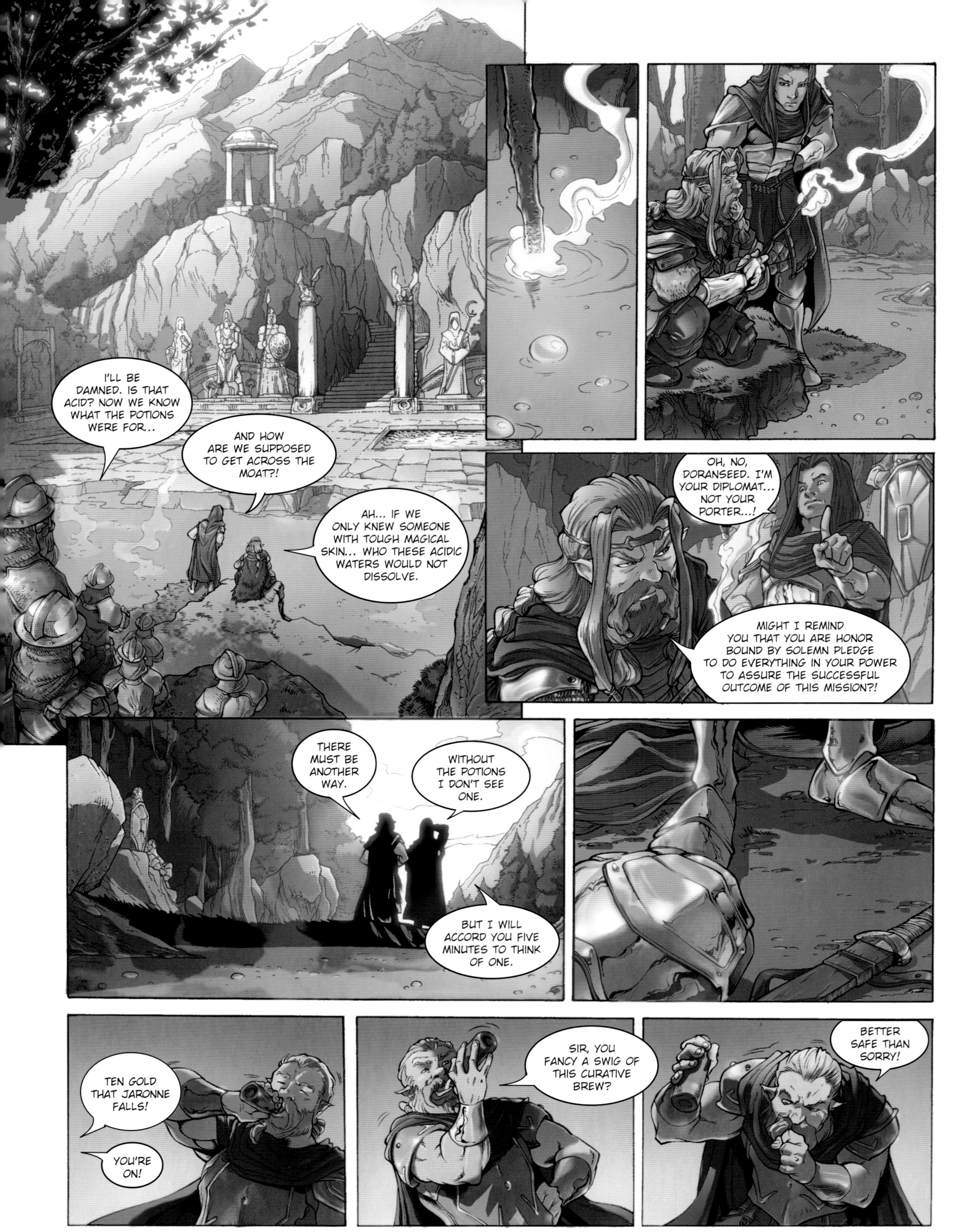
I'LL BE DAMNED. IS THAT ACID? NOW WE KNOW WHAT THE POTIONS WERE FOR...
AND HOW ARE WE SUPPOSED TO GET ACROSS THE MOAT?!
AH... IF WE ONLY KNEW SOMEONE WITH TOUGH MAGICAL SKIN... WHO THESE ACIDIC WATERS WOULD NOT DISSOLVE.
OH, NO, DORANSEED. I'M YOUR DIPLOMAT... NOT YOUR PORTER...!
MIGHT I REMIND YOU THAT YOU ARE HONOR BOUND BY SOLEMN PLEDGE TO DO EVERYTHING IN YOUR POWER TO ASSURE THE SUCCESSFUL OUTCOME OF THIS MISSION?!
THERE MUST BE ANOTHER WAY.
WITHOUT THE POTIONS I DON'T SEE ONE.
BUT I WILL ACCORD YOU FIVE MINUTES TO THINK OF ONE.
TEN GOLD THAT JARONNE FALLS!
YOU'RE ON!
SIR, YOU FANCY A SWIG OF THIS CURATIVE BREW?
BETTER SAFE THAN SORRY!

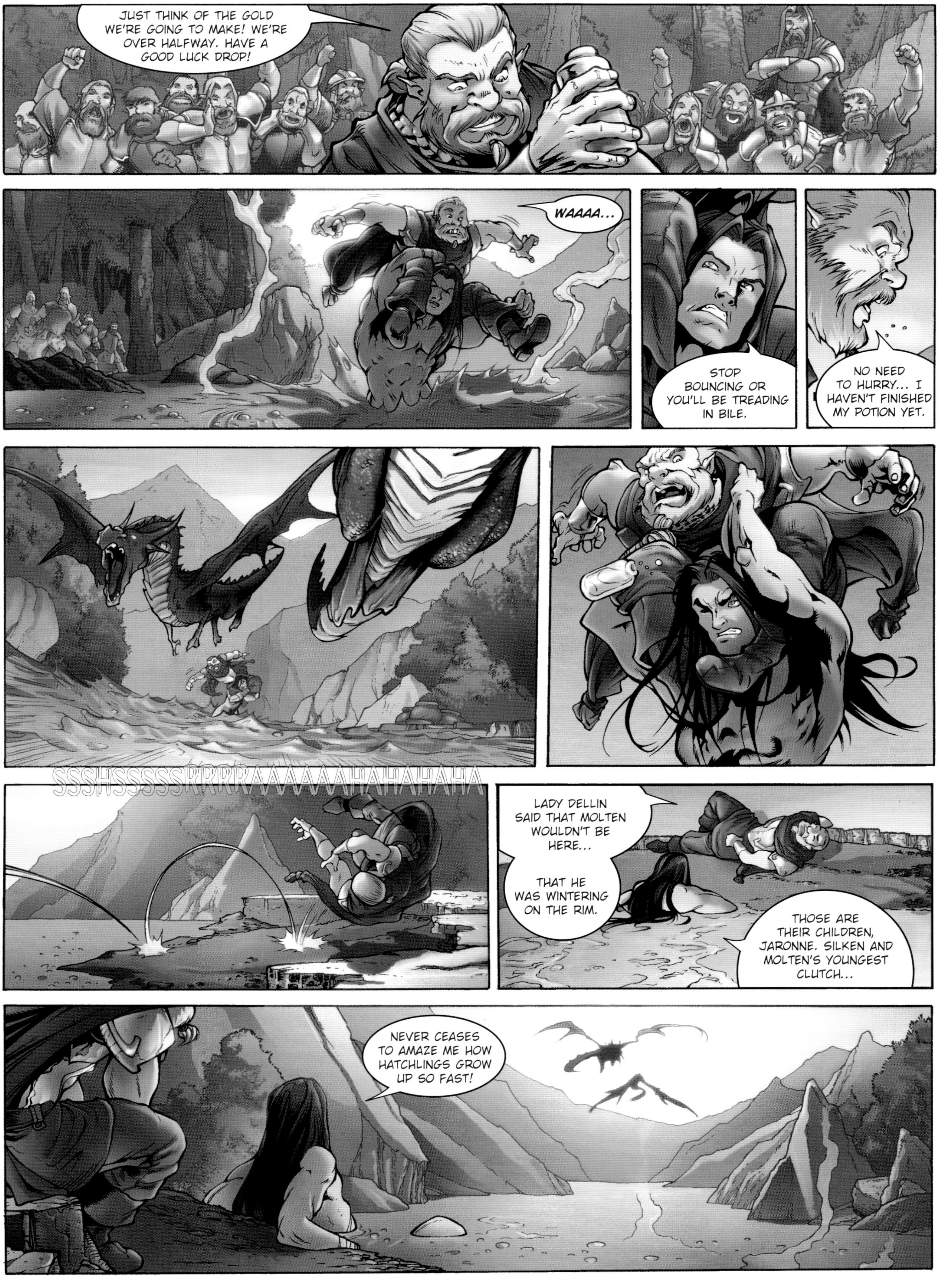

JUST THINK OF THE GOLD WE'RE GOING TO MAKE! WE'RE OVER HALFWAY. HAVE A GOOD LUCK DROP!
WAAAA...
STOP BOUNCING OR YOU'LL BE TREADING IN BILE.
NO NEED TO HURRY... I HAVEN'T FINISHED MY POTION YET.
SSSHSSSSSSRRRRAAAAAAHAHAHAHA
LADY DELLIN SAID THAT MOLTEN WOULDN'T BE HERE...
THAT HE WAS WINTERING ON THE RIM.
THOSE ARE THEIR CHILDREN, JARONNE. SILKEN AND MOLTEN'S YOUNGEST CLUTCH...
NEVER CEASES TO AMAZE ME HOW HATCHLINGS GROW UP SO FAST!

FIFTEEN TRIPS OVER THE MOAT LATER...

THE REMWEL SILKENSEED? WASN'T THAT HALF-ELF THROWN OUT OF SCHOOL FOR BURNING DOWN THE STABLES?!?

THE STORY WAS EXAGGERATED. YOU KNOW THE DRUIDS AT THE COLLEGE...

TWO HUNDRED MAGICAL CREATURES ROASTED LIKE CHICKENS.

A HUNDRED AND FIFTY-SIX... WENT UNACCOUNTED FOR... BUT YES, *THAT* REMWEL SILKENSEED.

WHO'S SIDE WILL HE BE ON IF HE'S UP THERE? THE PACT LORDS' OR HIS MOTHER'S?

YOU DON'T GET IT, TAARON. THERE IS ONLY ONE SIDE. AND THAT IS SILKEN'S. HER MOOD AND PRIORITIES WILL DETERMINE THE OUTCOME...

HE'LL BE ON HIS MOTHER'S SIDE, THEN.

HOW DO I LOOK?

YOU ARE QUITE REGAL. CAREFUL OR YOU'LL ATTRACT A MATE.

MAYBE IT *IS* TIME I STARTED LOOKING FOR MY LADY.

IF YOU'RE LUCKY SILKEN WILL TAKE A FANCY. SHE'S NOT ONE TO DEVOUR HER SUITORS.

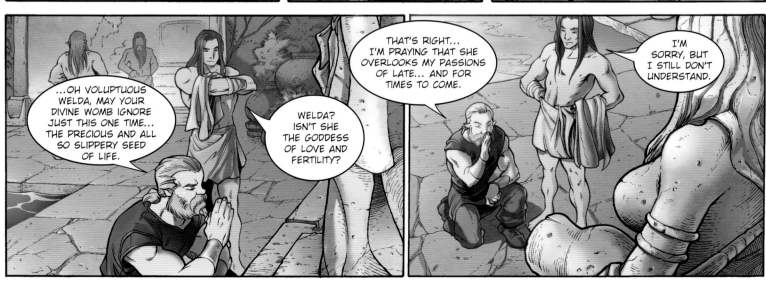

...OH VOLUPTUOUS WELDA, MAY YOUR DIVINE WOMB IGNORE JUST THIS ONE TIME... THE PRECIOUS AND ALL SO SLIPPERY SEED OF LIFE.

WELDA? ISN'T SHE THE GODDESS OF LOVE AND FERTILITY?

THAT'S RIGHT... I'M PRAYING THAT SHE OVERLOOKS MY PASSIONS OF LATE... AND FOR TIMES TO COME.

I'M SORRY, BUT I STILL DON'T UNDERSTAND.

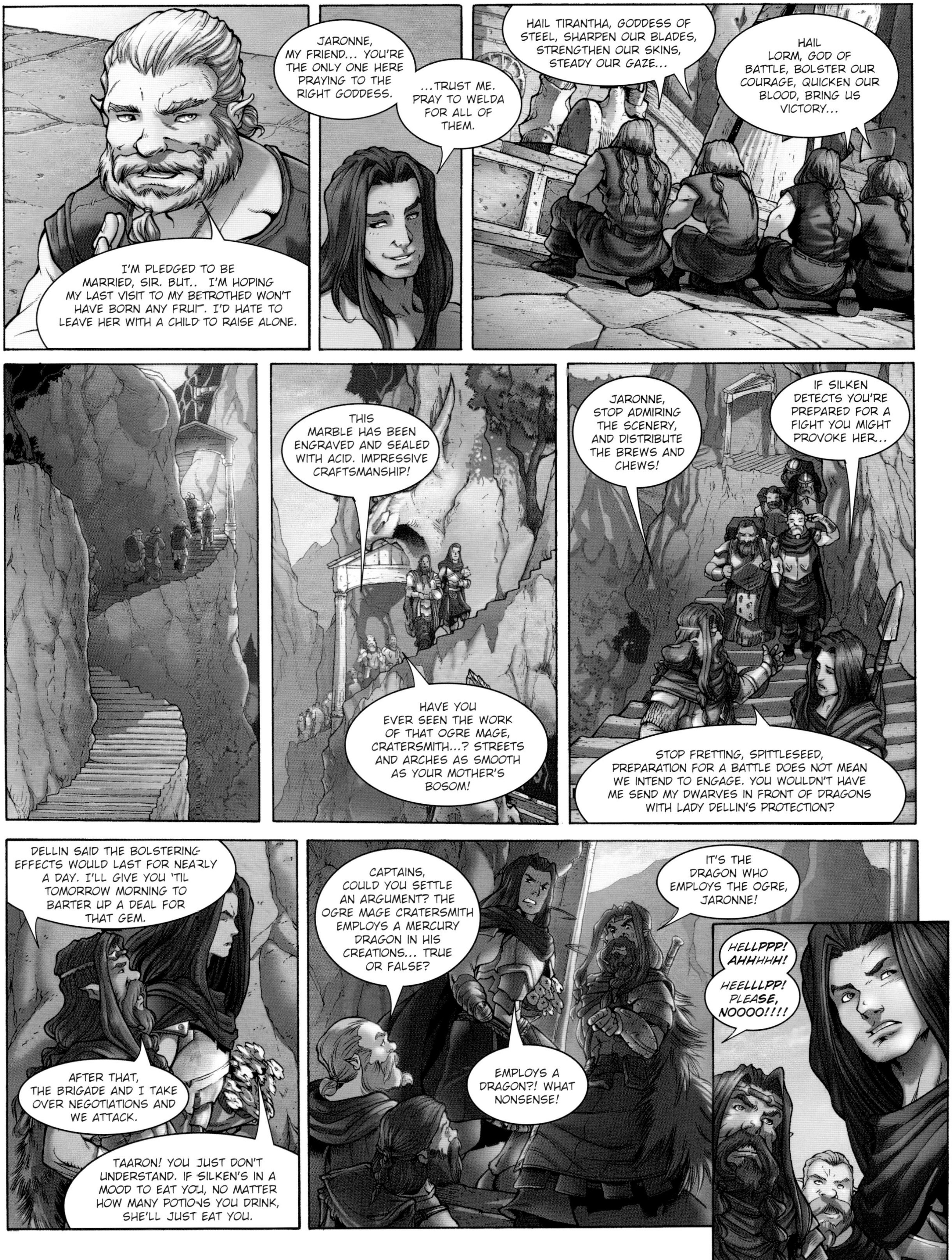
I'M PLEDGED TO BE MARRIED, SIR. BUT.. I'M HOPING MY LAST VISIT TO MY BETROTHED WON'T HAVE BORN ANY FRUIT. I'D HATE TO LEAVE HER WITH A CHILD TO RAISE ALONE.
JARONNE, MY FRIEND... YOU'RE THE ONLY ONE HERE PRAYING TO THE RIGHT GODDESS.
...TRUST ME. PRAY TO WELDA FOR ALL OF THEM.
HAIL TIRANTHA, GODDESS OF STEEL, SHARPEN OUR BLADES, STRENGTHEN OUR SKINS, STEADY OUR GAZE...
HAIL LORM, GOD OF BATTLE, BOLSTER OUR COURAGE, QUICKEN OUR BLOOD, BRING US VICTORY...
THIS MARBLE HAS BEEN ENGRAVED AND SEALED WITH ACID. IMPRESSIVE CRAFTSMANSHIP!
HAVE YOU EVER SEEN THE WORK OF THAT OGRE MAGE, CRATERSMITH...? STREETS AND ARCHES AS SMOOTH AS YOUR MOTHER'S BOSOM!
JARONNE, STOP ADMIRING THE SCENERY, AND DISTRIBUTE THE BREWS AND CHEWS!
IF SILKEN DETECTS YOU'RE PREPARED FOR A FIGHT YOU MIGHT PROVOKE HER...
STOP FRETTING, SPITTLESEED, PREPARATION FOR A BATTLE DOES NOT MEAN WE INTEND TO ENGAGE. YOU WOULDN'T HAVE ME SEND MY DWARVES IN FRONT OF DRAGONS WITH LADY DELLIN'S PROTECTION?
DELLIN SAID THE BOLSTERING EFFECTS WOULD LAST FOR NEARLY A DAY. I'LL GIVE YOU 'TIL TOMORROW MORNING TO BARTER UP A DEAL FOR THAT GEM.
AFTER THAT, THE BRIGADE AND I TAKE OVER NEGOTIATIONS AND WE ATTACK.
TAARON! YOU JUST DON'T UNDERSTAND. IF SILKEN'S IN A MOOD TO EAT YOU, NO MATTER HOW MANY POTIONS YOU DRINK, SHE'LL JUST EAT YOU.
CAPTAINS, COULD YOU SETTLE AN ARGUMENT? THE OGRE MAGE CRATERSMITH EMPLOYS A MERCURY DRAGON IN HIS CREATIONS... TRUE OR FALSE?
IT'S THE DRAGON WHO EMPLOYS THE OGRE, JARONNE!
EMPLOYS A DRAGON?! WHAT NONSENSE!
HELLPPP! AHHHHH!
HEELLLPP! PLEASE, NOOOO!!!!

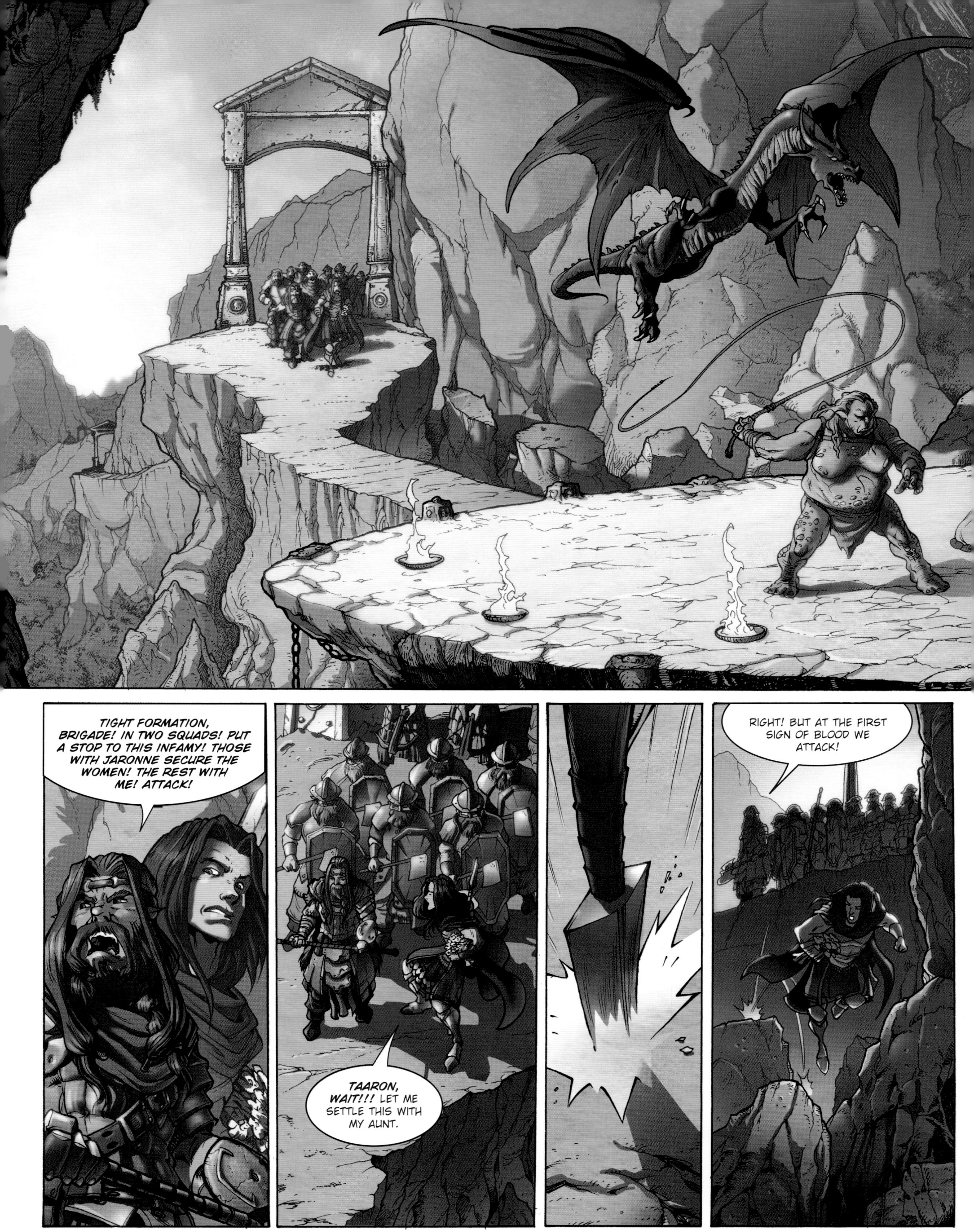
TIGHT FORMATION, BRIGADE! IN TWO SQUADS! PUT A STOP TO THIS INFAMY! THOSE WITH JARONNE SECURE THE WOMEN! THE REST WITH ME! ATTACK!
TAARON, WAIT!!! LET ME SETTLE THIS WITH MY AUNT.
RIGHT! BUT AT THE FIRST SIGN OF BLOOD WE ATTACK!

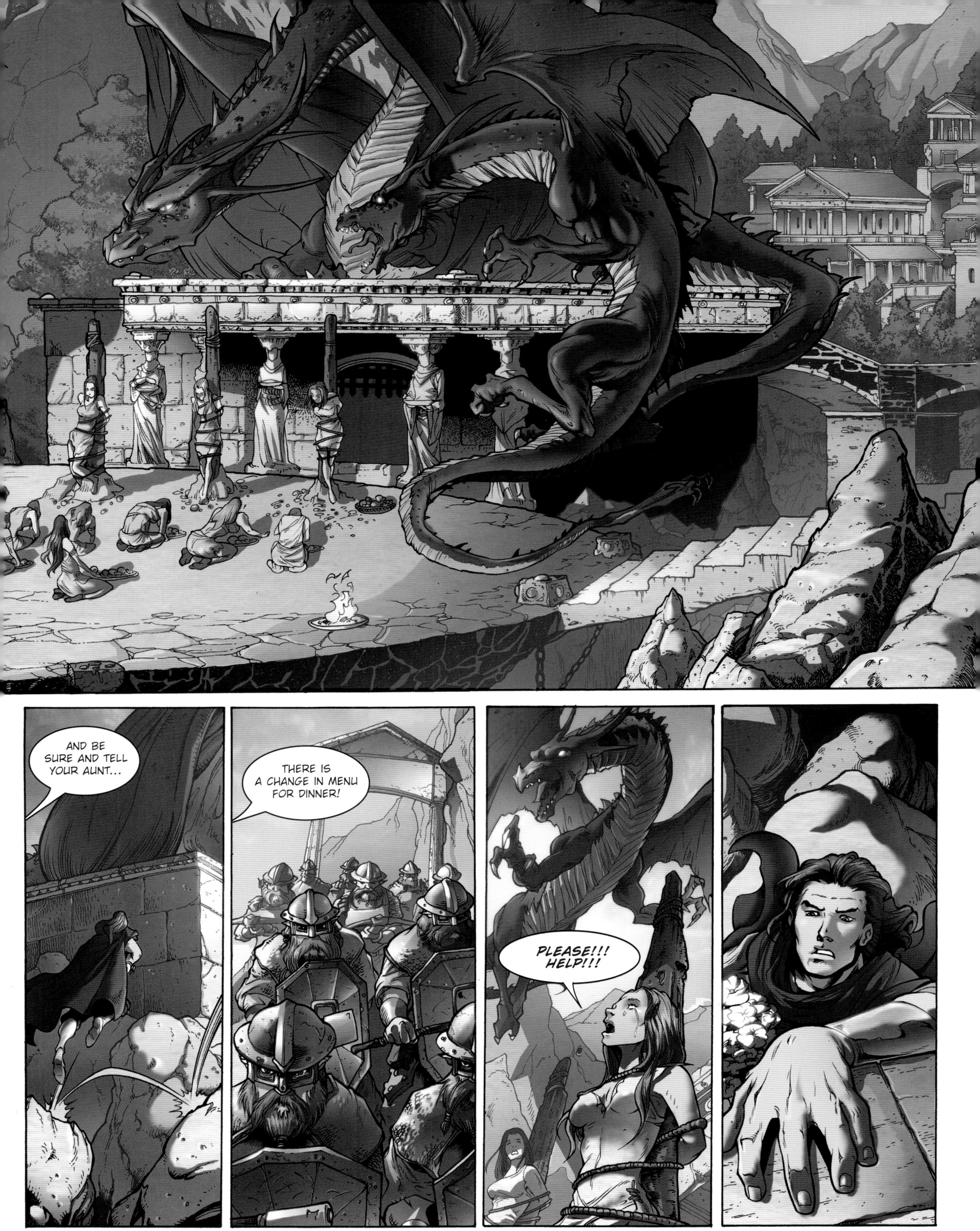
AND BE SURE AND TELL YOUR AUNT...
THERE IS A CHANGE IN MENU FOR DINNER!
PLEASE!!! HELP!!!

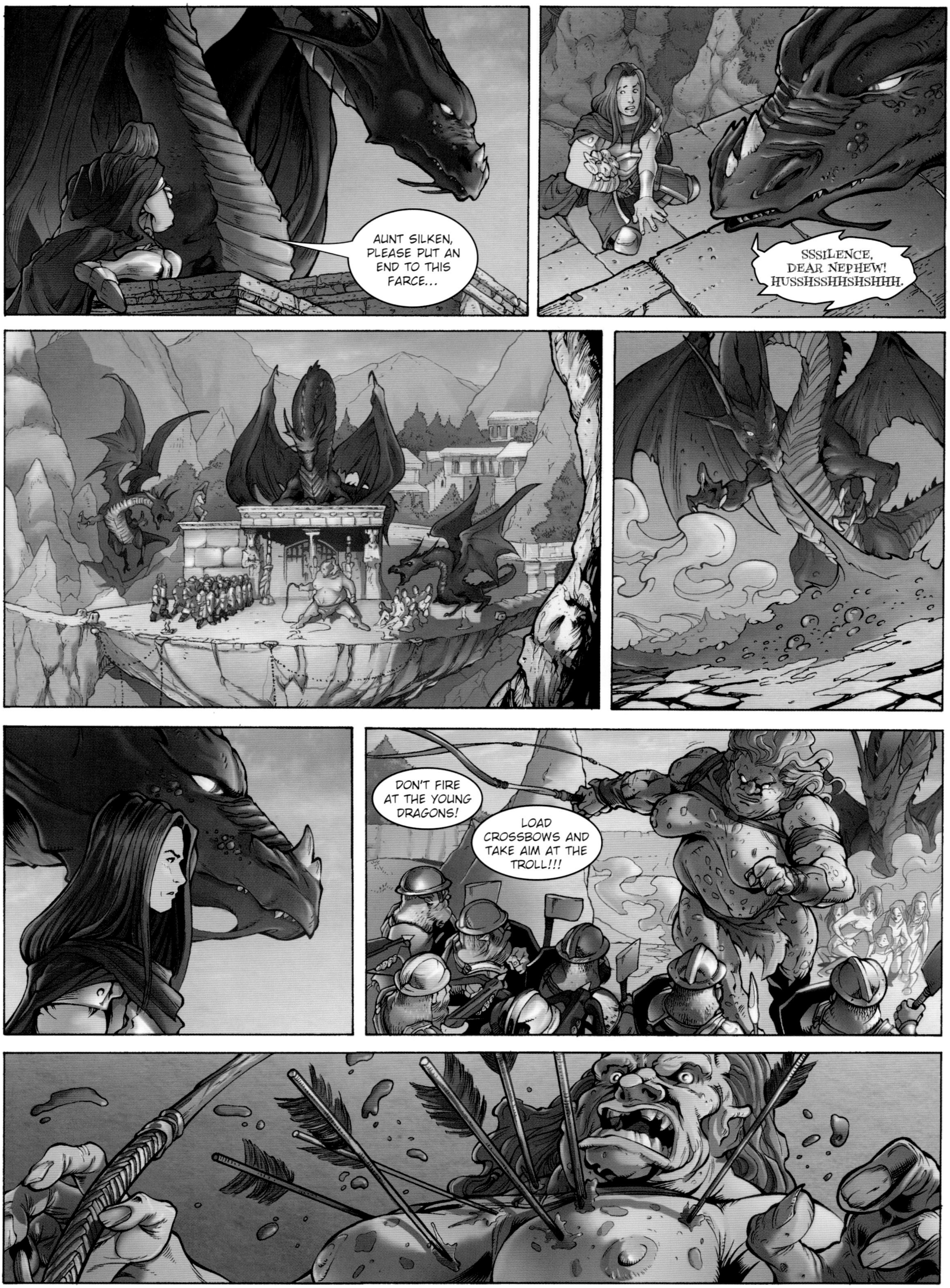
AUNT SILKEN, PLEASE PUT AN END TO THIS FARCE...
SSSILENCE, DEAR NEPHEW! HUSSHSSHHSHSHHH.
DON'T FIRE AT THE YOUNG DRAGONS!
LOAD CROSSBOWS AND TAKE AIM AT THE TROLL!!!

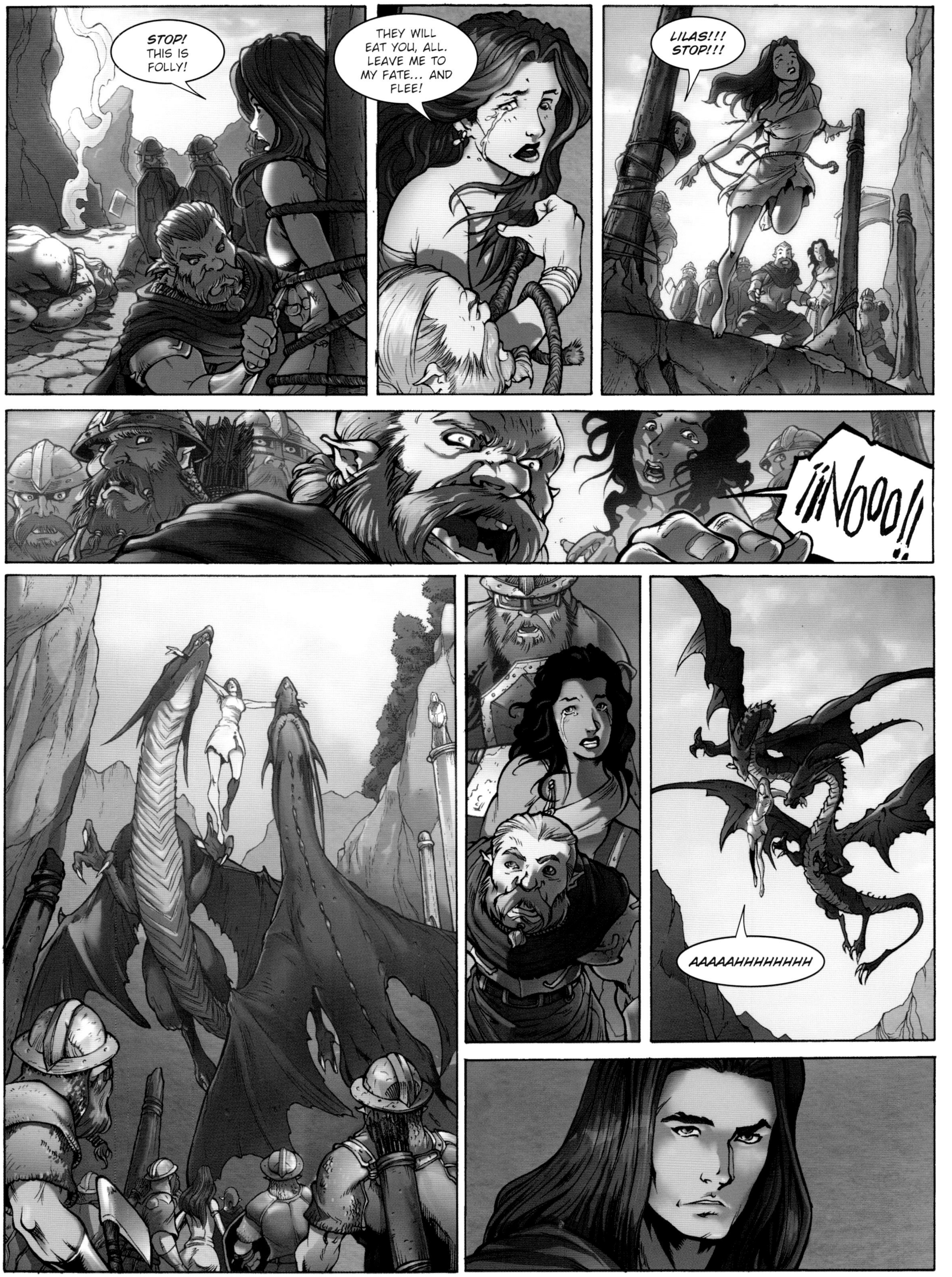
STOP! THIS IS FOLLY!
THEY WILL EAT YOU, ALL. LEAVE ME TO MY FATE... AND FLEE!
LILAS!!! STOP!!!
¡¡NOOO!!
AAAAAHHHHHHHH

I THOUGHT DRAGONS COULD ONLY CRY ONCE IN A LIFETIME.

THAT'SSS TRUE... IN OUR DRAGON FORM.

BUT IN HUMAN SSSHAPE...

...WE CAN SSSHED TEARSSS TO FILL AN OCEAN.

MY DEAR NEPHEW, YOU ARE SSSO SSSWEET...

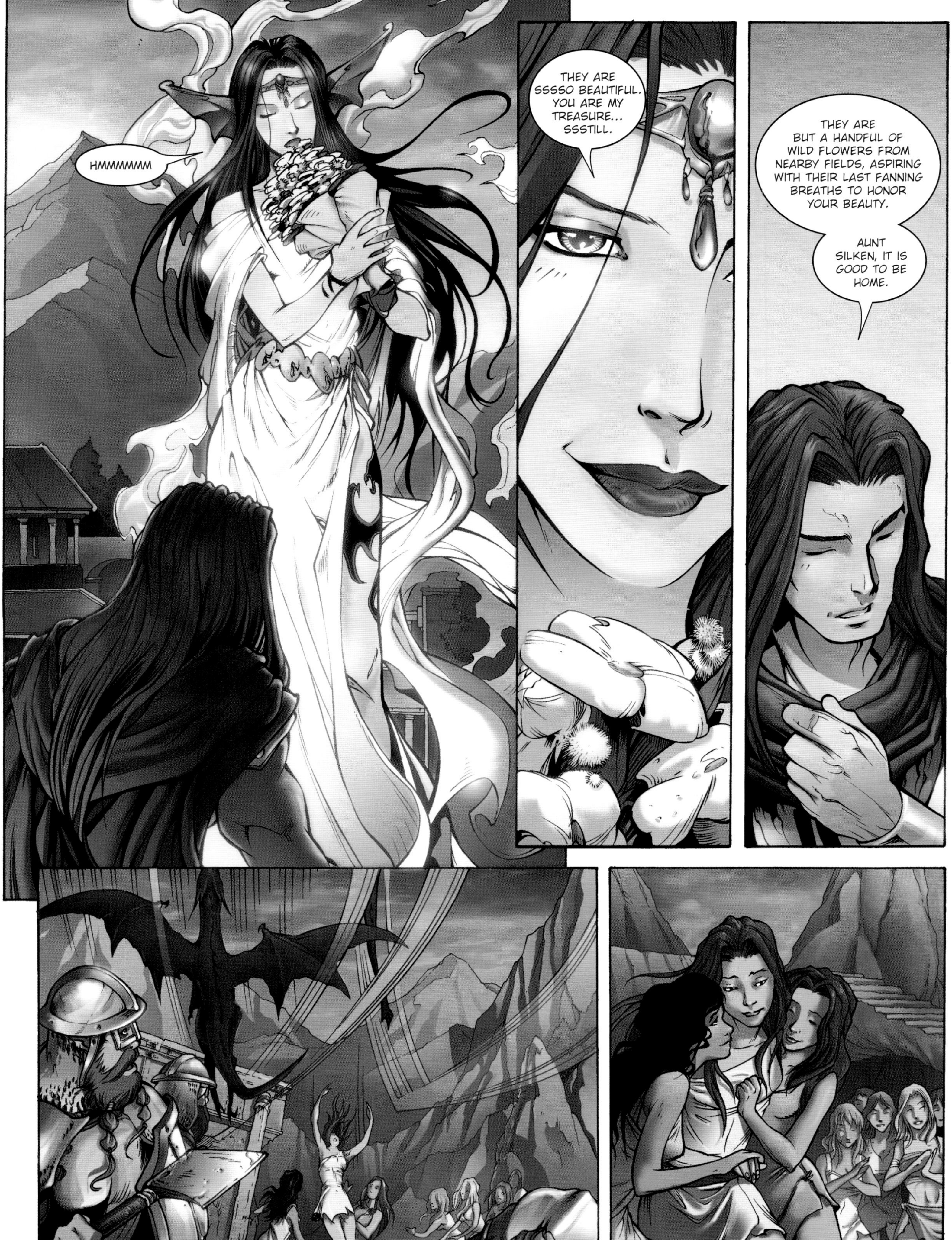
HMMMMMMM
THEY ARE SSSSO BEAUTIFUL. YOU ARE MY TREASURE... SSSTILL.
THEY ARE BUT A HANDFUL OF WILD FLOWERS FROM NEARBY FIELDS, ASPIRING WITH THEIR LAST FANNING BREATHS TO HONOR YOUR BEAUTY.
AUNT SILKEN, IT IS GOOD TO BE HOME.

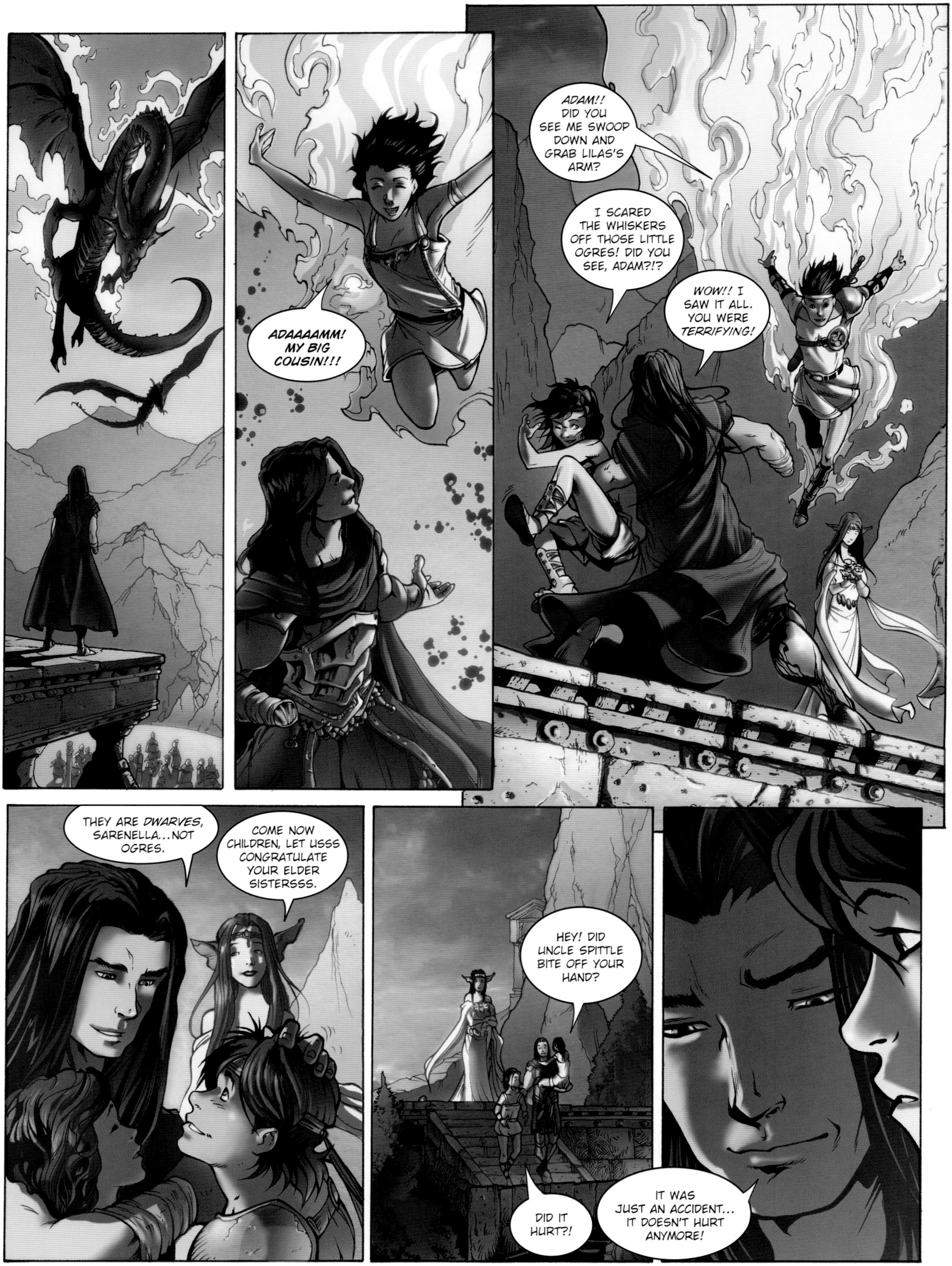
ADAAAAMM! MY BIG COUSIN!!!
ADAM!! DID YOU SEE ME SWOOP DOWN AND GRAB LILAS'S ARM?
I SCARED THE WHISKERS OFF THOSE LITTLE OGRES! DID YOU SEE, ADAM?!?
WOW!! I SAW IT ALL. YOU WERE TERRIFYING!
THEY ARE DWARVES, SARENELLA...NOT OGRES.
COME NOW CHILDREN, LET USSS CONGRATULATE YOUR ELDER SISTERSSS.
HEY! DID UNCLE SPITTLE BITE OFF YOUR HAND?
DID IT HURT?!
IT WAS JUST AN ACCIDENT... IT DOESN'T HURT ANYMORE!

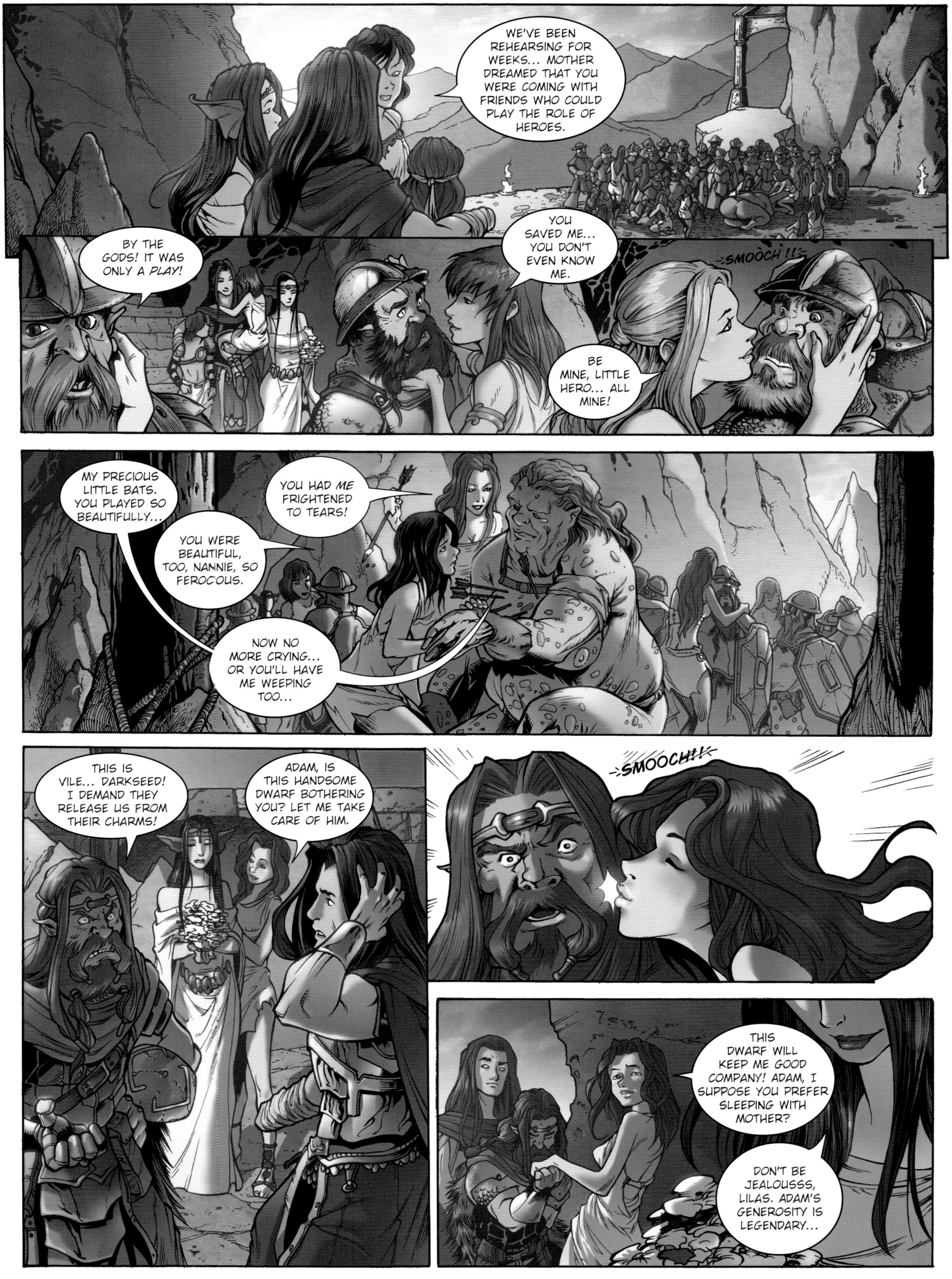
WE'VE BEEN REHEARSING FOR WEEKS... MOTHER DREAMED THAT YOU WERE COMING WITH FRIENDS WHO COULD PLAY THE ROLE OF HEROES.
BY THE GODS! IT WAS ONLY A *PLAY*!
YOU SAVED ME... YOU DON'T EVEN KNOW ME.
-SMOOCH!!-
BE MINE, LITTLE HERO... ALL MINE!
MY PRECIOUS LITTLE BATS. YOU PLAYED SO BEAUTIFULLY...
YOU HAD *ME* FRIGHTENED TO TEARS!
YOU WERE BEAUTIFUL, TOO, NANNIE, SO FEROCIOUS.
NOW NO MORE CRYING... OR YOU'LL HAVE ME WEEPING TOO...
THIS IS VILE... DARKSEED! I DEMAND THEY RELEASE US FROM THEIR CHARMS!
ADAM, IS THIS HANDSOME DWARF BOTHERING YOU? LET ME TAKE CARE OF HIM.
-SMOOCH!!-
THIS DWARF WILL KEEP ME GOOD COMPANY! ADAM, I SUPPOSE YOU PREFER SLEEPING WITH MOTHER?
DON'T BE JEALOUSSS, LILAS. ADAM'S GENEROSITY IS LEGENDARY...

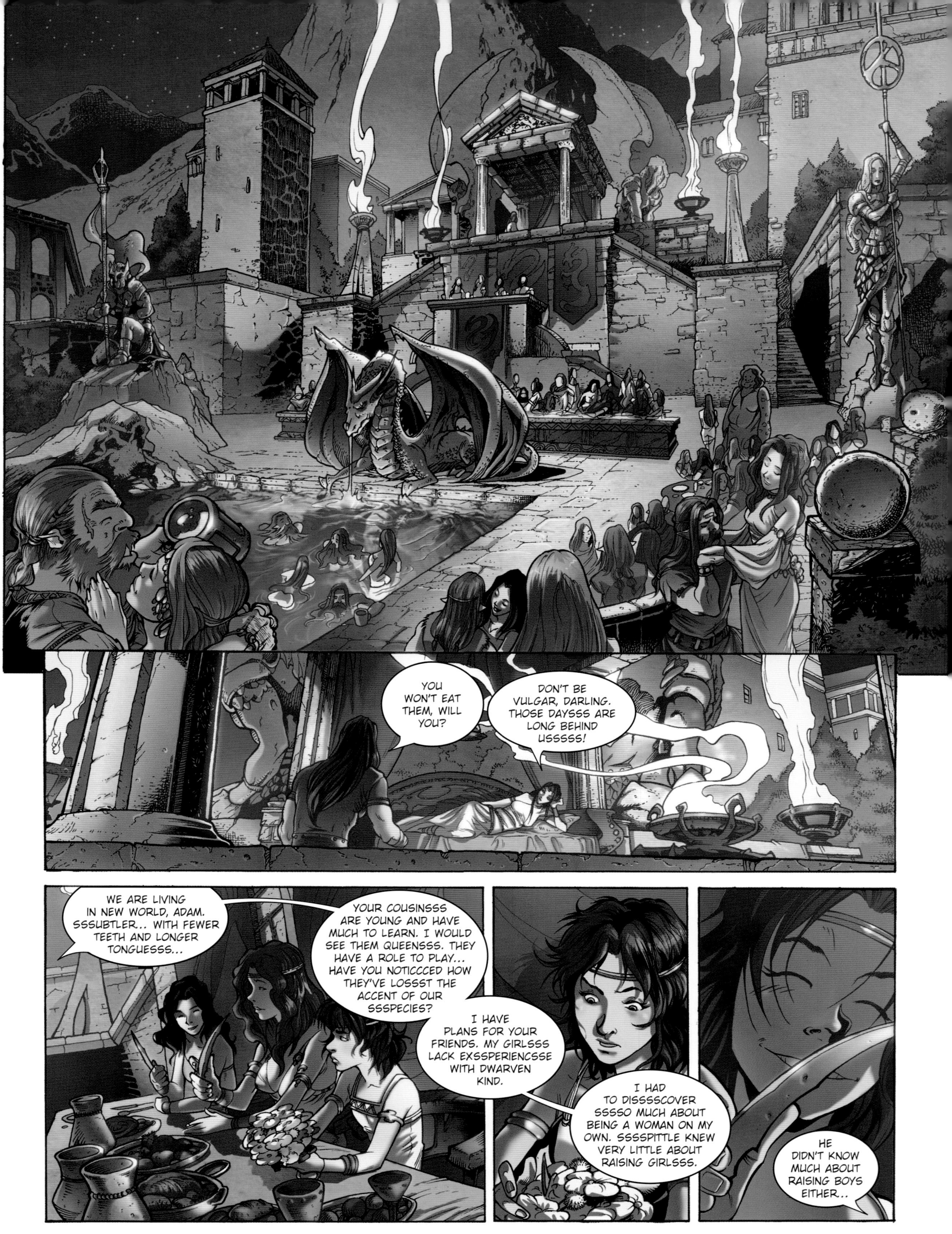
YOU WON'T EAT THEM, WILL YOU?
DON'T BE VULGAR, DARLING. THOSE DAYSSS ARE LONG BEHIND USSSSS!
WE ARE LIVING IN NEW WORLD, ADAM. SSSUBTLER... WITH FEWER TEETH AND LONGER TONGUESSS...
YOUR COUSINSSS ARE YOUNG AND HAVE MUCH TO LEARN. I WOULD SEE THEM QUEENSSS. THEY HAVE A ROLE TO PLAY... HAVE YOU NOTICCCED HOW THEY'VE LOSSST THE ACCENT OF OUR SSSPECIES?
I HAVE PLANS FOR YOUR FRIENDS. MY GIRLSSS LACK EXSSPERIENCSSE WITH DWARVEN KIND.
I HAD TO DISSSSCOVER SSSSO MUCH ABOUT BEING A WOMAN ON MY OWN. SSSSPITTLE KNEW VERY LITTLE ABOUT RAISING GIRLSSS.
HE DIDN'T KNOW MUCH ABOUT RAISING BOYS EITHER...

WAIT! MY FATHER RAISED YOU? I ALWAYS THOUGHT YOU HIS ELDER.

ADAM! HOW INSSSSENSSSITIVE! I'M A CSSSSENTURY AND A HALF HISSS YOUNGER. DO YOU WANT ME TO BITE OFF YOUR OTHER HAND?!

FORGIVE ME, AUNT SILKEN... IT'S JUST THAT YOU WERE ALWAYS THERE... EVEN MY MOTHER'S FUNERAL.

...WHILE SPITTLE WAS ALWAYS SLEEPING...

COME HERE, ADAM.

HOW OLD WERE YOU WHEN YOUR MOTHER RELEASSSED HER FINAL BREATH? BARELY A DECADE...NO?

I WAS TWELVE.

YOU'RE FATHER ASSSKED ME TO TAKE YOU UNDER WING...

YOU WERE SSSO HEARTBROKEN. I CRIED MANY TEARSSS TO SSSEE SSSUCH SSSADNESS.

YOU CRIED FOR MY MOTHER... JUST LIKE MY FATHER CRIED FOR YOURS?

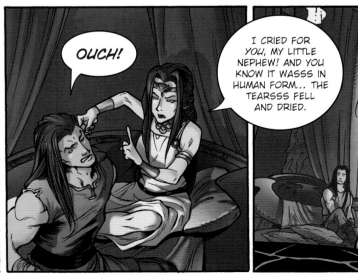

OUCH!

I CRIED FOR YOU, MY LITTLE NEPHEW! AND YOU KNOW IT WASSS IN HUMAN FORM... THE TEARSSS FELL AND DRIED.

I SHALL CRY BUT ONE DRAGON TEAR AND THE HOUR HASSS FAILED TO COME. DRAGONSSS ONLY CRY WHEN THEIR DESSSTINY IS REVEALED TO THEM.

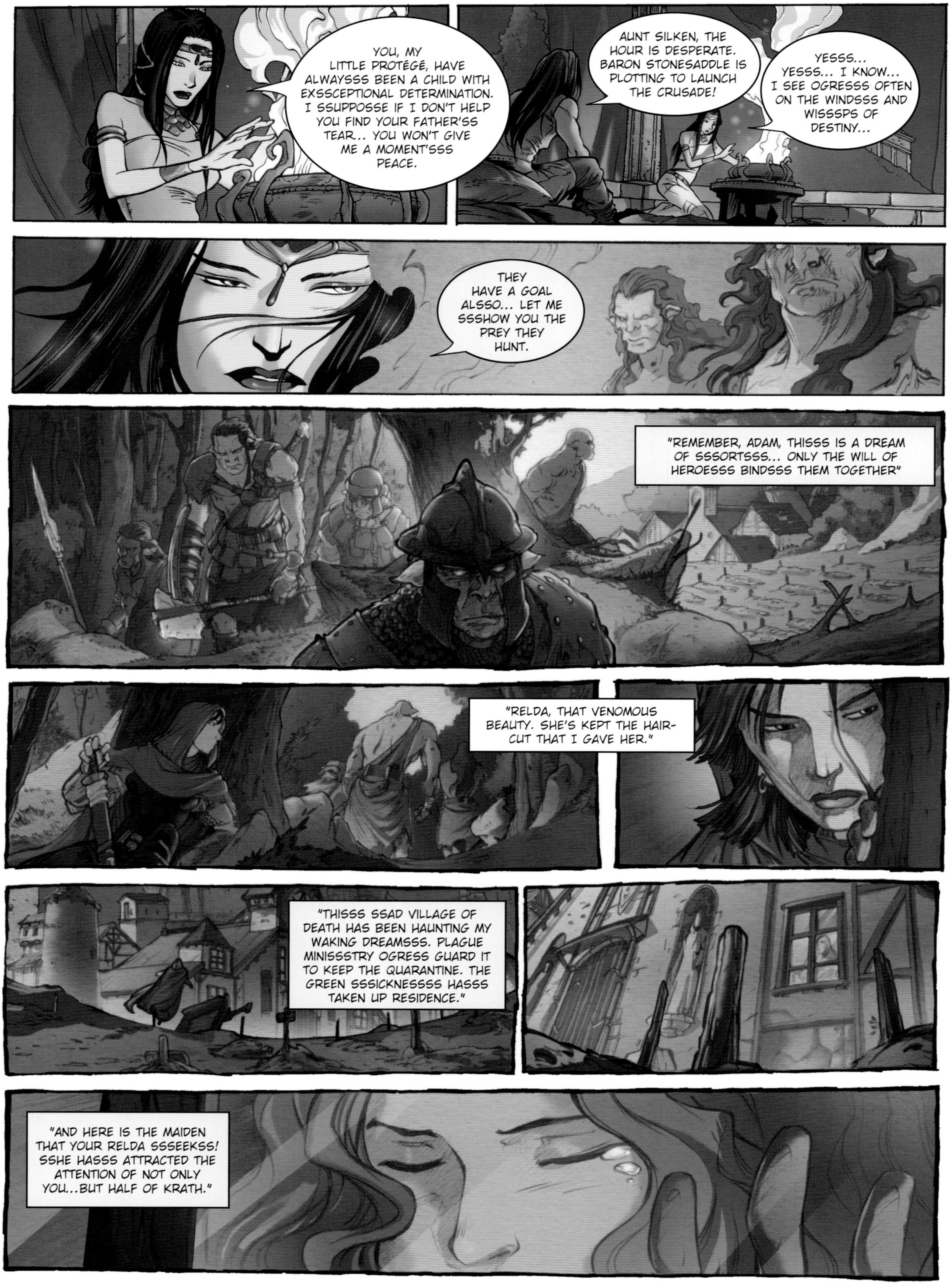
YOU, MY LITTLE PROTÉGÉ, HAVE ALWAYSSS BEEN A CHILD WITH EXSSCEPTIONAL DETERMINATION. I SSUPPOSSE IF I DON'T HELP YOU FIND YOUR FATHER'SS TEAR... YOU WON'T GIVE ME A MOMENT'SSS PEACE.
AUNT SILKEN, THE HOUR IS DESPERATE. BARON STONESADDLE IS PLOTTING TO LAUNCH THE CRUSADE!
YESSS... YESSS... I KNOW... I SEE OGRESSS OFTEN ON THE WINDSSS AND WISSSPS OF DESTINY...
THEY HAVE A GOAL ALSSO... LET ME SSSHOW YOU THE PREY THEY HUNT.
"REMEMBER, ADAM, THISSS IS A DREAM OF SSSORTSSS... ONLY THE WILL OF HEROESSS BINDSSS THEM TOGETHER"
"RELDA, THAT VENOMOUS BEAUTY. SHE'S KEPT THE HAIR-CUT THAT I GAVE HER."
"THISSS SSAD VILLAGE OF DEATH HAS BEEN HAUNTING MY WAKING DREAMSSS. PLAGUE MINISSSTRY OGRESS GUARD IT TO KEEP THE QUARANTINE. THE GREEN SSSICKNESSSS HASSS TAKEN UP RESIDENCE."
"AND HERE IS THE MAIDEN THAT YOUR RELDA SSSEEKSS! SSHE HASSS ATTRACTED THE ATTENTION OF NOT ONLY YOU...BUT HALF OF KRATH."

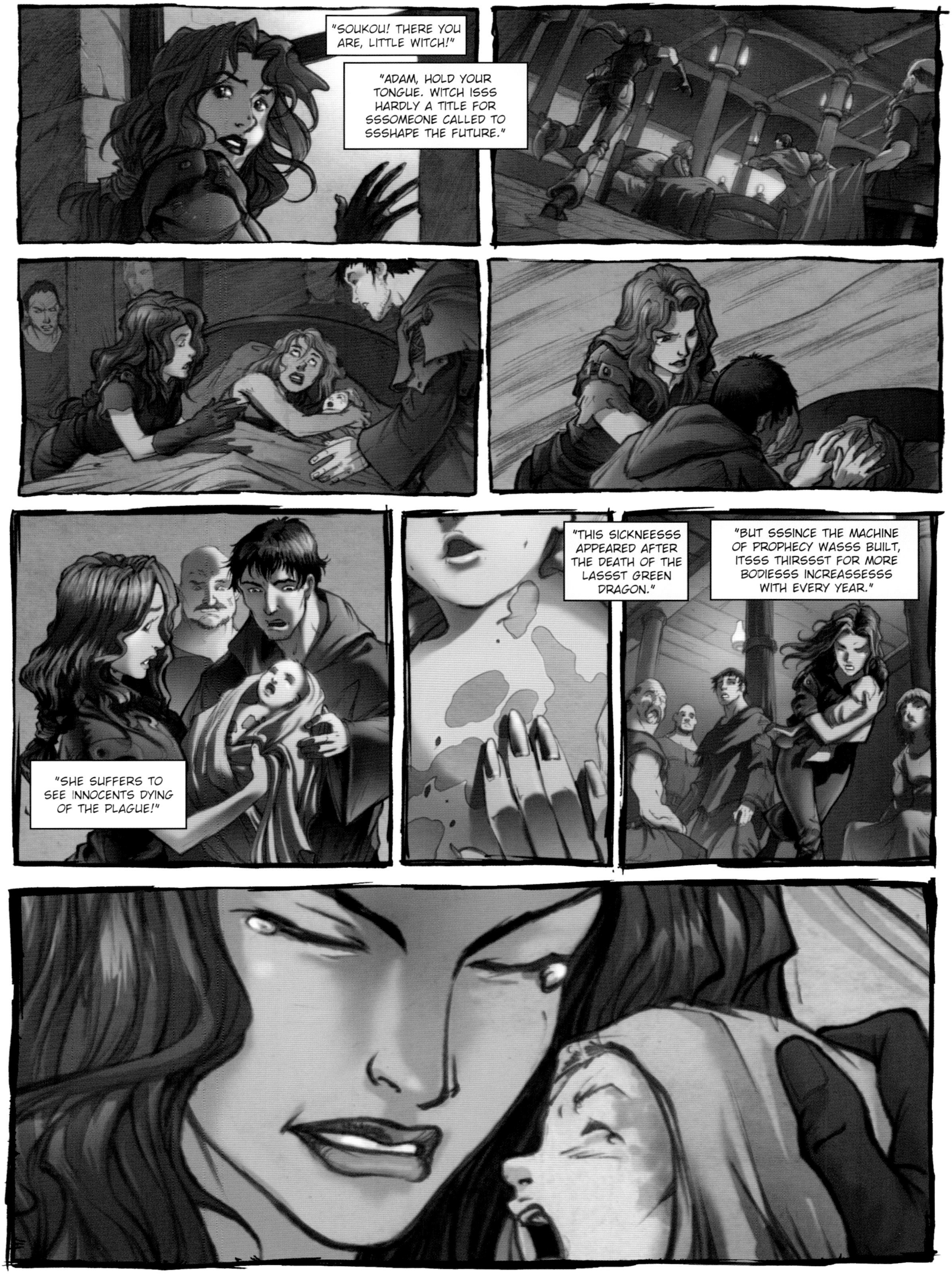
"SOUKOU! THERE YOU ARE, LITTLE WITCH!"
"ADAM, HOLD YOUR TONGUE. WITCH ISSS HARDLY A TITLE FOR SSSOMEONE CALLED TO SSSHAPE THE FUTURE."
"SHE SUFFERS TO SEE INNOCENTS DYING OF THE PLAGUE!"
"THIS SICKNEESSS APPEARED AFTER THE DEATH OF THE LASSST GREEN DRAGON."
"BUT SSSINCE THE MACHINE OF PROPHECY WASSS BUILT, ITSSS THIRSSST FOR MORE BODIESSS INCREASSESSS WITH EVERY YEAR."

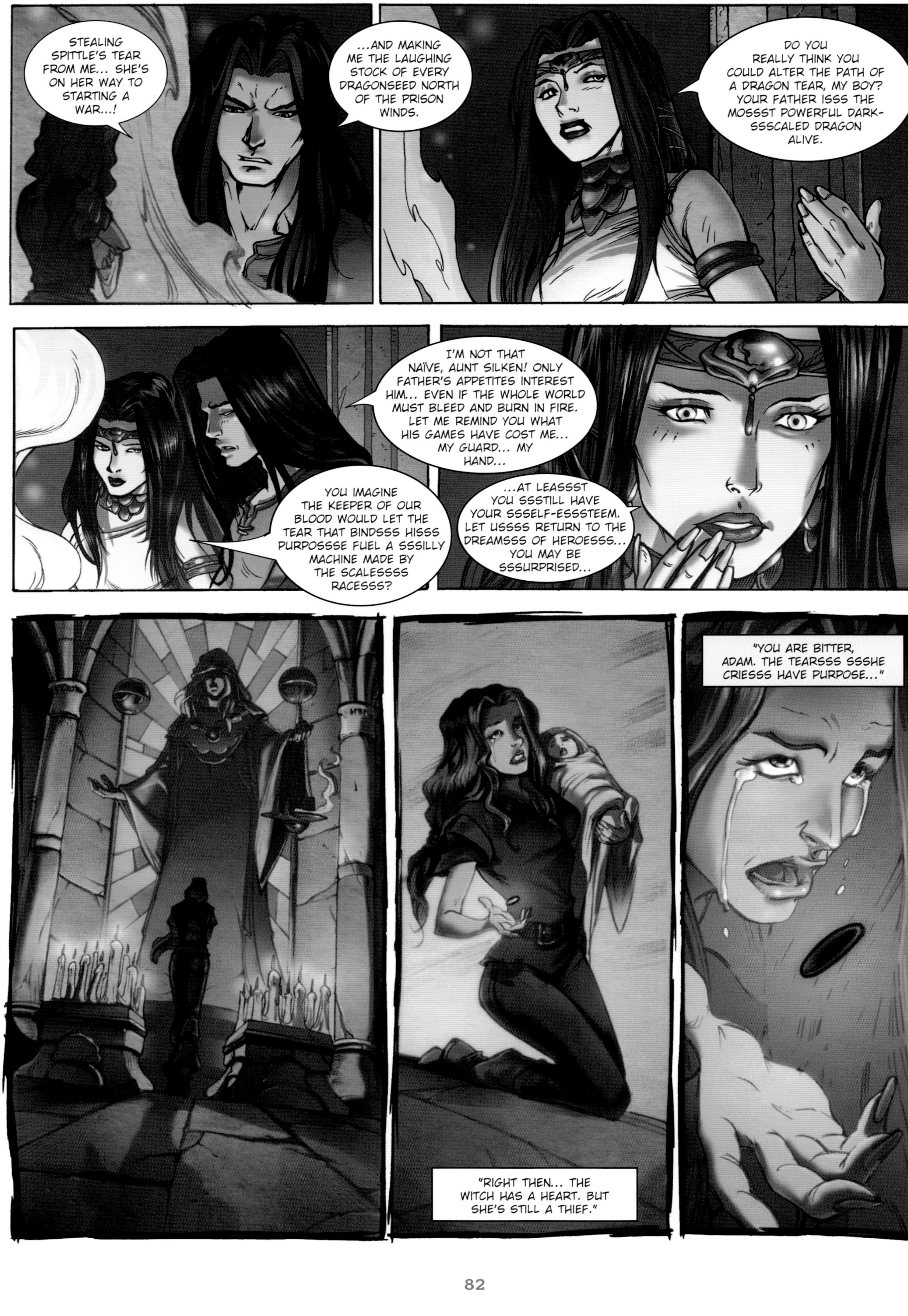
STEALING SPITTLE'S TEAR FROM ME... SHE'S ON HER WAY TO STARTING A WAR...!
...AND MAKING ME THE LAUGHING STOCK OF EVERY DRAGONSEED NORTH OF THE PRISON WINDS.
DO YOU REALLY THINK YOU COULD ALTER THE PATH OF A DRAGON TEAR, MY BOY? YOUR FATHER ISSS THE MOSSST POWERFUL DARK-SSSCALED DRAGON ALIVE.
YOU IMAGINE THE KEEPER OF OUR BLOOD WOULD LET THE TEAR THAT BINDSSS HISSS PURPOSSSE FUEL A SSSILLY MACHINE MADE BY THE SCALESSSS RACESSS?
I'M NOT THAT NAÏVE, AUNT SILKEN! ONLY FATHER'S APPETITES INTEREST HIM... EVEN IF THE WHOLE WORLD MUST BLEED AND BURN IN FIRE. LET ME REMIND YOU WHAT HIS GAMES HAVE COST ME... MY GUARD... MY HAND...
...AT LEASSST YOU SSSTILL HAVE YOUR SSSELF-ESSSTEEM. LET USSSS RETURN TO THE DREAMSSS OF HEROESSS... YOU MAY BE SSSURPRISED...
"RIGHT THEN... THE WITCH HAS A HEART. BUT SHE'S STILL A THIEF."
"YOU ARE BITTER, ADAM. THE TEARSSS SSSHE CRIESSS HAVE PURPOSE..."

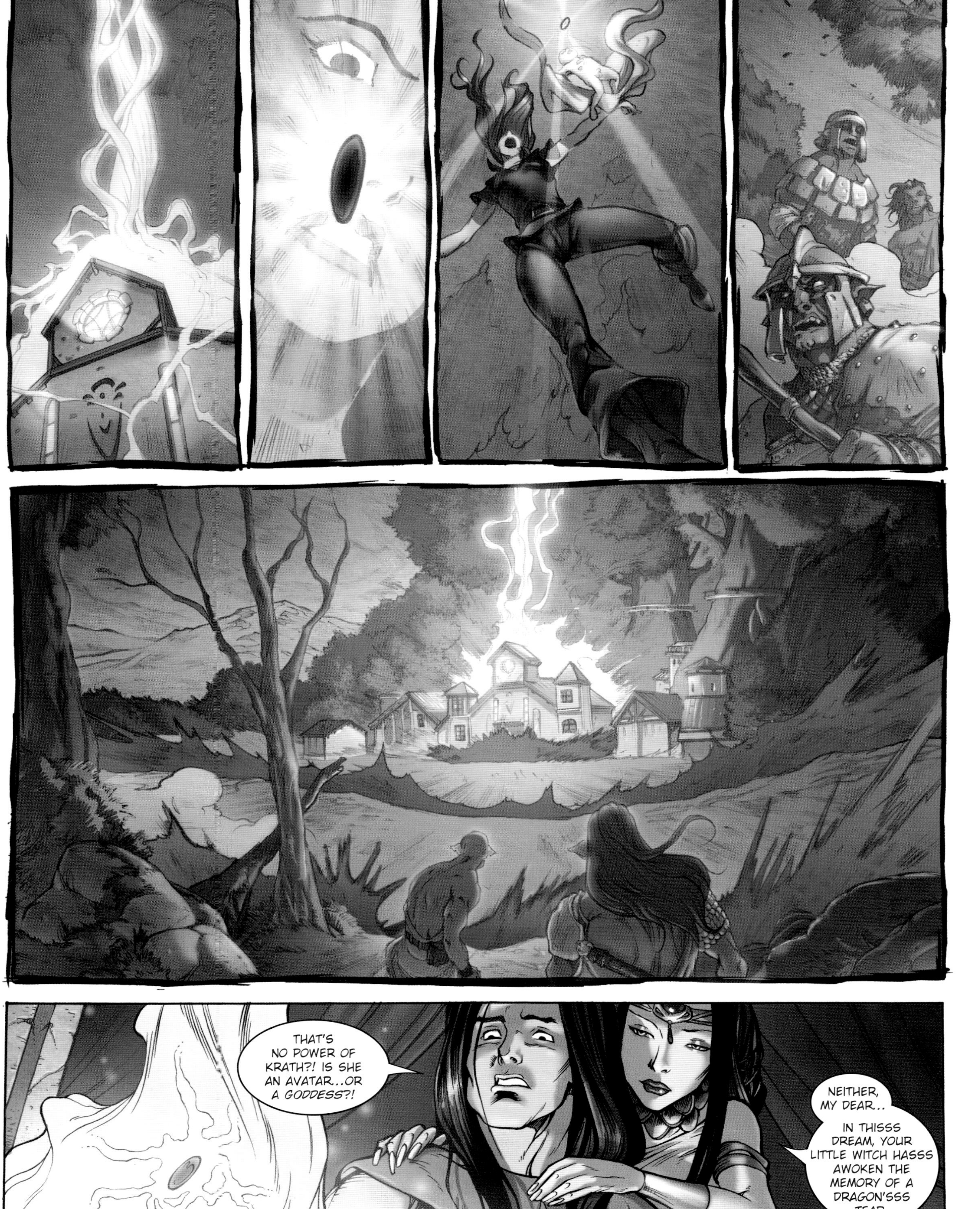
THAT'S NO POWER OF KRATH?! IS SHE AN AVATAR...OR A *GODDESS*?!
NEITHER, MY DEAR...
IN THISSS DREAM, YOUR LITTLE WITCH HASSS AWOKEN THE MEMORY OF A DRAGON'SSS TEAR.

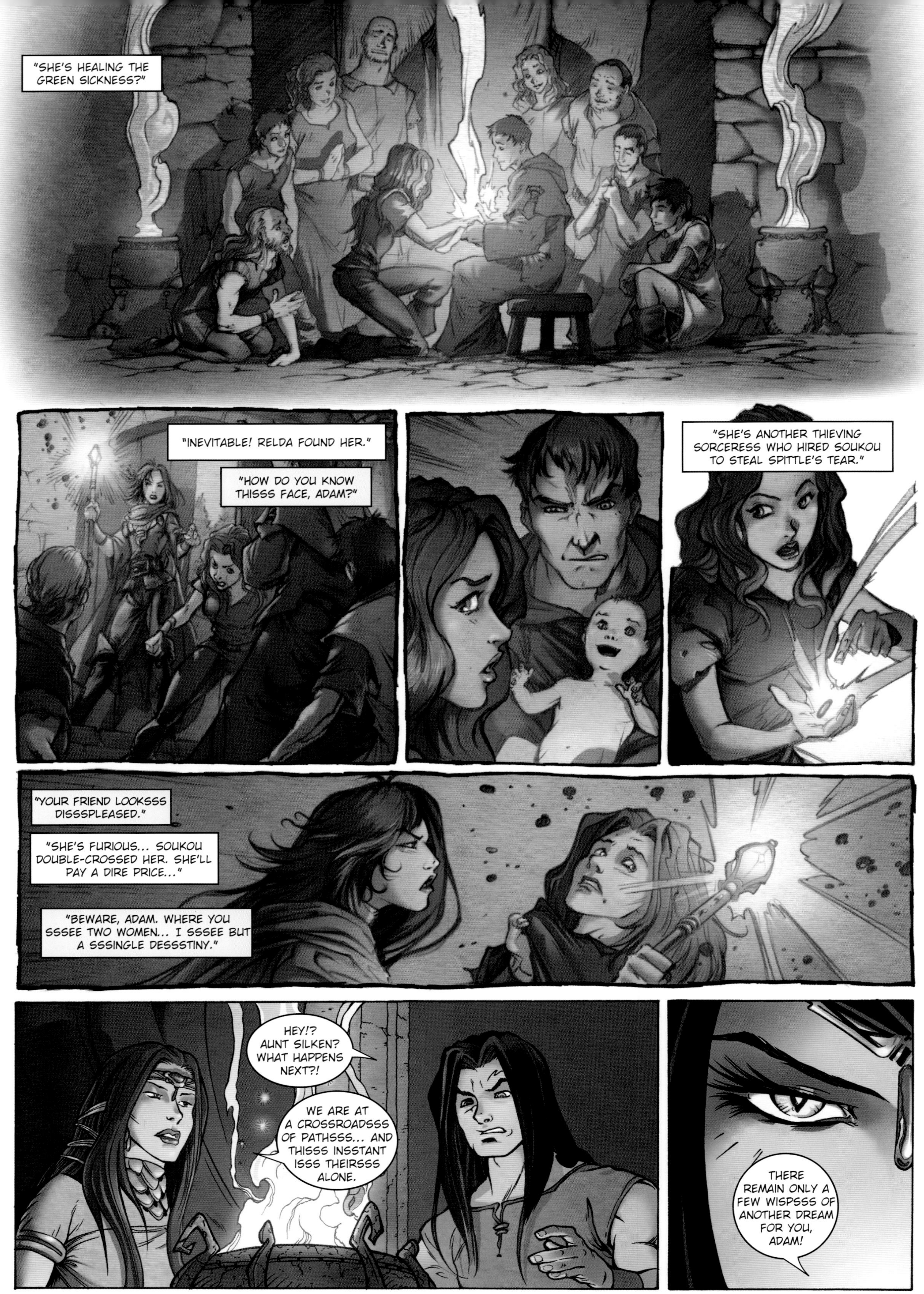
"SHE'S HEALING THE GREEN SICKNESS?"
"INEVITABLE! RELDA FOUND HER."
"HOW DO YOU KNOW THISSS FACE, ADAM?"
"SHE'S ANOTHER THIEVING SORCERESS WHO HIRED SOUKOU TO STEAL SPITTLE'S TEAR."
"YOUR FRIEND LOOKSSS DISSSPLEASED."
"SHE'S FURIOUS... SOUKOU DOUBLE-CROSSED HER. SHE'LL PAY A DIRE PRICE..."
"BEWARE, ADAM. WHERE YOU SSSEE TWO WOMEN... I SSSEE BUT A SSSINGLE DESSSTINY."
HEY!? AUNT SILKEN? WHAT HAPPENS NEXT?!
WE ARE AT A CROSSROADSSS OF PATHSSS... AND THISSS INSSTANT ISSS THEIRSSS ALONE.
THERE REMAIN ONLY A FEW WISPSSS OF ANOTHER DREAM FOR YOU, ADAM!

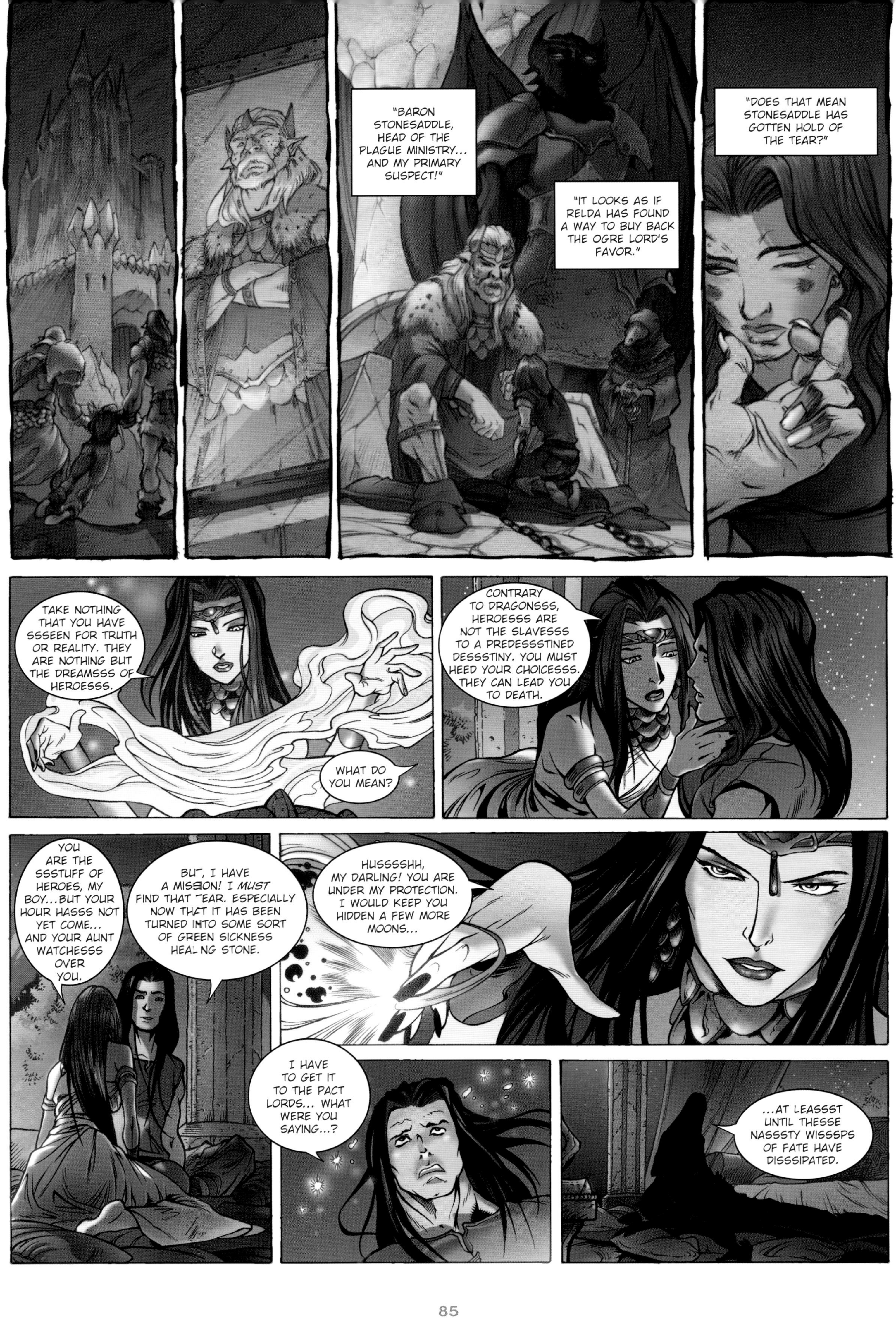

"BARON STONESADDLE, HEAD OF THE PLAGUE MINISTRY... AND MY PRIMARY SUSPECT!"
"IT LOOKS AS IF RELDA HAS FOUND A WAY TO BUY BACK THE OGRE LORD'S FAVOR."
"DOES THAT MEAN STONESADDLE HAS GOTTEN HOLD OF THE TEAR?"
TAKE NOTHING THAT YOU HAVE SSSEEN FOR TRUTH OR REALITY. THEY ARE NOTHING BUT THE DREAMSSS OF HEROESSS.
WHAT DO YOU MEAN?
CONTRARY TO DRAGONSSS, HEROESSS ARE NOT THE SLAVESSS TO A PREDESSSTINED DESSSTINY. YOU MUST HEED YOUR CHOICESSS. THEY CAN LEAD YOU TO DEATH.
YOU ARE THE SSSTUFF OF HEROES, MY BOY...BUT YOUR HOUR HASSS NOT YET COME... AND YOUR AUNT WATCHESSS OVER YOU.
BUT, I HAVE A MISSION! I MUST FIND THAT TEAR. ESPECIALLY NOW THAT IT HAS BEEN TURNED INTO SOME SORT OF GREEN SICKNESS HEALING STONE.
HUSSSSHH, MY DARLING! YOU ARE UNDER MY PROTECTION. I WOULD KEEP YOU HIDDEN A FEW MORE MOONS...
I HAVE TO GET IT TO THE PACT LORDS... WHAT WERE YOU SAYING...?
...AT LEASSST UNTIL THESSE NASSSTY WISSSPS OF FATE HAVE DISSSIPATED.

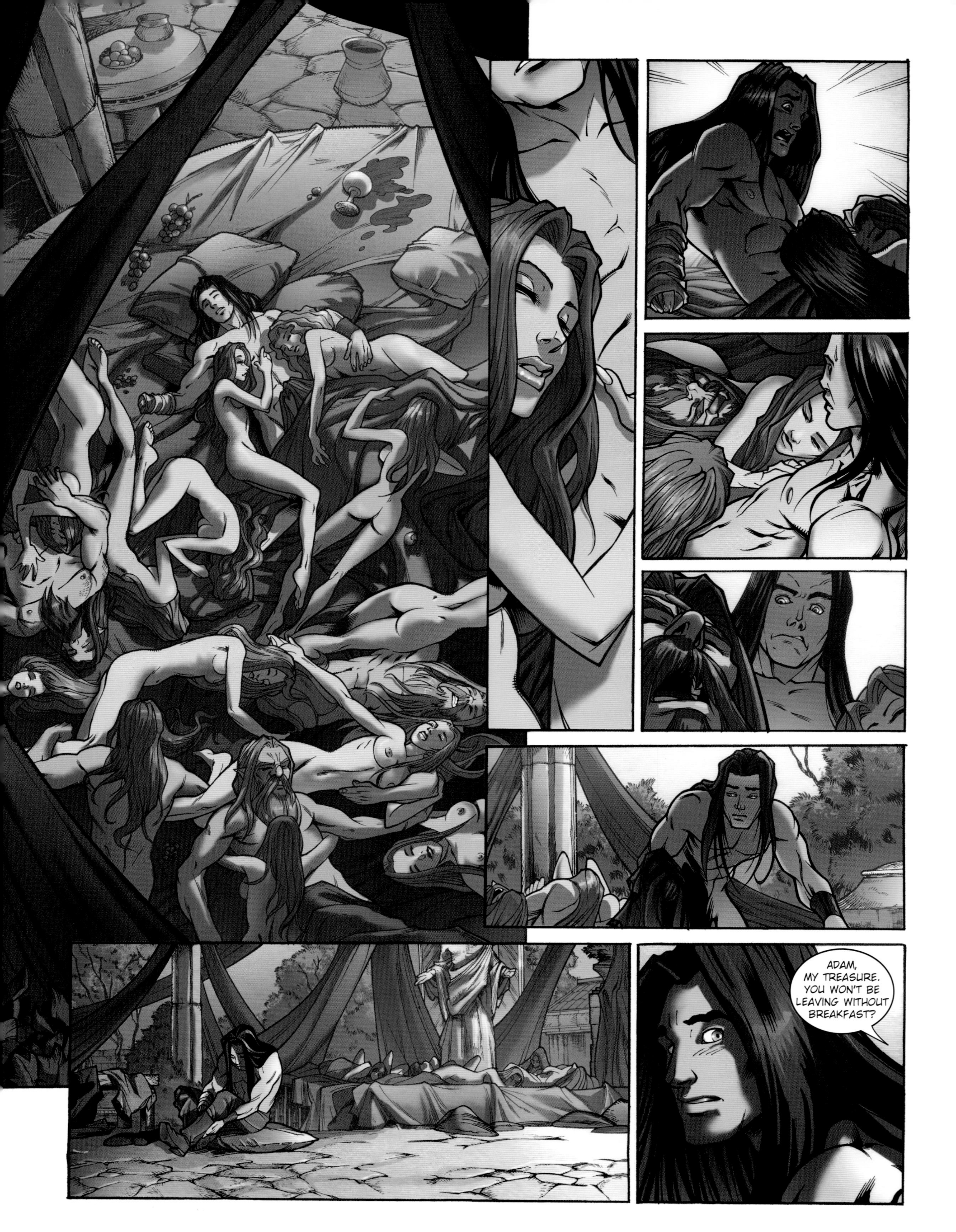
ADAM, MY TREASURE. YOU WON'T BE LEAVING WITHOUT BREAKFAST?

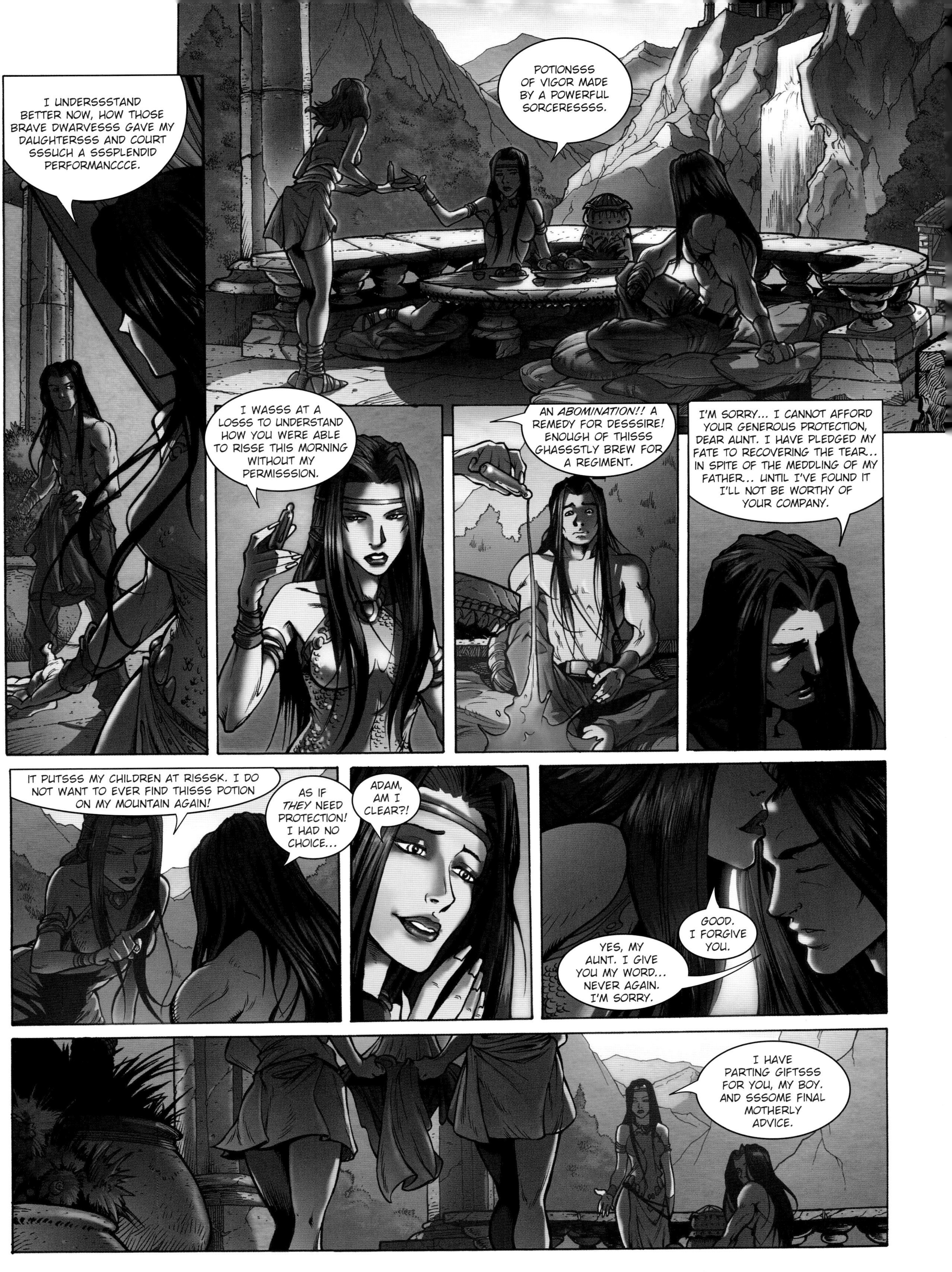

I UNDERSSSTAND BETTER NOW, HOW THOSE BRAVE DWARVESSS GAVE MY DAUGHTERSSS AND COURT SSSUCH A SSSPLENDID PERFORMANCCCE.
POTIONSSS OF VIGOR MADE BY A POWERFUL SORCERESSSS.
I WASSS AT A LOSSS TO UNDERSTAND HOW YOU WERE ABLE TO RISSE THIS MORNING WITHOUT MY PERMISSSSION.
AN *ABOMINATION!!* A REMEDY FOR DESSSIRE! ENOUGH OF THISSS GHASSSTLY BREW FOR A REGIMENT.
I'M SORRY... I CANNOT AFFORD YOUR GENEROUS PROTECTION, DEAR AUNT. I HAVE PLEDGED MY FATE TO RECOVERING THE TEAR... IN SPITE OF THE MEDDLING OF MY FATHER... UNTIL I'VE FOUND IT I'LL NOT BE WORTHY OF YOUR COMPANY.
IT PUTSSS MY CHILDREN AT RISSSK. I DO NOT WANT TO EVER FIND THISSS POTION ON MY MOUNTAIN AGAIN!
AS IF *THEY* NEED PROTECTION! I HAD NO CHOICE...
ADAM, AM I CLEAR?!
YES, MY AUNT. I GIVE YOU MY WORD... NEVER AGAIN. I'M SORRY.
GOOD. I FORGIVE YOU.
I HAVE PARTING GIFTSSS FOR YOU, MY BOY. AND SSSOME FINAL MOTHERLY ADVICE.

IF THIS WOMAN, SSSOUKOU, CALLED UPON THE POWER OF YOUR FATHER'SSSS TEAR, SSSHE HAD TO KNOW A MEMORY... THE MEMORY OF THE MOMENT HIS PURPOSSSE WASSS REVEALED.

I SUSPECT ELVEN IMPLICATION IN THISSS SSSTORY...

ARE YOU SUGGESTING I SEEK COUNCIL FROM ELVES?

NOT JUST ANY ELVESSS... DO YOU REMEMBER KHORRÉ DELZEWÉ... THE FATHER OF MY SON, REMWEL...? HE KNOWSSS THE SSSTORY OF THE TEAR.

THAT TEAR WILL DELIVER ITSSS POWERSSS TO NO ONE, AND IF YOU WANT ITSSS POWER YOU MUSSST CONVINCE IT TO GRANT YOU ITSSS FAVOR.

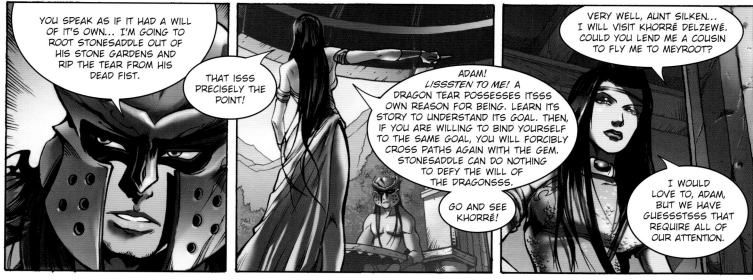

YOU SPEAK AS IF IT HAD A WILL OF IT'S OWN... I'M GOING TO ROOT STONESADDLE OUT OF HIS STONE GARDENS AND RIP THE TEAR FROM HIS DEAD FIST.

THAT ISSS PRECISELY THE POINT!

ADAM! LISSSTEN TO ME! A DRAGON TEAR POSSESSES ITSSS OWN REASON FOR BEING. LEARN ITS STORY TO UNDERSTAND ITS GOAL. THEN, IF YOU ARE WILLING TO BIND YOURSELF TO THE SAME GOAL, YOU WILL FORCIBLY CROSS PATHS AGAIN WITH THE GEM. STONESADDLE CAN DO NOTHING TO DEFY THE WILL OF THE DRAGONSSS.

GO AND SEE KHORRÉ!

VERY WELL, AUNT SILKEN... I WILL VISIT KHORRÉ DELZEWÉ. COULD YOU LEND ME A COUSIN TO FLY ME TO MEYROOT?

I WOULD LOVE TO, ADAM, BUT WE HAVE GUESSSTSSS THAT REQUIRE ALL OF OUR ATTENTION.

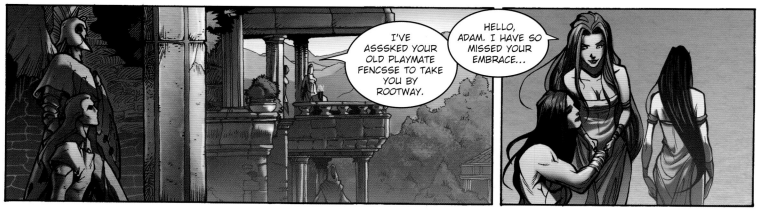

I'VE ASSSKED YOUR OLD PLAYMATE FENCSSE TO TAKE YOU BY ROOTWAY.

HELLO, ADAM. I HAVE SO MISSED YOUR EMBRACE...

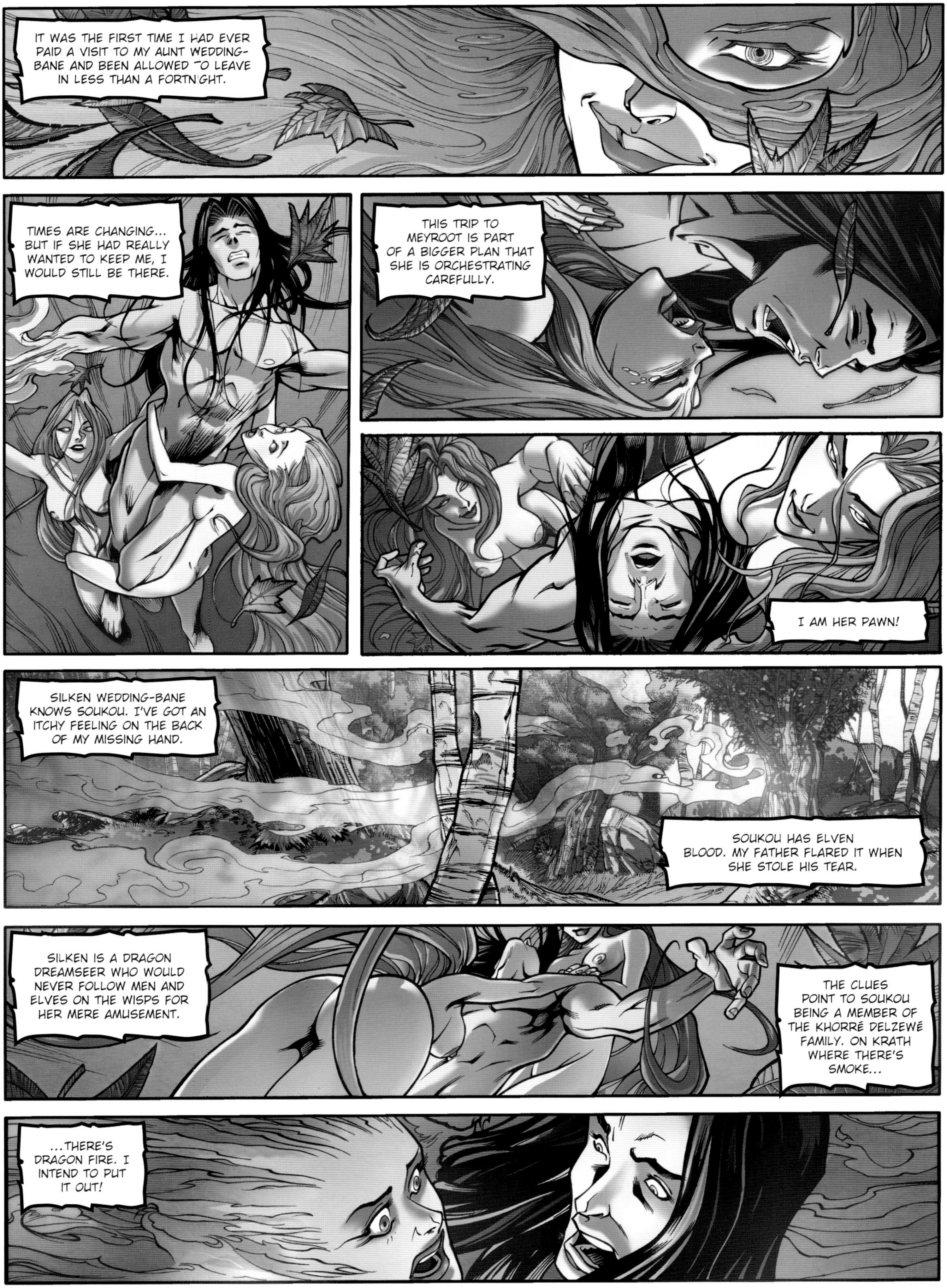
IT WAS THE FIRST TIME I HAD EVER PAID A VISIT TO MY AUNT WEDDING-BANE AND BEEN ALLOWED TO LEAVE IN LESS THAN A FORTNIGHT.
TIMES ARE CHANGING... BUT IF SHE HAD REALLY WANTED TO KEEP ME, I WOULD STILL BE THERE.
THIS TRIP TO MEYROOT IS PART OF A BIGGER PLAN THAT SHE IS ORCHESTRATING CAREFULLY.
I AM HER PAWN!
SILKEN WEDDING-BANE KNOWS SOUKOU. I'VE GOT AN ITCHY FEELING ON THE BACK OF MY MISSING HAND.
SOUKOU HAS ELVEN BLOOD. MY FATHER FLARED IT WHEN SHE STOLE HIS TEAR.
SILKEN IS A DRAGON DREAMSEER WHO WOULD NEVER FOLLOW MEN AND ELVES ON THE WISPS FOR HER MERE AMUSEMENT.
THE CLUES POINT TO SOUKOU BEING A MEMBER OF THE KHORRÉ DELZEWÉ FAMILY. ON KRATH WHERE THERE'S SMOKE...
...THERE'S DRAGON FIRE. I INTEND TO PUT IT OUT!

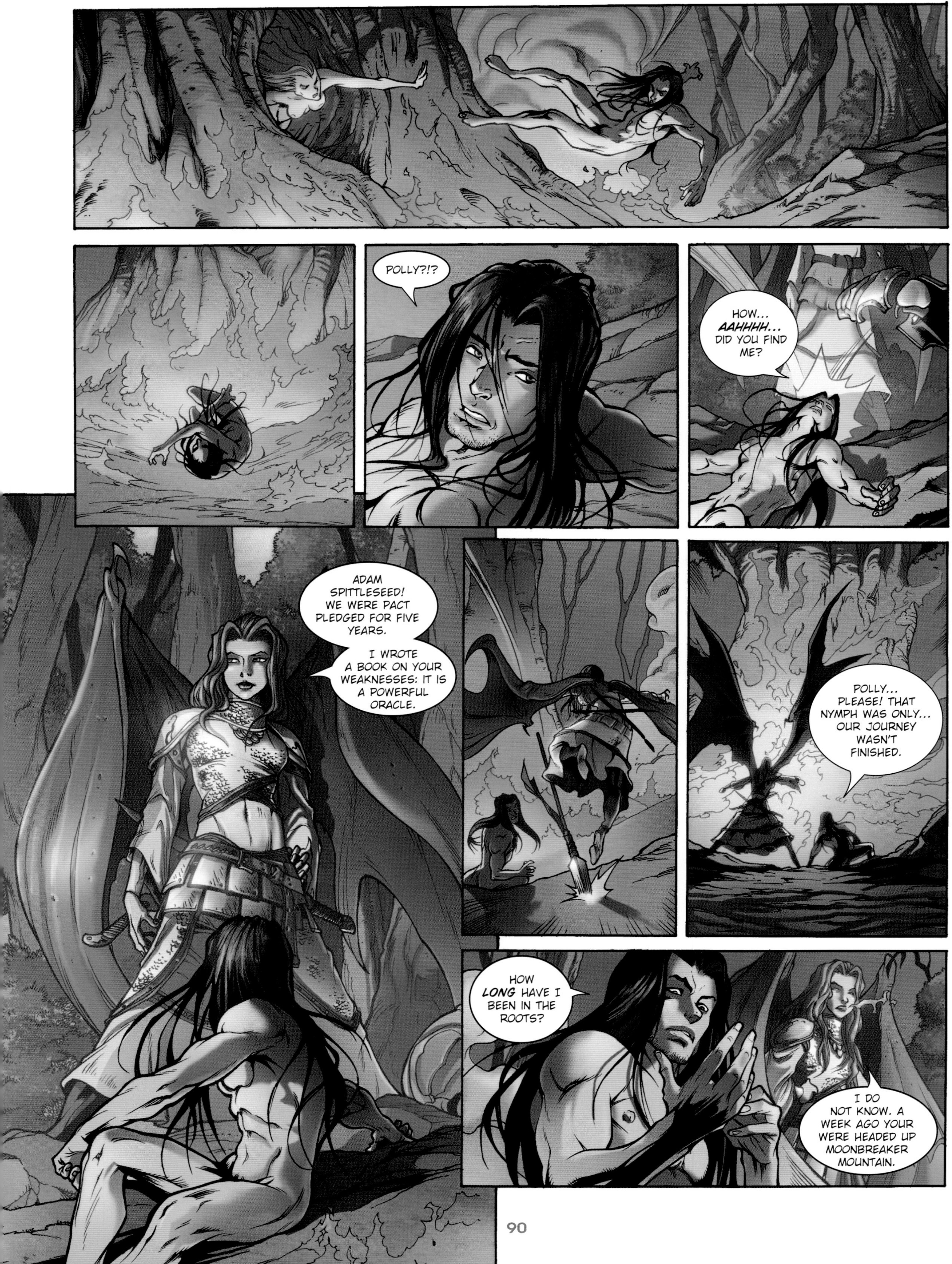
POLLY?!?
HOW... AAHHHH... DID YOU FIND ME?
ADAM SPITTLESEED! WE WERE PACT PLEDGED FOR FIVE YEARS.
I WROTE A BOOK ON YOUR WEAKNESSES: IT IS A POWERFUL ORACLE.
POLLY... PLEASE! THAT NYMPH WAS ONLY... OUR JOURNEY WASN'T FINISHED.
HOW LONG HAVE I BEEN IN THE ROOTS?
I DO NOT KNOW. A WEEK AGO YOUR WERE HEADED UP MOONBREAKER MOUNTAIN.

LADY DELLIN SPOTTED YOU IN THE ROOTWAY AND I TRACKED YOU TO THIS NECK OF THE MEYROOT FOREST.

FOR THREE DAYS THE ARBORESCENT NYMPHS HAVE BEEN PASSING YOU AROUND, SAPPING YOUR STRENGTH AND RESOLVE. I CAMPED BELOW A WEEPING WILLOW AND LISTENED FOR YOUR VOICE...

I KNEW IT. THAT WILLOW SOMEHOW SEEMED FAMILIAR...

THE THIRD TIME I SET FIRE TO THE TREE. YOU'RE LUCKY YOUR GENITALS ARE NOT GROWING BARK.

YOU COURTED REMWEL? HE'S TEN YEARS YOUR YOUNGER!!!

SIX YEARS MY YOUNGER... THAT'S HARDLY A DECADE.

YES!

YOU ARE NOT SAYING YOU'RE JEALOUS?

I KNOW YOU WANT CHILDREN... BUT THERE ARE DOZENS OF ELIGIBLE DRAGONSEED OUT THERE WHO MIGHT PROVE COMPATIBLE SIRES.

OUT OF RESPECT FOR ME, I WOULD THINK MY COUSIN WOULD BE THE LAST ON YOUR LIST.

WHO SAYS HE WASN'T...?

HOW MANY DRAGON SONS HAVE YOU BEDDED WITH?

NOT ENOUGH, APPARENTLY! YOU HAVE A LESSER RIGHT THAN ANYONE TO JUDGE ME.

OF ALL THOSE WHO TOUCHED MY BODY, ONLY YOU HAVE BROKEN MY HEART.

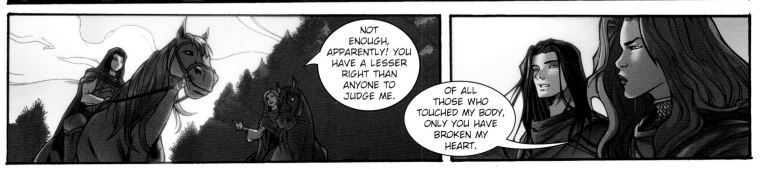

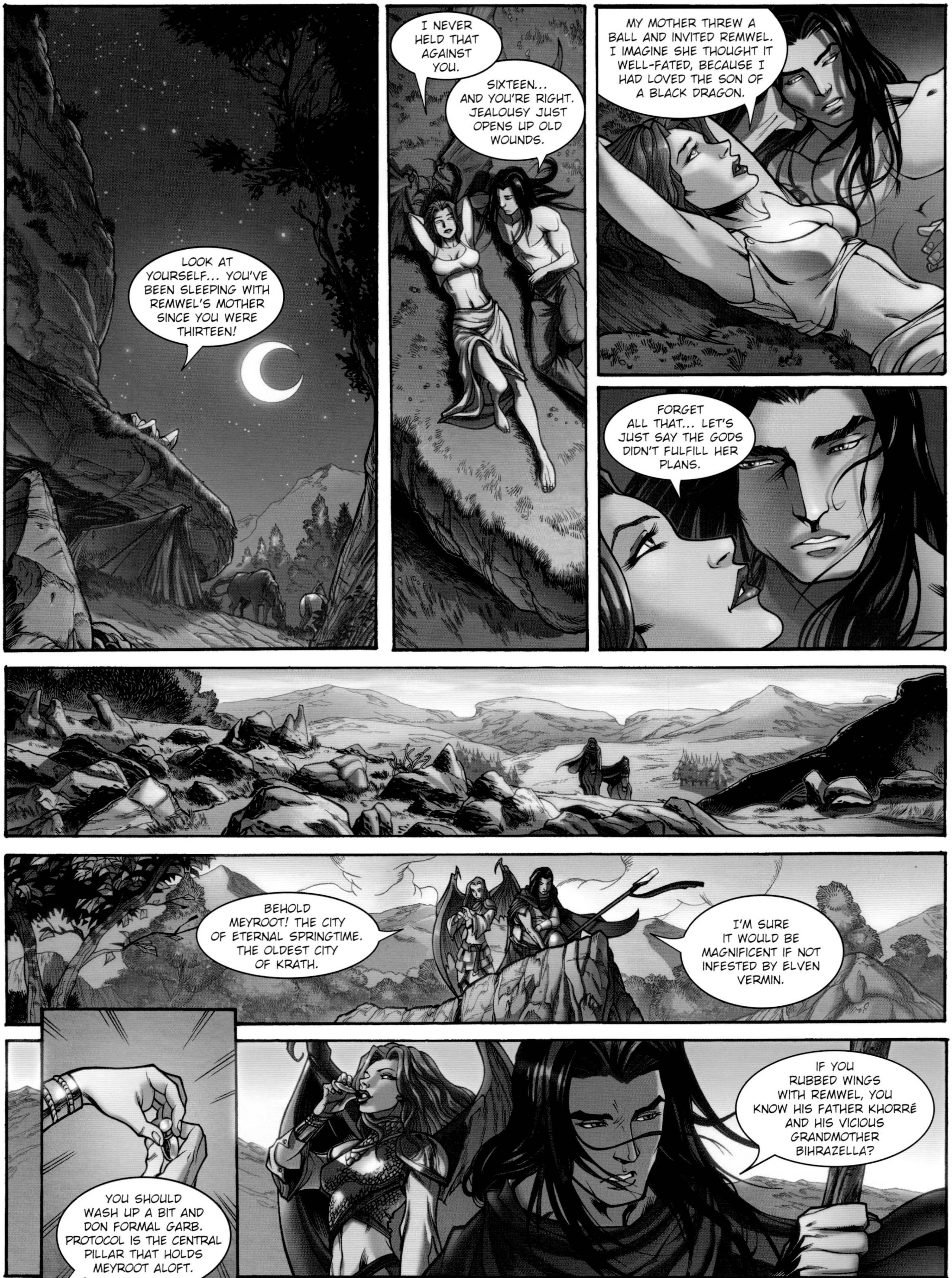
LOOK AT YOURSELF... YOU'VE BEEN SLEEPING WITH REMWEL'S MOTHER SINCE YOU WERE THIRTEEN!
I NEVER HELD THAT AGAINST YOU.
SIXTEEN... AND YOU'RE RIGHT. JEALOUSY JUST OPENS UP OLD WOUNDS.
MY MOTHER THREW A BALL AND INVITED REMWEL. I IMAGINE SHE THOUGHT IT WELL-FATED, BECAUSE I HAD LOVED THE SON OF A BLACK DRAGON.
FORGET ALL THAT... LET'S JUST SAY THE GODS DIDN'T FULFILL HER PLANS.
BEHOLD MEYROOT! THE CITY OF ETERNAL SPRINGTIME. THE OLDEST CITY OF KRATH.
I'M SURE IT WOULD BE MAGNIFICENT IF NOT INFESTED BY ELVEN VERMIN.
YOU SHOULD WASH UP A BIT AND DON FORMAL GARB. PROTOCOL IS THE CENTRAL PILLAR THAT HOLDS MEYROOT ALOFT.
IF YOU RUBBED WINGS WITH REMWEL, YOU KNOW HIS FATHER KHORRÉ AND HIS VICIOUS GRANDMOTHER BIHRAZELLA?

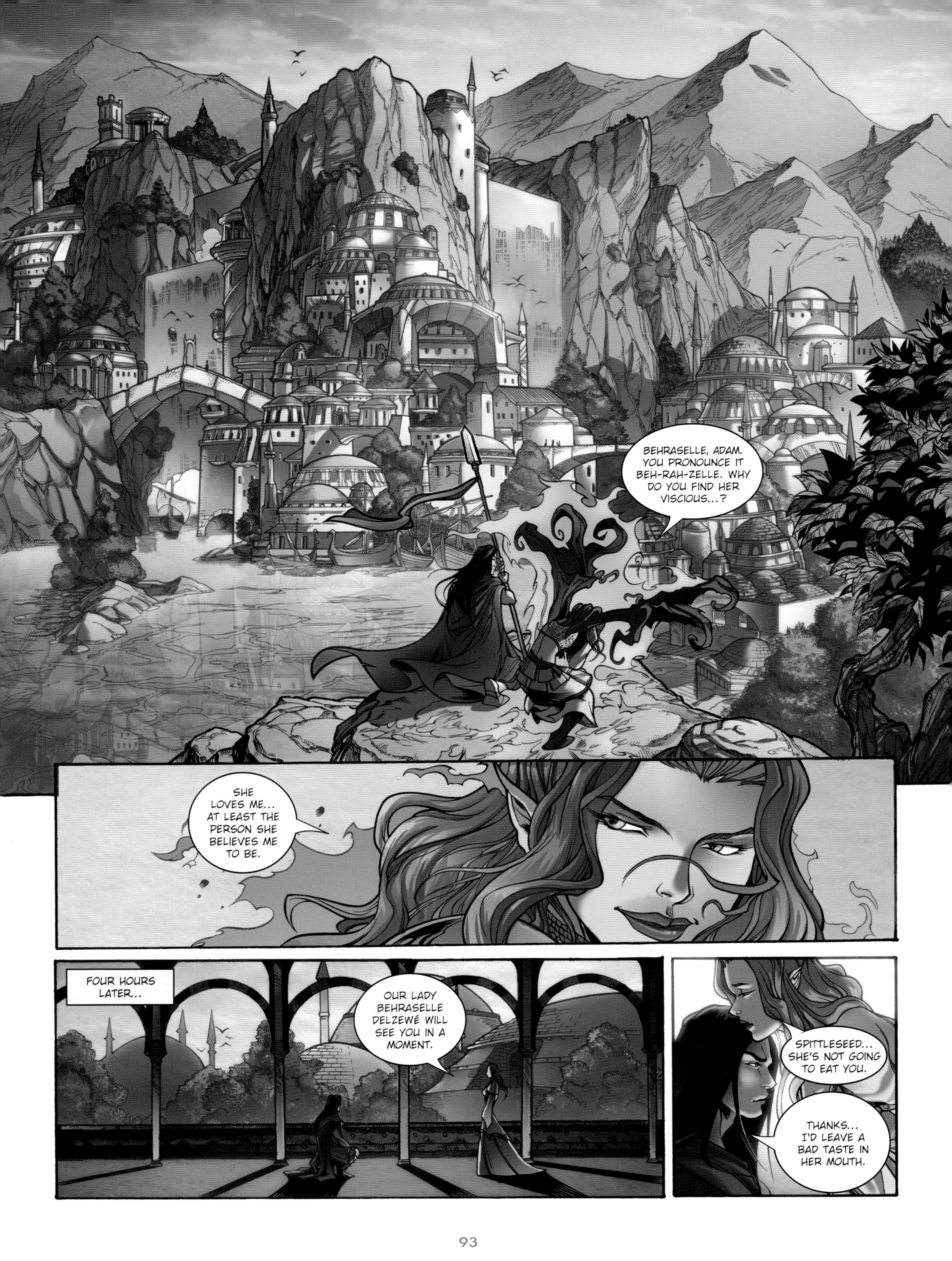
BEHRASELLE, ADAM. YOU PRONOUNCE IT BEH-RAH-ZELLE. WHY DO YOU FIND HER VISCIOUS...?
SHE LOVES ME... AT LEAST THE PERSON SHE BELIEVES ME TO BE.
FOUR HOURS LATER...
OUR LADY BEHRASELLE DELZEWÉ WILL SEE YOU IN A MOMENT.
SPITTLESEED... SHE'S NOT GOING TO EAT YOU.
THANKS... I'D LEAVE A BAD TASTE IN HER MOUTH.

SOUKOU? THAT WOULD BE A HUMAN NAME, NO?

IT IS QUITE CHARMING!

WELL... PERHAPS... IT IS NOVEL...

WE BELIEVE, MY DEAR LADY, THE GIRL TO BE HALF-ELF. YOUR VAST AND POWERFUL NETWORK MIGHT CERTAINLY PROVIDE A FEW CLUES TO FIND HER...

OF COURSE OUR MANDATE WITH THE PROPHECY CHAMBER OBLIGES US TO ACT WITH DISCRETION... ESPECIALLY REGARDING OUR SOURCES...

MY SWEET POLLANDERA, IT WOULD PLEASE ME IMMENSELY TO HELP YOU OUT. WE SHARE AN ARDENT LOVE FOR MY DEAR GRANDSON.

REMWEL WILL BE HEARTBROKEN WHEN HE LEARNS THAT YOU HAVE PAID ME A VISIT WHILE HE WAS OUT GALLIVANTING AT THE RIM WITH HIS BROTHERS AND HIS NOBLE FATHER MOLTEN.

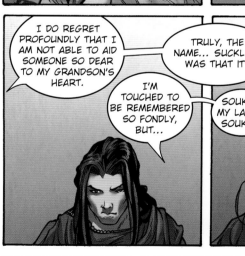

I DO REGRET PROFOUNDLY THAT I AM NOT ABLE TO AID SOMEONE SO DEAR TO MY GRANDSON'S HEART.

I'M TOUCHED TO BE REMEMBERED SO FONDLY, BUT...

TRULY, THE NAME... SUCKLE... WAS THAT IT?

SOUKOU, MY LADY... SOUKOU.

YES... SO SIMPLE THAT IT PAINS THE LIP. THE NAME RINGS NO BELLS.

ENOUGH OF THIS LADY BEHHHRAAA-SZZZELLLE!

SOUKOU DELZEWÉ IS YOUR GRANDCHILD. I HAVE THIS FROM A SURE SOURCE.

A DRAGON DREAMSEER! AND NOT JUST ANY DRAGON!

REMWEL'S MOTHER AND MY AUNT... SILKEN WEDDING-BANE!

CONFIDENTIAL SOURCES...? IF THAT'S HOW YOU KEEP THEM, POLLANDERA...

I *WOULD* ASK MY SON, BUT HE IS CURRENTLY UNABLE TO RESPOND.

NOW ISN'T THAT CONVENIENT, MILADY!

PLEASE, ADAM. CALM DOWN. THIS GETS US NOWHERE.

WHY DON'T YOU ASK HIM YOURSELF?

HE'S STANDING RIGHT BEHIND YOU...

I HAD TO PUT HIM IN AN ICY SLUMBER. HE'S SICK, YOU SEE. VERY SICK...

UNTIL I'VE FOUND A CURE, A CURE FOR THIS... GUTTER-BORN GREEN SICKNESS, HE STAYS THERE. IMMOBILE AS A STATUE... MY POOR SON.

I THOUGHT ELVES WERE IMMUNE...

I AM SORRY, LADY DEZELWÉ. I'M SO SORRY.

I FOUND KHORRÉ IN A SMALL QUARANTINED VILLAGE CALLED KETTLE LAKE. WHAT A HORRID PLACE TO DIE.

HIS NAME WAS INSCRIBED ON THE LIST... SENT BY THE PLAGUE MINISTRY.

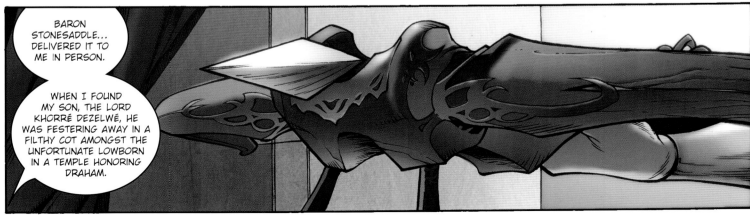

BARON STONESADDLE... DELIVERED IT TO ME IN PERSON.

WHEN I FOUND MY SON, THE LORD KHORRÉ DEZELWÉ, HE WAS FESTERING AWAY IN A FILTHY COT AMONGST THE UNFORTUNATE LOWBORN IN A TEMPLE HONORING DRAHAM.

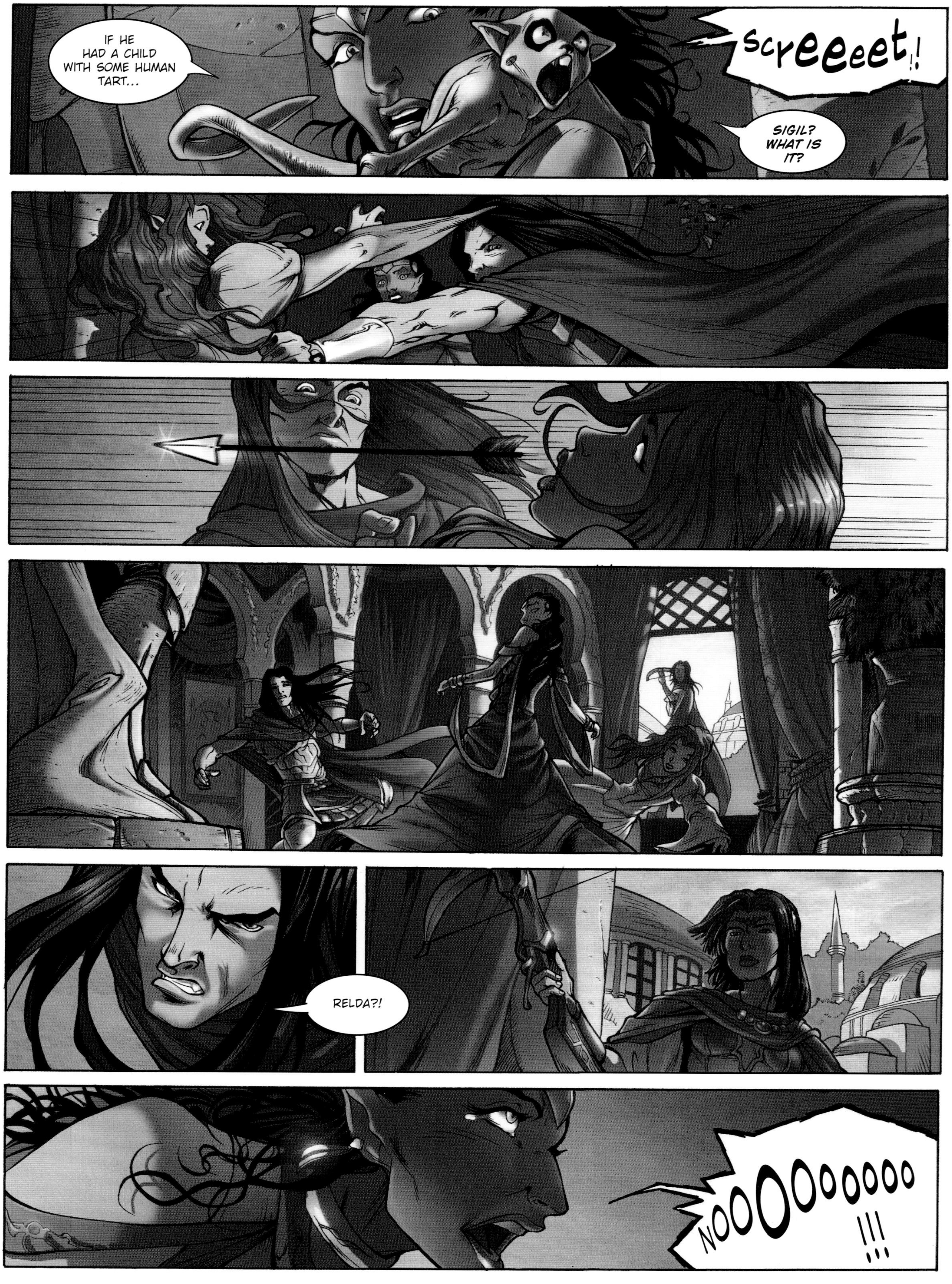
IF HE HAD A CHILD WITH SOME HUMAN TART...
SCREEEEET!!
SIGIL? WHAT IS IT?
RELDA?!
NOOOOOOOOO!!!

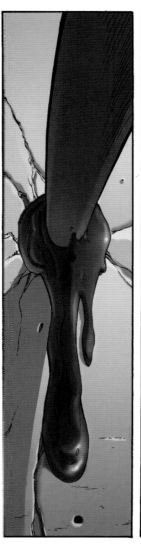

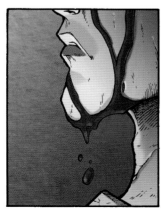

I MUST GO AND HELP ADAM, MILADY. I'LL BE BACK.

KHORRÉ, MY LITTLE STAR... OH KHORRÉ!

YOU KNOW REMWEL CANNOT PROCREATE... FIND SOUKOU... SHE IS THE LAST HEIR OF DELZEWÉ!

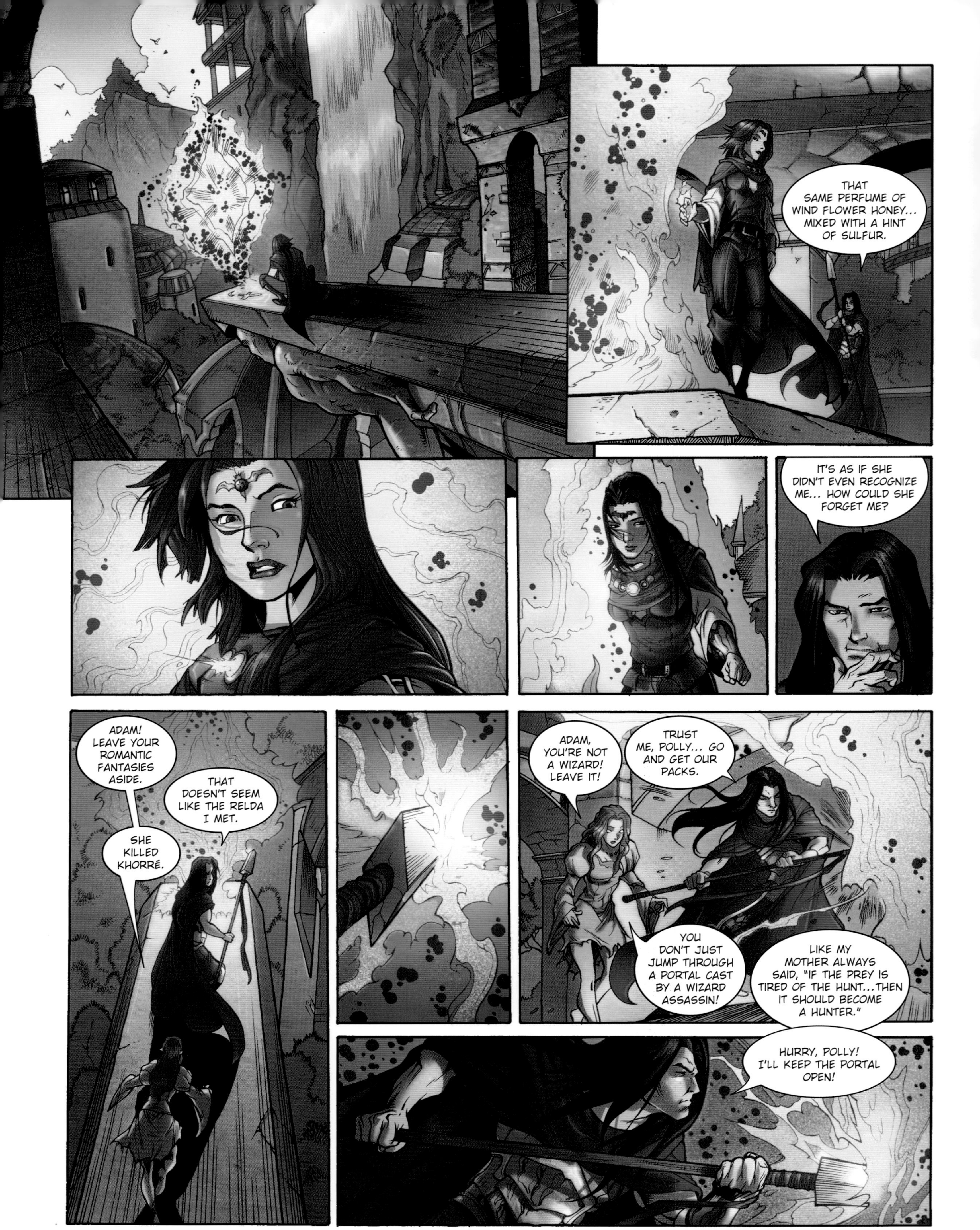
THAT SAME PERFUME OF WIND FLOWER HONEY... MIXED WITH A HINT OF SULFUR.
IT'S AS IF SHE DIDN'T EVEN RECOGNIZE ME... HOW COULD SHE FORGET ME?
ADAM! LEAVE YOUR ROMANTIC FANTASIES ASIDE.
THAT DOESN'T SEEM LIKE THE RELDA I MET.
SHE KILLED KHORRÉ.
ADAM, YOU'RE NOT A WIZARD! LEAVE IT!
TRUST ME, POLLY... GO AND GET OUR PACKS.
YOU DON'T JUST JUMP THROUGH A PORTAL CAST BY A WIZARD ASSASSIN!
LIKE MY MOTHER ALWAYS SAID, "IF THE PREY IS TIRED OF THE HUNT... THEN IT SHOULD BECOME A HUNTER."
HURRY, POLLY! I'LL KEEP THE PORTAL OPEN!

"...ALL SAID AND DONE, THERE IS A CERTAIN LOGIC TO THIS... FOLLOWING RELDA'S TRAIL WE END UP IN ROCKCRUSH... LAND OF THE OGRES, IN THE NATIVE COUNTRY OF BARON STONESADDLE."

"AFTER ALL...THE CLUES HAVE ALWAYS POINTED IN HIS DIRECTION..."

"WHAT I STILL FAIL TO UNDERSTAND...IS WHY, WHEN WE GOT HERE, YOU INSISTED ON BEING INVITED TO A FUNERAL!"

"THE OGRES HAVE AN ANCESTRAL RITUAL. WHEN ONE OF THEIR WARRIORS FALLS, HIS SPIRIT CAN BE KEPT IN A WEAPON..."

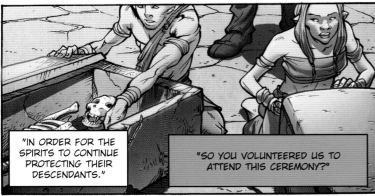

"IN ORDER FOR THE SPIRITS TO CONTINUE PROTECTING THEIR DESCENDANTS."

"SO YOU VOLUNTEERED US TO ATTEND THIS CEREMONY?"

"NOT EXACTLY... WE ARE ACTUALLY PART OF THE CEREMONY. WE WERE PRESENT DURING THEIR FINAL FIGHT AND CAN ATTEST TO THEIR COURAGE IN COMBAT."

"THOSE ARE THE CHILDREN OF STONESADDLE'S GUARDS... WHO WE KILLED AT THE TAVERN?"

"'BIND YOUR DESIRE TO THAT OF THE TEAR AND YOUR PATHS WILL CROSS ONCE AGAIN.'"

"ANOTHER ONE OF YOUR MOTHER'S CURSED PROVERBS?"

"NO... MY AUNT. BUT THERE IS SOMETHING THAT DOESN'T SEEM RIGHT."

YOU MEAN YOU JUST NOTICED THAT WE ARE TIED AND BOUND?

WE ARE ALL LINKED THROUGH SOMETHING... BY BLOOD...OR BY DESTINY...

"WHO WAS RELDA TARGETING... YOU OR ME?"

"WHETHER YOU, OR ME, OR A STATUE ON THE WALL...SHE WAS TARGETING SOMEONE... WHAT MORE IS THERE TO KNOW?"

ADAM, WHY ARE THOSE CHILDREN POINTING THEIR WEAPONS AT US...? YOU SAID WE HAD NOTHING TO WORRY ABOUT...

IT'S PART OF THE RITUAL.

"WHAT IF IT WAS THE STATUE–KHORRÉ–SHE WANTED TO KILL? TO KEEP US FROM TALKING TO HIM. OR TO PUNISH SOUKOU BY KILLING HER FATHER!"

"WHO GIVES A GRIFFIN'S ASS?! SHE TOOK A LIFE! YOU'RE COMPLICATING THINGS."

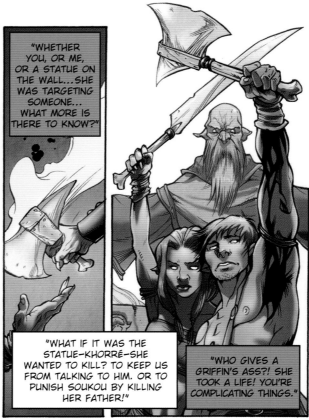

"WHAT RITUAL?"

"THE CEREMONY OF THE IMMORTAL BONE CRUSHER. IT'S TO INSURE THAT THE FIGHTING SPIRIT OF THEIR PARENTS WILL LIVE FOREVER."

AHHHHH.... THAT'S RIGHT. YOU ALREADY TOLD ME. NOW THEY'RE GOING TO PRETEND TO KILL US?

I PICKED THOSE UP OFF OF THE OGRES WE KILLED BACK AT STONESADDLE'S TAVERN.

DO YOU REMEMBER THOSE TWO PENDANTS THAT I GAVE THEM WHEN THEY CAUGHT US?

STOP WITH THE JESTS, ADAM. I HOPE YOU DIDN'T TELL THEM WE HAD KILLED THEIR FATHERS?

OF COURSE I DID. YOU CAN'T EVEN PERFORM THE RITUAL IF YOU DON'T HAVE THE FATHER SLAYERS.

HOLD YOUR BREATH! YOU WOULDN'T WANT TO COUGH UP FIRE ALL OVER THE KIDS.

DON'T WORRY. YOU'VE TAKEN MY BREATH AWAY.

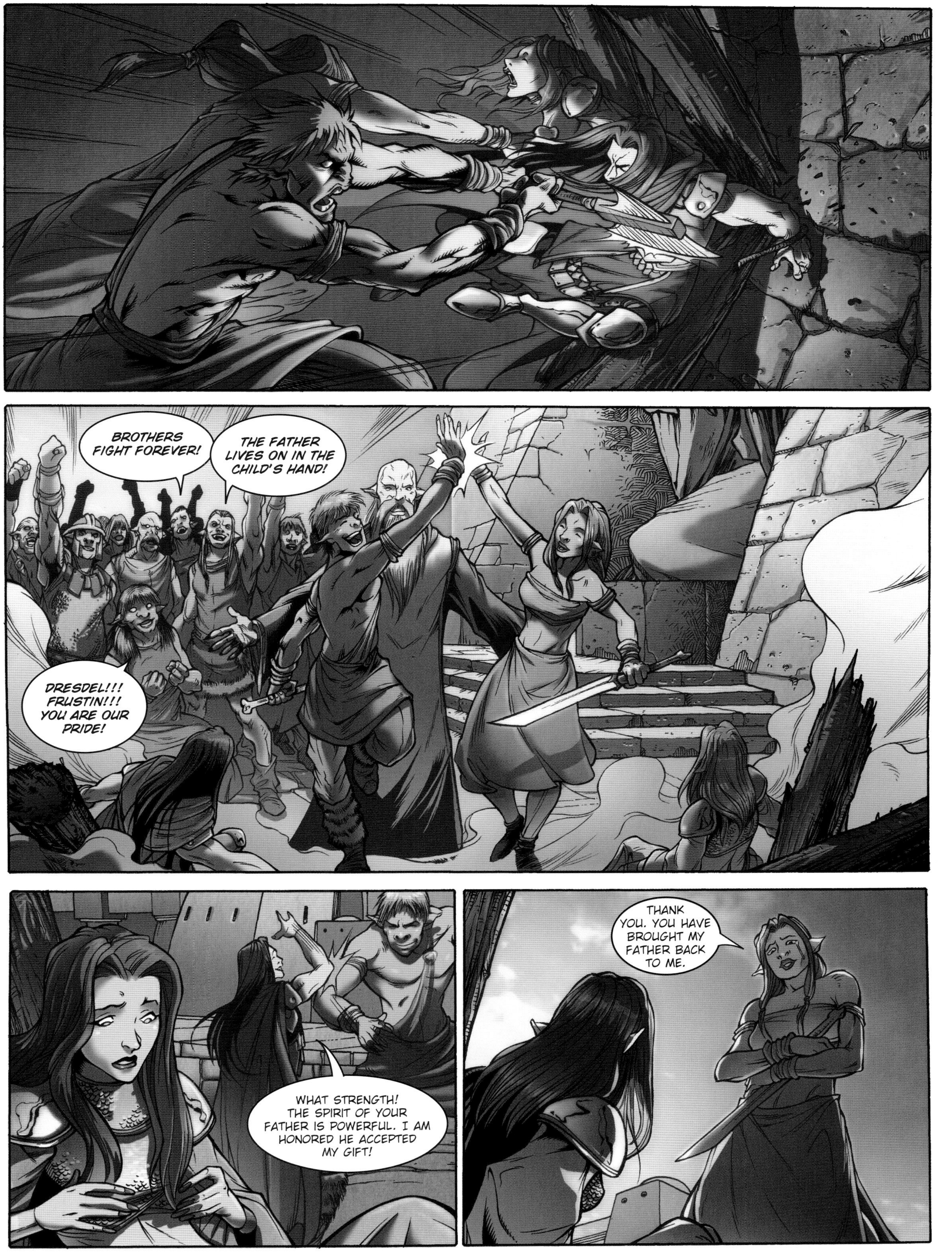
BROTHERS FIGHT FOREVER!
THE FATHER LIVES ON IN THE CHILD'S HAND!
DRESDEL!!! FRUSTIN!!! YOU ARE OUR PRIDE!
WHAT STRENGTH! THE SPIRIT OF YOUR FATHER IS POWERFUL. I AM HONORED HE ACCEPTED MY GIFT!
THANK YOU. YOU HAVE BROUGHT MY FATHER BACK TO ME.

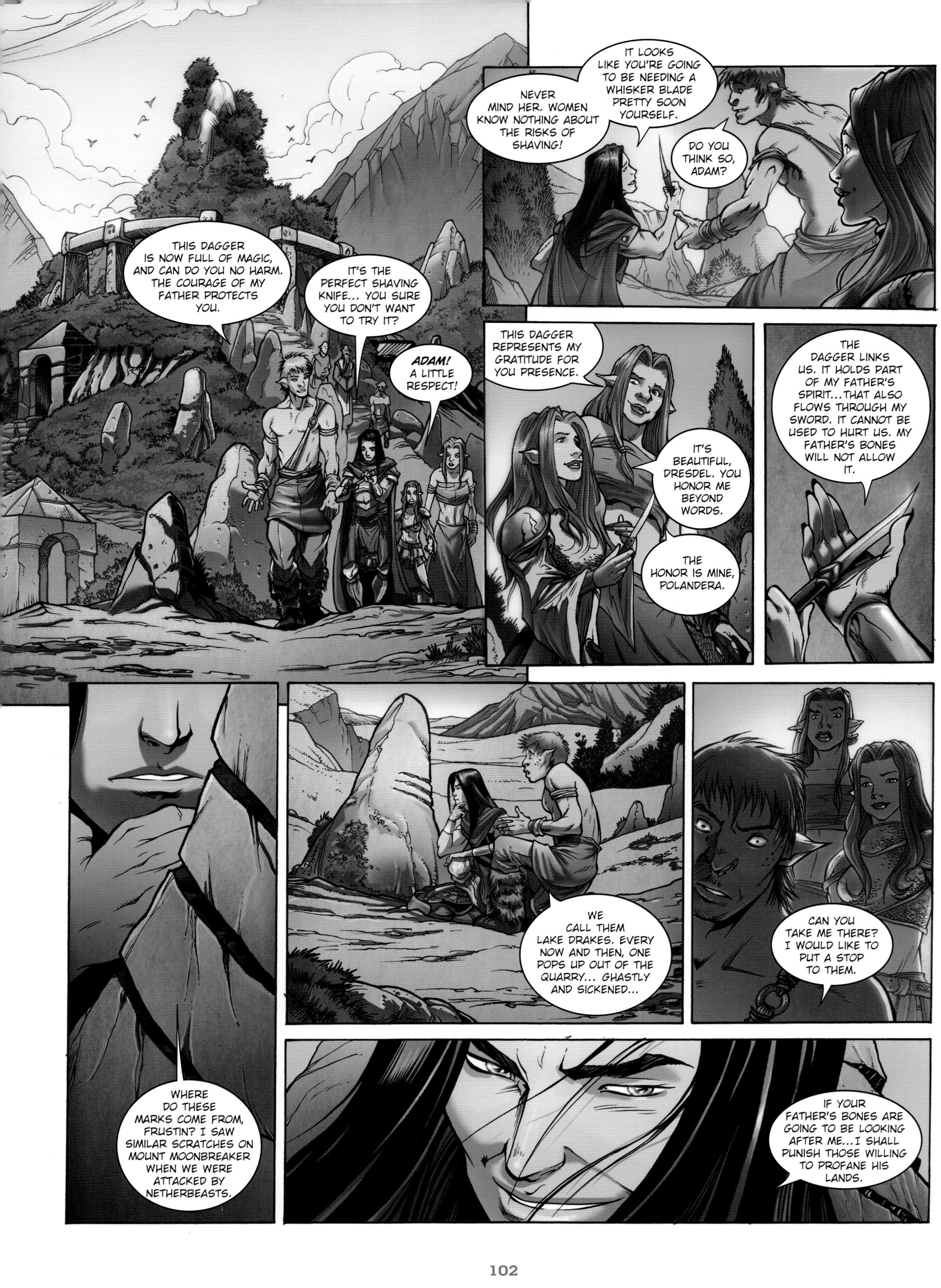
THIS DAGGER IS NOW FULL OF MAGIC, AND CAN DO YOU NO HARM. THE COURAGE OF MY FATHER PROTECTS YOU.
IT'S THE PERFECT SHAVING KNIFE... YOU SURE YOU DON'T WANT TO TRY IT?
ADAM! A LITTLE RESPECT!
NEVER MIND HER. WOMEN KNOW NOTHING ABOUT THE RISKS OF SHAVING!
IT LOOKS LIKE YOU'RE GOING TO BE NEEDING A WHISKER BLADE PRETTY SOON YOURSELF.
DO YOU THINK SO, ADAM?
THIS DAGGER REPRESENTS MY GRATITUDE FOR YOU PRESENCE.
IT'S BEAUTIFUL, DRESDEL. YOU HONOR ME BEYOND WORDS.
THE HONOR IS MINE, POLANDERA.
THE DAGGER LINKS US. IT HOLDS PART OF MY FATHER'S SPIRIT...THAT ALSO FLOWS THROUGH MY SWORD. IT CANNOT BE USED TO HURT US. MY FATHER'S BONES WILL NOT ALLOW IT.
WHERE DO THESE MARKS COME FROM, FRUSTIN? I SAW SIMILAR SCRATCHES ON MOUNT MOONBREAKER WHEN WE WERE ATTACKED BY NETHERBEASTS.
WE CALL THEM LAKE DRAKES. EVERY NOW AND THEN, ONE POPS UP OUT OF THE QUARRY... GHASTLY AND SICKENED...
CAN YOU TAKE ME THERE? I WOULD LIKE TO PUT A STOP TO THEM.
IF YOUR FATHER'S BONES ARE GOING TO BE LOOKING AFTER ME...I SHALL PUNISH THOSE WILLING TO PROFANE HIS LANDS.

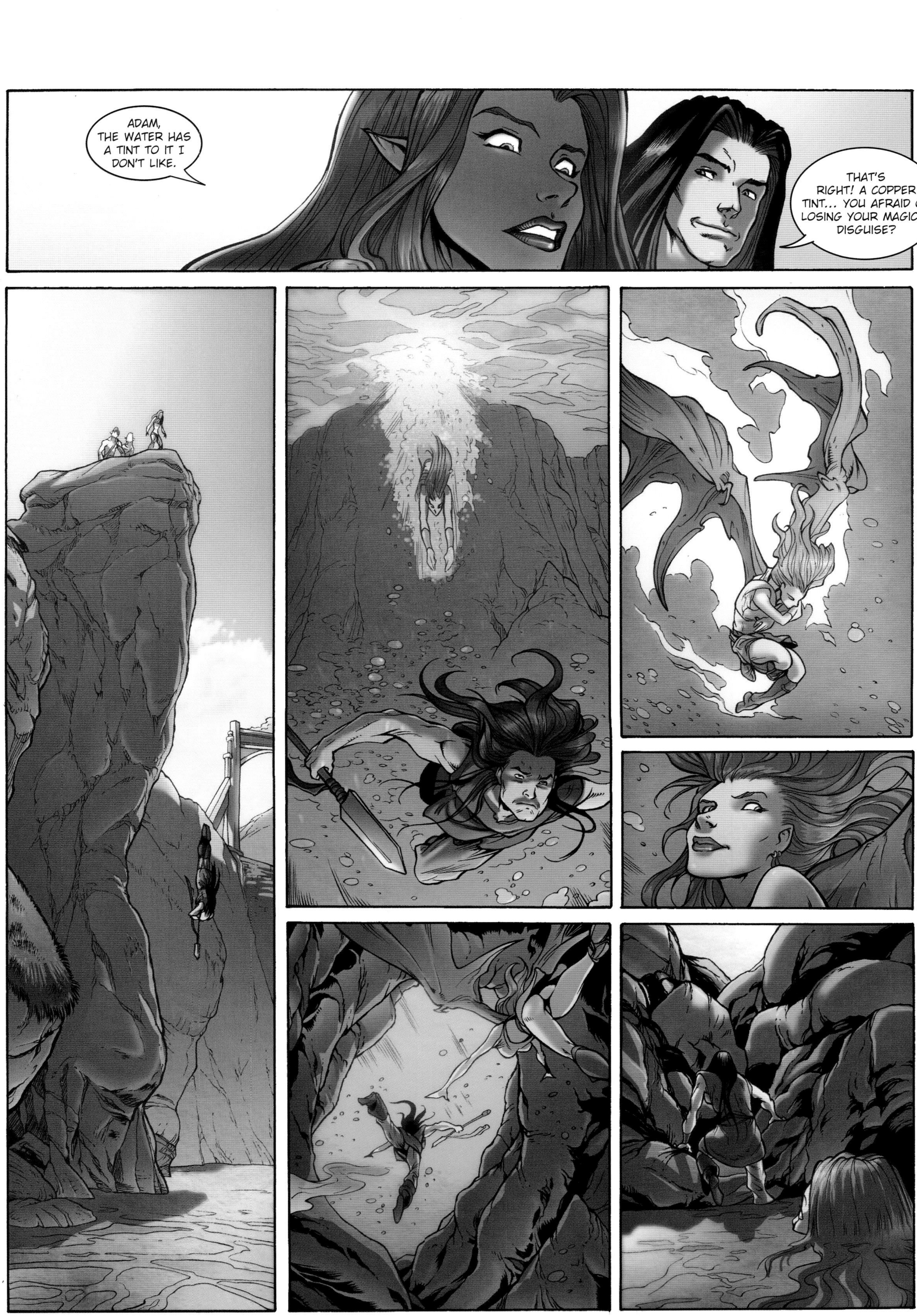
ADAM, THE WATER HAS A TINT TO IT I DON'T LIKE.
THAT'S RIGHT! A COPPER TINT... YOU AFRAID OF LOSING YOUR MAGICAL DISGUISE?

THOSE ARE THE SAME CREATURES THAT ATTACKED TAARON AND ME ON OUR TRIP TO SEE MY AUNT.

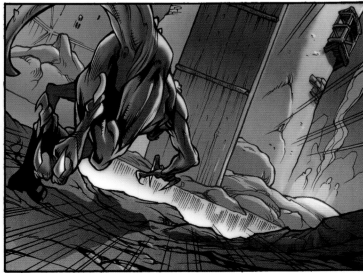

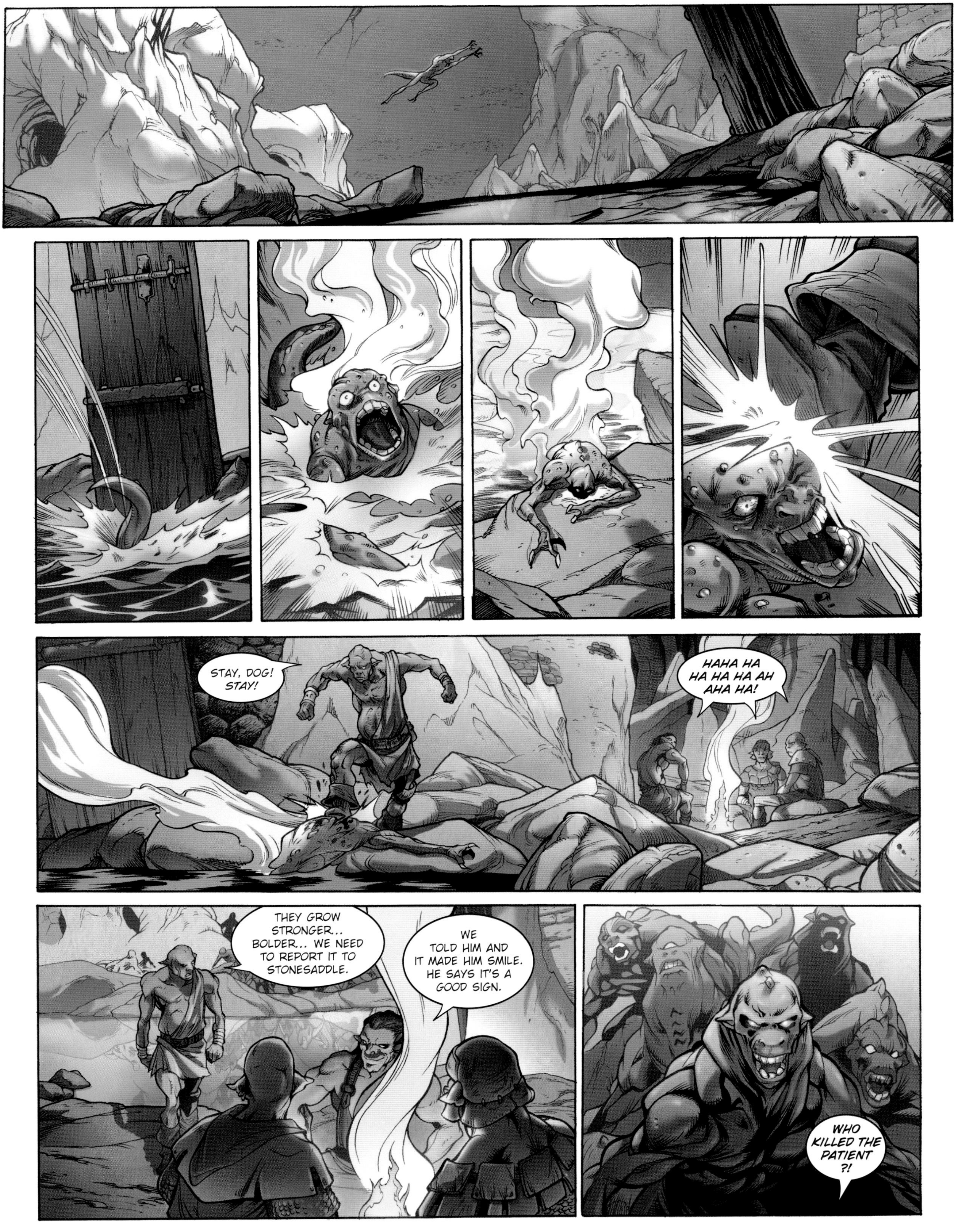
STAY, DOG! STAY!
HAHA HA HA HA HA AH AHA HA!
THEY GROW STRONGER.. BOLDER... WE NEED TO REPORT IT TO STONESADDLE.
WE TOLD HIM AND IT MADE HIM SMILE. HE SAYS IT'S A GOOD SIGN.
WHO KILLED THE PATIENT ?!

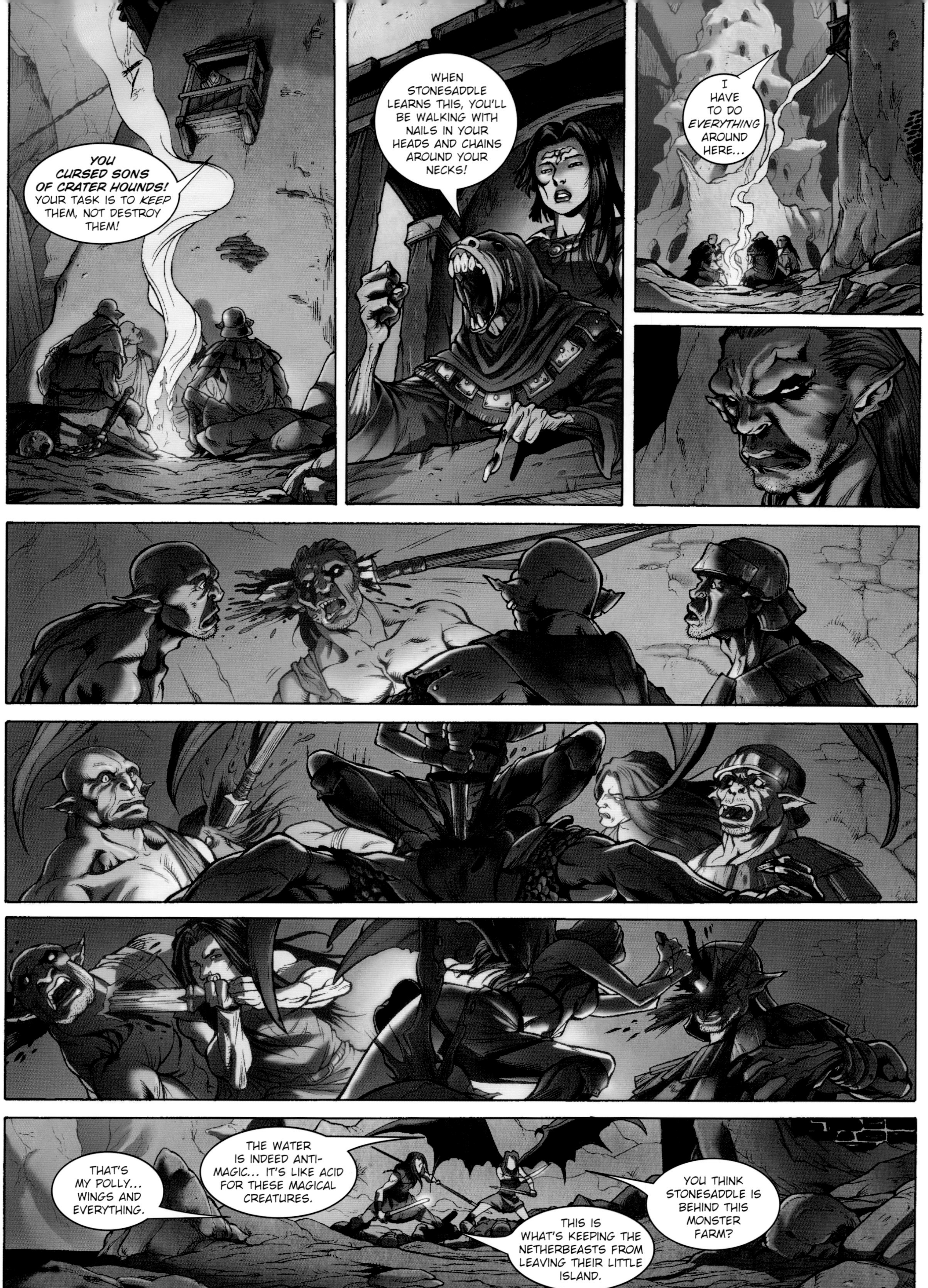
YOU CURSED SONS OF CRATER HOUNDS! YOUR TASK IS TO KEEP THEM, NOT DESTROY THEM!
WHEN STONESADDLE LEARNS THIS, YOU'LL BE WALKING WITH NAILS IN YOUR HEADS AND CHAINS AROUND YOUR NECKS!
I HAVE TO DO EVERYTHING AROUND HERE...
THAT'S MY POLLY... WINGS AND EVERYTHING.
THE WATER IS INDEED ANTI-MAGIC... IT'S LIKE ACID FOR THESE MAGICAL CREATURES.
THIS IS WHAT'S KEEPING THE NETHERBEASTS FROM LEAVING THEIR LITTLE ISLAND.
YOU THINK STONESADDLE IS BEHIND THIS MONSTER FARM?

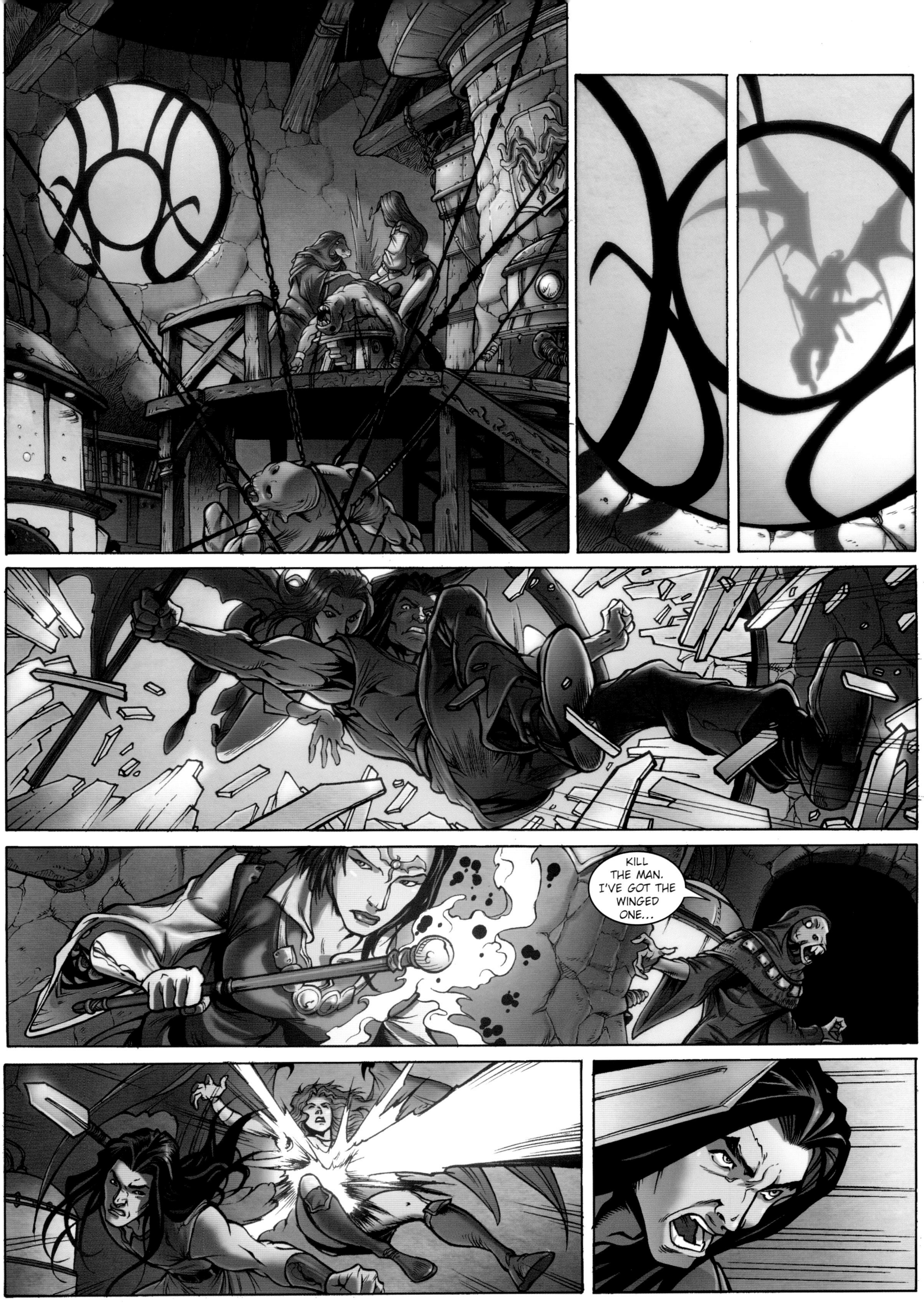
KILL THE MAN. I'VE GOT THE WINGED ONE...

WHAT ARE YOU WAITING FOR...? SNAP THE WITCH'S NECK!

SHE IS UNDER THE CONTROL OF A DOMINATION SPELL.

WE NEED TO TAKE HER TO LADY DELLIN.

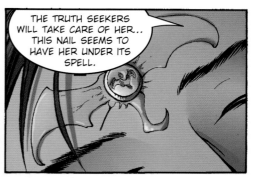

THE TRUTH SEEKERS WILL TAKE CARE OF HER... THIS NAIL SEEMS TO HAVE HER UNDER ITS SPELL.

THAT WENCH HAS MORE LIVES THAN A SWAMP-CAT.

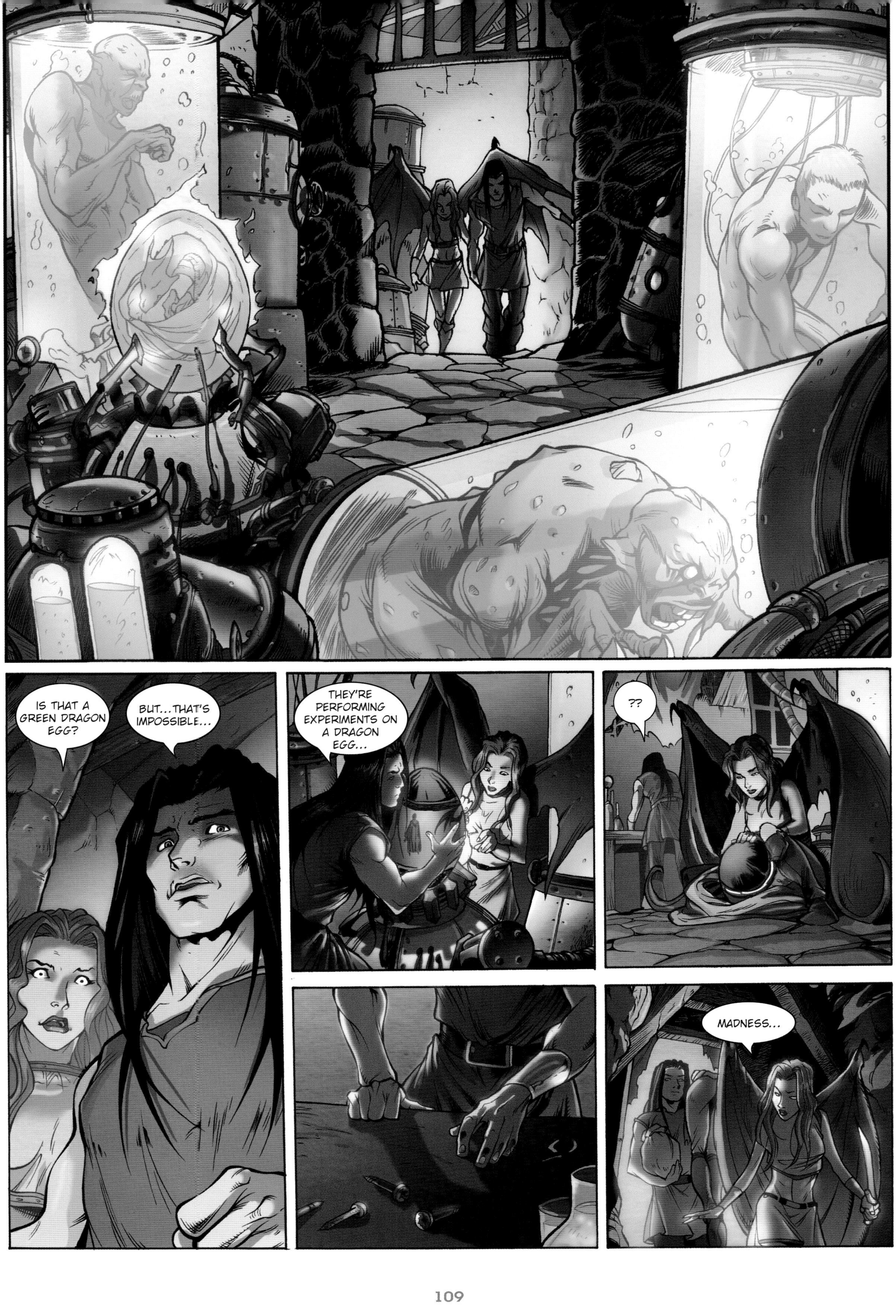
IS THAT A GREEN DRAGON EGG?
BUT...THAT'S IMPOSSIBLE...
THEY'RE PERFORMING EXPERIMENTS ON A DRAGON EGG...
??
MADNESS...

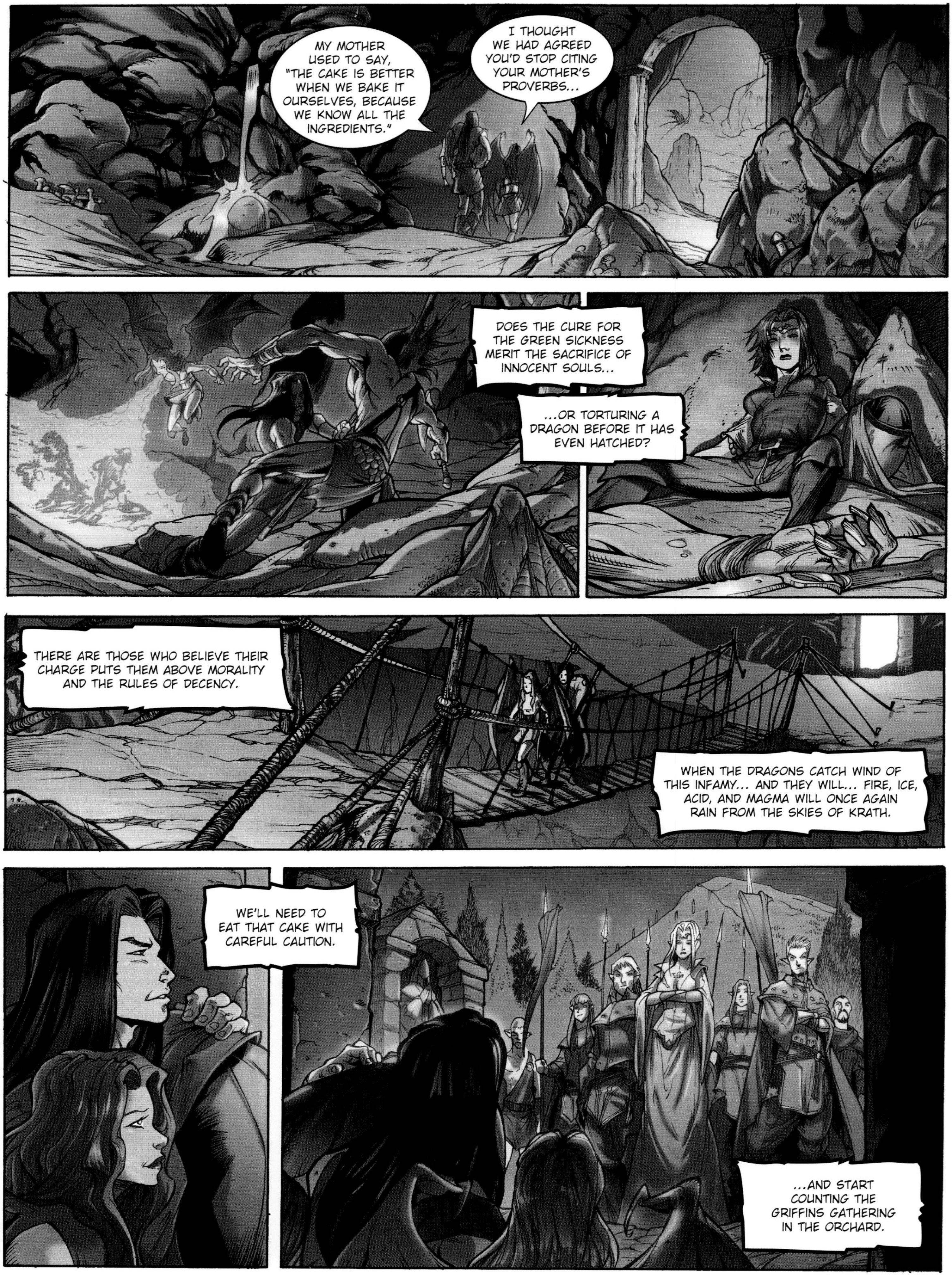
MY MOTHER USED TO SAY, "THE CAKE IS BETTER WHEN WE BAKE IT OURSELVES, BECAUSE WE KNOW ALL THE INGREDIENTS."
I THOUGHT WE HAD AGREED YOU'D STOP CITING YOUR MOTHER'S PROVERBS...
DOES THE CURE FOR THE GREEN SICKNESS MERIT THE SACRIFICE OF INNOCENT SOULS...
...OR TORTURING A DRAGON BEFORE IT HAS EVEN HATCHED?
THERE ARE THOSE WHO BELIEVE THEIR CHARGE PUTS THEM ABOVE MORALITY AND THE RULES OF DECENCY.
WHEN THE DRAGONS CATCH WIND OF THIS INFAMY... AND THEY WILL... FIRE, ICE, ACID, AND MAGMA WILL ONCE AGAIN RAIN FROM THE SKIES OF KRATH.
WE'LL NEED TO EAT THAT CAKE WITH CAREFUL CAUTION.
...AND START COUNTING THE GRIFFINS GATHERING IN THE ORCHARD.

LADY DELLIN TOOK THE NEWS FAR BETTER THAN I'D EXPECTED.

FOR STARTERS, SHE PARDONED ME FOR MISSING HER INTERROGATION. THEN SHE HAD THE LABORATORY OF THE BARON-MADE NETHERBEASTS DESTROYED BY THE WIZARDS OF THE MINER GUILD.

...BUT ONLY AFTER SHE HAD GATHERED ENOUGH EVIDENCE TO ACCUSE BARON STONESADDLE OF TREASON AGAINST THE PACT.

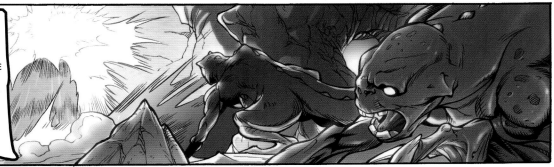

THE PROOF ACCUSES AN OGRE SO DESPERATE FOR A WAR THAT HE CONSPIRED TO START ONE. A CURE SO ELUSIVE, BARON ORLAND STONESADDLE, HEAD OF THE PLAGUE MINISTRY, WAS CONVINCED THE SICKNESS WAS DUE TO A SLOTHFUL PEACE. HIS RESEARCH PROVIDED A CASUS BELLI... RELEASING HIS CREATURES AT THE RIGHT TIME, WOULD ACCUSE THE NETHERWORLD, AND GET HIM HIS CURATIVE WAR!

A FINAL IRONY, THE WATER OF THE LAKE USED TO FENCE HIS MONSTERS IN... WAS WHAT WAS USED TO DESTROY THEM.

WE HAVE OUSTED THE GRIFFIN, BUT HE HASN'T LEFT THE ORCHARD. NOW THAT STONESADDLE HAS LOCKED HIMSELF IN HIS CASTLE, HE'LL RALLY ALL HIS ALLIES TO HIS CALL.

LADY DELLIN WILL TRY AND CONVINCE THE PACT LORDS TO ARREST STONESADDLE.

INSTEAD OF A CRUSADE... THE BARON GETS A CIVIL WAR BETWEEN THE PACT AND THE OGRES...

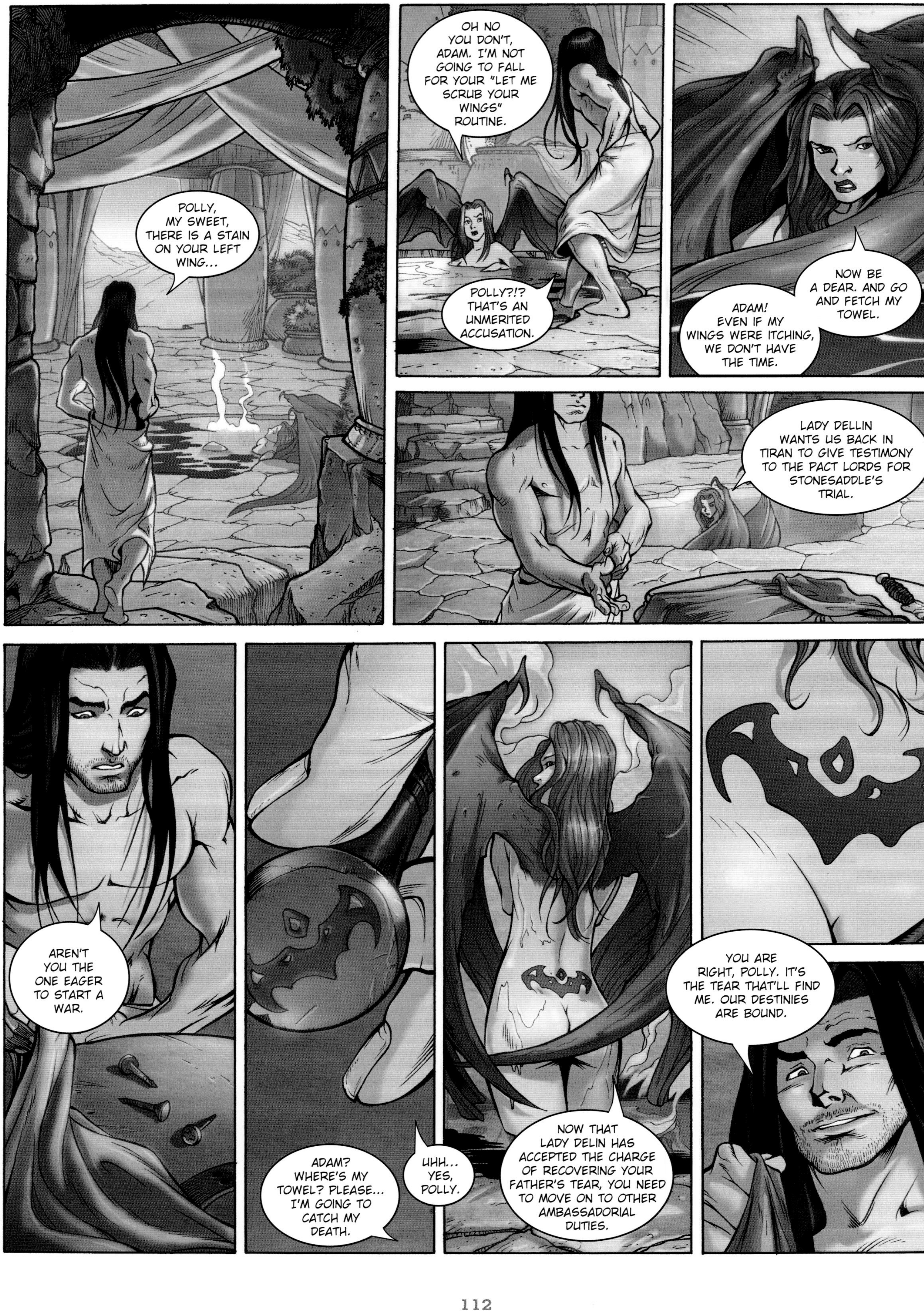
POLLY, MY SWEET, THERE IS A STAIN ON YOUR LEFT WING...
OH NO YOU DON'T, ADAM. I'M NOT GOING TO FALL FOR YOUR "LET ME SCRUB YOUR WINGS" ROUTINE.
POLLY?!? THAT'S AN UNMERITED ACCUSATION.
ADAM! EVEN IF MY WINGS WERE ITCHING, WE DON'T HAVE THE TIME.
NOW BE A DEAR. AND GO AND FETCH MY TOWEL.
LADY DELLIN WANTS US BACK IN TIRAN TO GIVE TESTIMONY TO THE PACT LORDS FOR STONESADDLE'S TRIAL.
AREN'T YOU THE ONE EAGER TO START A WAR.
ADAM? WHERE'S MY TOWEL? PLEASE... I'M GOING TO CATCH MY DEATH.
UHH... YES, POLLY.
NOW THAT LADY DELIN HAS ACCEPTED THE CHARGE OF RECOVERING YOUR FATHER'S TEAR, YOU NEED TO MOVE ON TO OTHER AMBASSADORIAL DUTIES.
YOU ARE RIGHT, POLLY. IT'S THE TEAR THAT'LL FIND ME. OUR DESTINIES ARE BOUND.

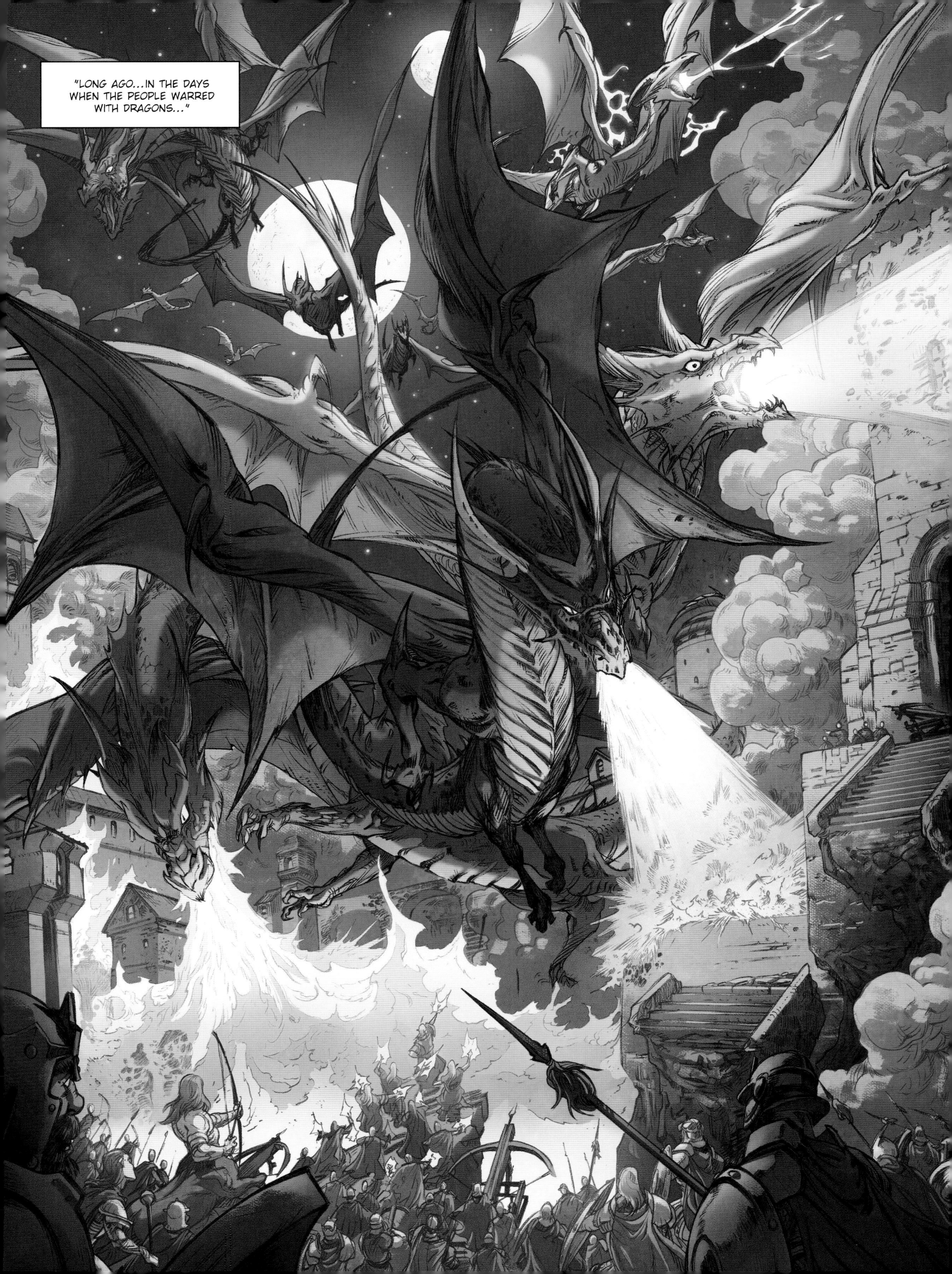
"LONG AGO...IN THE DAYS WHEN THE PEOPLE WARRED WITH DRAGONS..."

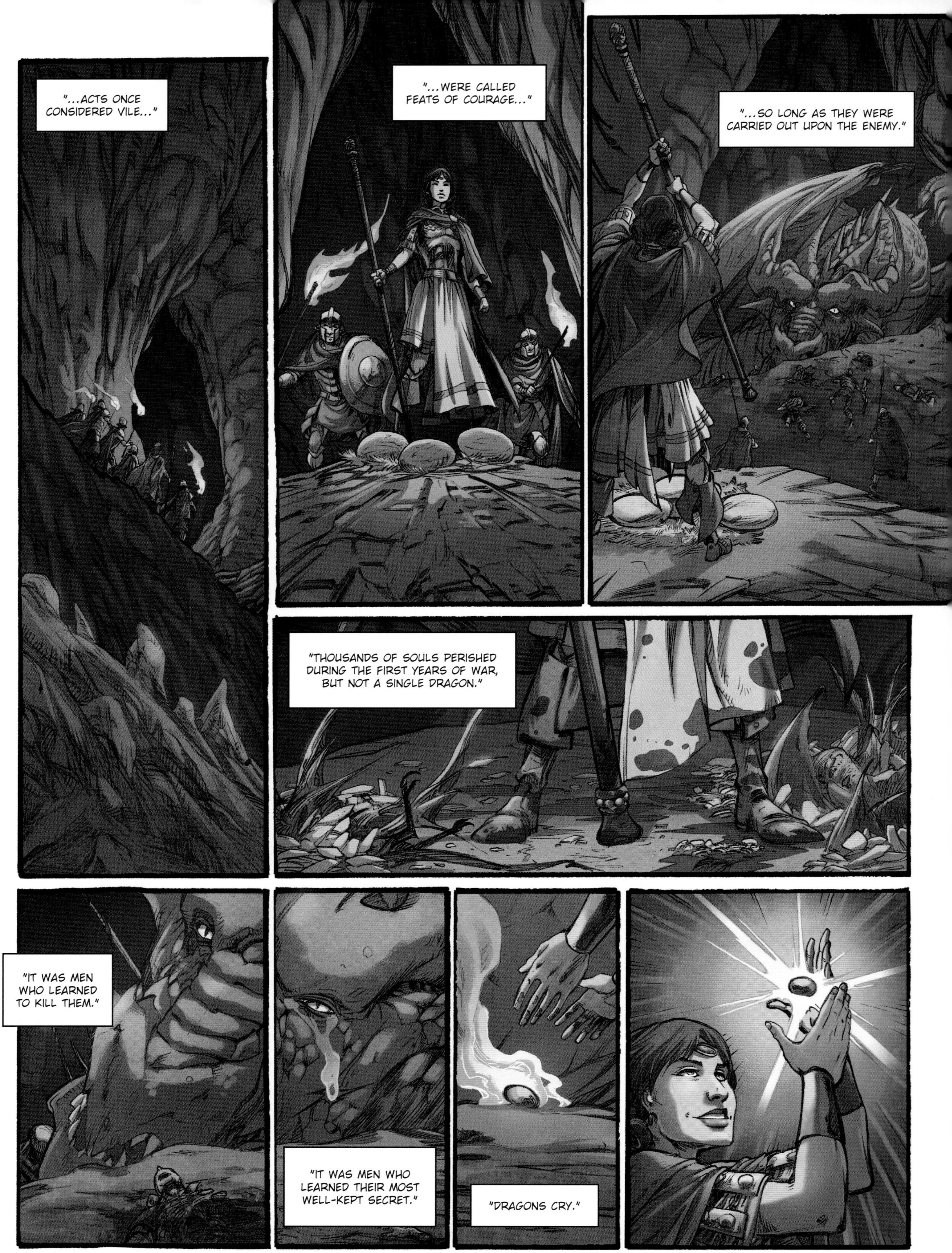
"...ACTS ONCE CONSIDERED VILE..."
"...WERE CALLED FEATS OF COURAGE..."
"...SO LONG AS THEY WERE CARRIED OUT UPON THE ENEMY."
"THOUSANDS OF SOULS PERISHED DURING THE FIRST YEARS OF WAR, BUT NOT A SINGLE DRAGON."
"IT WAS MEN WHO LEARNED TO KILL THEM."
"IT WAS MEN WHO LEARNED THEIR MOST WELL-KEPT SECRET."
"DRAGONS CRY."

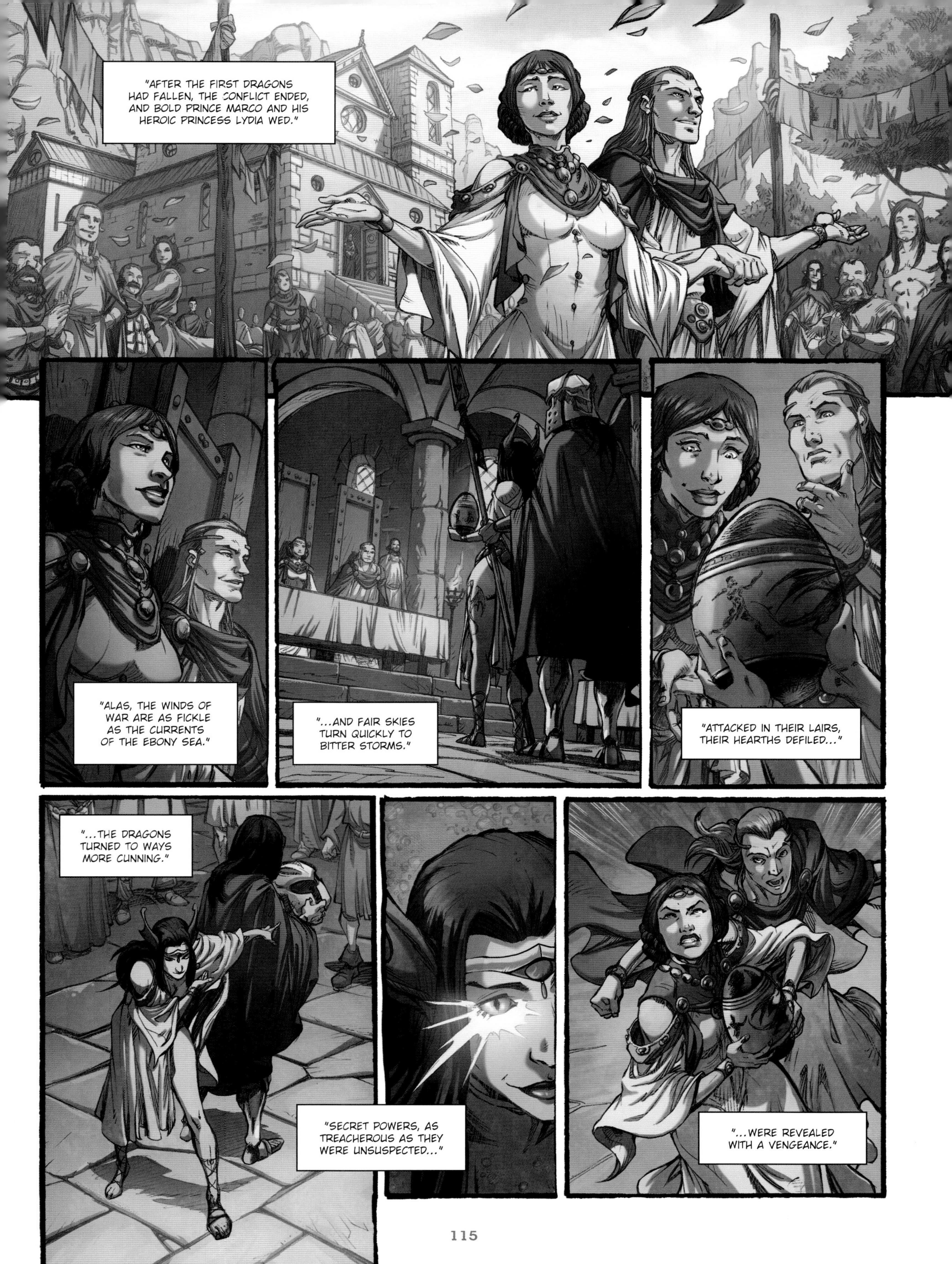
"AFTER THE FIRST DRAGONS HAD FALLEN, THE CONFLICT ENDED, AND BOLD PRINCE MARCO AND HIS HEROIC PRINCESS LYDIA WED."
"ALAS, THE WINDS OF WAR ARE AS FICKLE AS THE CURRENTS OF THE EBONY SEA."
"...AND FAIR SKIES TURN QUICKLY TO BITTER STORMS."
"ATTACKED IN THEIR LAIRS, THEIR HEARTHS DEFILED..."
"...THE DRAGONS TURNED TO WAYS MORE CUNNING."
"SECRET POWERS, AS TREACHEROUS AS THEY WERE UNSUSPECTED..."
"...WERE REVEALED WITH A VENGEANCE."

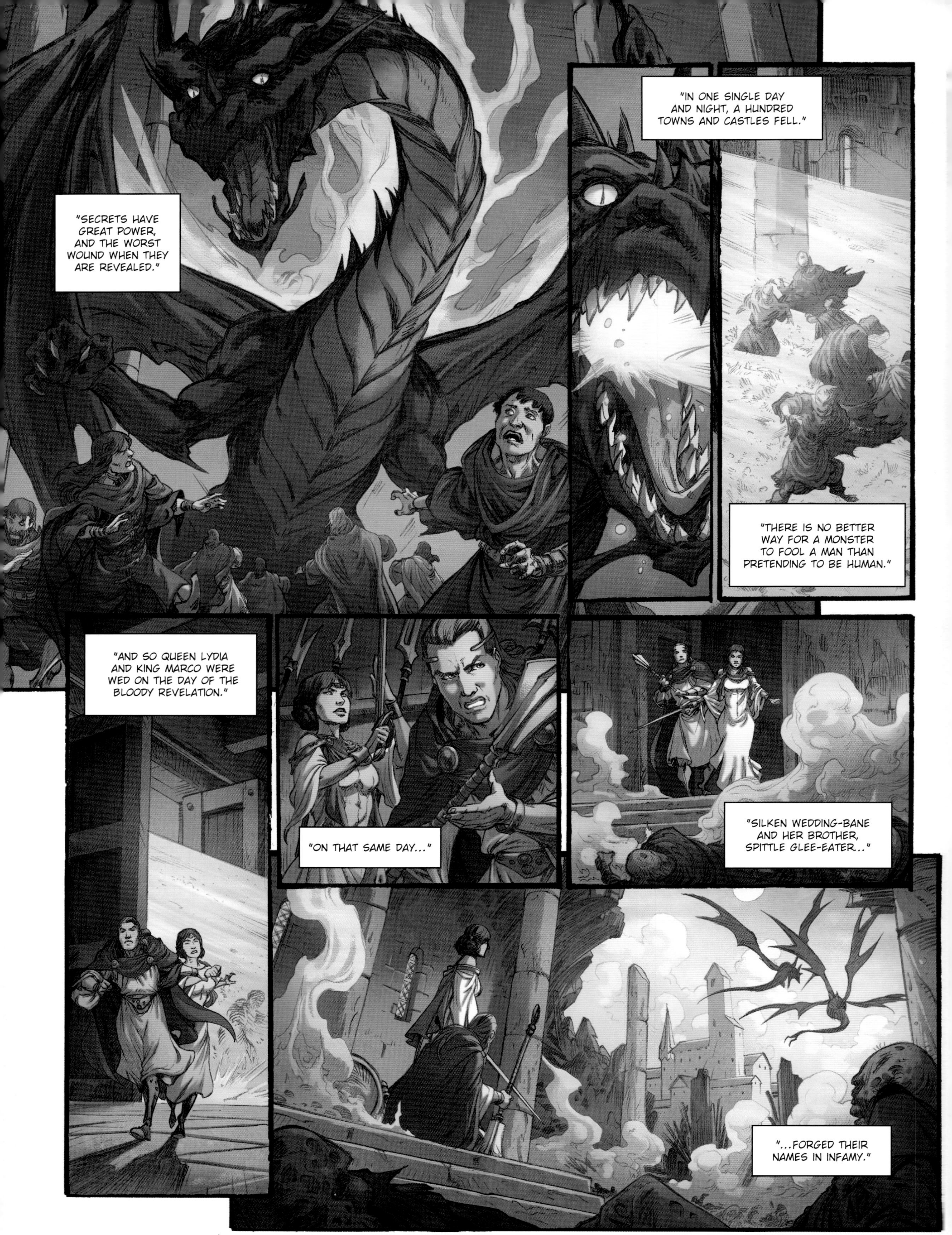
"SECRETS HAVE GREAT POWER, AND THE WORST WOUND WHEN THEY ARE REVEALED."
"IN ONE SINGLE DAY AND NIGHT, A HUNDRED TOWNS AND CASTLES FELL."
"THERE IS NO BETTER WAY FOR A MONSTER TO FOOL A MAN THAN PRETENDING TO BE HUMAN."
"AND SO QUEEN LYDIA AND KING MARCO WERE WED ON THE DAY OF THE BLOODY REVELATION."
"ON THAT SAME DAY..."
"SILKEN WEDDING-BANE AND HER BROTHER, SPITTLE GLEE-EATER..."
"...FORGED THEIR NAMES IN INFAMY."

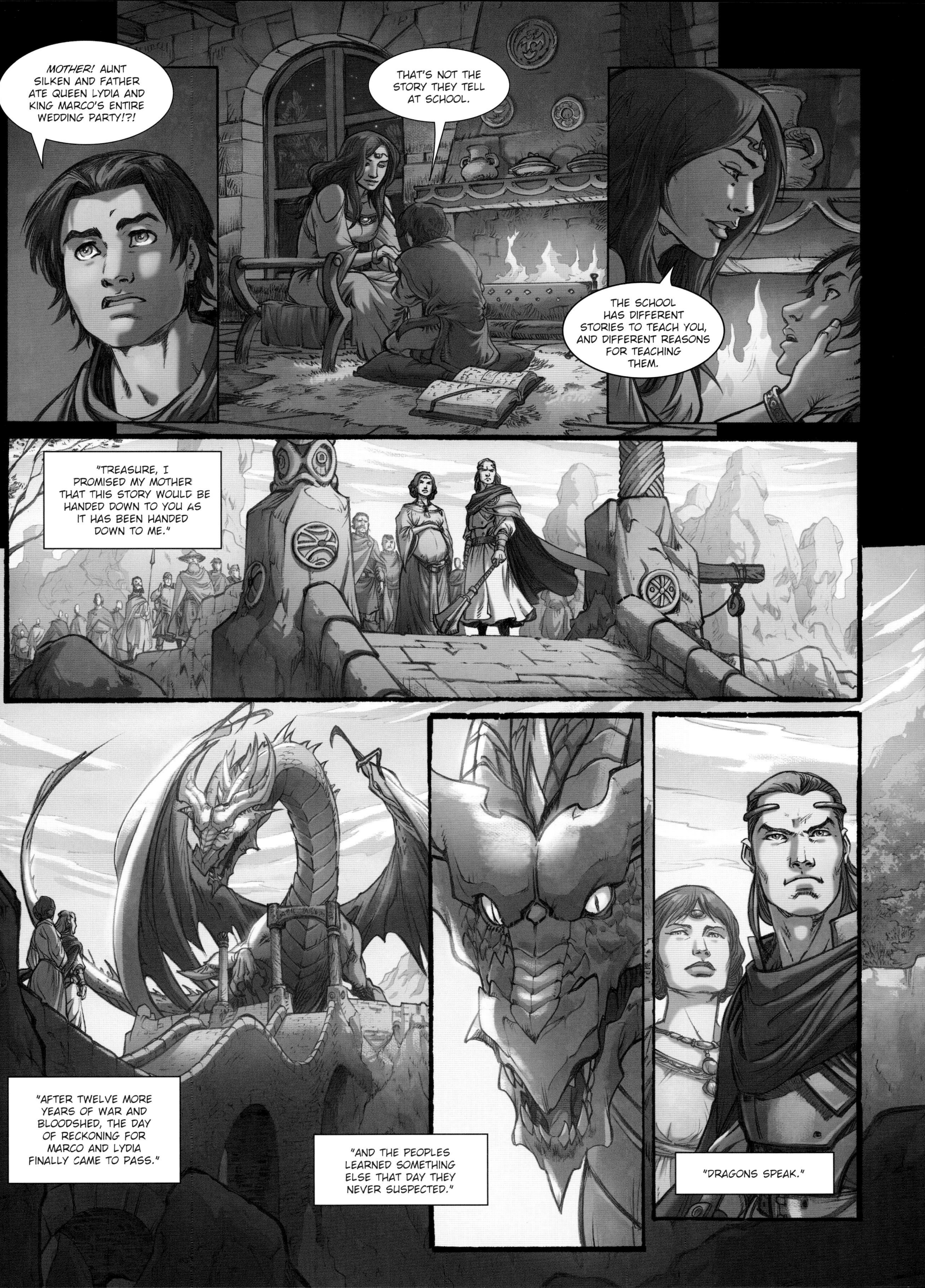
MOTHER! AUNT SILKEN AND FATHER ATE QUEEN LYDIA AND KING MARCO'S ENTIRE WEDDING PARTY!?!
THAT'S NOT THE STORY THEY TELL AT SCHOOL.
THE SCHOOL HAS DIFFERENT STORIES TO TEACH YOU, AND DIFFERENT REASONS FOR TEACHING THEM.
"TREASURE, I PROMISED MY MOTHER THAT THIS STORY WOULD BE HANDED DOWN TO YOU AS IT HAS BEEN HANDED DOWN TO ME."
"AFTER TWELVE MORE YEARS OF WAR AND BLOODSHED, THE DAY OF RECKONING FOR MARCO AND LYDIA FINALLY CAME TO PASS."
"AND THE PEOPLES LEARNED SOMETHING ELSE THAT DAY THEY NEVER SUSPECTED."
"DRAGONS SPEAK."

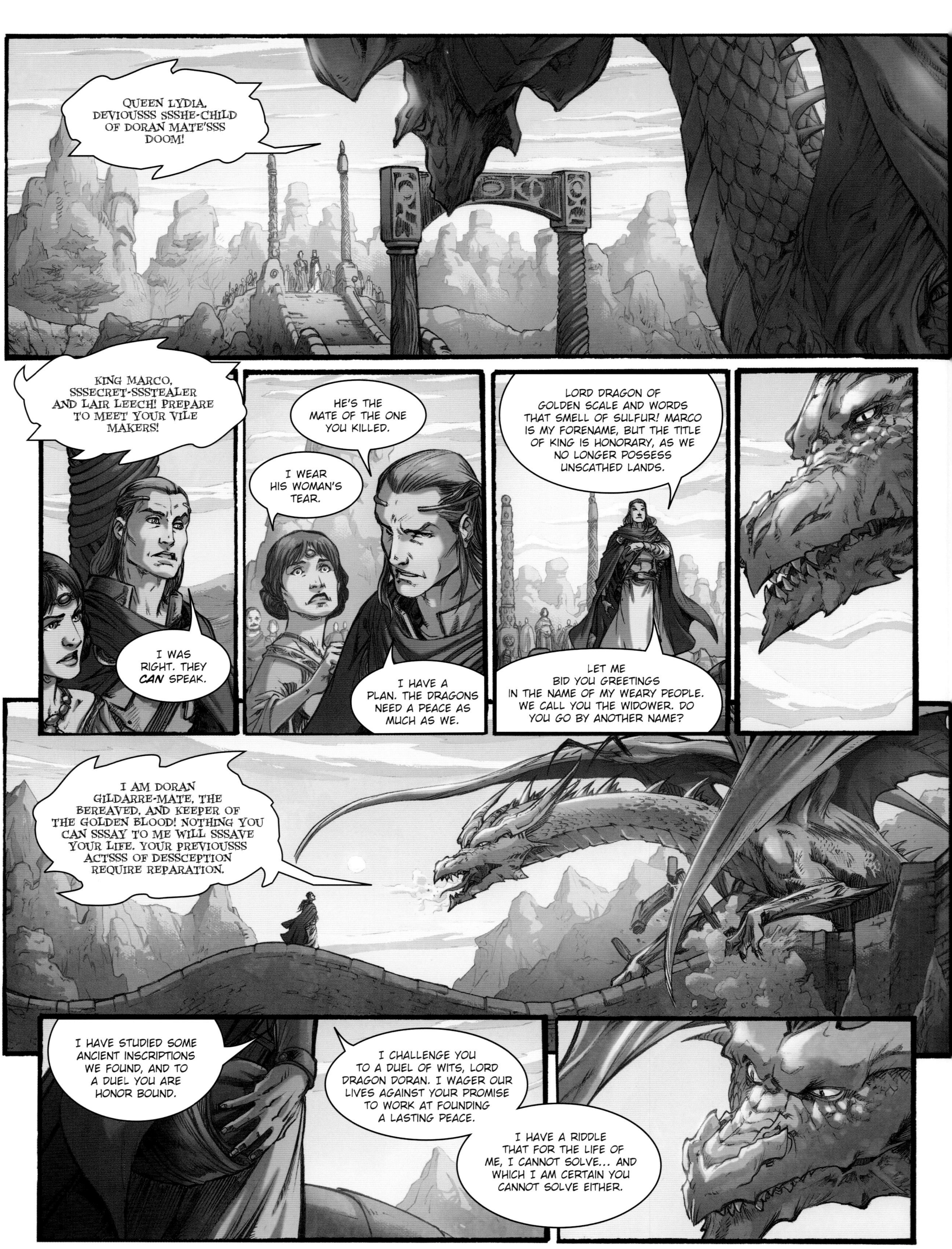
QUEEN LYDIA, DEVIOUSSS SSSHE-CHILD OF DORAN MATE'SSS DOOM!
KING MARCO, SSSECRET-SSSTEALER AND LAIR LEECH! PREPARE TO MEET YOUR VILE MAKERS!
I WAS RIGHT. THEY CAN SPEAK.
HE'S THE MATE OF THE ONE YOU KILLED.
I WEAR HIS WOMAN'S TEAR.
I HAVE A PLAN. THE DRAGONS NEED A PEACE AS MUCH AS WE.
LORD DRAGON OF GOLDEN SCALE AND WORDS THAT SMELL OF SULFUR! MARCO IS MY FORENAME, BUT THE TITLE OF KING IS HONORARY, AS WE NO LONGER POSSESS UNSCATHED LANDS.
LET ME BID YOU GREETINGS IN THE NAME OF MY WEARY PEOPLE. WE CALL YOU THE WIDOWER. DO YOU GO BY ANOTHER NAME?
I AM DORAN GILDARRE-MATE, THE BEREAVED, AND KEEPER OF THE GOLDEN BLOOD! NOTHING YOU CAN SSSAY TO ME WILL SSSAVE YOUR LIFE. YOUR PREVIOUSSS ACTSSS OF DESSCEPTION REQUIRE REPARATION.
I HAVE STUDIED SOME ANCIENT INSCRIPTIONS WE FOUND, AND TO A DUEL YOU ARE HONOR BOUND.
I CHALLENGE YOU TO A DUEL OF WITS, LORD DRAGON DORAN. I WAGER OUR LIVES AGAINST YOUR PROMISE TO WORK AT FOUNDING A LASTING PEACE.
I HAVE A RIDDLE THAT FOR THE LIFE OF ME, I CANNOT SOLVE... AND WHICH I AM CERTAIN YOU CANNOT SOLVE EITHER.

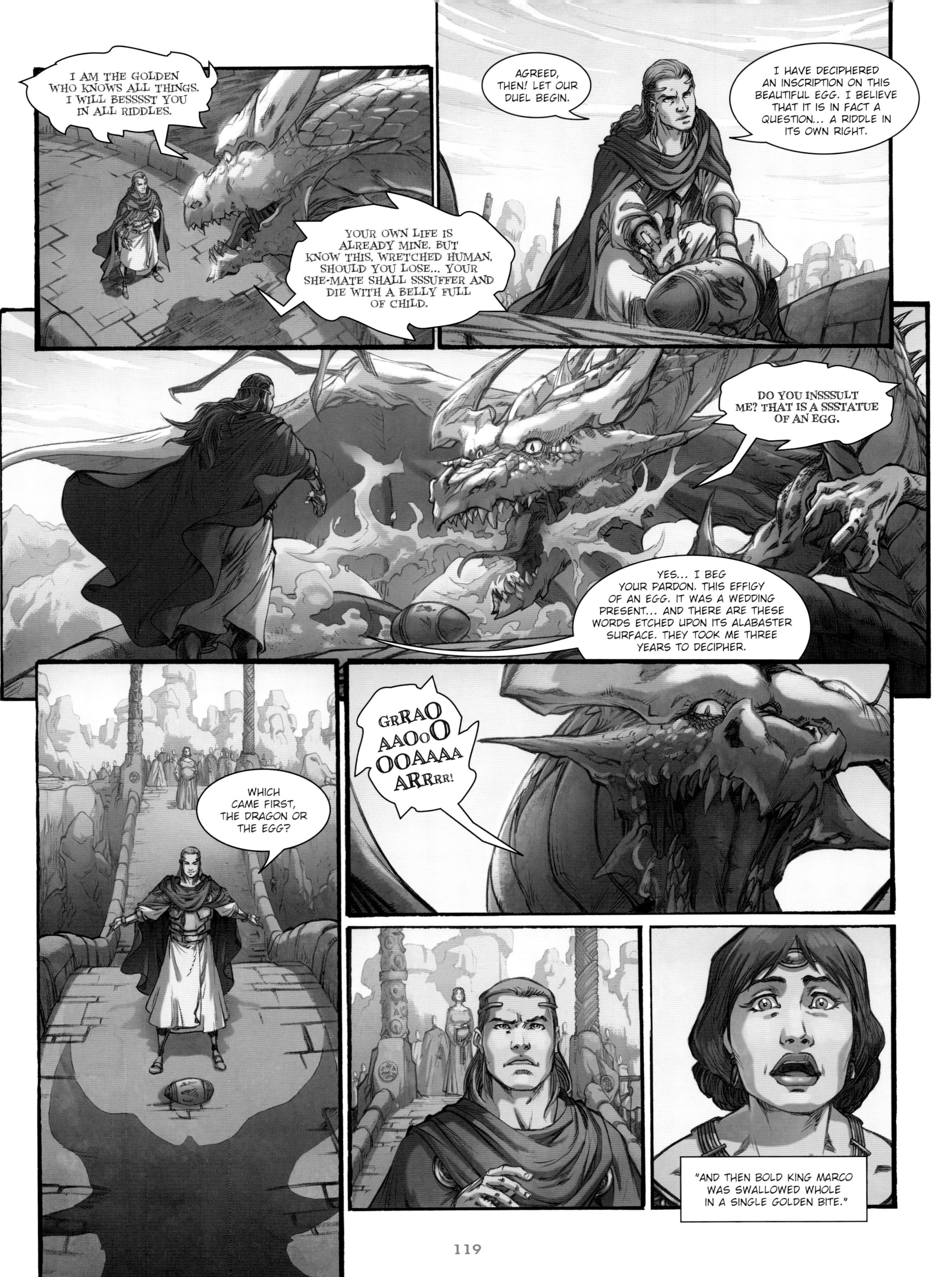
I AM THE GOLDEN WHO KNOWS ALL THINGS. I WILL BESSSST YOU IN ALL RIDDLES.
YOUR OWN LIFE IS ALREADY MINE. BUT KNOW THIS, WRETCHED HUMAN, SHOULD YOU LOSE... YOUR SHE-MATE SHALL SSSUFFER AND DIE WITH A BELLY FULL OF CHILD.
AGREED, THEN! LET OUR DUEL BEGIN.
I HAVE DECIPHERED AN INSCRIPTION ON THIS BEAUTIFUL EGG. I BELIEVE THAT IT IS IN FACT A QUESTION... A RIDDLE IN ITS OWN RIGHT.
DO YOU INSSSULT ME? THAT IS A SSSTATUE OF AN EGG.
YES... I BEG YOUR PARDON. THIS EFFIGY OF AN EGG. IT WAS A WEDDING PRESENT... AND THERE ARE THESE WORDS ETCHED UPON ITS ALABASTER SURFACE. THEY TOOK ME THREE YEARS TO DECIPHER.
WHICH CAME FIRST, THE DRAGON OR THE EGG?
GRRAOAAOOOOOAAAAARRRR!
"AND THEN BOLD KING MARCO WAS SWALLOWED WHOLE IN A SINGLE GOLDEN BITE."

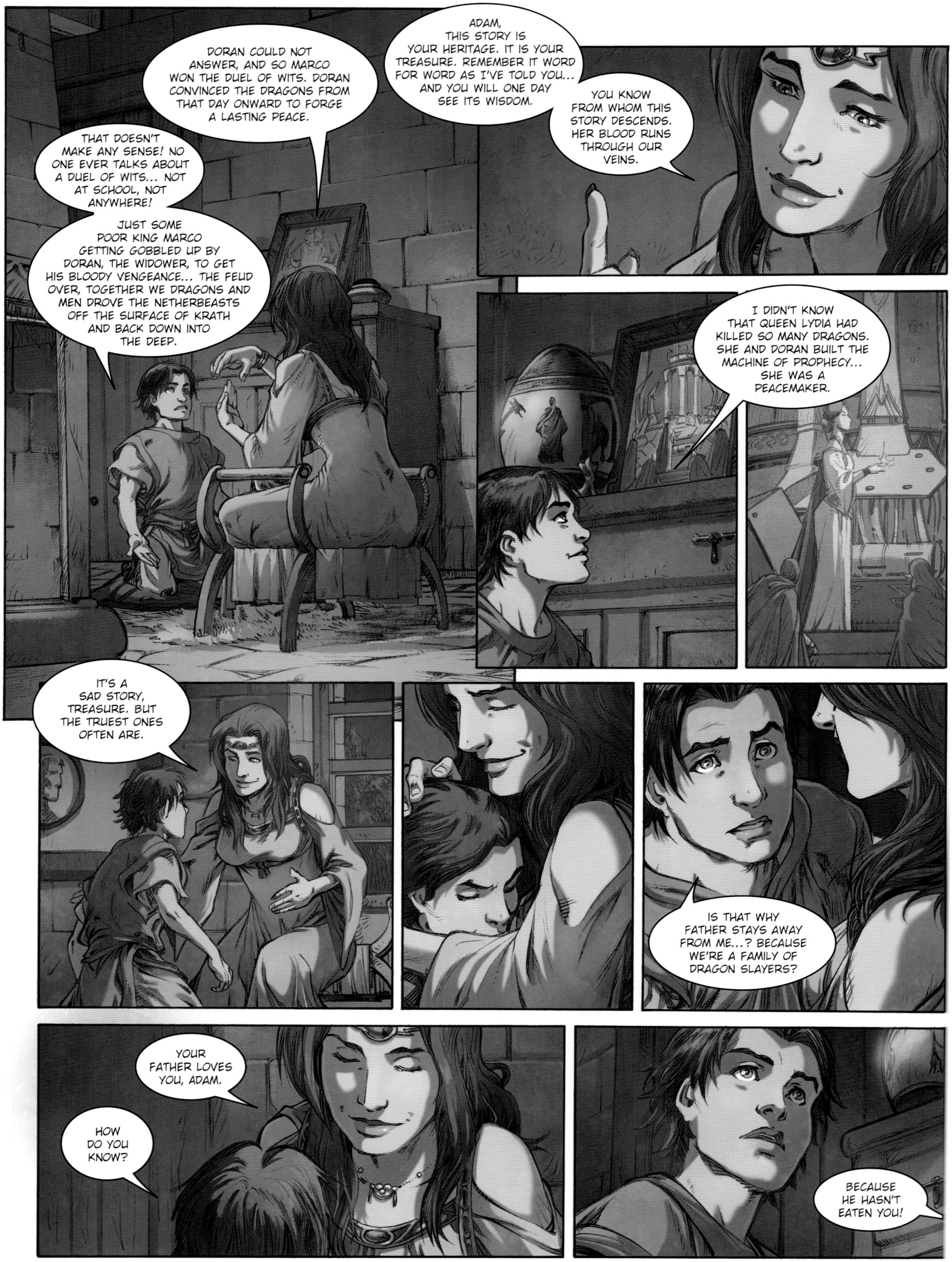
DORAN COULD NOT ANSWER, AND SO MARCO WON THE DUEL OF WITS. DORAN CONVINCED THE DRAGONS FROM THAT DAY ONWARD TO FORGE A LASTING PEACE.
THAT DOESN'T MAKE ANY SENSE! NO ONE EVER TALKS ABOUT A DUEL OF WITS... NOT AT SCHOOL, NOT ANYWHERE!
JUST SOME POOR KING MARCO GETTING GOBBLED UP BY DORAN, THE WIDOWER, TO GET HIS BLOODY VENGEANCE... THE FEUD OVER, TOGETHER WE DRAGONS AND MEN DROVE THE NETHERBEASTS OFF THE SURFACE OF KRATH AND BACK DOWN INTO THE DEEP.
ADAM, THIS STORY IS YOUR HERITAGE. IT IS YOUR TREASURE. REMEMBER IT WORD FOR WORD AS I'VE TOLD YOU... AND YOU WILL ONE DAY SEE ITS WISDOM.
YOU KNOW FROM WHOM THIS STORY DESCENDS. HER BLOOD RUNS THROUGH OUR VEINS.
I DIDN'T KNOW THAT QUEEN LYDIA HAD KILLED SO MANY DRAGONS. SHE AND DORAN BUILT THE MACHINE OF PROPHECY... SHE WAS A PEACEMAKER.
IT'S A SAD STORY, TREASURE. BUT THE TRUEST ONES OFTEN ARE.
IS THAT WHY FATHER STAYS AWAY FROM ME...? BECAUSE WE'RE A FAMILY OF DRAGON SLAYERS?
YOUR FATHER LOVES YOU, ADAM.
HOW DO YOU KNOW?
BECAUSE HE HASN'T EATEN YOU!

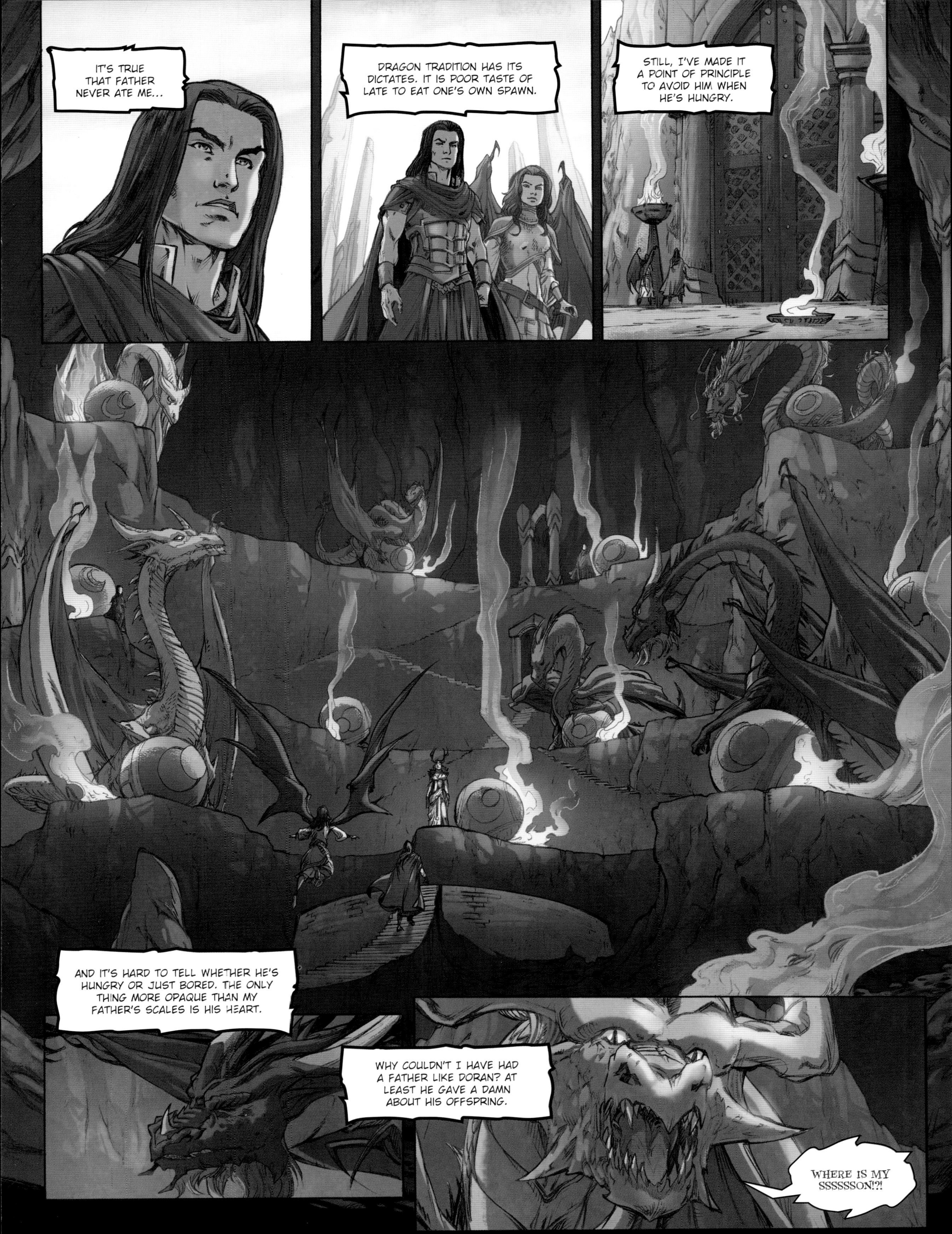
IT'S TRUE THAT FATHER NEVER ATE ME...
DRAGON TRADITION HAS ITS DICTATES. IT IS POOR TASTE OF LATE TO EAT ONE'S OWN SPAWN.
STILL, I'VE MADE IT A POINT OF PRINCIPLE TO AVOID HIM WHEN HE'S HUNGRY.
AND IT'S HARD TO TELL WHETHER HE'S HUNGRY OR JUST BORED. THE ONLY THING MORE OPAQUE THAN MY FATHER'S SCALES IS HIS HEART.
WHY COULDN'T I HAVE HAD A FATHER LIKE DORAN? AT LEAST HE GAVE A DAMN ABOUT HIS OFFSPRING.
WHERE IS MY SSSSSSON!?!

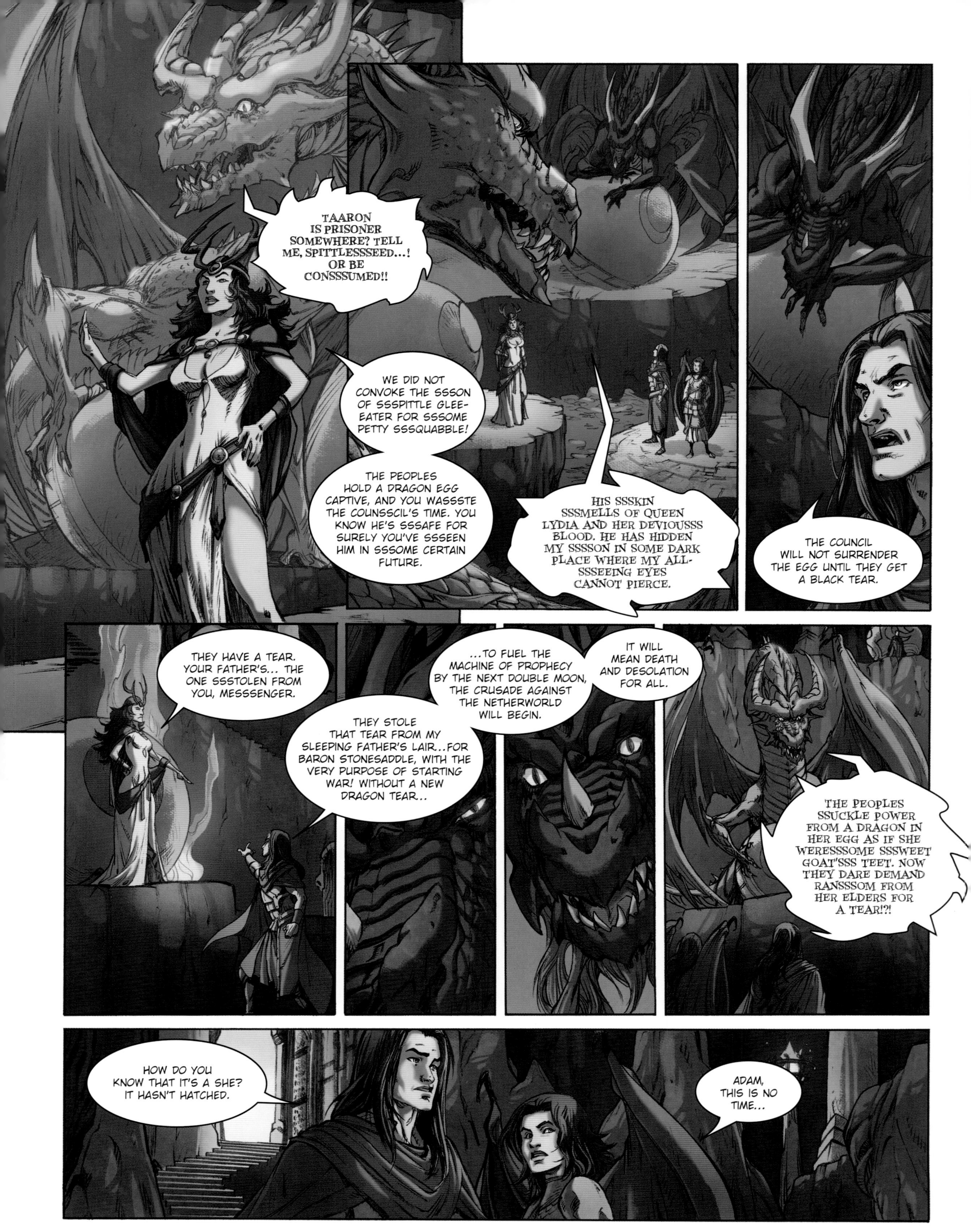
TAARON IS PRISONER SOMEWHERE? TELL ME, SPITTLESSSEED...! OR BE CONSSSUMED!!
WE DID NOT CONVOKE THE SSSON OF SSSPITTLE GLEE-EATER FOR SSSOME PETTY SSSQUABBLE!
THE PEOPLES HOLD A DRAGON EGG CAPTIVE, AND YOU WASSSTE THE COUNSSCIL'S TIME. YOU KNOW HE'S SSSAFE FOR SURELY YOU'VE SSSEEN HIM IN SSSOME CERTAIN FUTURE.
HIS SSSKIN SSSMELLS OF QUEEN LYDIA AND HER DEVIOUSSS BLOOD. HE HAS HIDDEN MY SSSSON IN SOME DARK PLACE WHERE MY ALL-SSSEEING EYES CANNOT PIERCE.
THE COUNCIL WILL NOT SURRENDER THE EGG UNTIL THEY GET A BLACK TEAR.
THEY HAVE A TEAR. YOUR FATHER'S... THE ONE SSSTOLEN FROM YOU, MESSSENGER.
THEY STOLE THAT TEAR FROM MY SLEEPING FATHER'S LAIR...FOR BARON STONESADDLE, WITH THE VERY PURPOSE OF STARTING WAR! WITHOUT A NEW DRAGON TEAR...
...TO FUEL THE MACHINE OF PROPHECY BY THE NEXT DOUBLE MOON, THE CRUSADE AGAINST THE NETHERWORLD WILL BEGIN.
IT WILL MEAN DEATH AND DESOLATION FOR ALL.
THE PEOPLES SSUCKLE POWER FROM A DRAGON IN HER EGG AS IF SHE WERESSSOME SSSWEET GOAT'SSS TEET. NOW THEY DARE DEMAND RANSSSOM FROM HER ELDERS FOR A TEAR!?!
HOW DO YOU KNOW THAT IT'S A SHE? IT HASN'T HATCHED.
ADAM, THIS IS NO TIME...

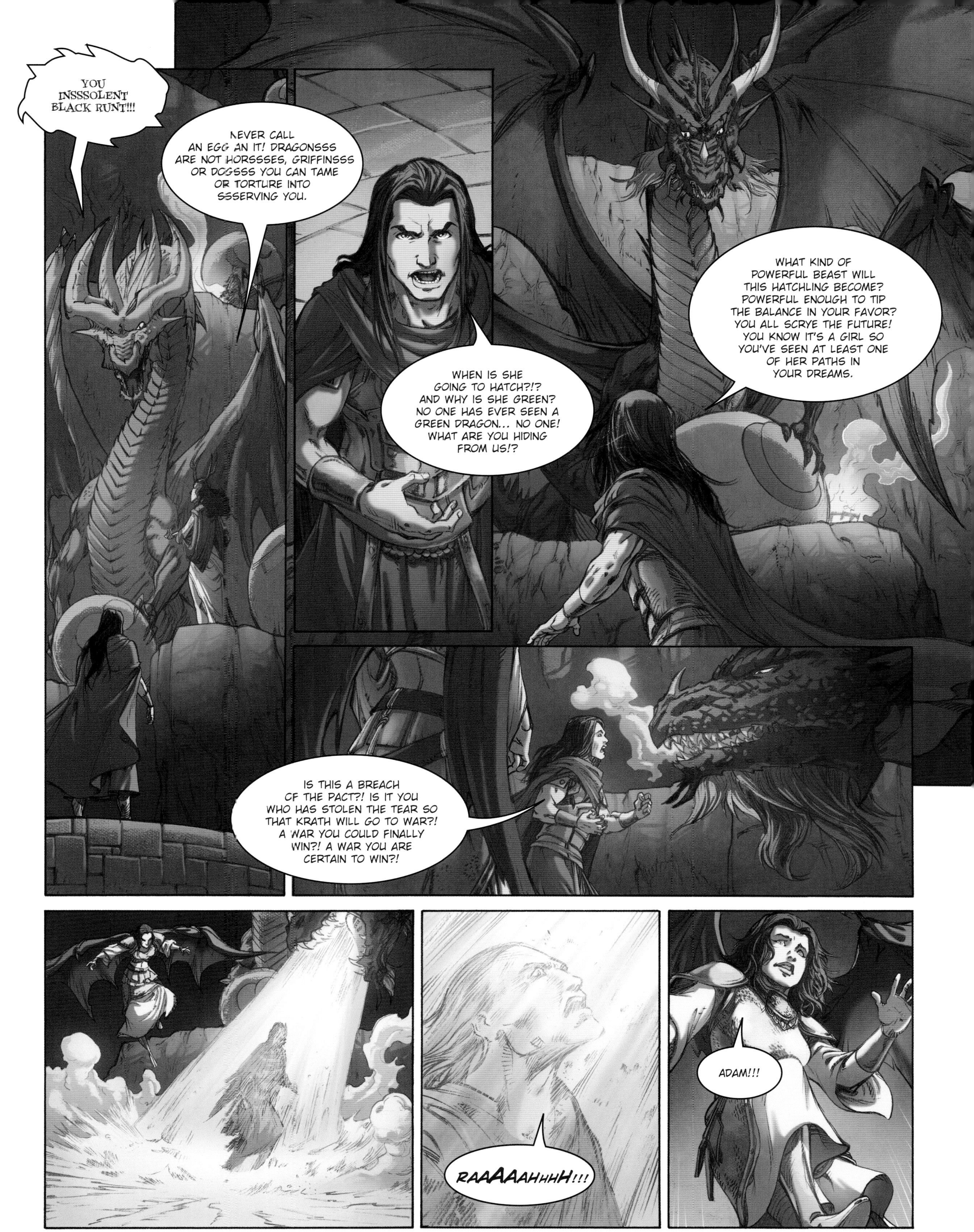
YOU INSSSOLENT BLACK RUNT!!!
NEVER CALL AN EGG AN IT! DRAGONSSS ARE NOT HORSSSES, GRIFFINSSS OR DOGSSS YOU CAN TAME OR TORTURE INTO SSSERVING YOU.
WHEN IS SHE GOING TO HATCH?!? AND WHY IS SHE GREEN? NO ONE HAS EVER SEEN A GREEN DRAGON... NO ONE! WHAT ARE YOU HIDING FROM US!?
WHAT KIND OF POWERFUL BEAST WILL THIS HATCHLING BECOME? POWERFUL ENOUGH TO TIP THE BALANCE IN YOUR FAVOR? YOU ALL SCRYE THE FUTURE! YOU KNOW IT'S A GIRL SO YOU'VE SEEN AT LEAST ONE OF HER PATHS IN YOUR DREAMS.
IS THIS A BREACH OF THE PACT?! IS IT YOU WHO HAS STOLEN THE TEAR SO THAT KRATH WILL GO TO WAR?! A WAR YOU COULD FINALLY WIN?! A WAR YOU ARE CERTAIN TO WIN?!
RAAAAAHHHH!!!
ADAM!!!

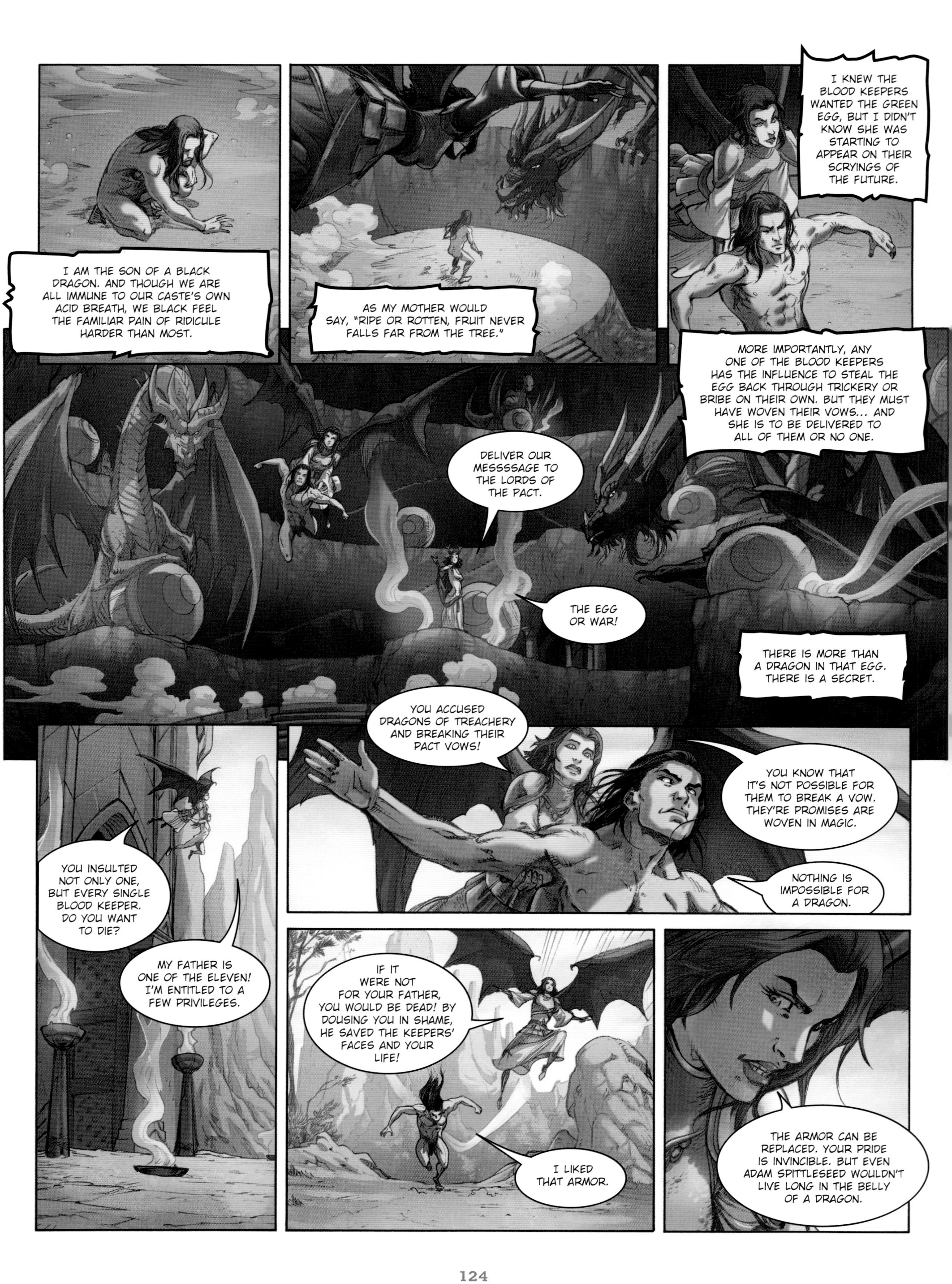
I AM THE SON OF A BLACK DRAGON. AND THOUGH WE ARE ALL IMMUNE TO OUR CASTE'S OWN ACID BREATH, WE BLACK FEEL THE FAMILIAR PAIN OF RIDICULE HARDER THAN MOST.
AS MY MOTHER WOULD SAY, "RIPE OR ROTTEN, FRUIT NEVER FALLS FAR FROM THE TREE."
I KNEW THE BLOOD KEEPERS WANTED THE GREEN EGG, BUT I DIDN'T KNOW SHE WAS STARTING TO APPEAR ON THEIR SCRYINGS OF THE FUTURE.
MORE IMPORTANTLY, ANY ONE OF THE BLOOD KEEPERS HAS THE INFLUENCE TO STEAL THE EGG BACK THROUGH TRICKERY OR BRIBE ON THEIR OWN. BUT THEY MUST HAVE WOVEN THEIR VOWS... AND SHE IS TO BE DELIVERED TO ALL OF THEM OR NO ONE.
DELIVER OUR MESSSSAGE TO THE LORDS OF THE PACT.
THE EGG OR WAR!
THERE IS MORE THAN A DRAGON IN THAT EGG. THERE IS A SECRET.
YOU INSULTED NOT ONLY ONE, BUT EVERY SINGLE BLOOD KEEPER. DO YOU WANT TO DIE?
MY FATHER IS ONE OF THE ELEVEN! I'M ENTITLED TO A FEW PRIVILEGES.
YOU ACCUSED DRAGONS OF TREACHERY AND BREAKING THEIR PACT VOWS!
YOU KNOW THAT IT'S NOT POSSIBLE FOR THEM TO BREAK A VOW. THEY'RE PROMISES ARE WOVEN IN MAGIC.
NOTHING IS IMPOSSIBLE FOR A DRAGON.
IF IT WERE NOT FOR YOUR FATHER, YOU WOULD BE DEAD! BY DOUSING YOU IN SHAME, HE SAVED THE KEEPERS' FACES AND YOUR LIFE!
I LIKED THAT ARMOR.
THE ARMOR CAN BE REPLACED. YOUR PRIDE IS INVINCIBLE. BUT EVEN ADAM SPITTLESEED WOULDN'T LIVE LONG IN THE BELLY OF A DRAGON.

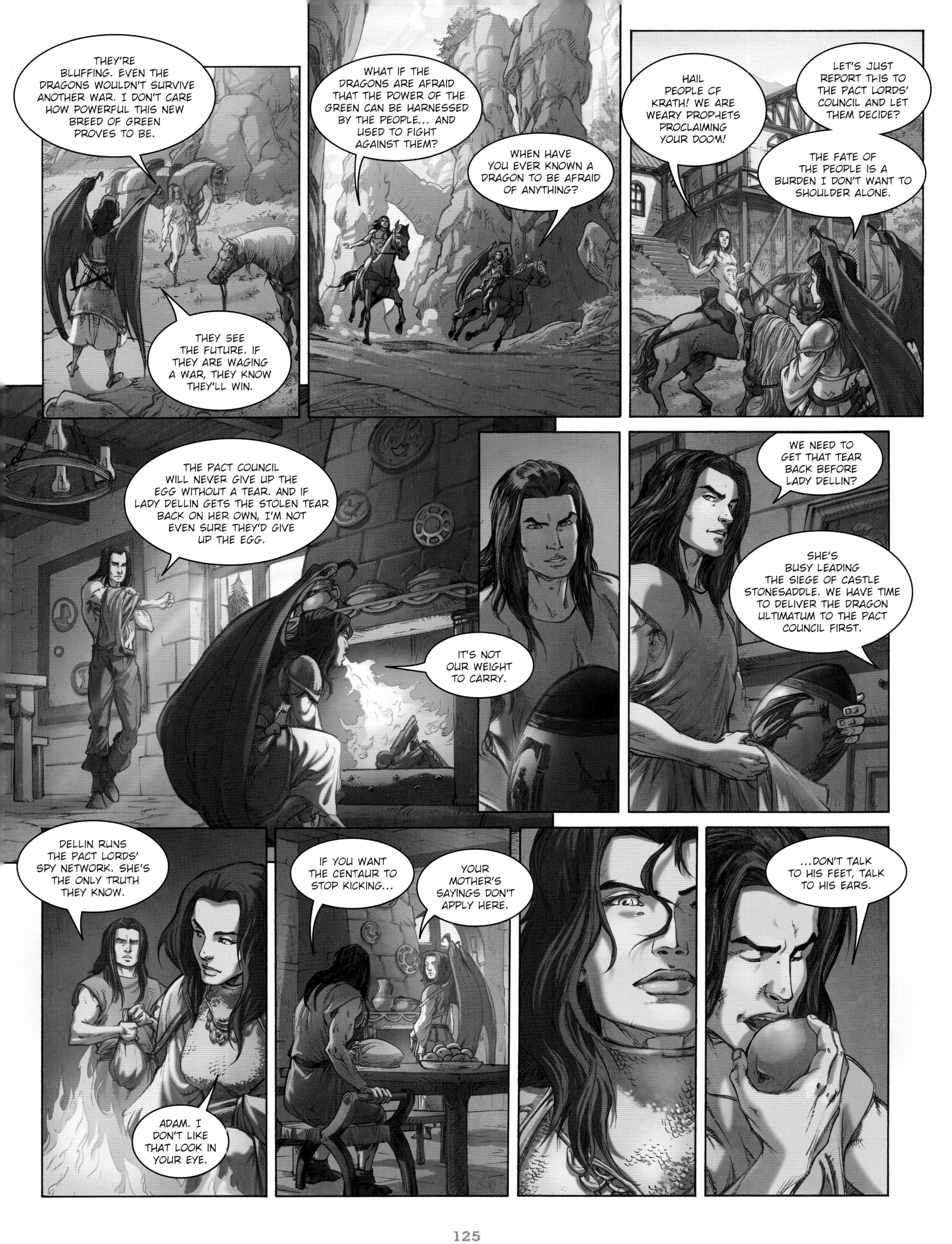
THEY'RE BLUFFING. EVEN THE DRAGONS WOULDN'T SURVIVE ANOTHER WAR. I DON'T CARE HOW POWERFUL THIS NEW BREED OF GREEN PROVES TO BE.
THEY SEE THE FUTURE. IF THEY ARE WAGING A WAR, THEY'LL KNOW THEY'LL WIN.
WHAT IF THE DRAGONS ARE AFRAID THAT THE POWER OF THE GREEN CAN BE HARNESSED BY THE PEOPLE... AND USED TO FIGHT AGAINST THEM?
WHEN HAVE YOU EVER KNOWN A DRAGON TO BE AFRAID OF ANYTHING?
HAIL PEOPLE OF KRATH! WE ARE WEARY PROPHETS PROCLAIMING YOUR DOOM!
LET'S JUST REPORT THIS TO THE PACT LORDS' COUNCIL AND LET THEM DECIDE?
THE FATE OF THE PEOPLE IS A BURDEN I DON'T WANT TO SHOULDER ALONE.
THE PACT COUNCIL WILL NEVER GIVE UP THE EGG WITHOUT A TEAR. AND IF LADY DELLIN GETS THE STOLEN TEAR BACK ON HER OWN, I'M NOT EVEN SURE THEY'D GIVE UP THE EGG.
IT'S NOT OUR WEIGHT TO CARRY.
WE NEED TO GET THAT TEAR BACK BEFORE LADY DELLIN?
SHE'S BUSY LEADING THE SIEGE OF CASTLE STONESADDLE. WE HAVE TIME TO DELIVER THE DRAGON ULTIMATUM TO THE PACT COUNCIL FIRST.
DELLIN RUNS THE PACT LORDS' SPY NETWORK. SHE'S THE ONLY TRUTH THEY KNOW.
ADAM. I DON'T LIKE THAT LOOK IN YOUR EYE.
IF YOU WANT THE CENTAUR TO STOP KICKING...
YOUR MOTHER'S SAYINGS DON'T APPLY HERE.
...DON'T TALK TO HIS FEET, TALK TO HIS EARS.

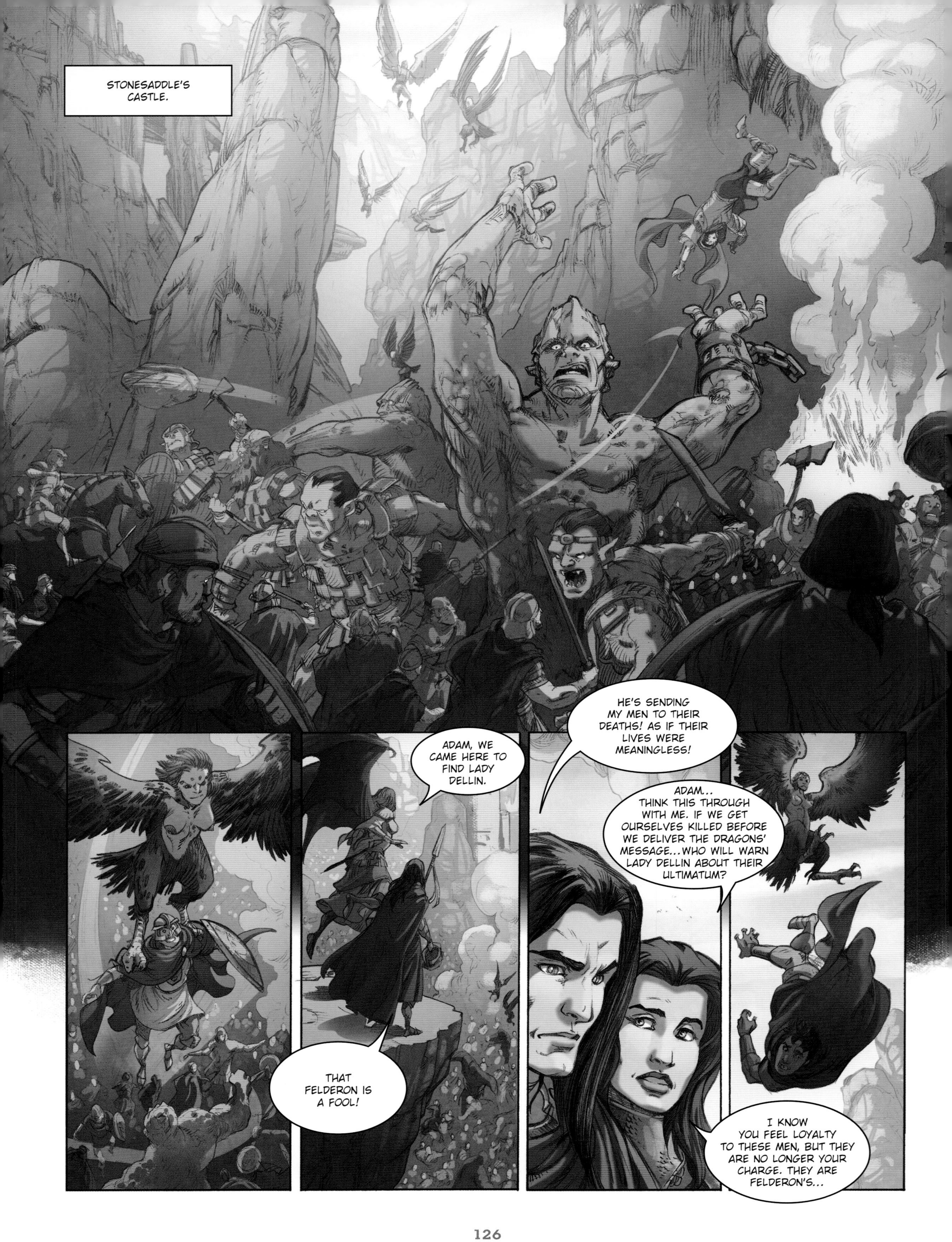
STONESADDLE'S CASTLE.
ADAM, WE CAME HERE TO FIND LADY DELLIN.
THAT FELDERON IS A FOOL!
HE'S SENDING MY MEN TO THEIR DEATHS! AS IF THEIR LIVES WERE MEANINGLESS!
ADAM... THINK THIS THROUGH WITH ME. IF WE GET OURSELVES KILLED BEFORE WE DELIVER THE DRAGONS' MESSAGE...WHO WILL WARN LADY DELLIN ABOUT THEIR ULTIMATUM?
I KNOW YOU FEEL LOYALTY TO THESE MEN, BUT THEY ARE NO LONGER YOUR CHARGE. THEY ARE FELDERON'S...

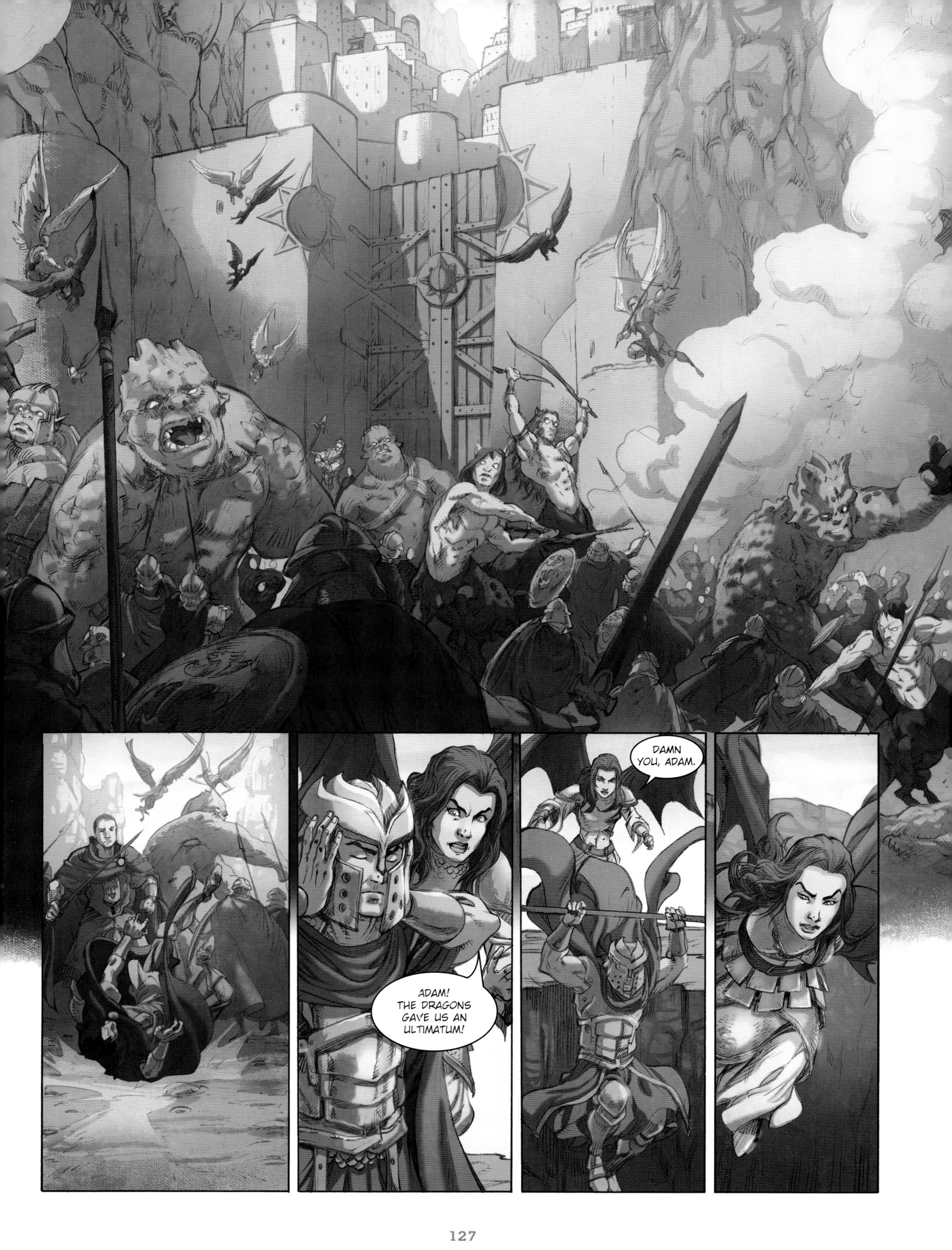
ADAM! THE DRAGONS GAVE US AN ULTIMATUM!
DAMN YOU, ADAM.

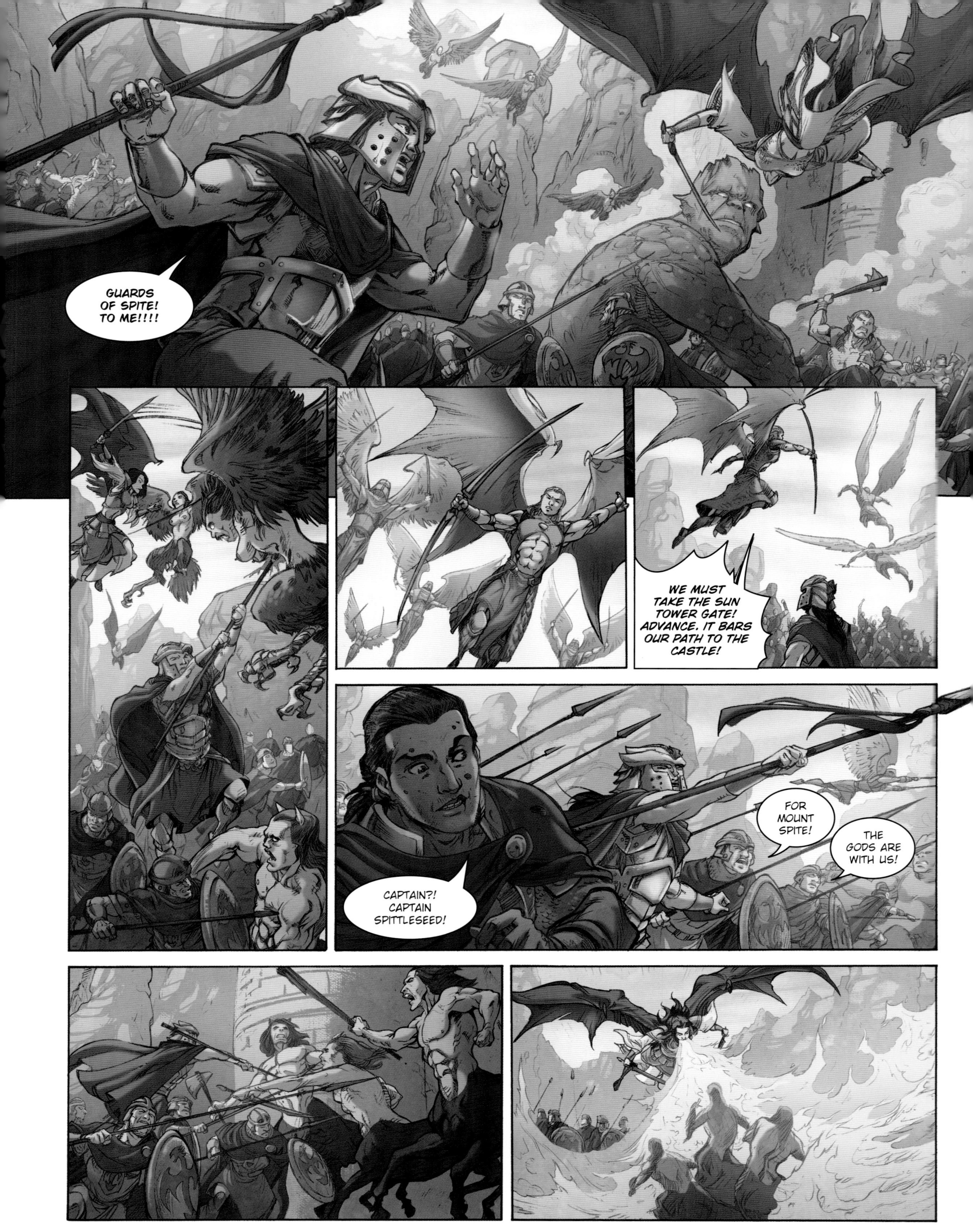
GUARDS OF SPITE! TO ME!!!!
WE MUST TAKE THE SUN TOWER GATE! ADVANCE. IT BARS OUR PATH TO THE CASTLE!
CAPTAIN?! CAPTAIN SPITTLESEED!
FOR MOUNT SPITE!
THE GODS ARE WITH US!

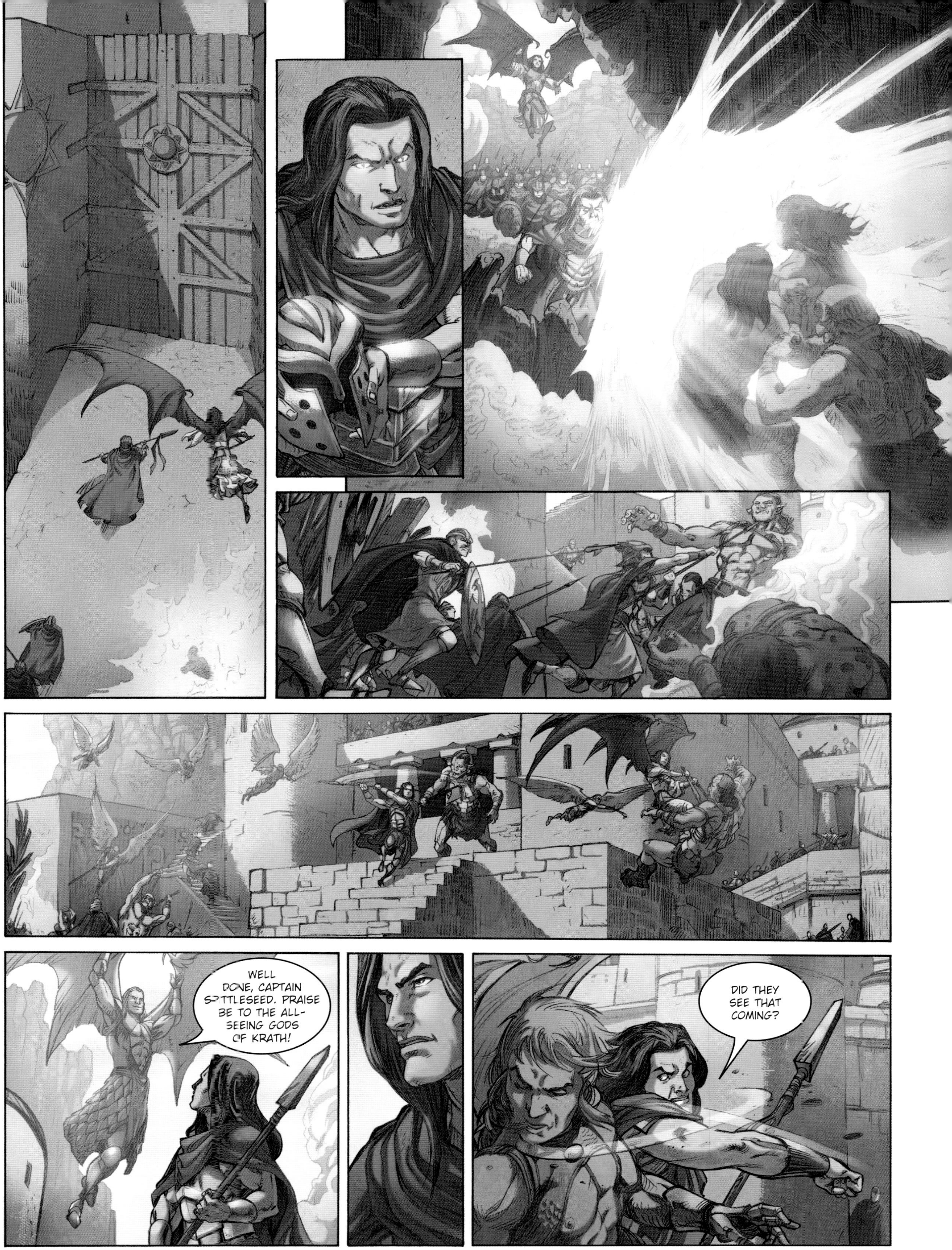
WELL DONE, CAPTAIN SPITTLESEED. PRAISE BE TO THE ALL-SEEING GODS OF KRATH!
DID THEY SEE THAT COMING?

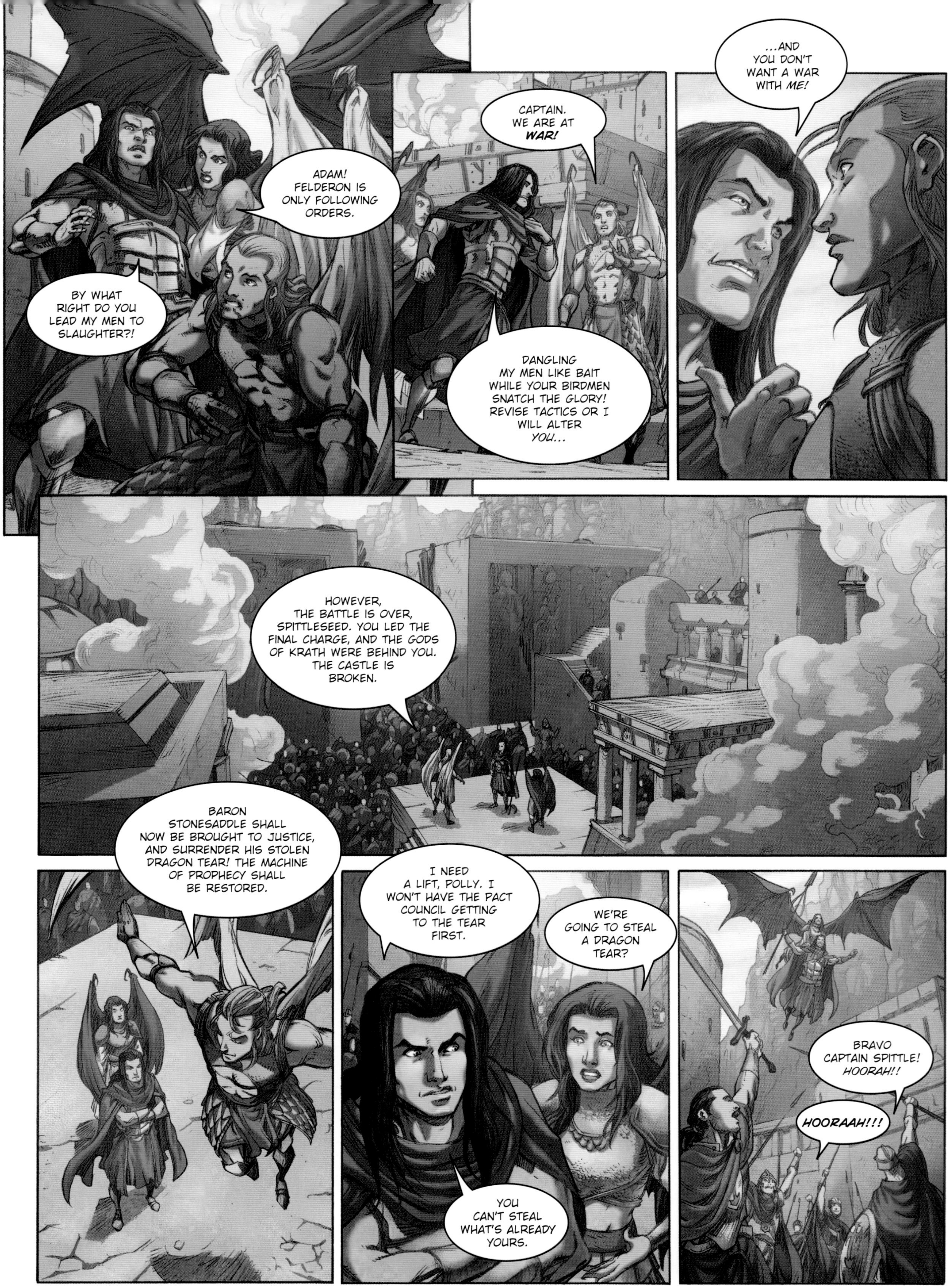
BY WHAT RIGHT DO YOU LEAD MY MEN TO SLAUGHTER?!
ADAM! FELDERON IS ONLY FOLLOWING ORDERS.
CAPTAIN. WE ARE AT *WAR!*
DANGLING MY MEN LIKE BAIT WHILE YOUR BIRDMEN SNATCH THE GLORY! REVISE TACTICS OR I WILL ALTER *YOU...*
...AND YOU DON'T WANT A WAR WITH *ME!*
HOWEVER, THE BATTLE IS OVER, SPITTLESEED. YOU LED THE FINAL CHARGE, AND THE GODS OF KRATH WERE BEHIND YOU. THE CASTLE IS BROKEN.
BARON STONESADDLE SHALL NOW BE BROUGHT TO JUSTICE, AND SURRENDER HIS STOLEN DRAGON TEAR! THE MACHINE OF PROPHECY SHALL BE RESTORED.
I NEED A LIFT, POLLY. I WON'T HAVE THE PACT COUNCIL GETTING TO THE TEAR FIRST.
WE'RE GOING TO STEAL A DRAGON TEAR?
YOU CAN'T STEAL WHAT'S ALREADY YOURS.
BRAVO CAPTAIN SPITTLE! *HOORAH!!*
HOORAAH!!!

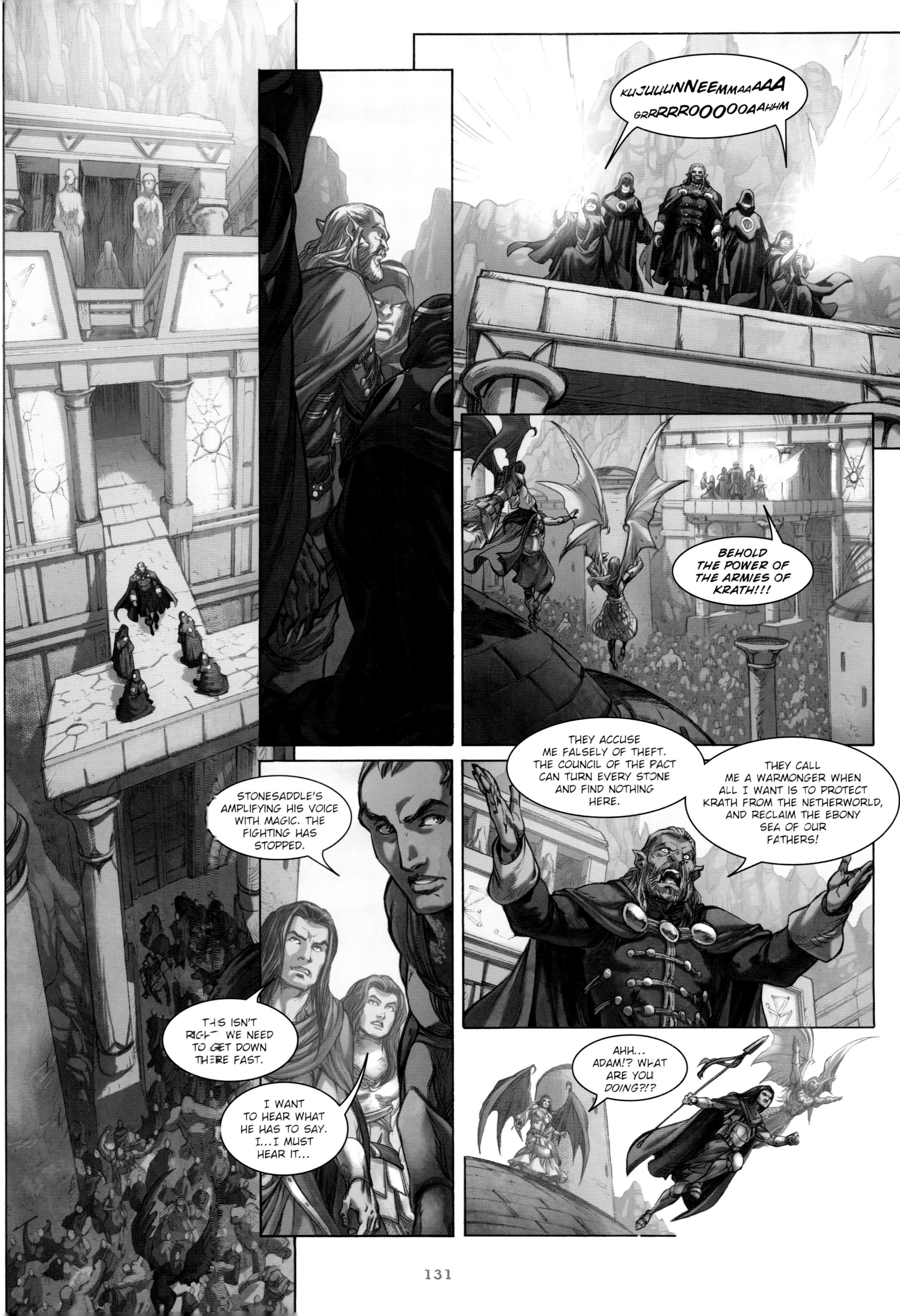
KUJUUUNNEEMMAAAAA GRRRRROOOOOAAHHM
BEHOLD THE POWER OF THE ARMIES OF KRATH!!!
STONESADDLE'S AMPLIFYING HIS VOICE WITH MAGIC. THE FIGHTING HAS STOPPED.
THEY ACCUSE ME FALSELY OF THEFT. THE COUNCIL OF THE PACT CAN TURN EVERY STONE AND FIND NOTHING HERE.
THEY CALL ME A WARMONGER WHEN ALL I WANT IS TO PROTECT KRATH FROM THE NETHERWORLD, AND RECLAIM THE EBONY SEA OF OUR FATHERS!
THIS ISN'T RIGHT. WE NEED TO GET DOWN THERE FAST.
I WANT TO HEAR WHAT HE HAS TO SAY. I...I MUST HEAR IT...
AHH... ADAM!? WHAT ARE YOU DOING?!?

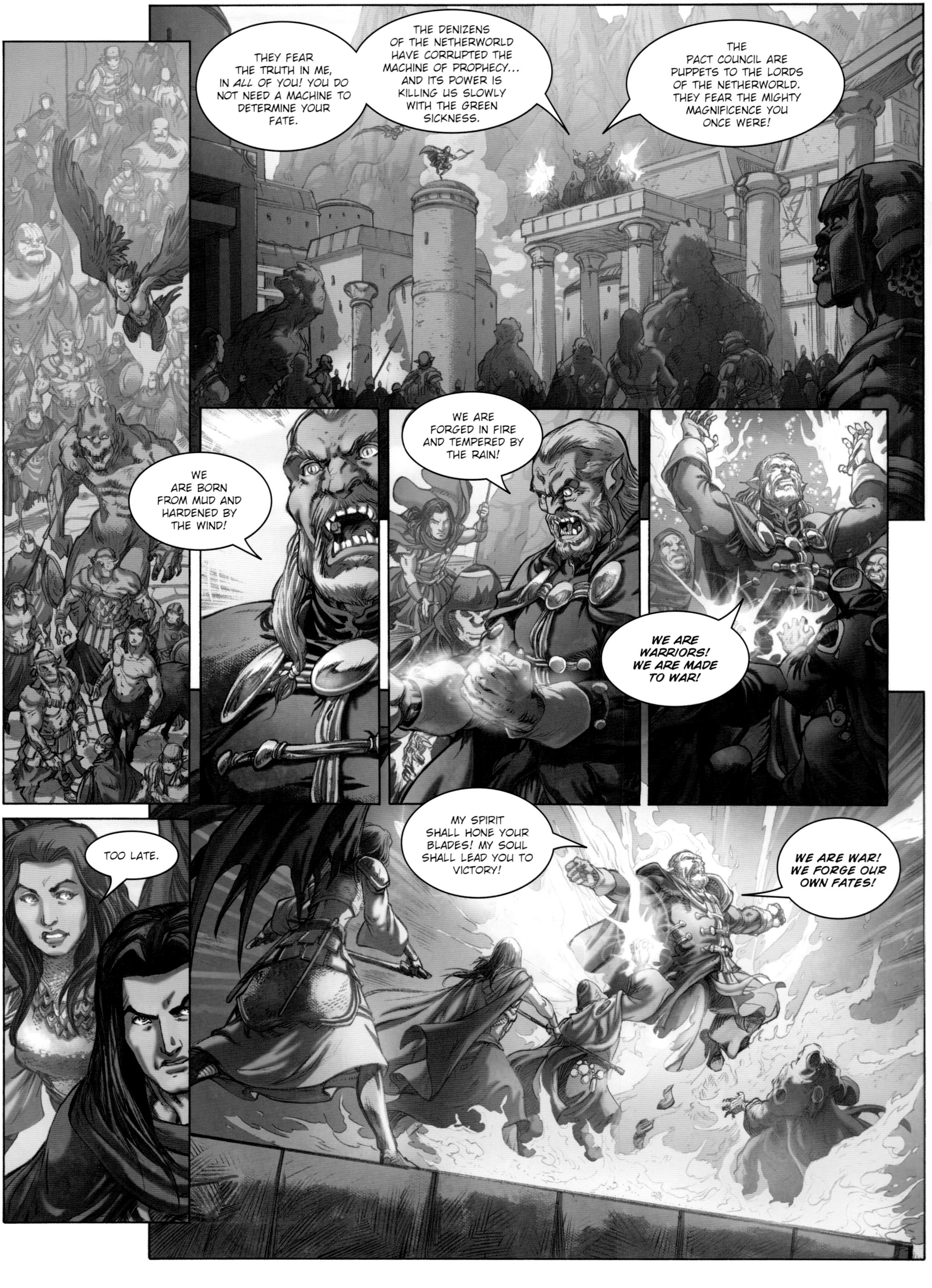
THEY FEAR THE TRUTH IN ME, IN *ALL* OF YOU! YOU DO NOT NEED A MACHINE TO DETERMINE YOUR FATE.
THE DENIZENS OF THE NETHERWORLD HAVE CORRUPTED THE MACHINE OF PROPHECY... AND ITS POWER IS KILLING US SLOWLY WITH THE GREEN SICKNESS.
THE PACT COUNCIL ARE PUPPETS TO THE LORDS OF THE NETHERWORLD. THEY FEAR THE MIGHTY MAGNIFICENCE YOU ONCE WERE!
WE ARE BORN FROM MUD AND HARDENED BY THE WIND!
WE ARE FORGED IN FIRE AND TEMPERED BY THE RAIN!
WE ARE WARRIORS! WE ARE MADE TO WAR!
TOO LATE.
MY SPIRIT SHALL HONE YOUR BLADES! MY SOUL SHALL LEAD YOU TO VICTORY!
WE ARE WAR! WE FORGE OUR OWN FATES!

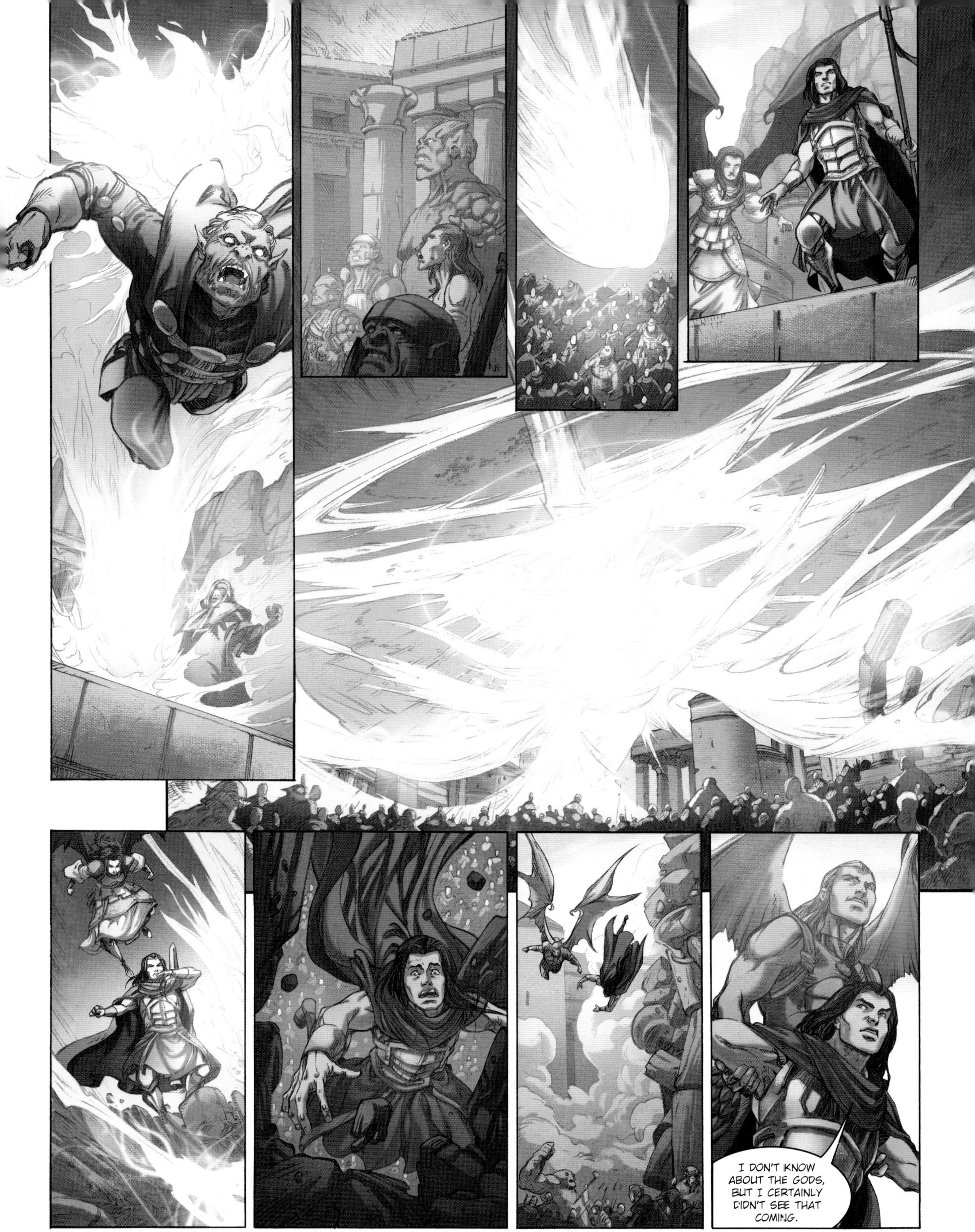
I DON'T KNOW ABOUT THE GODS, BUT I CERTAINLY DIDN'T SEE THAT COMING.

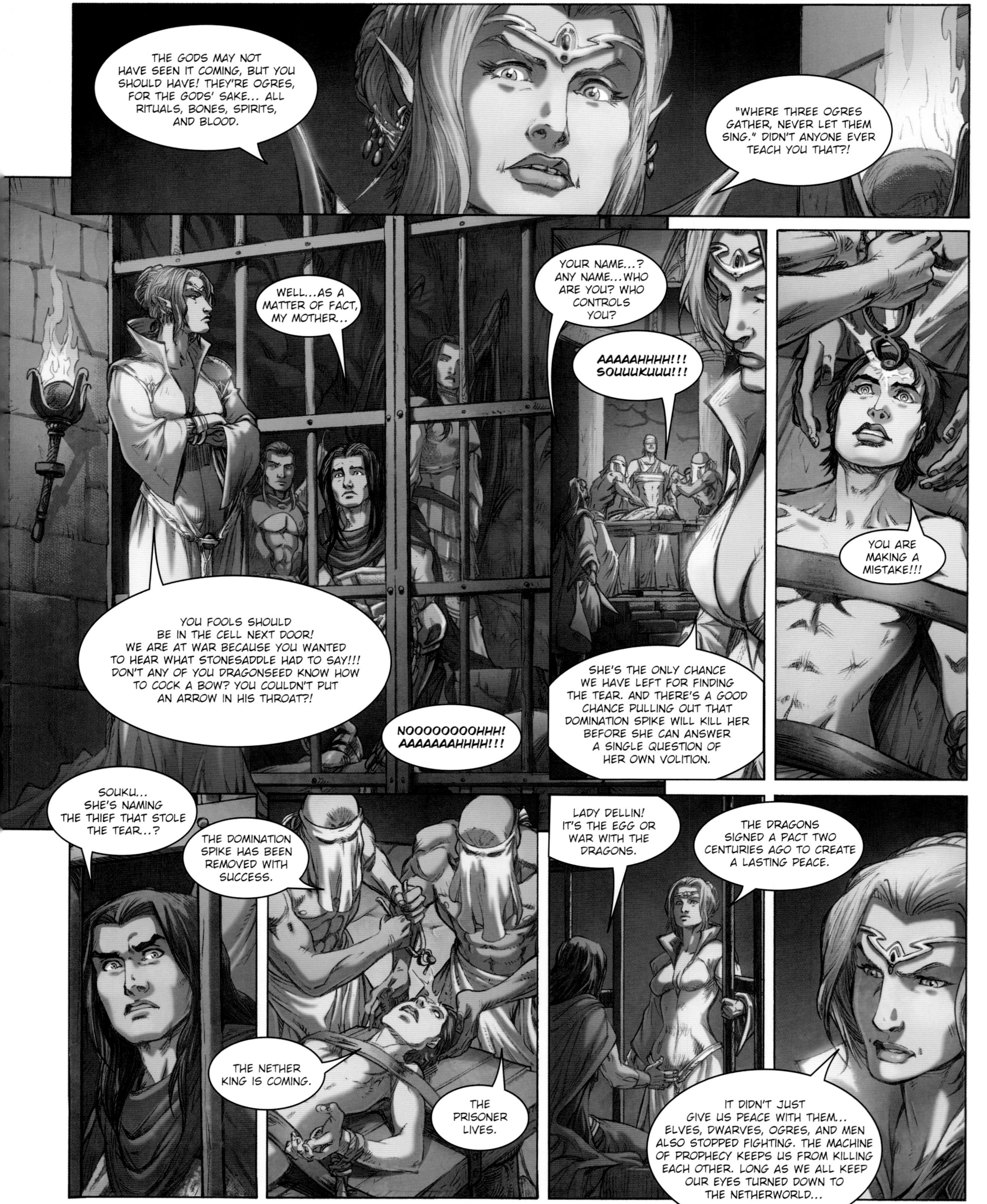
THE GODS MAY NOT HAVE SEEN IT COMING, BUT YOU SHOULD HAVE! THEY'RE OGRES, FOR THE GODS' SAKE... ALL RITUALS, BONES, SPIRITS, AND BLOOD.
"WHERE THREE OGRES GATHER, NEVER LET THEM SING." DIDN'T ANYONE EVER TEACH YOU THAT?!
WELL...AS A MATTER OF FACT, MY MOTHER...
YOU FOOLS SHOULD BE IN THE CELL NEXT DOOR! WE ARE AT WAR BECAUSE YOU WANTED TO HEAR WHAT STONESADDLE HAD TO SAY!!! DON'T ANY OF YOU DRAGONSEED KNOW HOW TO COCK A BOW? YOU COULDN'T PUT AN ARROW IN HIS THROAT?!
NOOOOOOOOHHH! AAAAAAAHHHH!!!
YOUR NAME...? ANY NAME...WHO ARE YOU? WHO CONTROLS YOU?
AAAAAHHHH!!! SOUUUKUUU!!!
SHE'S THE ONLY CHANCE WE HAVE LEFT FOR FINDING THE TEAR. AND THERE'S A GOOD CHANCE PULLING OUT THAT DOMINATION SPIKE WILL KILL HER BEFORE SHE CAN ANSWER A SINGLE QUESTION OF HER OWN VOLITION.
YOU ARE MAKING A MISTAKE!!!
SOUKU... SHE'S NAMING THE THIEF THAT STOLE THE TEAR...?
THE DOMINATION SPIKE HAS BEEN REMOVED WITH SUCCESS.
THE NETHER KING IS COMING.
THE PRISONER LIVES.
LADY DELLIN! IT'S THE EGG OR WAR WITH THE DRAGONS.
THE DRAGONS SIGNED A PACT TWO CENTURIES AGO TO CREATE A LASTING PEACE.
IT DIDN'T JUST GIVE US PEACE WITH THEM... ELVES, DWARVES, OGRES, AND MEN ALSO STOPPED FIGHTING. THE MACHINE OF PROPHECY KEEPS US FROM KILLING EACH OTHER. LONG AS WE ALL KEEP OUR EYES TURNED DOWN TO THE NETHERWORLD...

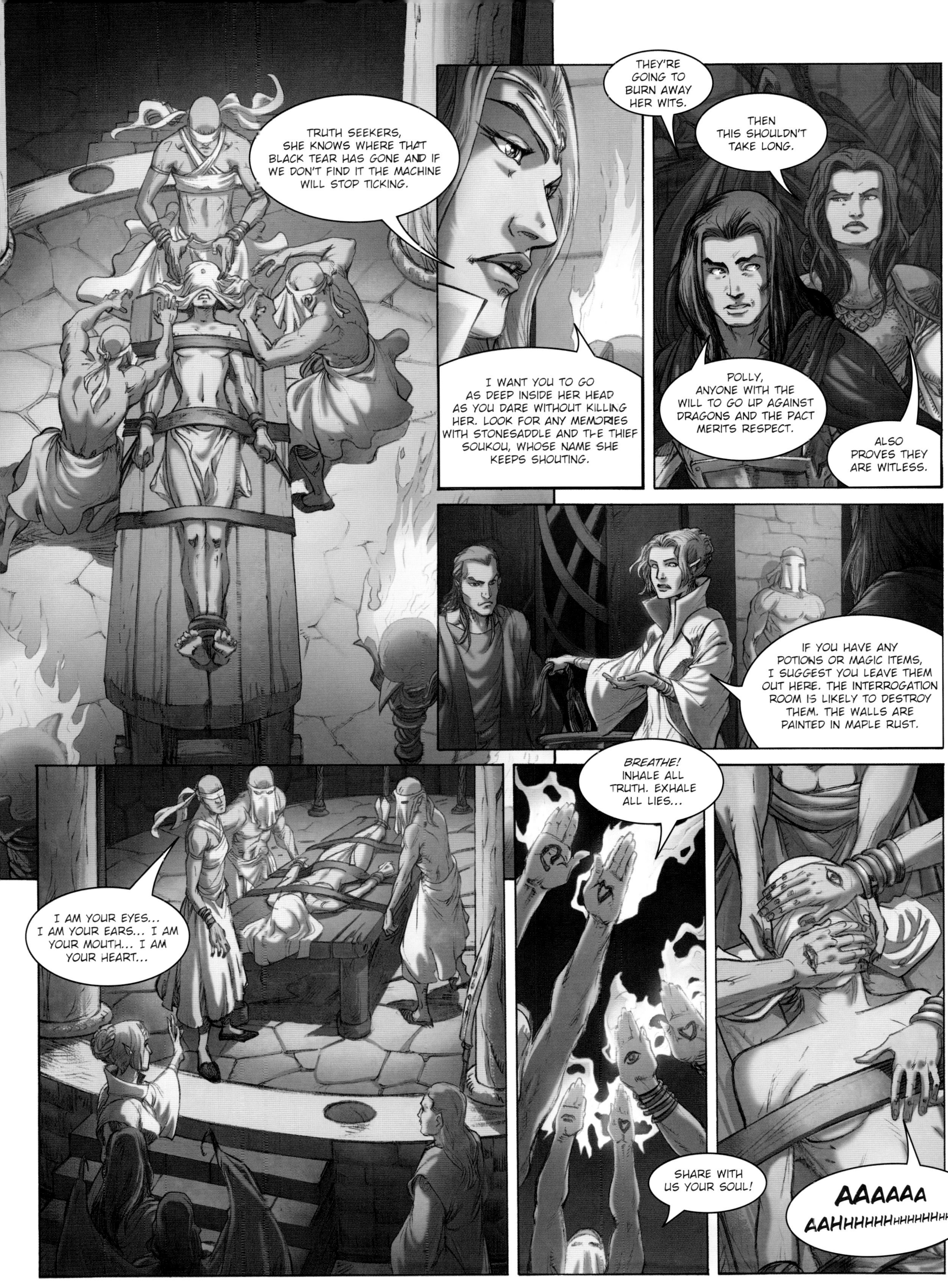
TRUTH SEEKERS, SHE KNOWS WHERE THAT BLACK TEAR HAS GONE AND IF WE DON'T FIND IT THE MACHINE WILL STOP TICKING.
I WANT YOU TO GO AS DEEP INSIDE HER HEAD AS YOU DARE WITHOUT KILLING HER. LOOK FOR ANY MEMORIES WITH STONESADDLE AND THE THIEF SOUKOU, WHOSE NAME SHE KEEPS SHOUTING.
THEY'RE GOING TO BURN AWAY HER WITS.
THEN THIS SHOULDN'T TAKE LONG.
POLLY, ANYONE WITH THE WILL TO GO UP AGAINST DRAGONS AND THE PACT MERITS RESPECT.
ALSO PROVES THEY ARE WITLESS.
IF YOU HAVE ANY POTIONS OR MAGIC ITEMS, I SUGGEST YOU LEAVE THEM OUT HERE. THE INTERROGATION ROOM IS LIKELY TO DESTROY THEM. THE WALLS ARE PAINTED IN MAPLE RUST.
I AM YOUR EYES... I AM YOUR EARS... I AM YOUR MOUTH... I AM YOUR HEART...
BREATHE! INHALE ALL TRUTH. EXHALE ALL LIES...
SHARE WITH US YOUR SOUL!
AAAAAA AAHHHHHHHHHHHHHH!

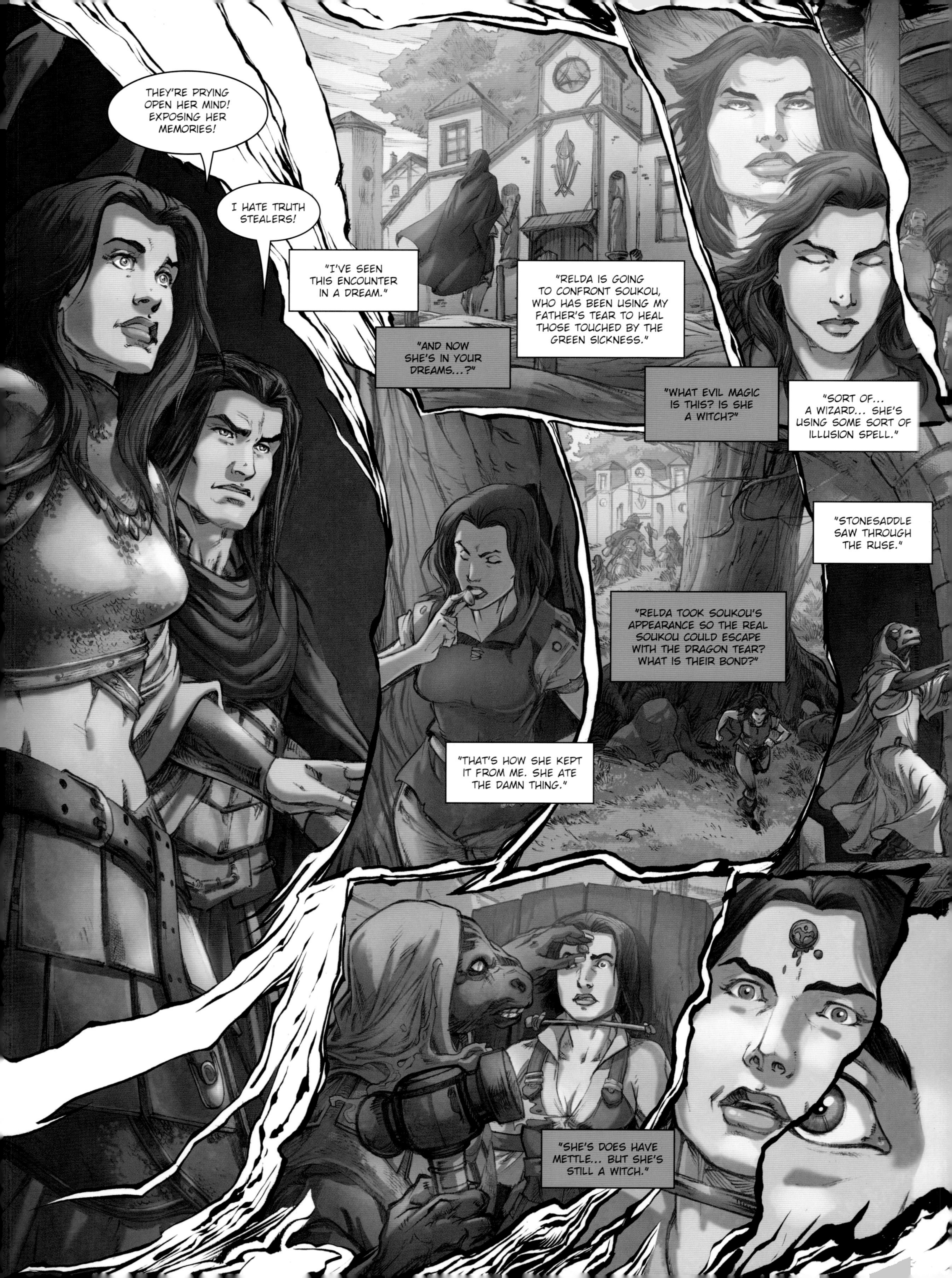
THEY'RE PRYING OPEN HER MIND! EXPOSING HER MEMORIES!
I HATE TRUTH STEALERS!
"I'VE SEEN THIS ENCOUNTER IN A DREAM."
"AND NOW SHE'S IN YOUR DREAMS...?"
"RELDA IS GOING TO CONFRONT SOUKOU, WHO HAS BEEN USING MY FATHER'S TEAR TO HEAL THOSE TOUCHED BY THE GREEN SICKNESS."
"WHAT EVIL MAGIC IS THIS? IS SHE A WITCH?"
"SORT OF... A WIZARD... SHE'S USING SOME SORT OF ILLUSION SPELL."
"STONESADDLE SAW THROUGH THE RUSE."
"RELDA TOOK SOUKOU'S APPEARANCE SO THE REAL SOUKOU COULD ESCAPE WITH THE DRAGON TEAR? WHAT IS THEIR BOND?"
"THAT'S HOW SHE KEPT IT FROM ME. SHE ATE THE DAMN THING."
"SHE'S DOES HAVE METTLE... BUT SHE'S STILL A WITCH."

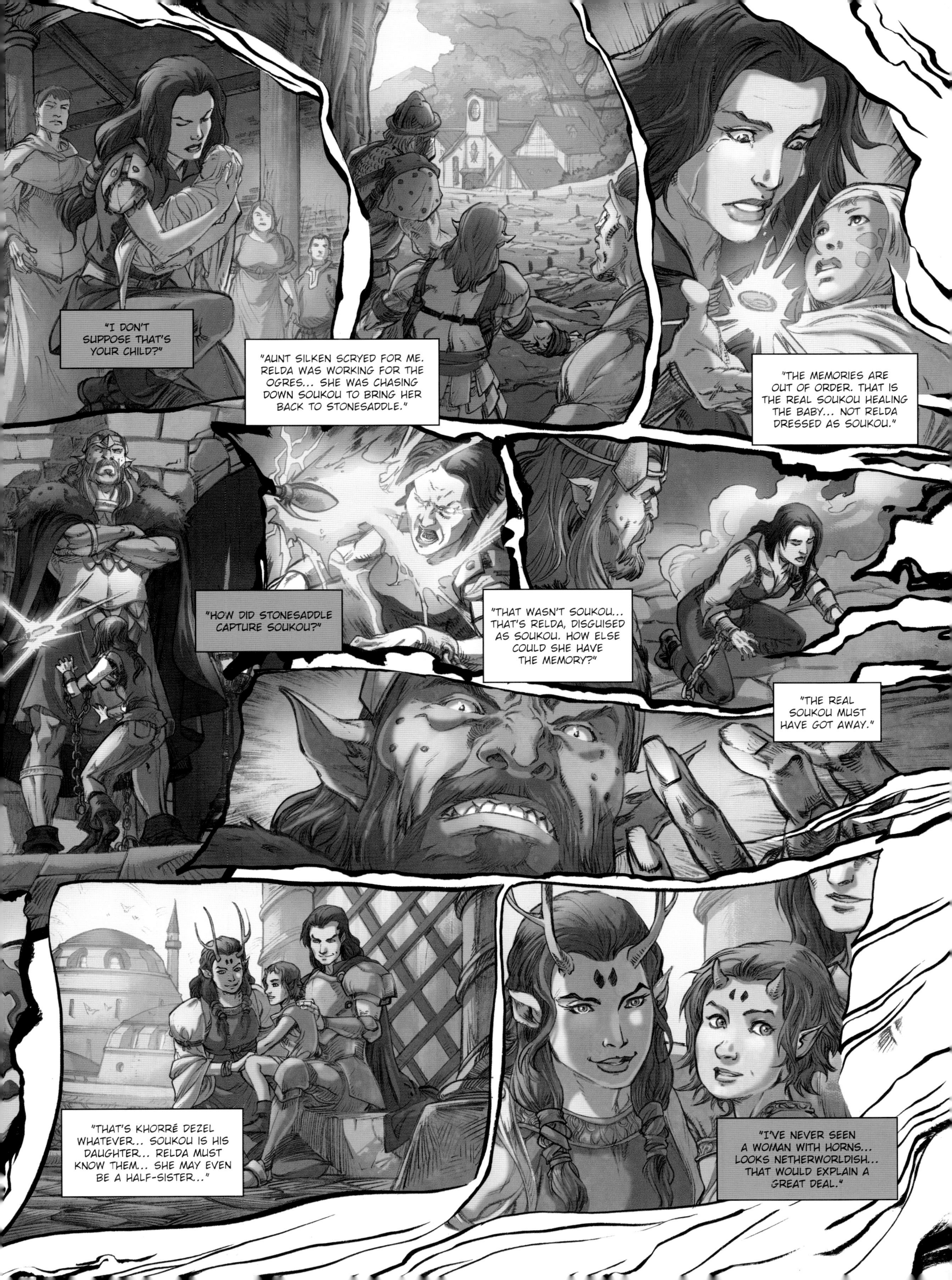
"I DON'T SUPPOSE THAT'S YOUR CHILD?"
"AUNT SILKEN SCRYED FOR ME. RELDA WAS WORKING FOR THE OGRES... SHE WAS CHASING DOWN SOUKOU TO BRING HER BACK TO STONESADDLE."
"THE MEMORIES ARE OUT OF ORDER. THAT IS THE REAL SOUKOU HEALING THE BABY... NOT RELDA DRESSED AS SOUKOU."
"HOW DID STONESADDLE CAPTURE SOUKOU?"
"THAT WASN'T SOUKOU... THAT'S RELDA, DISGUISED AS SOUKOU. HOW ELSE COULD SHE HAVE THE MEMORY?"
"THE REAL SOUKOU MUST HAVE GOT AWAY."
"THAT'S KHORRÉ DEZEL WHATEVER... SOUKOU IS HIS DAUGHTER... RELDA MUST KNOW THEM... SHE MAY EVEN BE A HALF-SISTER..."
"I'VE NEVER SEEN A WOMAN WITH HORNS... LOOKS NETHERWORLDISH... THAT WOULD EXPLAIN A GREAT DEAL."

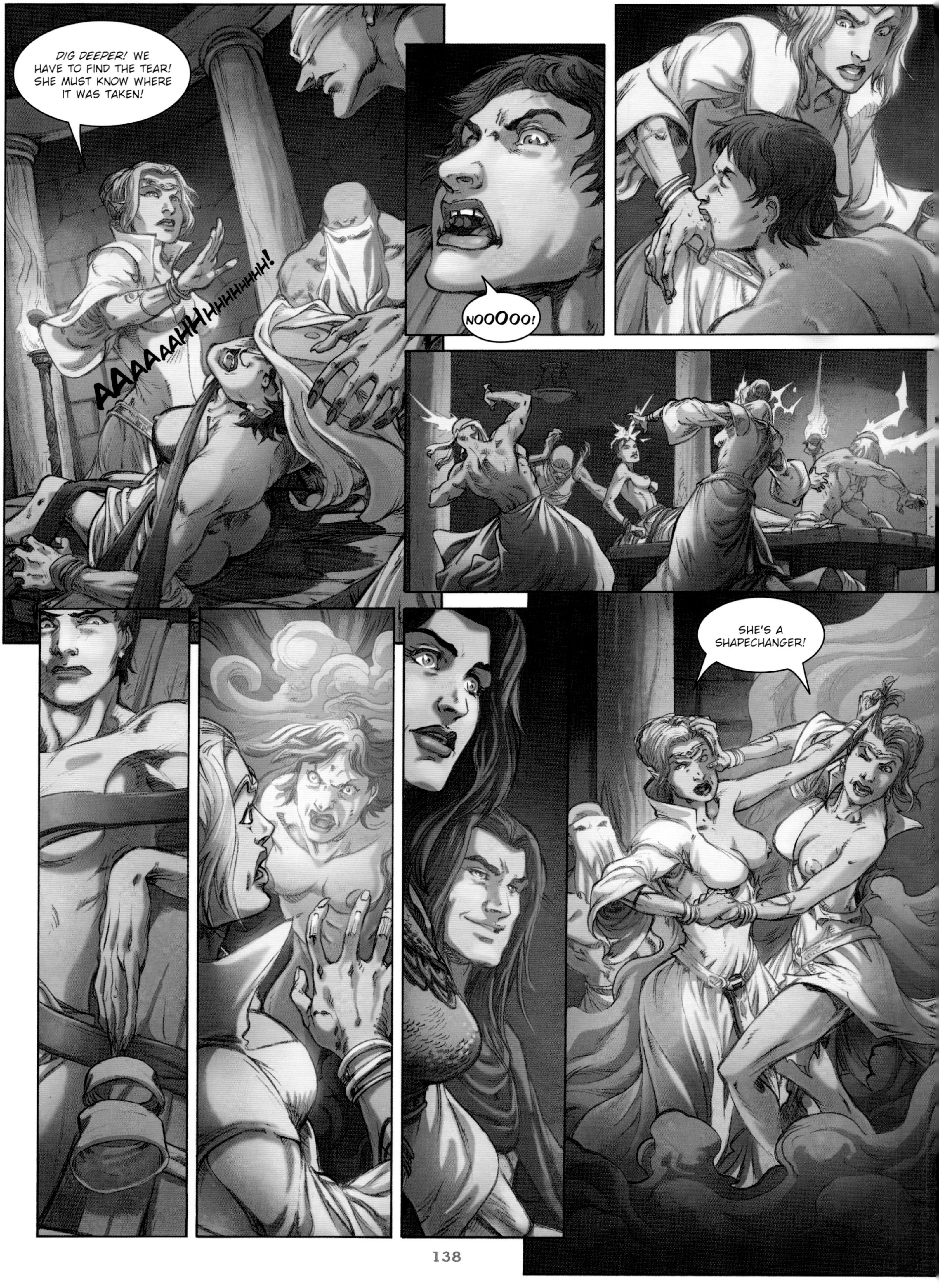
DIG DEEPER! WE HAVE TO FIND THE TEAR! SHE MUST KNOW WHERE IT WAS TAKEN!
AAAAAAHHHHHHHHH!
NOOOOO!
SHE'S A SHAPECHANGER!

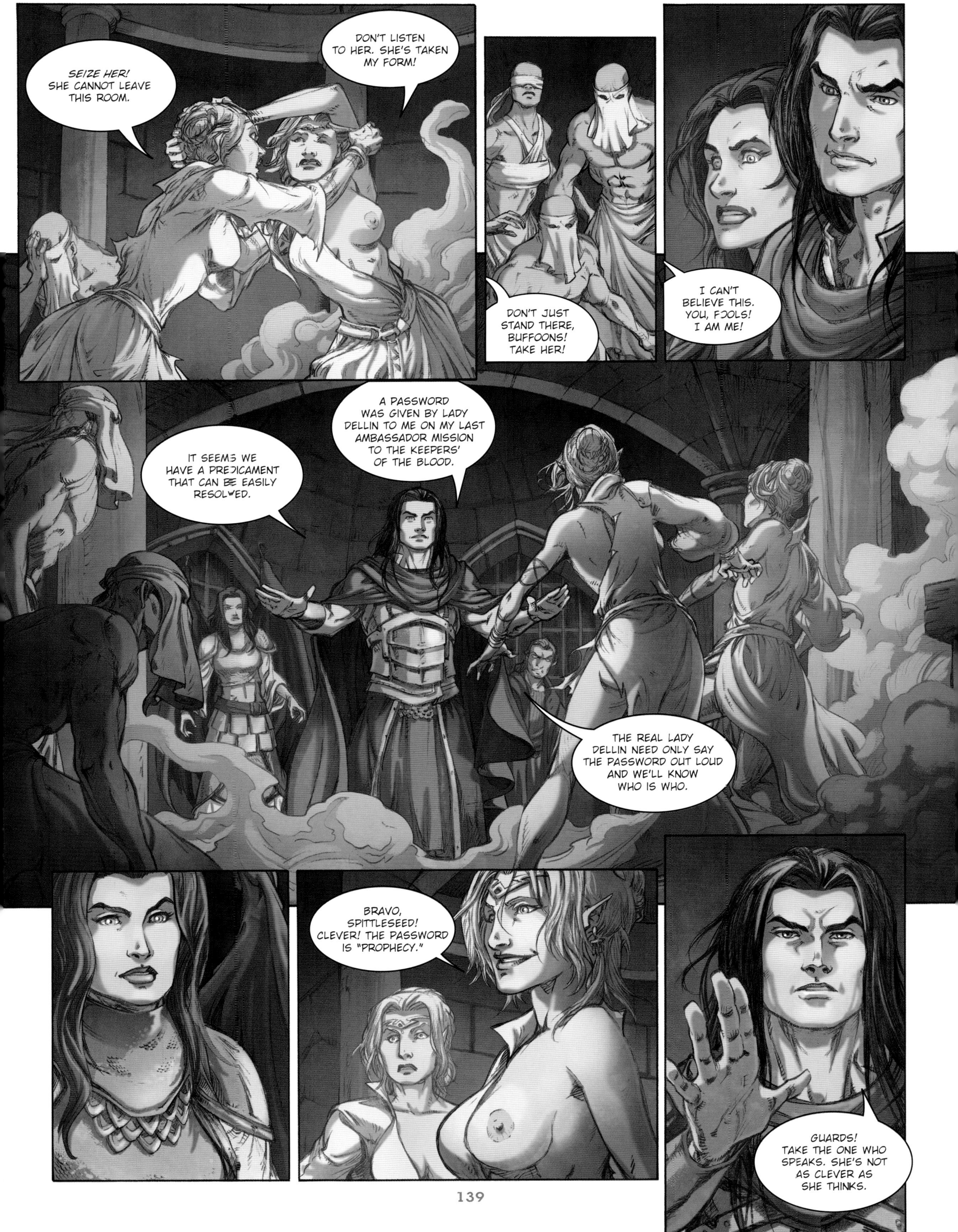

SEIZE HER! SHE CANNOT LEAVE THIS ROOM.
DON'T LISTEN TO HER. SHE'S TAKEN MY FORM!
DON'T JUST STAND THERE, BUFFOONS! TAKE HER!
I CAN'T BELIEVE THIS. YOU, FOOLS! I AM ME!
IT SEEMS WE HAVE A PREDICAMENT THAT CAN BE EASILY RESOLVED.
A PASSWORD WAS GIVEN BY LADY DELLIN TO ME ON MY LAST AMBASSADOR MISSION TO THE KEEPERS' OF THE BLOOD.
THE REAL LADY DELLIN NEED ONLY SAY THE PASSWORD OUT LOUD AND WE'LL KNOW WHO IS WHO.
BRAVO, SPITTLESEED! CLEVER! THE PASSWORD IS "PROPHECY."
GUARDS! TAKE THE ONE WHO SPEAKS. SHE'S NOT AS CLEVER AS SHE THINKS.

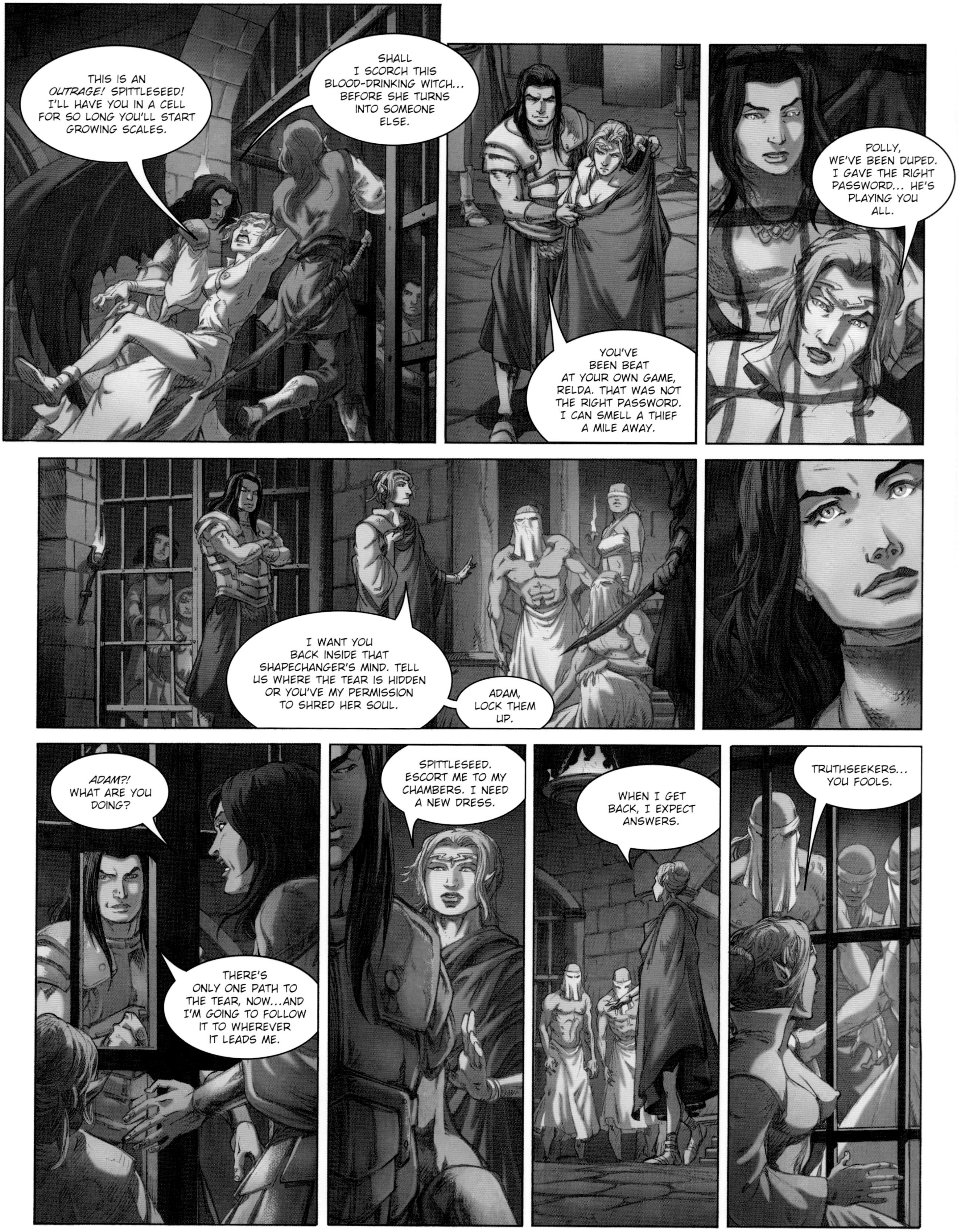
THIS IS AN *OUTRAGE!* SPITTLESEED! I'LL HAVE YOU IN A CELL FOR SO LONG YOU'LL START GROWING SCALES.
SHALL I SCORCH THIS BLOOD-DRINKING WITCH... BEFORE SHE TURNS INTO SOMEONE ELSE.
YOU'VE BEEN BEAT AT YOUR OWN GAME, RELDA. THAT WAS NOT THE RIGHT PASSWORD. I CAN SMELL A THIEF A MILE AWAY.
POLLY, WE'VE BEEN DUPED. I GAVE THE RIGHT PASSWORD... HE'S PLAYING YOU ALL.
I WANT YOU BACK INSIDE THAT SHAPECHANGER'S MIND. TELL US WHERE THE TEAR IS HIDDEN OR YOU'VE MY PERMISSION TO SHRED HER SOUL.
ADAM, LOCK THEM UP.
ADAM?! WHAT ARE YOU DOING?
THERE'S ONLY ONE PATH TO THE TEAR, NOW...AND I'M GOING TO FOLLOW IT TO WHEREVER IT LEADS ME.
SPITTLESEED. ESCORT ME TO MY CHAMBERS. I NEED A NEW DRESS.
WHEN I GET BACK, I EXPECT ANSWERS.
TRUTHSEEKERS... YOU FOOLS.

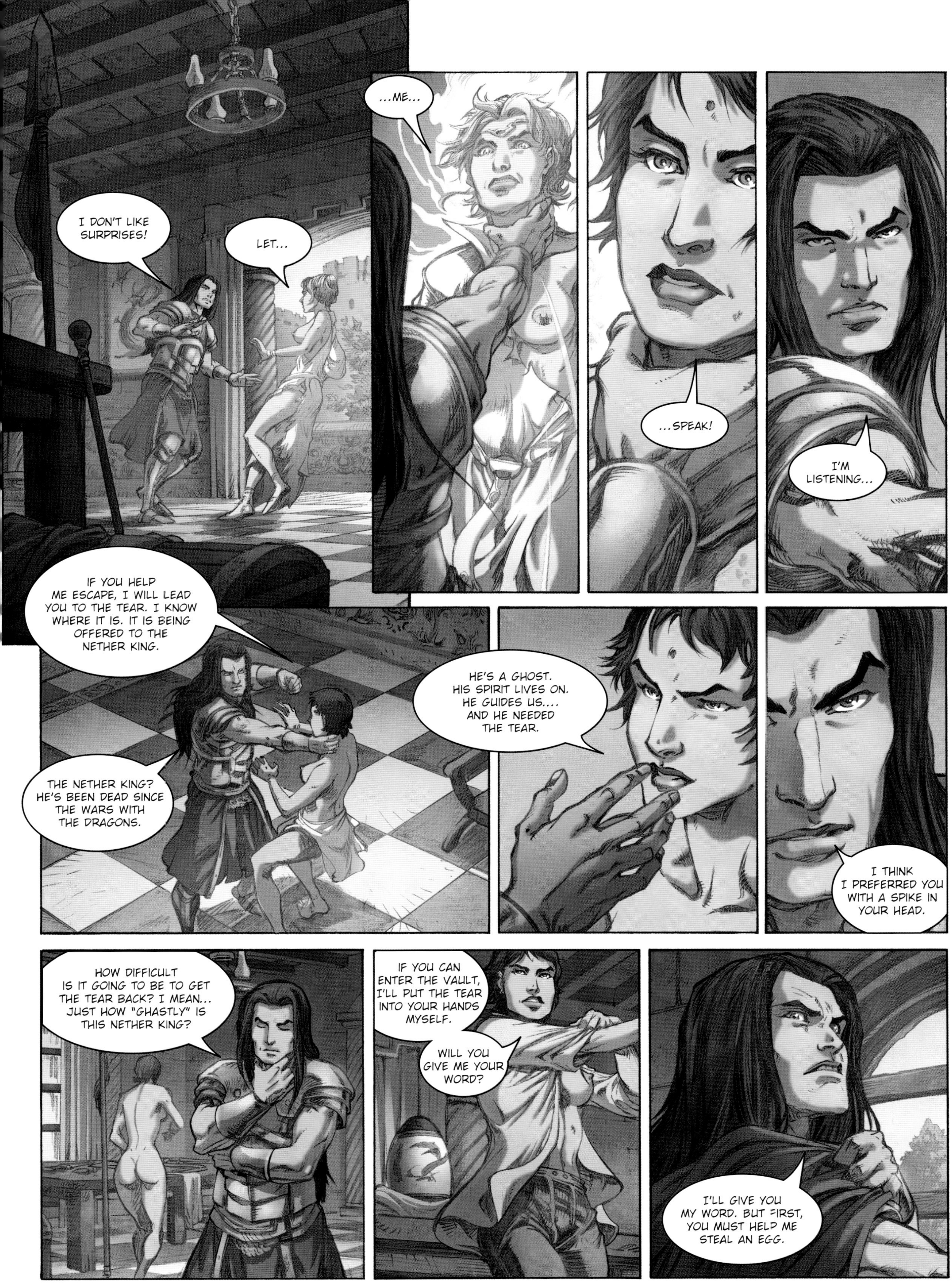
I DON'T LIKE SURPRISES!
LET...
...ME...
...SPEAK!
I'M LISTENING...
IF YOU HELP ME ESCAPE, I WILL LEAD YOU TO THE TEAR. I KNOW WHERE IT IS. IT IS BEING OFFERED TO THE NETHER KING.
THE NETHER KING? HE'S BEEN DEAD SINCE THE WARS WITH THE DRAGONS.
HE'S A GHOST. HIS SPIRIT LIVES ON. HE GUIDES US.... AND HE NEEDED THE TEAR.
I THINK I PREFERRED YOU WITH A SPIKE IN YOUR HEAD.
HOW DIFFICULT IS IT GOING TO BE TO GET THE TEAR BACK? I MEAN... JUST HOW "GHASTLY" IS THIS NETHER KING?
IF YOU CAN ENTER THE VAULT, I'LL PUT THE TEAR INTO YOUR HANDS MYSELF.
WILL YOU GIVE ME YOUR WORD?
I'LL GIVE YOU MY WORD. BUT FIRST, YOU MUST HELP ME STEAL AN EGG.

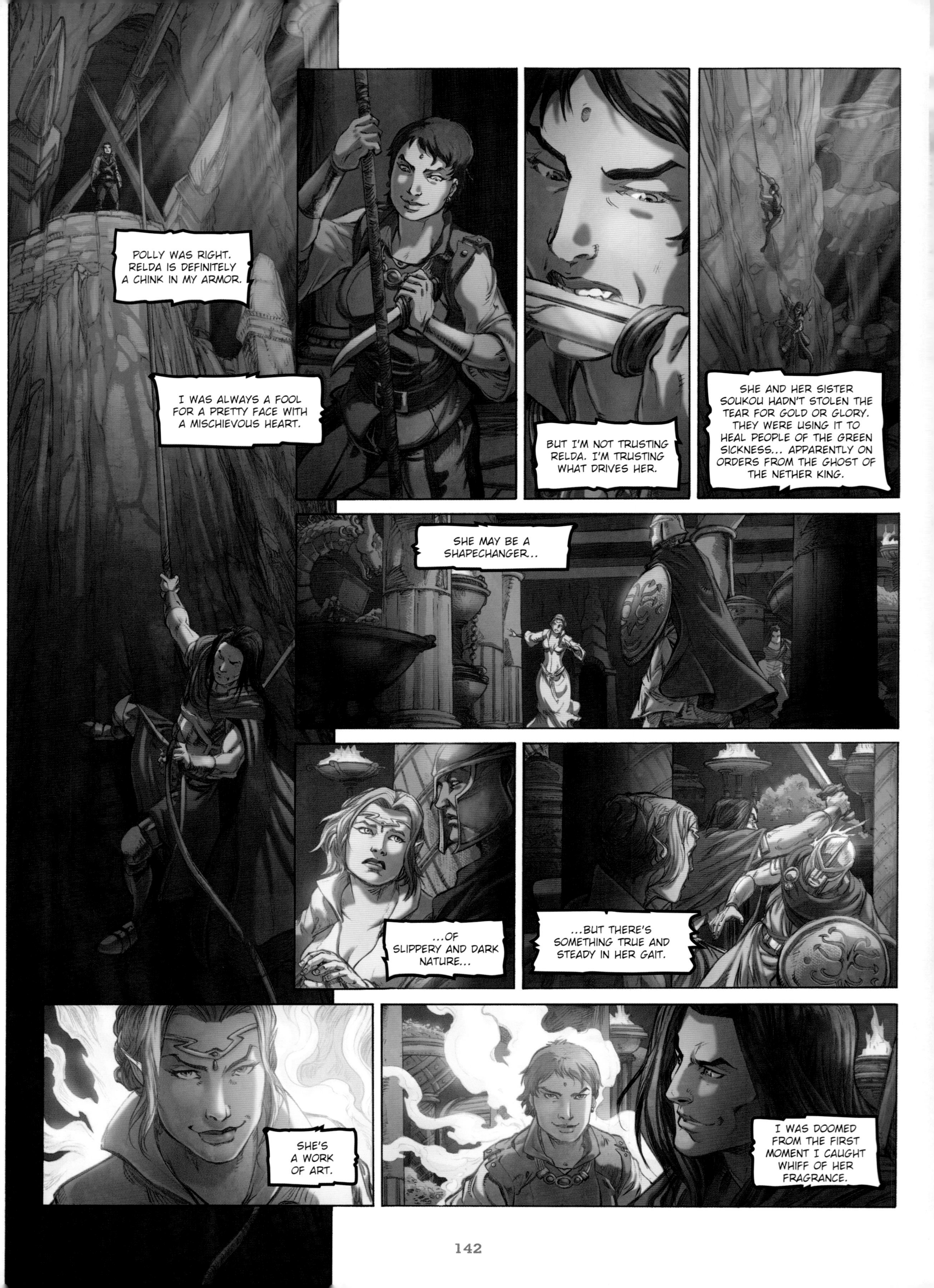
POLLY WAS RIGHT. RELDA IS DEFINITELY A CHINK IN MY ARMOR.
I WAS ALWAYS A FOOL FOR A PRETTY FACE WITH A MISCHIEVOUS HEART.
BUT I'M NOT TRUSTING RELDA. I'M TRUSTING WHAT DRIVES HER.
SHE AND HER SISTER SOUKOU HADN'T STOLEN THE TEAR FOR GOLD OR GLORY. THEY WERE USING IT TO HEAL PEOPLE OF THE GREEN SICKNESS... APPARENTLY ON ORDERS FROM THE GHOST OF THE NETHER KING.
SHE MAY BE A SHAPECHANGER..
...OF SLIPPERY AND DARK NATURE...
...BUT THERE'S SOMETHING TRUE AND STEADY IN HER GAIT.
SHE'S A WORK OF ART.
I WAS DOOMED FROM THE FIRST MOMENT I CAUGHT WHIFF OF HER FRAGRANCE.

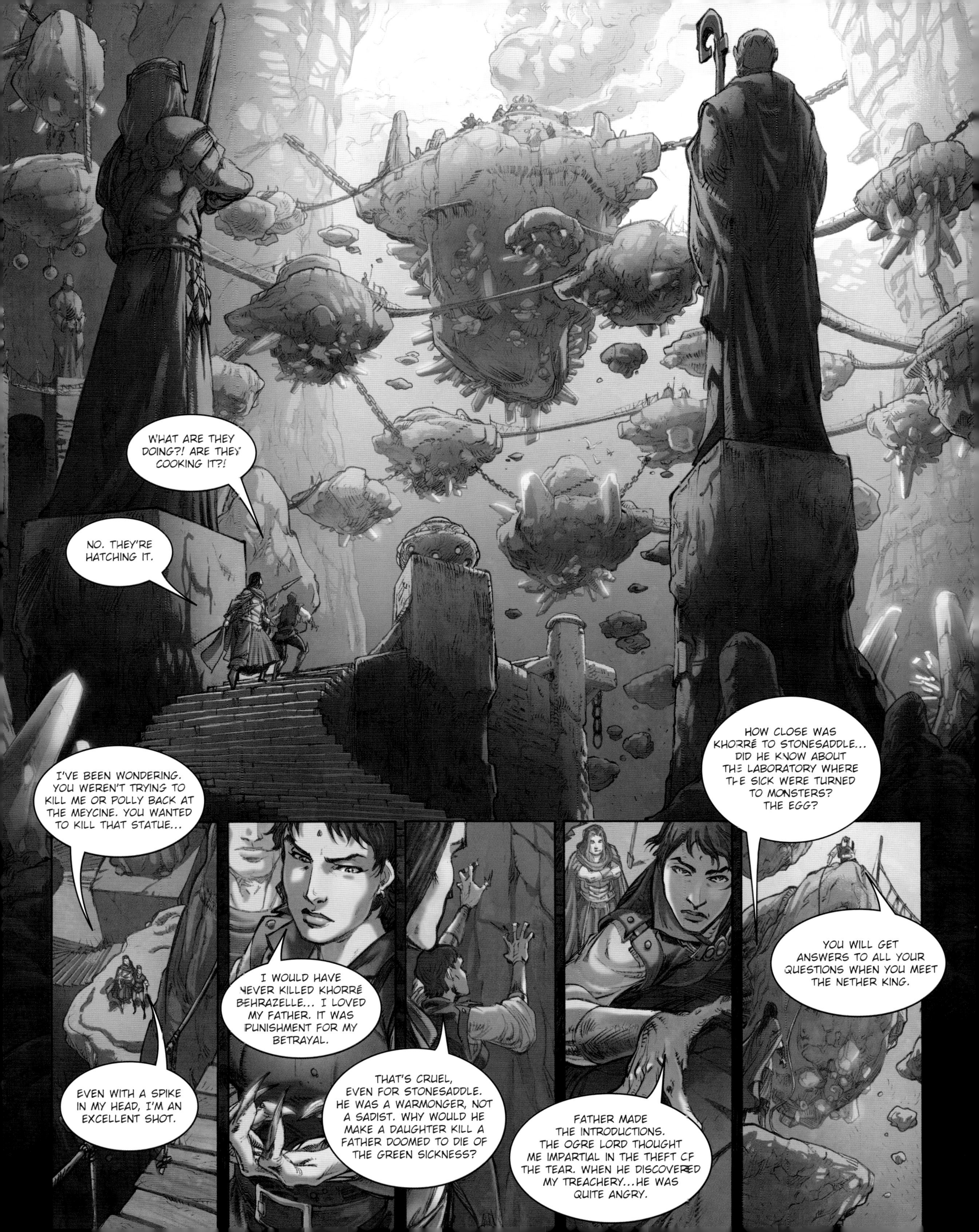
WHAT ARE THEY DOING?! ARE THEY COOKING IT?!
NO. THEY'RE HATCHING IT.
I'VE BEEN WONDERING. YOU WEREN'T TRYING TO KILL ME OR POLLY BACK AT THE MEYCINE. YOU WANTED TO KILL THAT STATUE...
EVEN WITH A SPIKE IN MY HEAD, I'M AN EXCELLENT SHOT.
I WOULD HAVE NEVER KILLED KHORRÉ BEHRAZELLE... I LOVED MY FATHER. IT WAS PUNISHMENT FOR MY BETRAYAL.
THAT'S CRUEL, EVEN FOR STONESADDLE. HE WAS A WARMONGER, NOT A SADIST. WHY WOULD HE MAKE A DAUGHTER KILL A FATHER DOOMED TO DIE OF THE GREEN SICKNESS?
FATHER MADE THE INTRODUCTIONS. THE OGRE LORD THOUGHT ME IMPARTIAL IN THE THEFT OF THE TEAR. WHEN HE DISCOVERED MY TREACHERY...HE WAS QUITE ANGRY.
HOW CLOSE WAS KHORRÉ TO STONESADDLE... DID HE KNOW ABOUT THE LABORATORY WHERE THE SICK WERE TURNED TO MONSTERS? THE EGG?
YOU WILL GET ANSWERS TO ALL YOUR QUESTIONS WHEN YOU MEET THE NETHER KING.

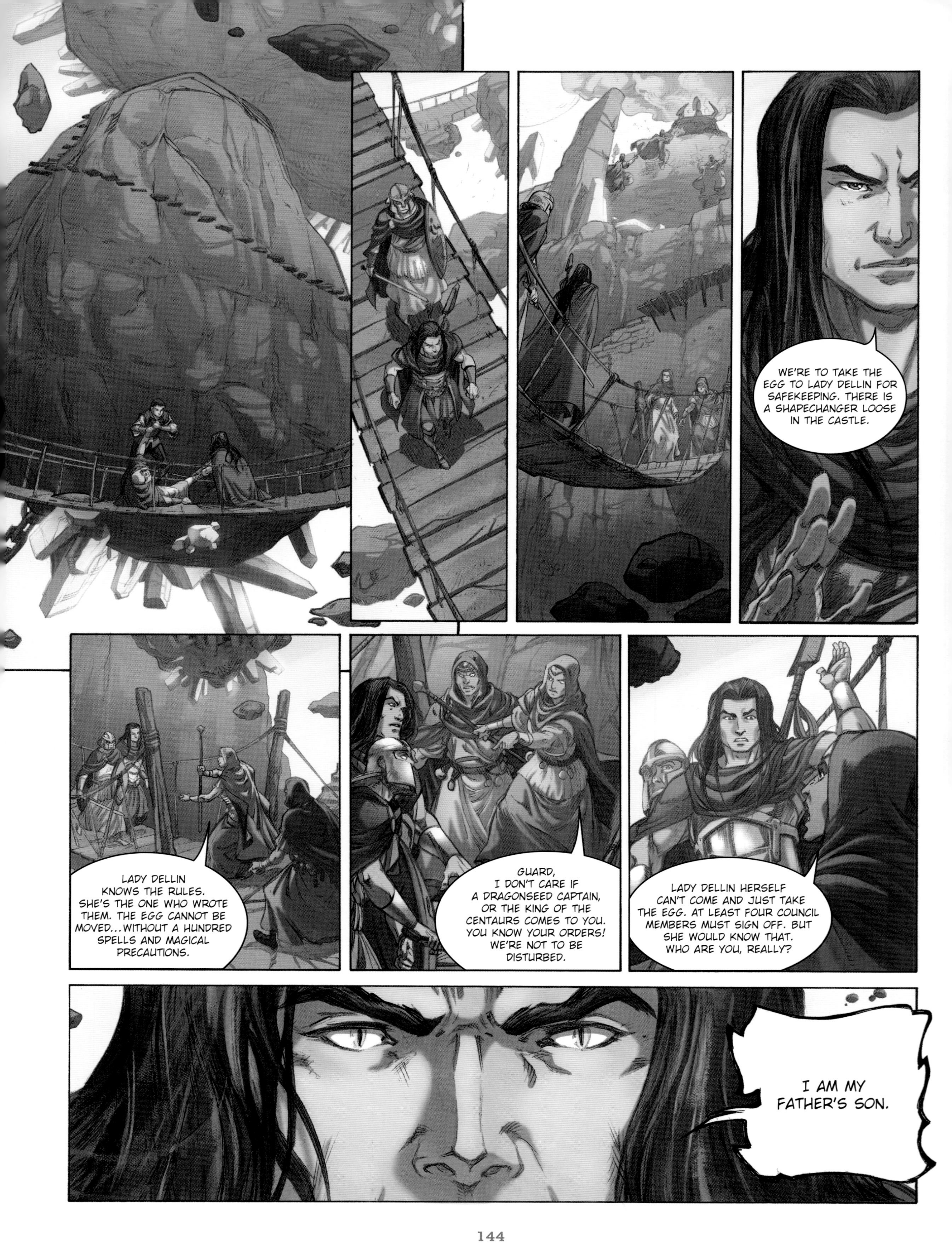
WE'RE TO TAKE THE EGG TO LADY DELLIN FOR SAFEKEEPING. THERE IS A SHAPECHANGER LOOSE IN THE CASTLE.
LADY DELLIN KNOWS THE RULES. SHE'S THE ONE WHO WROTE THEM. THE EGG CANNOT BE MOVED...WITHOUT A HUNDRED SPELLS AND MAGICAL PRECAUTIONS.
GUARD, I DON'T CARE IF A DRAGONSEED CAPTAIN, OR THE KING OF THE CENTAURS COMES TO YOU. YOU KNOW YOUR ORDERS! WE'RE NOT TO BE DISTURBED.
LADY DELLIN HERSELF CAN'T COME AND JUST TAKE THE EGG. AT LEAST FOUR COUNCIL MEMBERS MUST SIGN OFF. BUT SHE WOULD KNOW THAT. WHO ARE YOU, REALLY?
I AM MY FATHER'S SON.

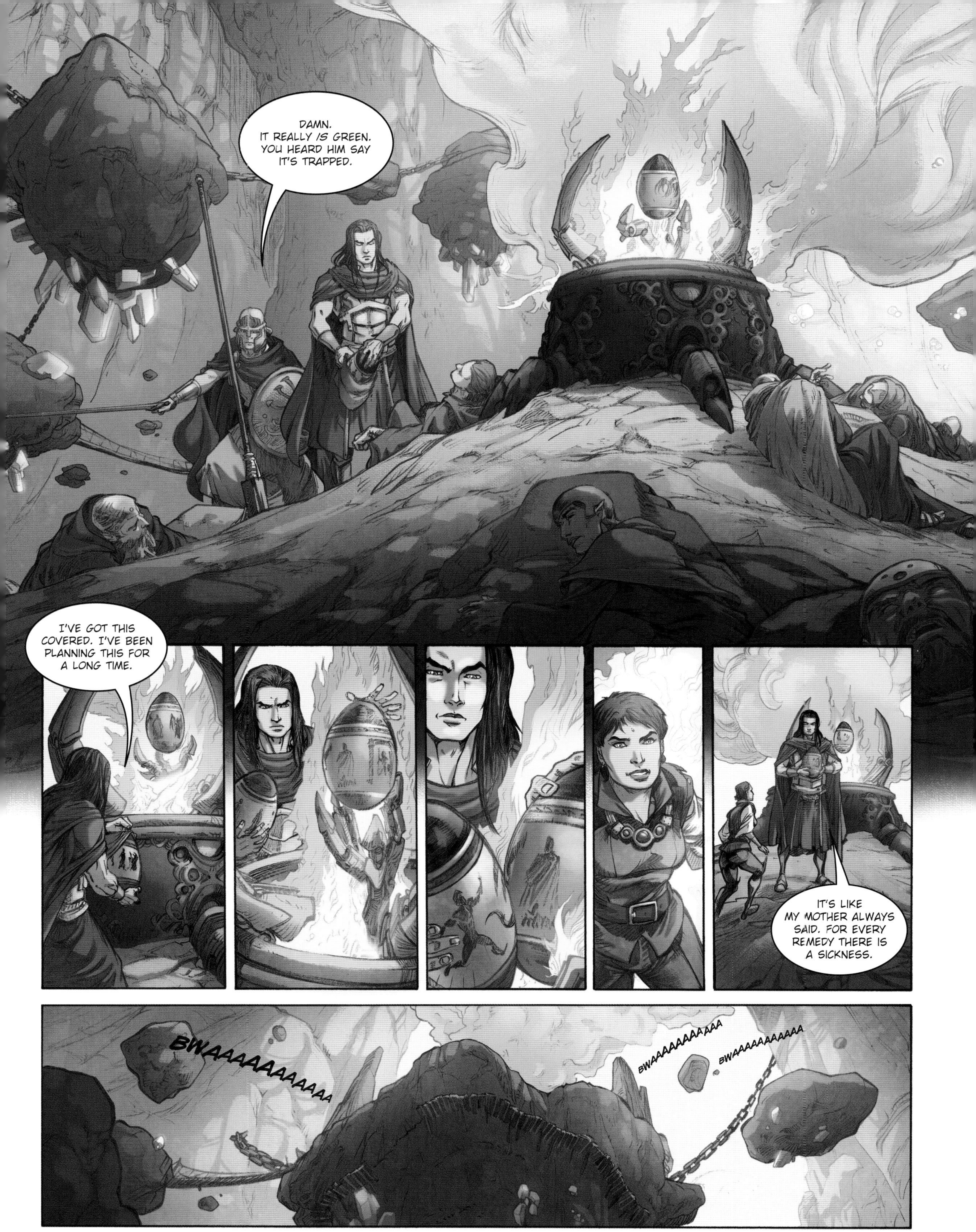
DAMN. IT REALLY IS GREEN. YOU HEARD HIM SAY IT'S TRAPPED.
I'VE GOT THIS COVERED. I'VE BEEN PLANNING THIS FOR A LONG TIME.
IT'S LIKE MY MOTHER ALWAYS SAID. FOR EVERY REMEDY THERE IS A SICKNESS.
BWAAAAAAAAAAAA
BWAAAAAAAAAAA
BWAAAAAAAAAAA

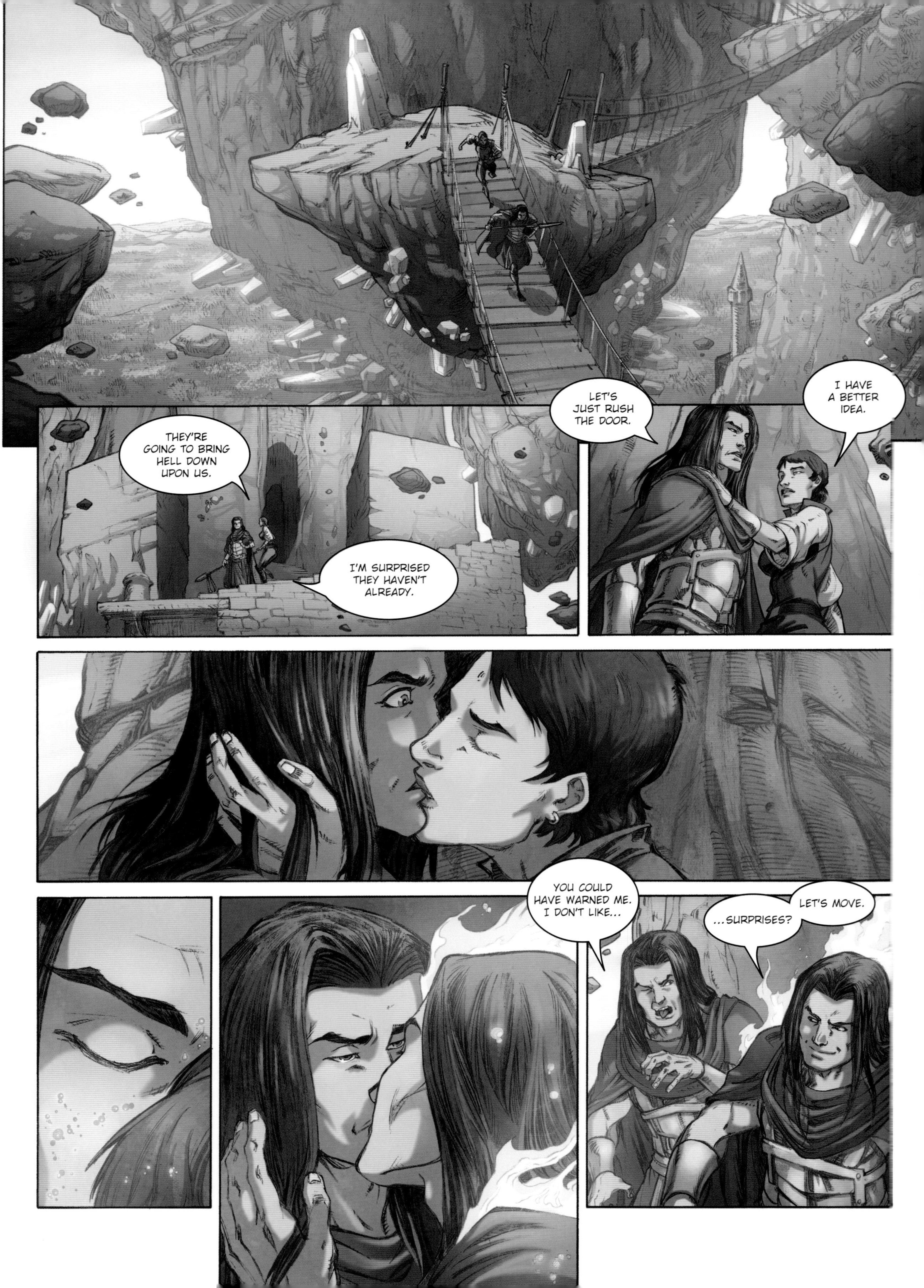
THEY'RE GOING TO BRING HELL DOWN UPON US.
I'M SURPRISED THEY HAVEN'T ALREADY.
LET'S JUST RUSH THE DOOR.
I HAVE A BETTER IDEA.
YOU COULD HAVE WARNED ME. I DON'T LIKE...
...SURPRISES?
LET'S MOVE.

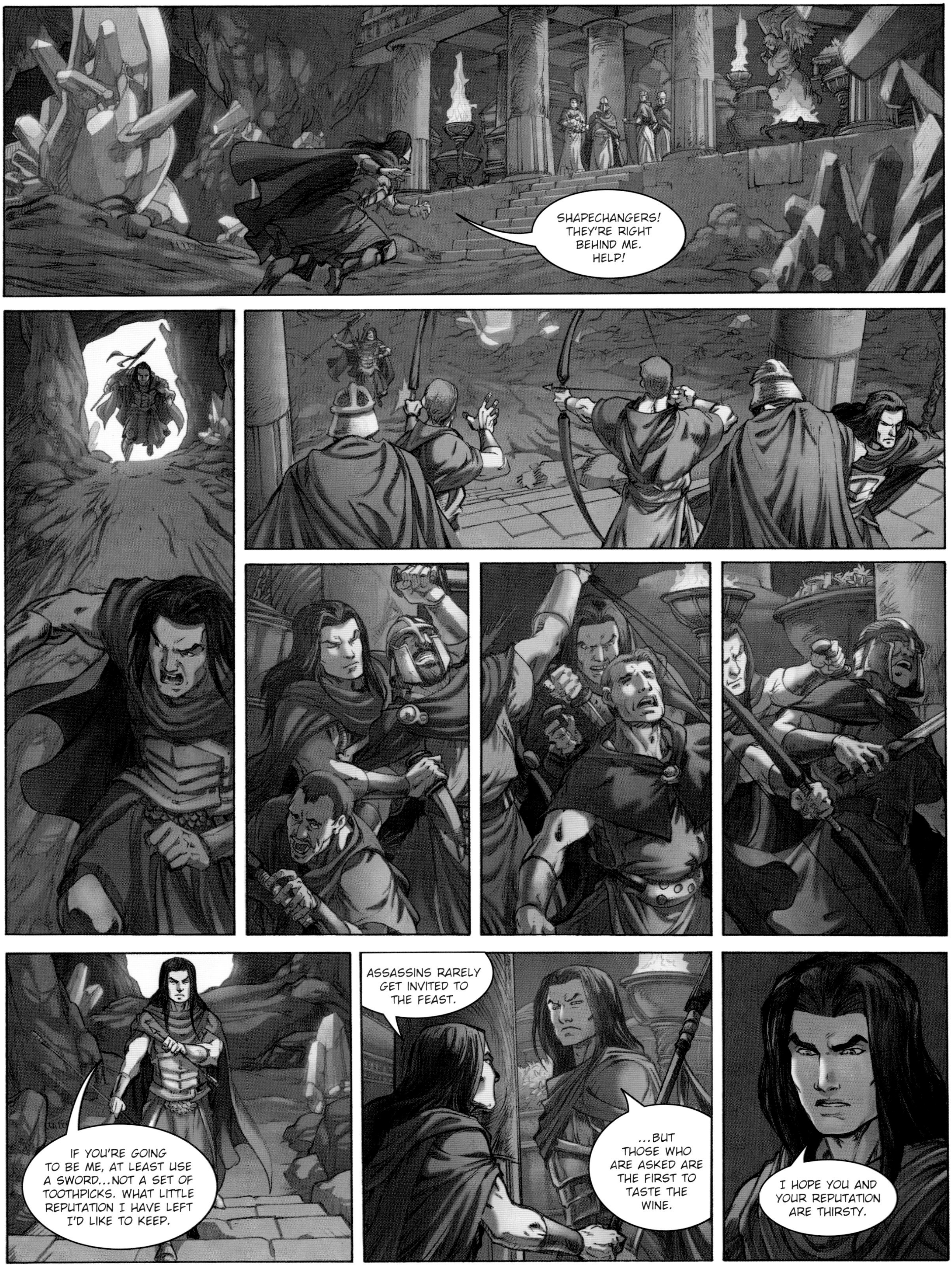
SHAPECHANGERS! THEY'RE RIGHT BEHIND ME. HELP!
IF YOU'RE GOING TO BE ME, AT LEAST USE A SWORD...NOT A SET OF TOOTHPICKS. WHAT LITTLE REPUTATION I HAVE LEFT I'D LIKE TO KEEP.
ASSASSINS RARELY GET INVITED TO THE FEAST.
...BUT THOSE WHO ARE ASKED ARE THE FIRST TO TASTE THE WINE.
I HOPE YOU AND YOUR REPUTATION ARE THIRSTY.

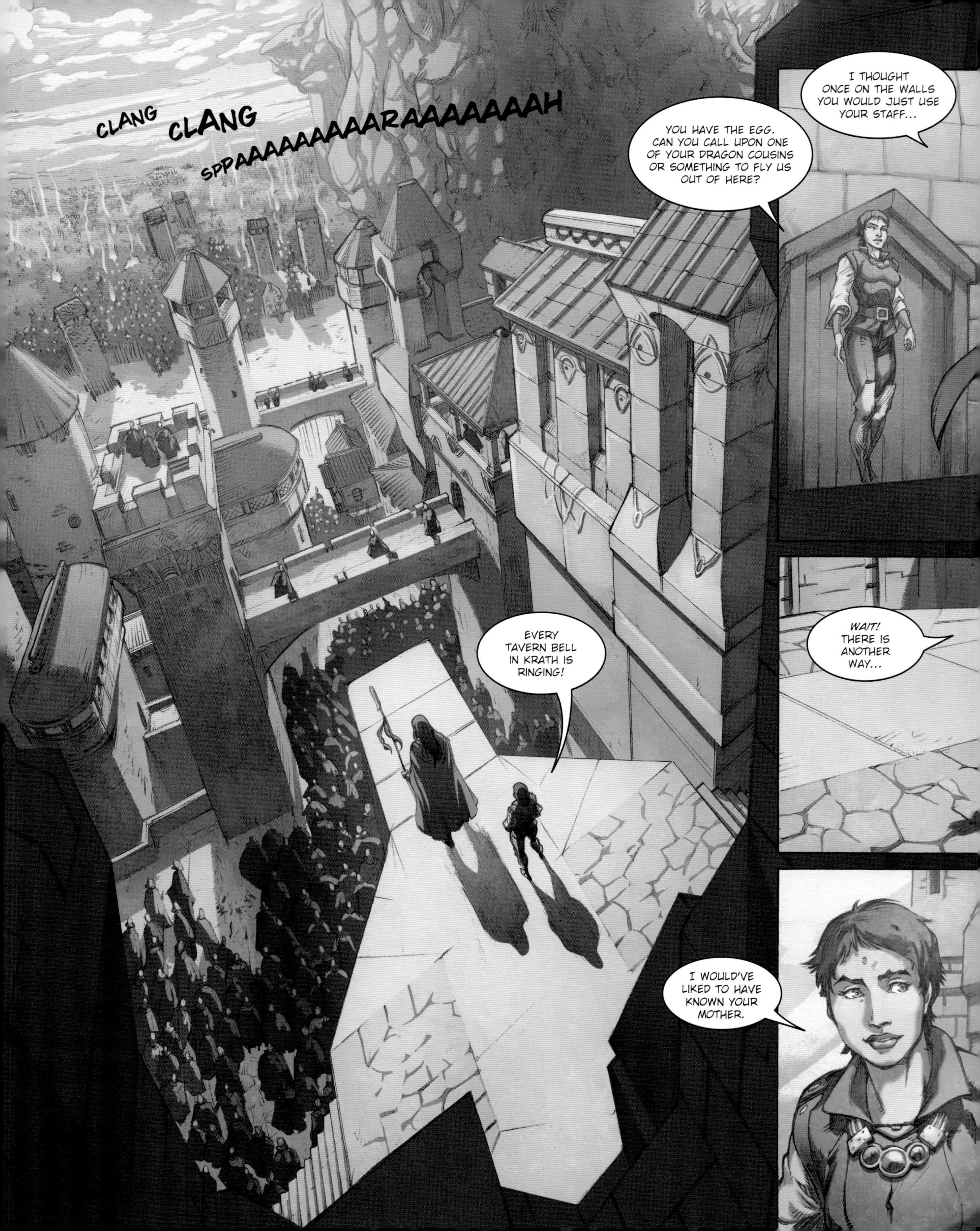
CLANG
CLANG
SPPAAAAAAAAAARAAAAAAAAH
EVERY TAVERN BELL IN KRATH IS RINGING!
YOU HAVE THE EGG. CAN YOU CALL UPON ONE OF YOUR DRAGON COUSINS OR SOMETHING TO FLY US OUT OF HERE?
I THOUGHT ONCE ON THE WALLS YOU WOULD JUST USE YOUR STAFF...
WAIT! THERE IS ANOTHER WAY...
I WOULD'VE LIKED TO HAVE KNOWN YOUR MOTHER.

I CANNOT USE A TRAVELLING SPELL ON CAPITOL MOUNTAIN.

EVERYSTONE IS IMBUED WITH CHARMS SO STRONG THAT A GATE MADE HERE COULD SEND US INTO THE TWELVE WINDS...OR WORSE.

CAN'T YOU JUST TELEPORT LIKE YOU DID BACK IN MEYCINE?

I WAS HOPING FOR ONCE WE COULD DO THIS THE EASY WAY.

...BUT YOU MUST TRUST ME.

LIKE MY MOTHER ALWAYS SAID, "WHEN CHAINS GO TO RUST, AND ROPES TO DUST, WE'VE NOTHING LEFT TO BIND BUT TRUST."

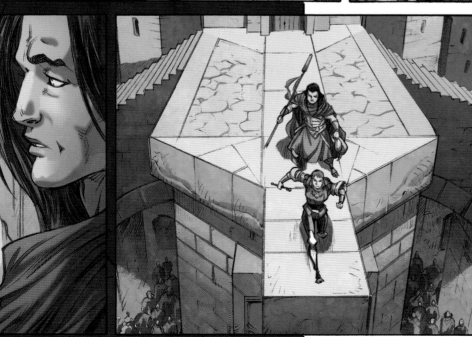

FOLLOW...

...MEEEEEE!!!

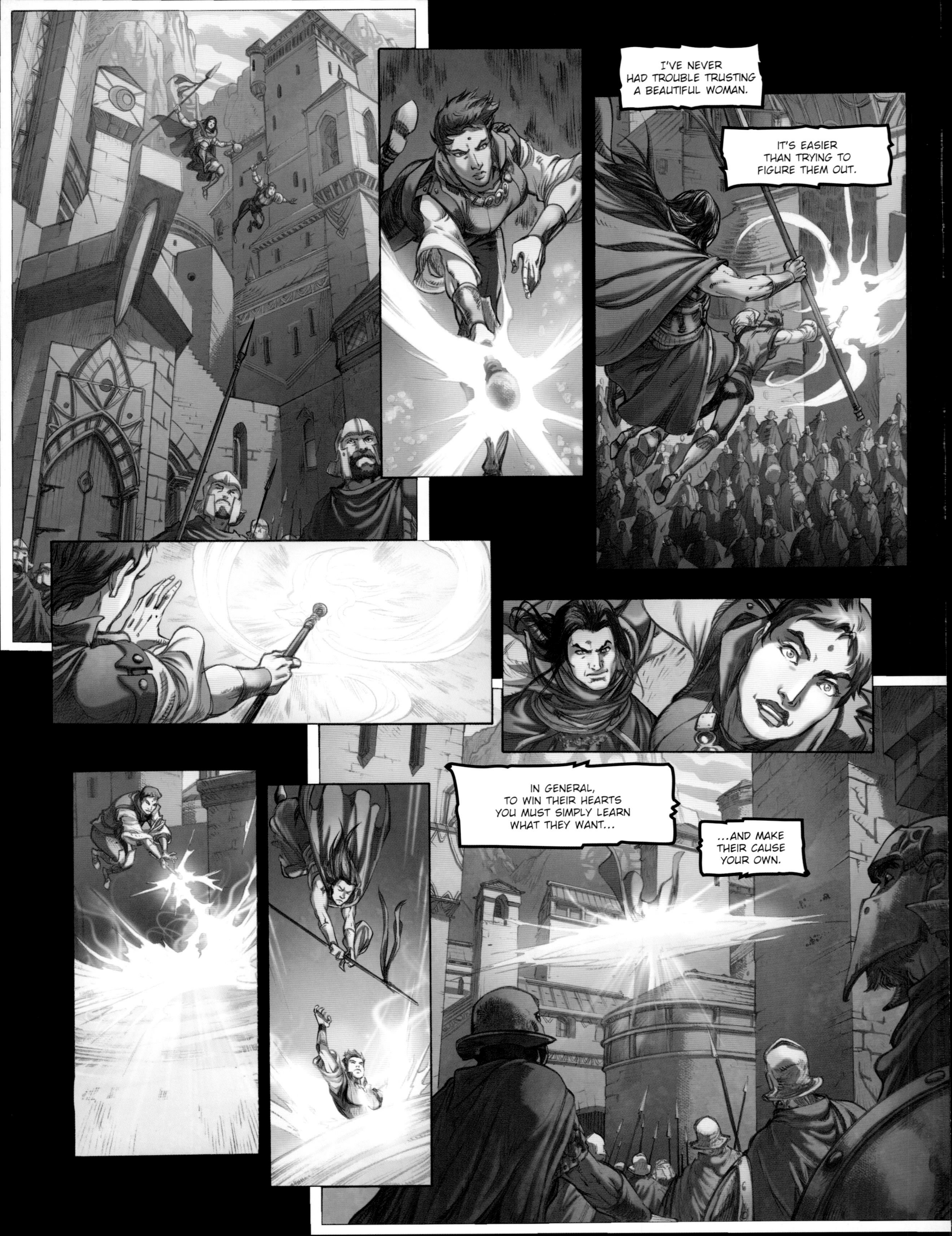
I'VE NEVER HAD TROUBLE TRUSTING A BEAUTIFUL WOMAN.
IT'S EASIER THAN TRYING TO FIGURE THEM OUT.
IN GENERAL, TO WIN THEIR HEARTS YOU MUST SIMPLY LEARN WHAT THEY WANT...
...AND MAKE THEIR CAUSE YOUR OWN.

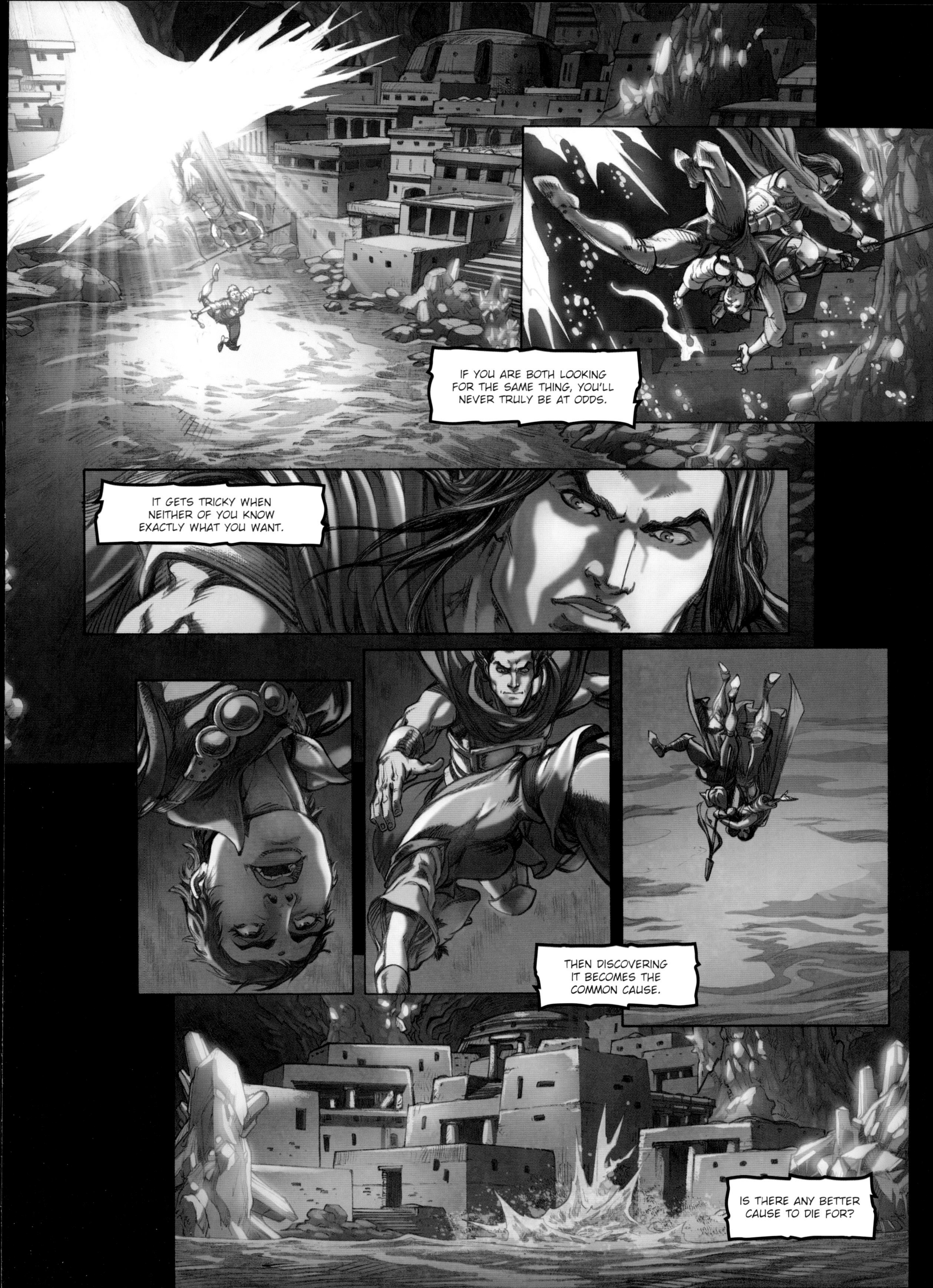
IF YOU ARE BOTH LOOKING FOR THE SAME THING, YOU'LL NEVER TRULY BE AT ODDS.
IT GETS TRICKY WHEN NEITHER OF YOU KNOW EXACTLY WHAT YOU WANT.
THEN DISCOVERING IT BECOMES THE COMMON CAUSE.
IS THERE ANY BETTER CAUSE TO DIE FOR?

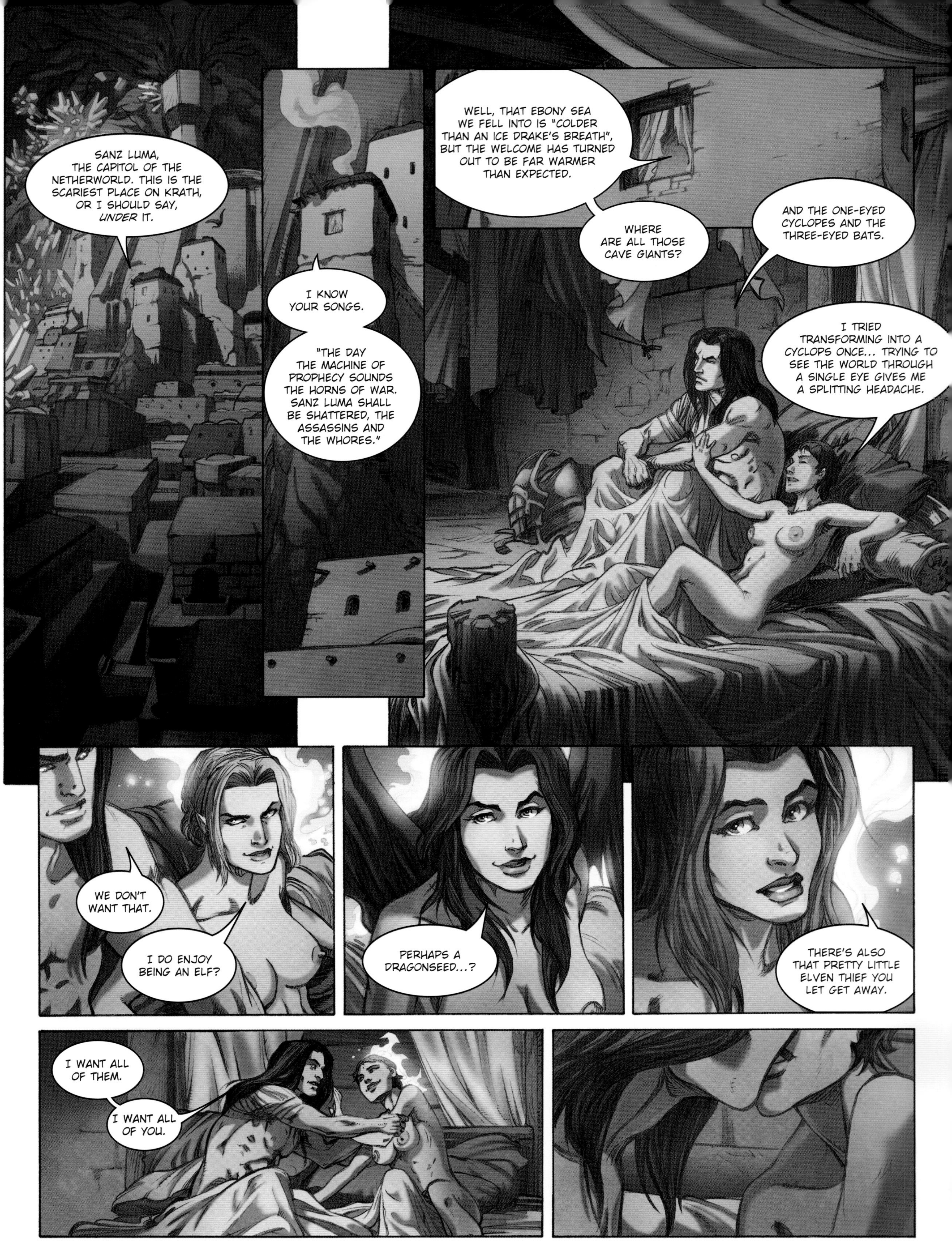
SANZ LUMA, THE CAPITOL OF THE NETHERWORLD. THIS IS THE SCARIEST PLACE ON KRATH, OR I SHOULD SAY, *UNDER* IT.
I KNOW YOUR SONGS.
"THE DAY THE MACHINE OF PROPHECY SOUNDS THE HORNS OF WAR. SANZ LUMA SHALL BE SHATTERED, THE ASSASSINS AND THE WHORES."
WELL, THAT EBONY SEA WE FELL INTO IS "COLDER THAN AN ICE DRAKE'S BREATH", BUT THE WELCOME HAS TURNED OUT TO BE FAR WARMER THAN EXPECTED.
WHERE ARE ALL THOSE CAVE GIANTS?
AND THE ONE-EYED CYCLOPES AND THE THREE-EYED BATS.
I TRIED TRANSFORMING INTO A CYCLOPS ONCE... TRYING TO SEE THE WORLD THROUGH A SINGLE EYE GIVES ME A SPLITTING HEADACHE.
WE DON'T WANT THAT.
I DO ENJOY BEING AN ELF?
PERHAPS A DRAGONSEED...?
THERE'S ALSO THAT PRETTY LITTLE ELVEN THIEF YOU LET GET AWAY.
I WANT ALL OF THEM.
I WANT ALL OF YOU.

HOW DID YOU REALLY KNOW WHICH ONE WAS ME IN THAT PRISON CELL?

YOU SMELL OF BITTERSWEET... AND ALMONDS... AND SOMETHING ELSE. I WOULD KNOW YOUR SMELL ANYWHERE. THE BETTER QUESTION WOULD BE, "WHY DID I LET YOU GO?"

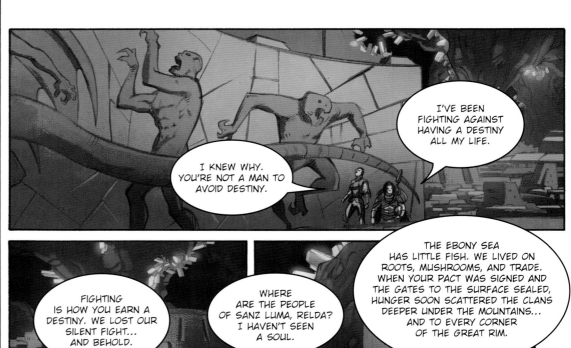

I KNEW WHY. YOU'RE NOT A MAN TO AVOID DESTINY.

I'VE BEEN FIGHTING AGAINST HAVING A DESTINY ALL MY LIFE.

FIGHTING IS HOW YOU EARN A DESTINY. WE LOST OUR SILENT FIGHT... AND BEHOLD.

WHERE ARE THE PEOPLE OF SANZ LUMA, RELDA? I HAVEN'T SEEN A SOUL.

THE EBONY SEA HAS LITTLE FISH. WE LIVED ON ROOTS, MUSHROOMS, AND TRADE. WHEN YOUR PACT WAS SIGNED AND THE GATES TO THE SURFACE SEALED, HUNGER SOON SCATTERED THE CLANS DEEPER UNDER THE MOUNTAINS... AND TO EVERY CORNER OF THE GREAT RIM.

THOSE OF US WHO COULD MOVED UP INTO THE LIGHT, INFILTRATING YOUR MASSES, DISGUISED AS ORDINARY PEOPLE.

MY FAMILY HAS BEEN LIVING ON THE SURFACE OF KRATH FOR FIVE GENERATIONS.

"...LIKE STOUT DRINK CHEERILY FLOWING INTO AN EARLY GRAVE."

"THEY KNEW WAR'S GLORIES LED TO MADNESS, AND STILL THEY CRAVED IT..."

I, TOO, AM FOND OF THE SHADOW SONNETS.

THIS IS YOUR LAST CHANCE TO TURN BACK, ADAM. YOUR LIFE DOES NOT NEED TO END LIKE SOME HERO OF THE DARK POEMS.

I CAN FIND US PASSAGE ON A SHIP TO CROSS THE EBONY SEA. THERE ARE OTHER REALMS AND OTHER WORLDS...

...AND OTHER WARS.

YOU CAN'T OUTRUN YOUR OWN SHADOW. TAKE ME TO THE NETHER KING.

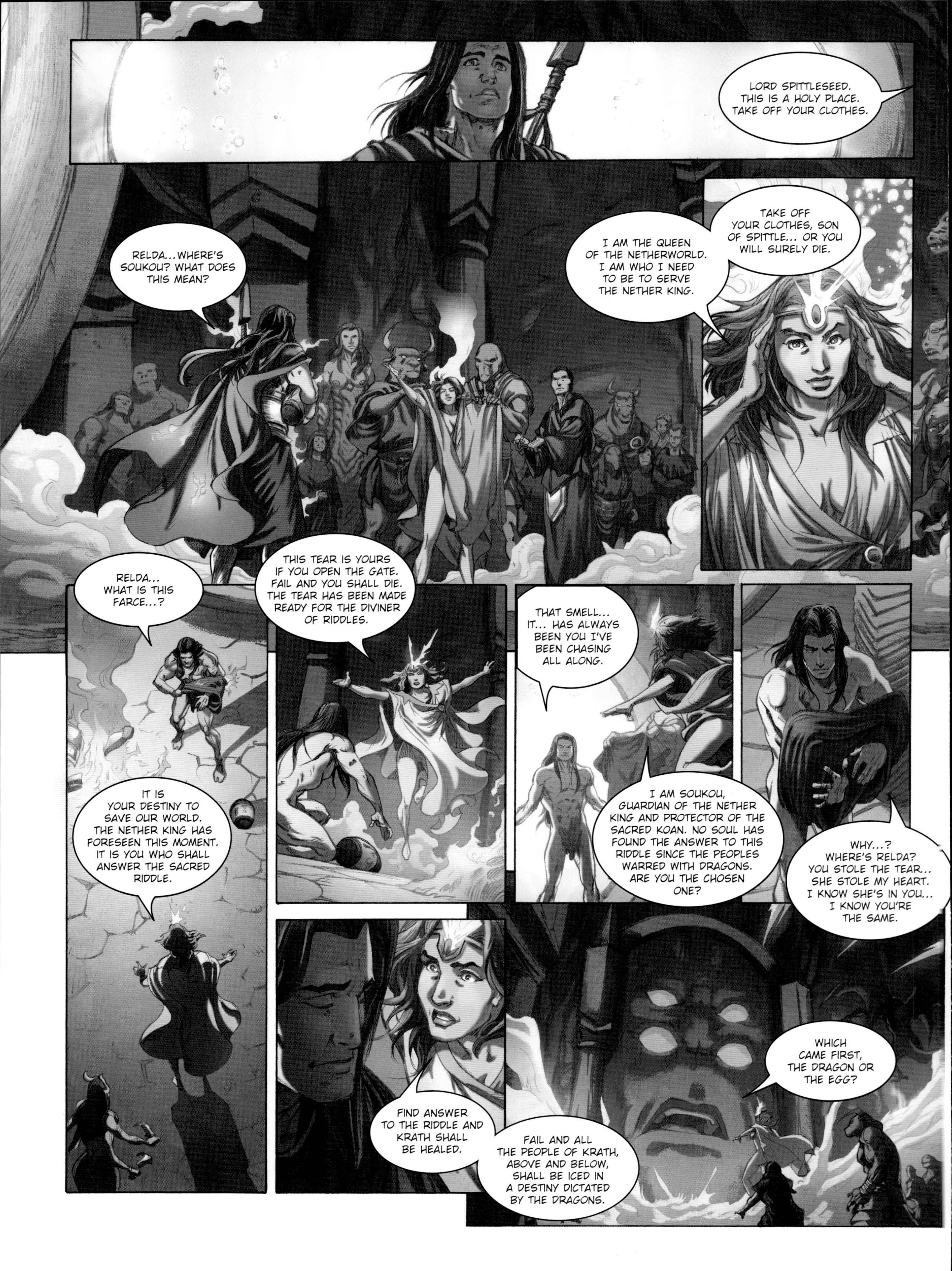

LORD SPITTLESEED. THIS IS A HOLY PLACE. TAKE OFF YOUR CLOTHES.
RELDA...WHERE'S SOUKOU? WHAT DOES THIS MEAN?
I AM THE QUEEN OF THE NETHERWORLD. I AM WHO I NEED TO BE TO SERVE THE NETHER KING.
TAKE OFF YOUR CLOTHES, SON OF SPITTLE... OR YOU WILL SURELY DIE.
RELDA... WHAT IS THIS FARCE...?
IT IS YOUR DESTINY TO SAVE OUR WORLD. THE NETHER KING HAS FORESEEN THIS MOMENT. IT IS YOU WHO SHALL ANSWER THE SACRED RIDDLE.
THIS TEAR IS YOURS IF YOU OPEN THE GATE. FAIL AND YOU SHALL DIE. THE TEAR HAS BEEN MADE READY FOR THE DIVINER OF RIDDLES.
THAT SMELL... IT... HAS ALWAYS BEEN YOU I'VE BEEN CHASING ALL ALONG.
I AM SOUKOU, GUARDIAN OF THE NETHER KING AND PROTECTOR OF THE SACRED KOAN. NO SOUL HAS FOUND THE ANSWER TO THIS RIDDLE SINCE THE PEOPLES WARRED WITH DRAGONS. ARE YOU THE CHOSEN ONE?
WHY...? WHERE'S RELDA? YOU STOLE THE TEAR... SHE STOLE MY HEART. I KNOW SHE'S IN YOU... I KNOW YOU'RE THE SAME.
FIND ANSWER TO THE RIDDLE AND KRATH SHALL BE HEALED.
FAIL AND ALL THE PEOPLE OF KRATH, ABOVE AND BELOW, SHALL BE ICED IN A DESTINY DICTATED BY THE DRAGONS.
WHICH CAME FIRST, THE DRAGON OR THE EGG?

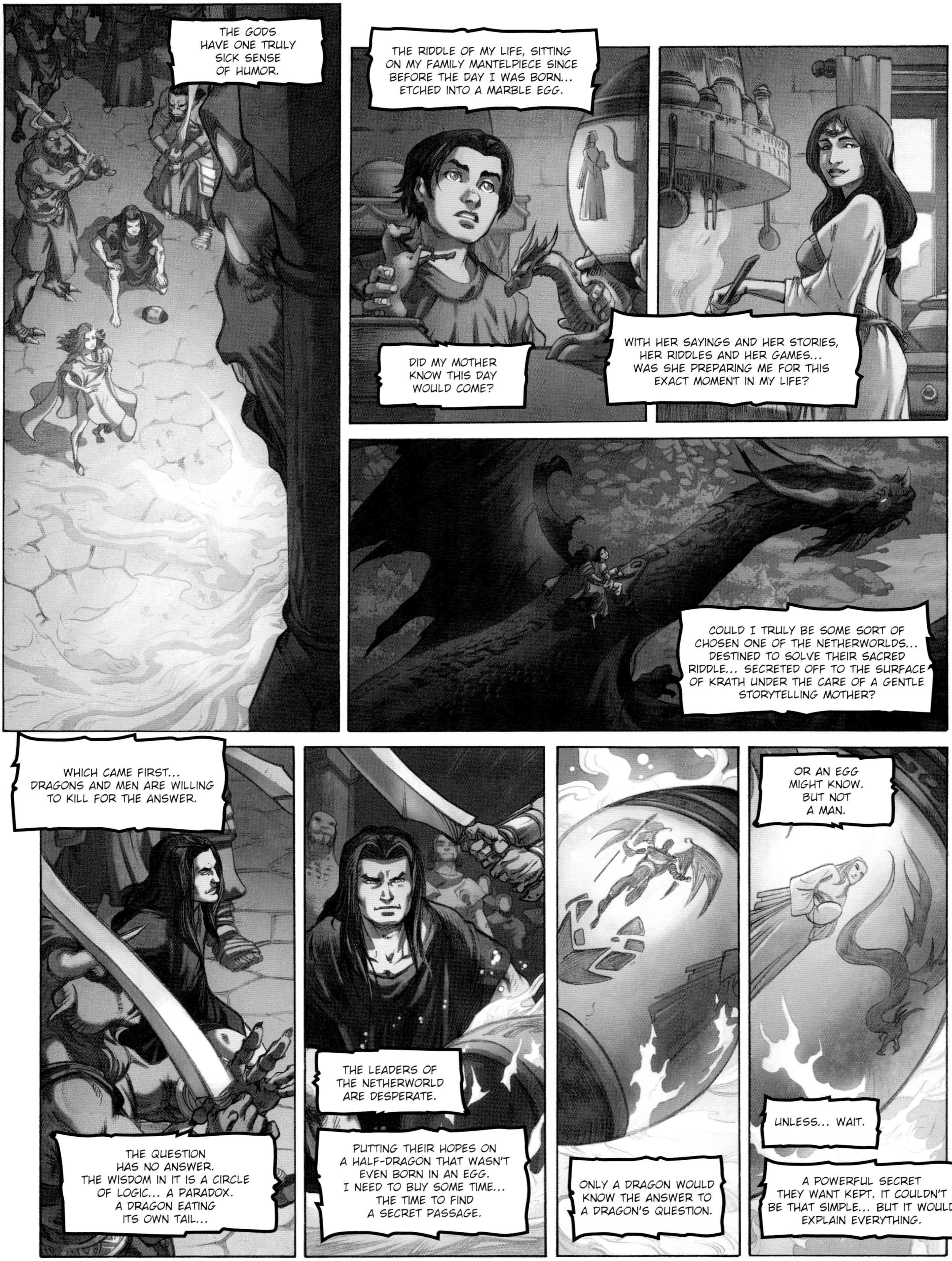
THE GODS HAVE ONE TRULY SICK SENSE OF HUMOR.
THE RIDDLE OF MY LIFE, SITTING ON MY FAMILY MANTELPIECE SINCE BEFORE THE DAY I WAS BORN... ETCHED INTO A MARBLE EGG.
DID MY MOTHER KNOW THIS DAY WOULD COME?
WITH HER SAYINGS AND HER STORIES, HER RIDDLES AND HER GAMES... WAS SHE PREPARING ME FOR THIS EXACT MOMENT IN MY LIFE?
COULD I TRULY BE SOME SORT OF CHOSEN ONE OF THE NETHERWORLDS... DESTINED TO SOLVE THEIR SACRED RIDDLE... SECRETED OFF TO THE SURFACE OF KRATH UNDER THE CARE OF A GENTLE STORYTELLING MOTHER?
WHICH CAME FIRST... DRAGONS AND MEN ARE WILLING TO KILL FOR THE ANSWER.
THE QUESTION HAS NO ANSWER. THE WISDOM IN IT IS A CIRCLE OF LOGIC... A PARADOX. A DRAGON EATING ITS OWN TAIL...
THE LEADERS OF THE NETHERWORLD ARE DESPERATE.
PUTTING THEIR HOPES ON A HALF-DRAGON THAT WASN'T EVEN BORN IN AN EGG. I NEED TO BUY SOME TIME... THE TIME TO FIND A SECRET PASSAGE.
ONLY A DRAGON WOULD KNOW THE ANSWER TO A DRAGON'S QUESTION.
OR AN EGG MIGHT KNOW. BUT NOT A MAN.
UNLESS... WAIT.
A POWERFUL SECRET THEY WANT KEPT. IT COULDN'T BE THAT SIMPLE... BUT IT WOULD EXPLAIN EVERYTHING.

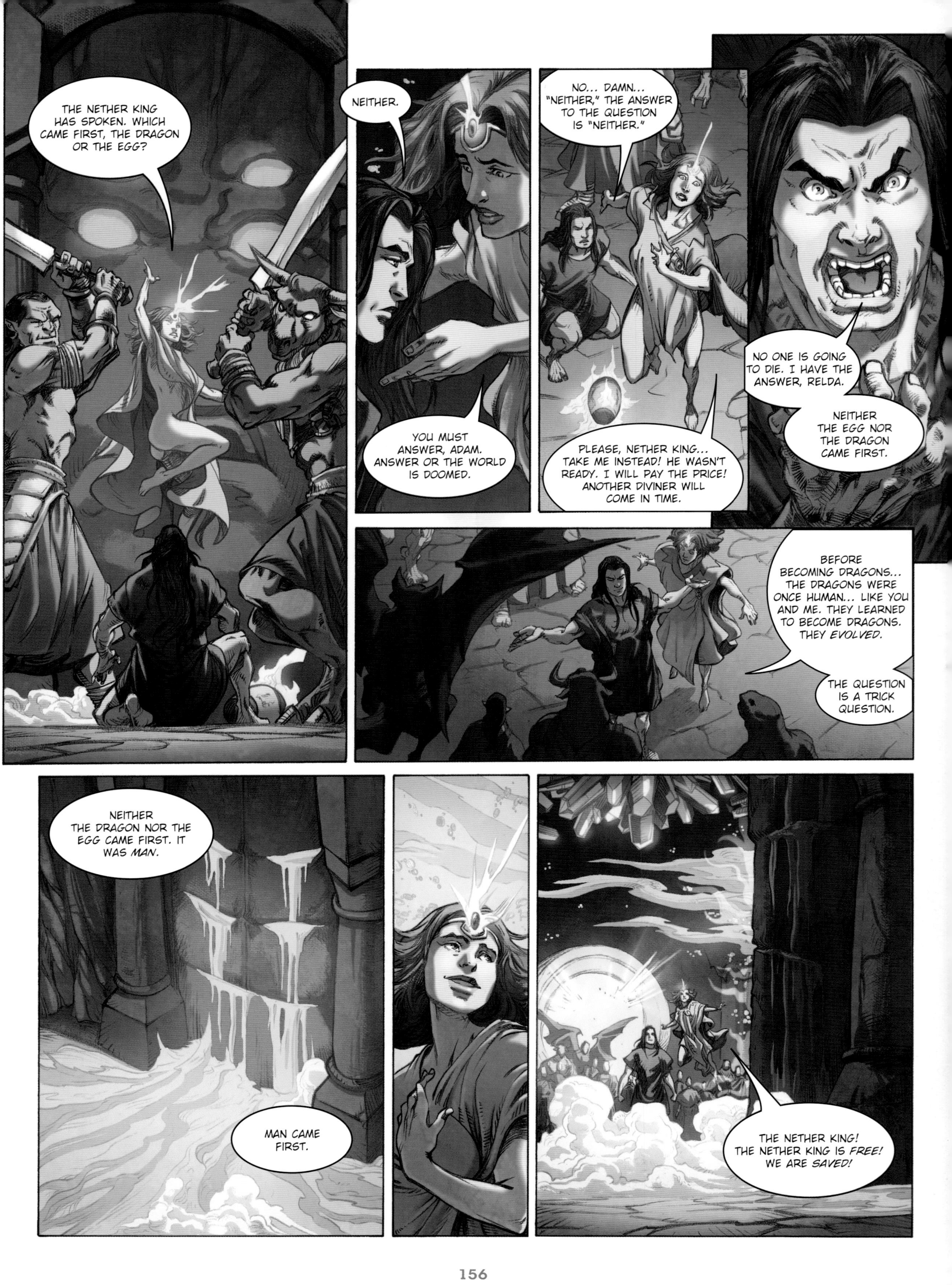
THE NETHER KING HAS SPOKEN. WHICH CAME FIRST, THE DRAGON OR THE EGG?
NEITHER.
YOU MUST ANSWER, ADAM. ANSWER OR THE WORLD IS DOOMED.
NO... DAMN... "NEITHER," THE ANSWER TO THE QUESTION IS "NEITHER."
PLEASE, NETHER KING... TAKE ME INSTEAD! HE WASN'T READY. I WILL PAY THE PRICE! ANOTHER DIVINER WILL COME IN TIME.
NO ONE IS GOING TO DIE. I HAVE THE ANSWER, RELDA.
NEITHER THE EGG NOR THE DRAGON CAME FIRST.
BEFORE BECOMING DRAGONS... THE DRAGONS WERE ONCE HUMAN... LIKE YOU AND ME. THEY LEARNED TO BECOME DRAGONS. THEY *EVOLVED*.
THE QUESTION IS A TRICK QUESTION.
NEITHER THE DRAGON NOR THE EGG CAME FIRST. IT WAS *MAN*.
MAN CAME FIRST.
THE NETHER KING! THE NETHER KING IS *FREE*! WE ARE *SAVED*!

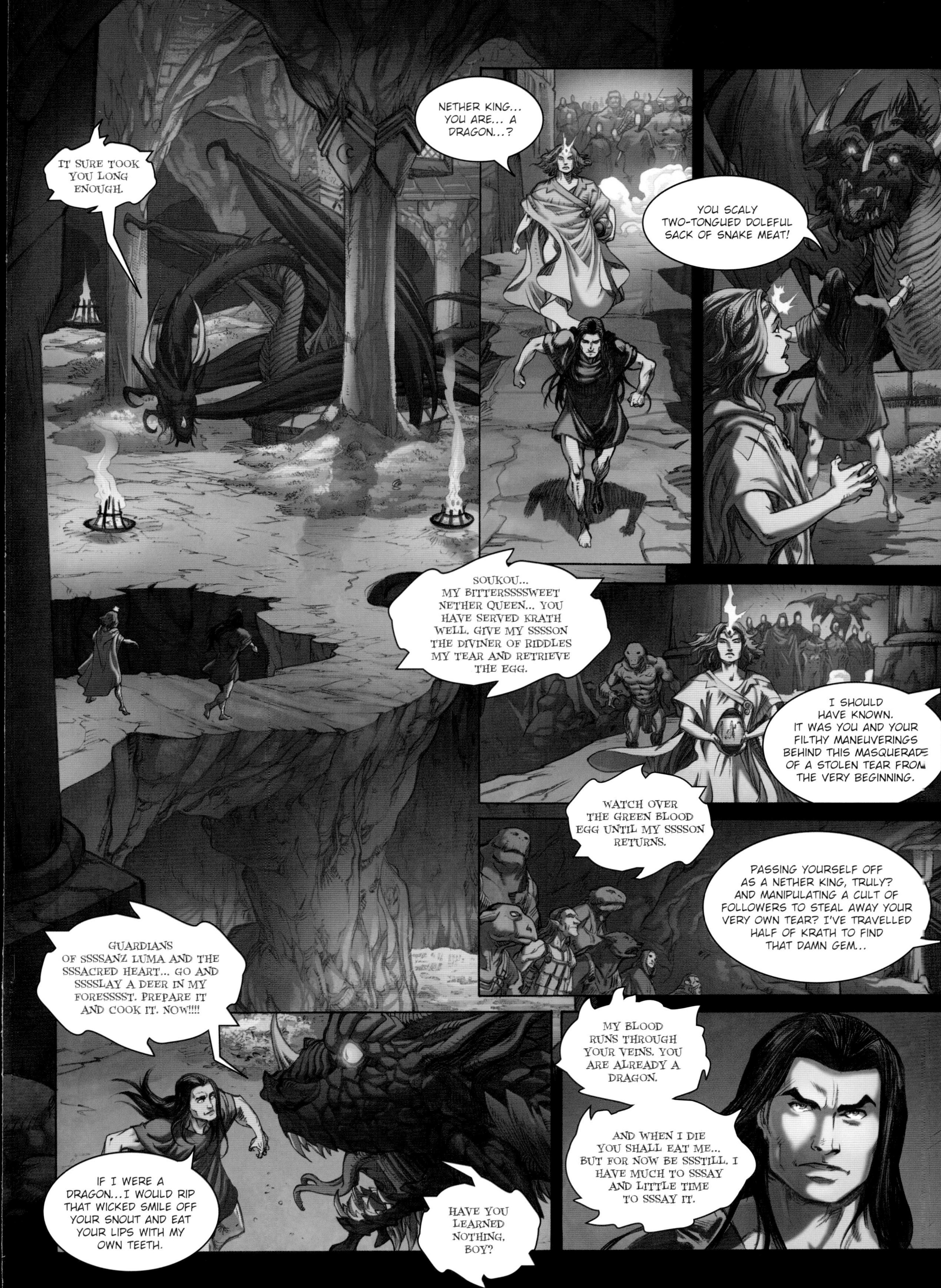

IT SURE TOOK YOU LONG ENOUGH.
NETHER KING... YOU ARE... A DRAGON...?
YOU SCALY TWO-TONGUED DOLEFUL SACK OF SNAKE MEAT!
SOUKOU... MY BITTERSSSSWEET NETHER QUEEN... YOU HAVE SERVED KRATH WELL. GIVE MY SSSSON THE DIVINER OF RIDDLES MY TEAR AND RETRIEVE THE EGG.
I SHOULD HAVE KNOWN. IT WAS YOU AND YOUR FILTHY MANEUVERINGS BEHIND THIS MASQUERADE OF A STOLEN TEAR FROM THE VERY BEGINNING.
WATCH OVER THE GREEN BLOOD EGG UNTIL MY SSSSON RETURNS.
PASSING YOURSELF OFF AS A NETHER KING, TRULY? AND MANIPULATING A CULT OF FOLLOWERS TO STEAL AWAY YOUR VERY OWN TEAR? I'VE TRAVELLED HALF OF KRATH TO FIND THAT DAMN GEM...
GUARDIANS OF SSSSANZ LUMA AND THE SSSACRED HEART... GO AND SSSSLAY A DEER IN MY FORESSSST. PREPARE IT AND COOK IT. NOW!!!!
IF I WERE A DRAGON... I WOULD RIP THAT WICKED SMILE OFF YOUR SNOUT AND EAT YOUR LIPS WITH MY OWN TEETH.
HAVE YOU LEARNED NOTHING, BOY?
MY BLOOD RUNS THROUGH YOUR VEINS. YOU ARE ALREADY A DRAGON.
AND WHEN I DIE YOU SHALL EAT ME... BUT FOR NOW BE SSSTILL. I HAVE MUCH TO SSSAY AND LITTLE TIME TO SSSAY IT.

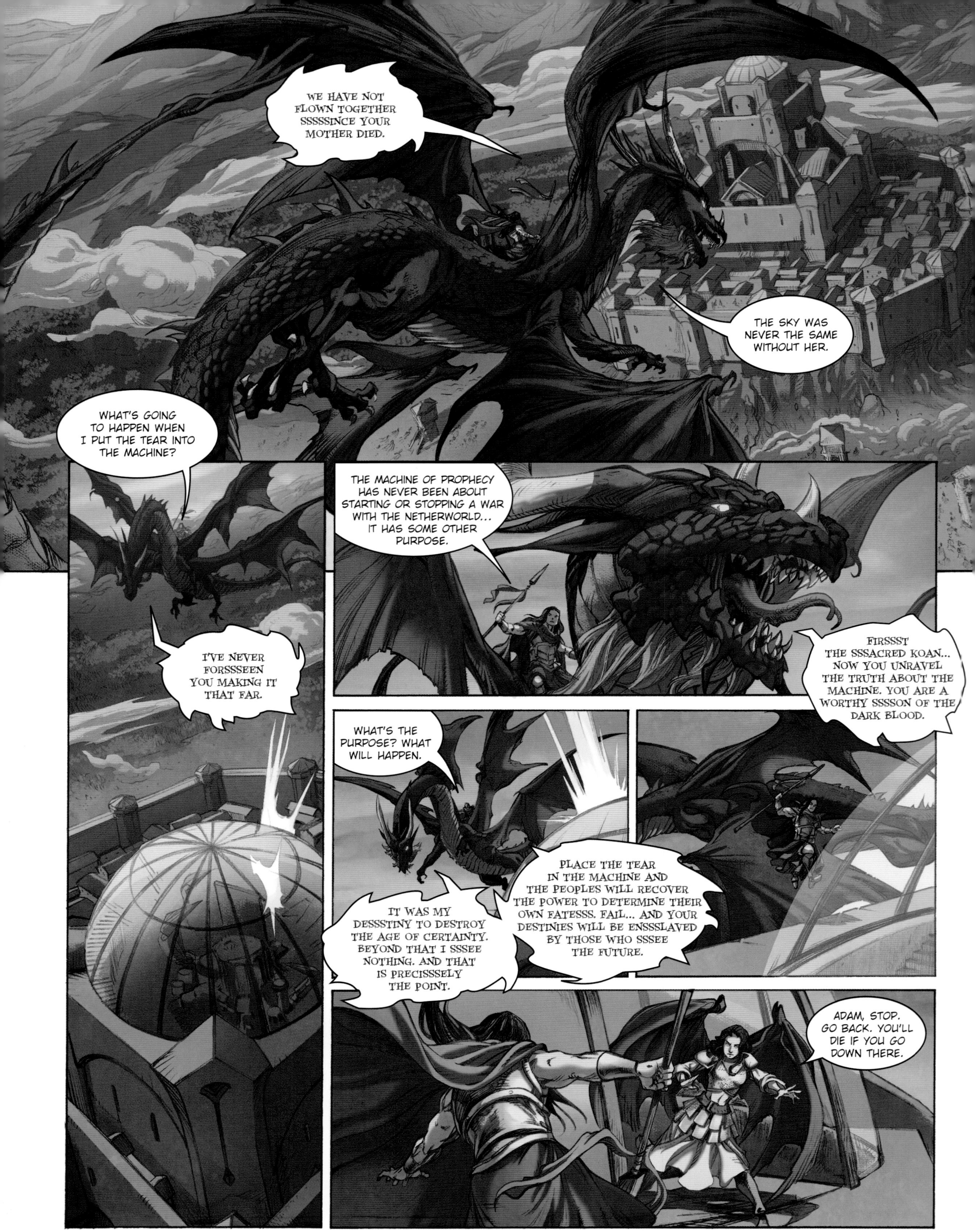

WE HAVE NOT FLOWN TOGETHER SSSSSINCE YOUR MOTHER DIED.
THE SKY WAS NEVER THE SAME WITHOUT HER.
WHAT'S GOING TO HAPPEN WHEN I PUT THE TEAR INTO THE MACHINE?
I'VE NEVER FORSSSEEN YOU MAKING IT THAT FAR.
THE MACHINE OF PROPHECY HAS NEVER BEEN ABOUT STARTING OR STOPPING A WAR WITH THE NETHERWORLD... IT HAS SOME OTHER PURPOSE.
FIRSSST THE SSSACRED KOAN... NOW YOU UNRAVEL THE TRUTH ABOUT THE MACHINE. YOU ARE A WORTHY SSSSON OF THE DARK BLOOD.
WHAT'S THE PURPOSE? WHAT WILL HAPPEN.
IT WAS MY DESSSTINY TO DESTROY THE AGE OF CERTAINTY. BEYOND THAT I SSSEE NOTHING. AND THAT IS PRECISSSELY THE POINT.
PLACE THE TEAR IN THE MACHINE AND THE PEOPLES WILL RECOVER THE POWER TO DETERMINE THEIR OWN FATESSS. FAIL... AND YOUR DESTINIES WILL BE ENSSSLAVED BY THOSE WHO SSSEE THE FUTURE.
ADAM, STOP. GO BACK. YOU'LL DIE IF YOU GO DOWN THERE.

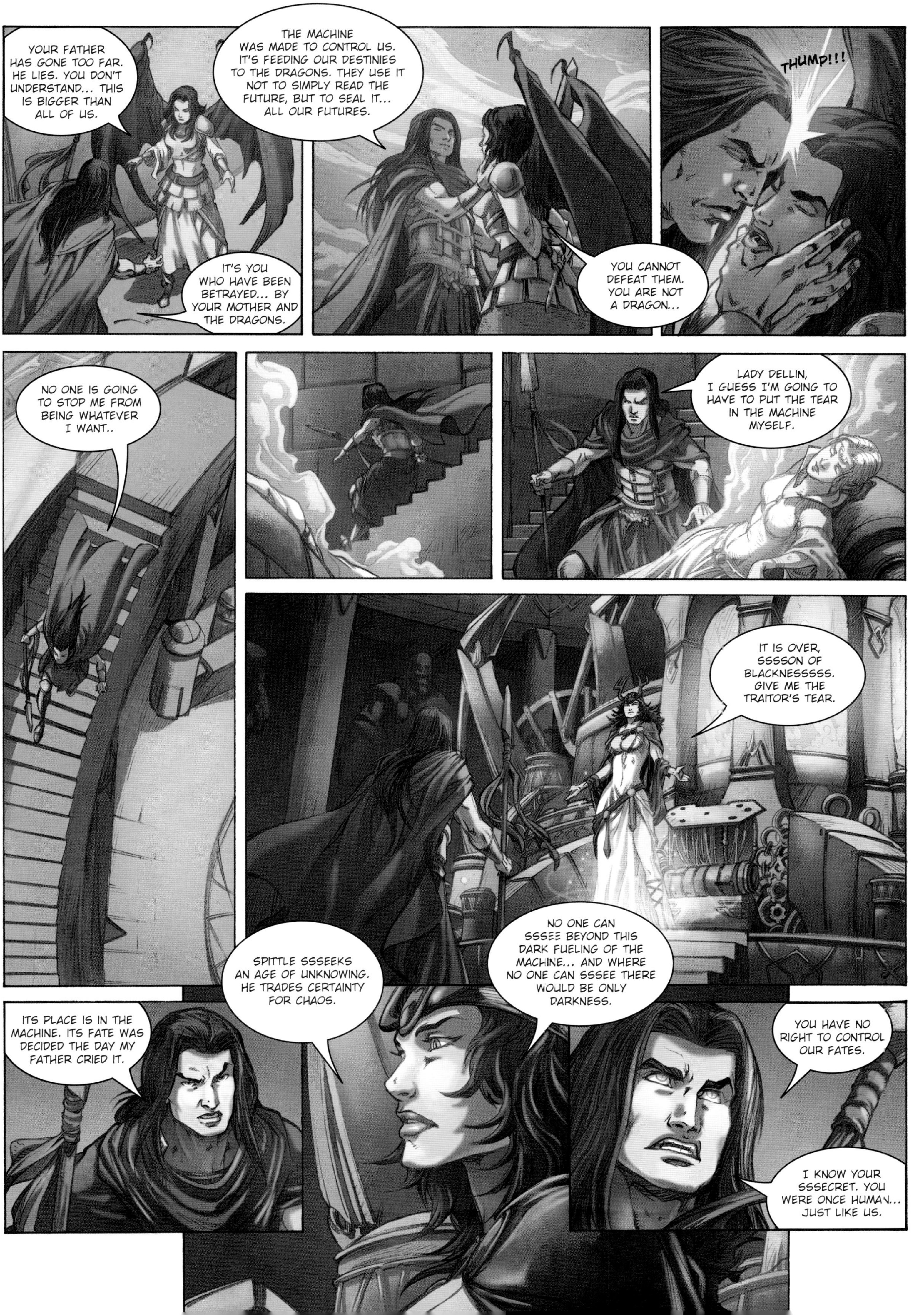

YOUR FATHER HAS GONE TOO FAR. HE LIES. YOU DON'T UNDERSTAND... THIS IS BIGGER THAN ALL OF US.
IT'S YOU WHO HAVE BEEN BETRAYED... BY YOUR MOTHER AND THE DRAGONS.
THE MACHINE WAS MADE TO CONTROL US. IT'S FEEDING OUR DESTINIES TO THE DRAGONS. THEY USE IT NOT TO SIMPLY READ THE FUTURE, BUT TO SEAL IT... ALL OUR FUTURES.
YOU CANNOT DEFEAT THEM. YOU ARE NOT A DRAGON...
THUMP!!!
NO ONE IS GOING TO STOP ME FROM BEING WHATEVER I WANT..
LADY DELLIN, I GUESS I'M GOING TO HAVE TO PUT THE TEAR IN THE MACHINE MYSELF.
IT IS OVER, SSSSON OF BLACKNESSSSS. GIVE ME THE TRAITOR'S TEAR.
ITS PLACE IS IN THE MACHINE. ITS FATE WAS DECIDED THE DAY MY FATHER CRIED IT.
SPITTLE SSSEEKS AN AGE OF UNKNOWING. HE TRADES CERTAINTY FOR CHAOS.
NO ONE CAN SSSEE BEYOND THIS DARK FUELING OF THE MACHINE... AND WHERE NO ONE CAN SSSEE THERE WOULD BE ONLY DARKNESS.
YOU HAVE NO RIGHT TO CONTROL OUR FATES.
I KNOW YOUR SSSECRET. YOU WERE ONCE HUMAN... JUST LIKE US.

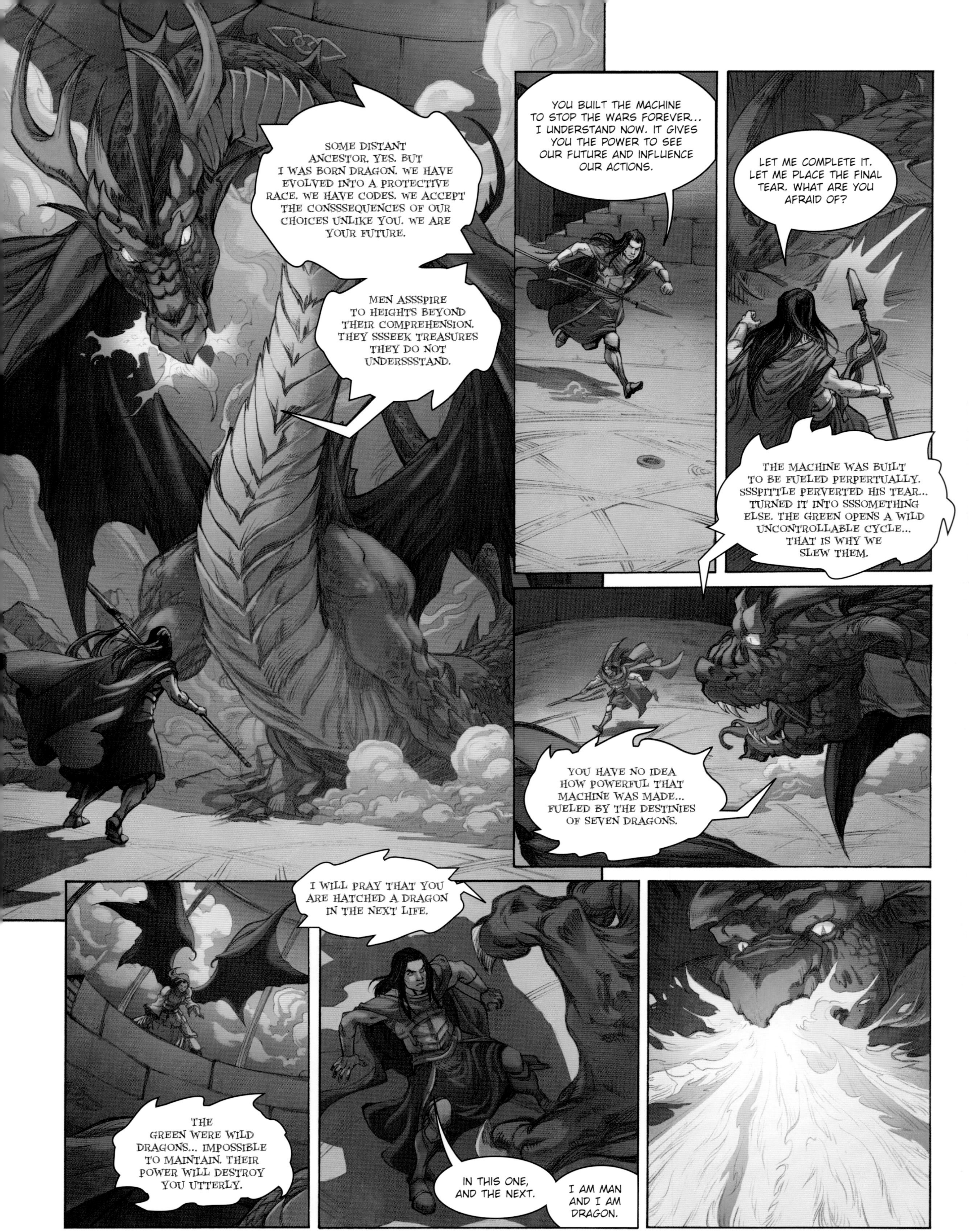

SOME DISTANT ANCESTOR, YES. BUT I WAS BORN DRAGON. WE HAVE EVOLVED INTO A PROTECTIVE RACE. WE HAVE CODES. WE ACCEPT THE CONSSSEQUENCES OF OUR CHOICES UNLIKE YOU. WE ARE YOUR FUTURE.
MEN ASSSPIRE TO HEIGHTS BEYOND THEIR COMPREHENSION. THEY SSSEEK TREASURES THEY DO NOT UNDERSSSTAND.
YOU BUILT THE MACHINE TO STOP THE WARS FOREVER... I UNDERSTAND NOW. IT GIVES YOU THE POWER TO SEE OUR FUTURE AND INFLUENCE OUR ACTIONS.
LET ME COMPLETE IT. LET ME PLACE THE FINAL TEAR. WHAT ARE YOU AFRAID OF?
THE MACHINE WAS BUILT TO BE FUELED PERPERTUALLY. SSSPITTLE PERVERTED HIS TEAR... TURNED IT INTO SSSOMETHING ELSE. THE GREEN OPENS A WILD UNCONTROLLABLE CYCLE... THAT IS WHY WE SLEW THEM.
YOU HAVE NO IDEA HOW POWERFUL THAT MACHINE WAS MADE... FUELED BY THE DESTINIES OF SEVEN DRAGONS.
THE GREEN WERE WILD DRAGONS... IMPOSSIBLE TO MAINTAIN. THEIR POWER WILL DESTROY YOU UTTERLY.
I WILL PRAY THAT YOU ARE HATCHED A DRAGON IN THE NEXT LIFE.
IN THIS ONE, AND THE NEXT.
I AM MAN AND I AM DRAGON.

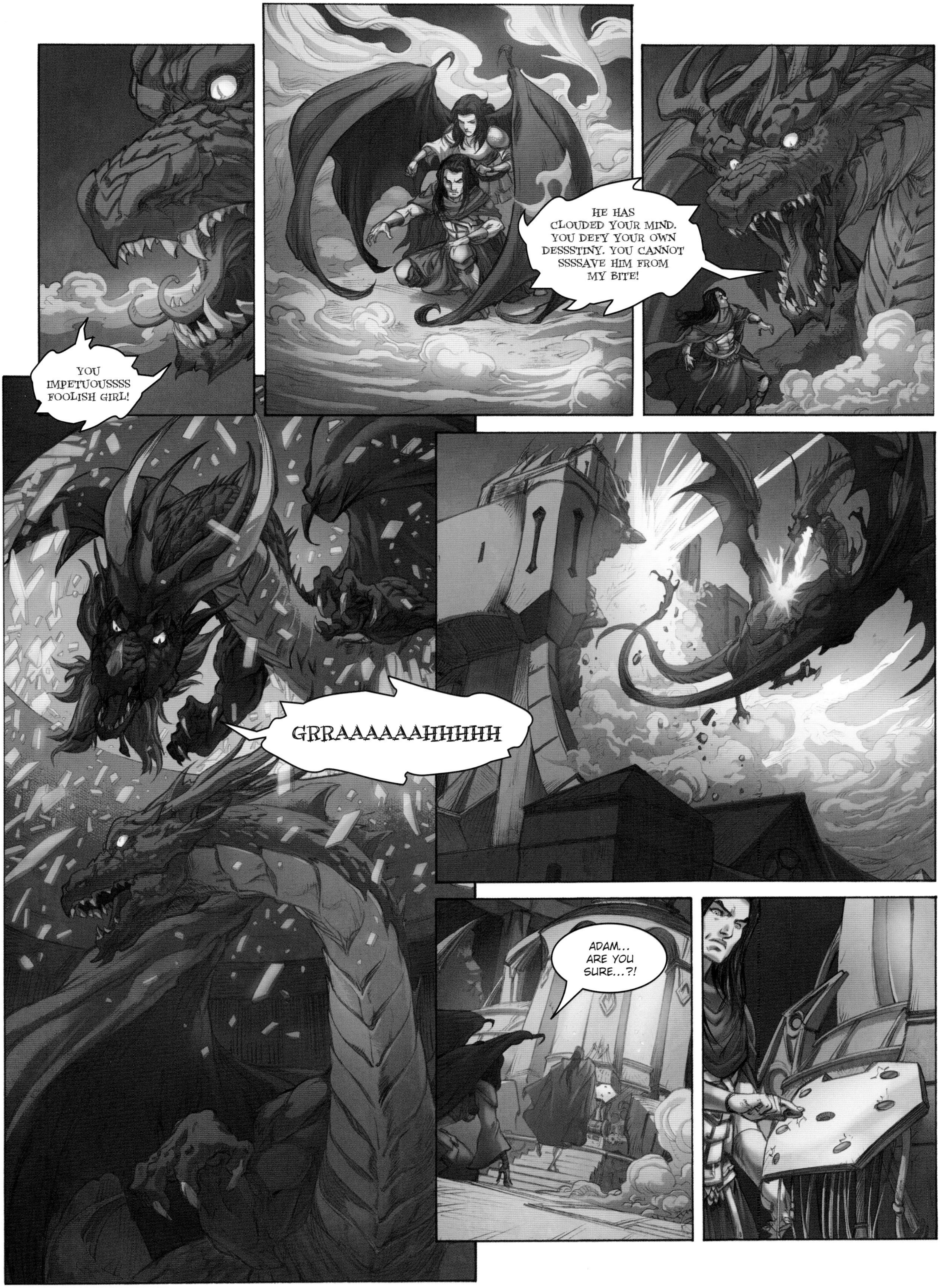
YOU IMPETUOUSSSS FOOLISH GIRL!
HE HAS CLOUDED YOUR MIND. YOU DEFY YOUR OWN DESSSTINY. YOU CANNOT SSSSAVE HIM FROM MY BITE!
GRRAAAAAAAHHHHH
ADAM... ARE YOU SURE...?!

THOSE WHO SAY THEY KNOW FOR CERTAIN WHAT HAPPENED THAT DAY ENTIRELY MISSED THE POINT.

EVEN I DON'T KNOW THE HALF OF IT... AND I SPARKED THE EXPLOSION.

NO ONE CAN KNOW EVERYTHING. THE WHOLE TRUTH IS HIDDEN IN LITTLE PIECES IN THE HEARTS OF EVERY MAN, ELF, AND DRAGON.

IN ONE BLINDING FLASH OF GREEN THE AGE OF CERTAINTY THE DRAGONS HAD CREATED WAS BLOWN AWAY.

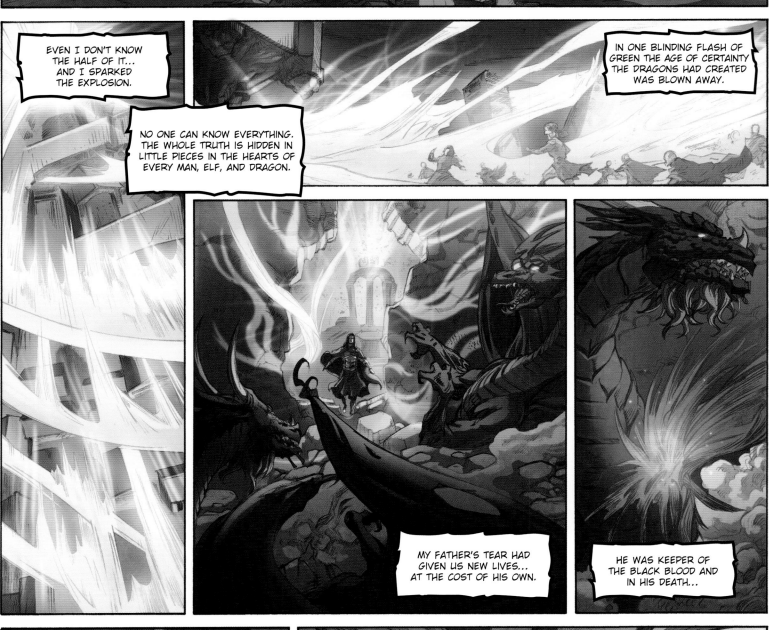

MY FATHER'S TEAR HAD GIVEN US NEW LIVES... AT THE COST OF HIS OWN.

HE WAS KEEPER OF THE BLACK BLOOD AND IN HIS DEATH...

...PASSED HIS POWER AND HIS SECRETS DOWN TO ME.

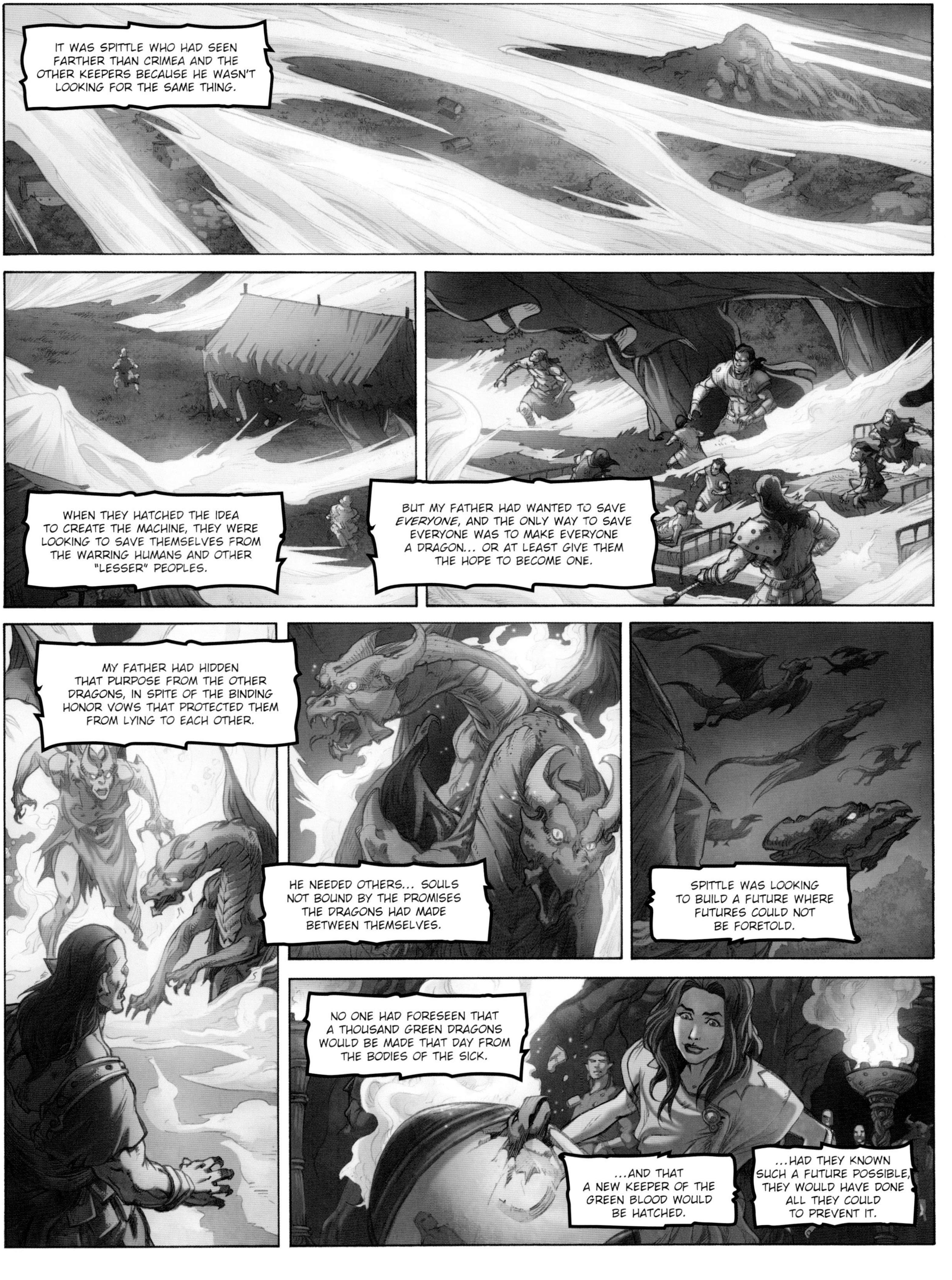
IT WAS SPITTLE WHO HAD SEEN FARTHER THAN CRIMEA AND THE OTHER KEEPERS BECAUSE HE WASN'T LOOKING FOR THE SAME THING.
WHEN THEY HATCHED THE IDEA TO CREATE THE MACHINE, THEY WERE LOOKING TO SAVE THEMSELVES FROM THE WARRING HUMANS AND OTHER "LESSER" PEOPLES.
BUT MY FATHER HAD WANTED TO SAVE *EVERYONE*, AND THE ONLY WAY TO SAVE EVERYONE WAS TO MAKE EVERYONE A DRAGON... OR AT LEAST GIVE THEM THE HOPE TO BECOME ONE.
MY FATHER HAD HIDDEN THAT PURPOSE FROM THE OTHER DRAGONS, IN SPITE OF THE BINDING HONOR VOWS THAT PROTECTED THEM FROM LYING TO EACH OTHER.
HE NEEDED OTHERS... SOULS NOT BOUND BY THE PROMISES THE DRAGONS HAD MADE BETWEEN THEMSELVES.
SPITTLE WAS LOOKING TO BUILD A FUTURE WHERE FUTURES COULD NOT BE FORETOLD.
NO ONE HAD FORESEEN THAT A THOUSAND GREEN DRAGONS WOULD BE MADE THAT DAY FROM THE BODIES OF THE SICK.
...AND THAT A NEW KEEPER OF THE GREEN BLOOD WOULD BE HATCHED.
...HAD THEY KNOWN SUCH A FUTURE POSSIBLE, THEY WOULD HAVE DONE ALL THEY COULD TO PREVENT IT.

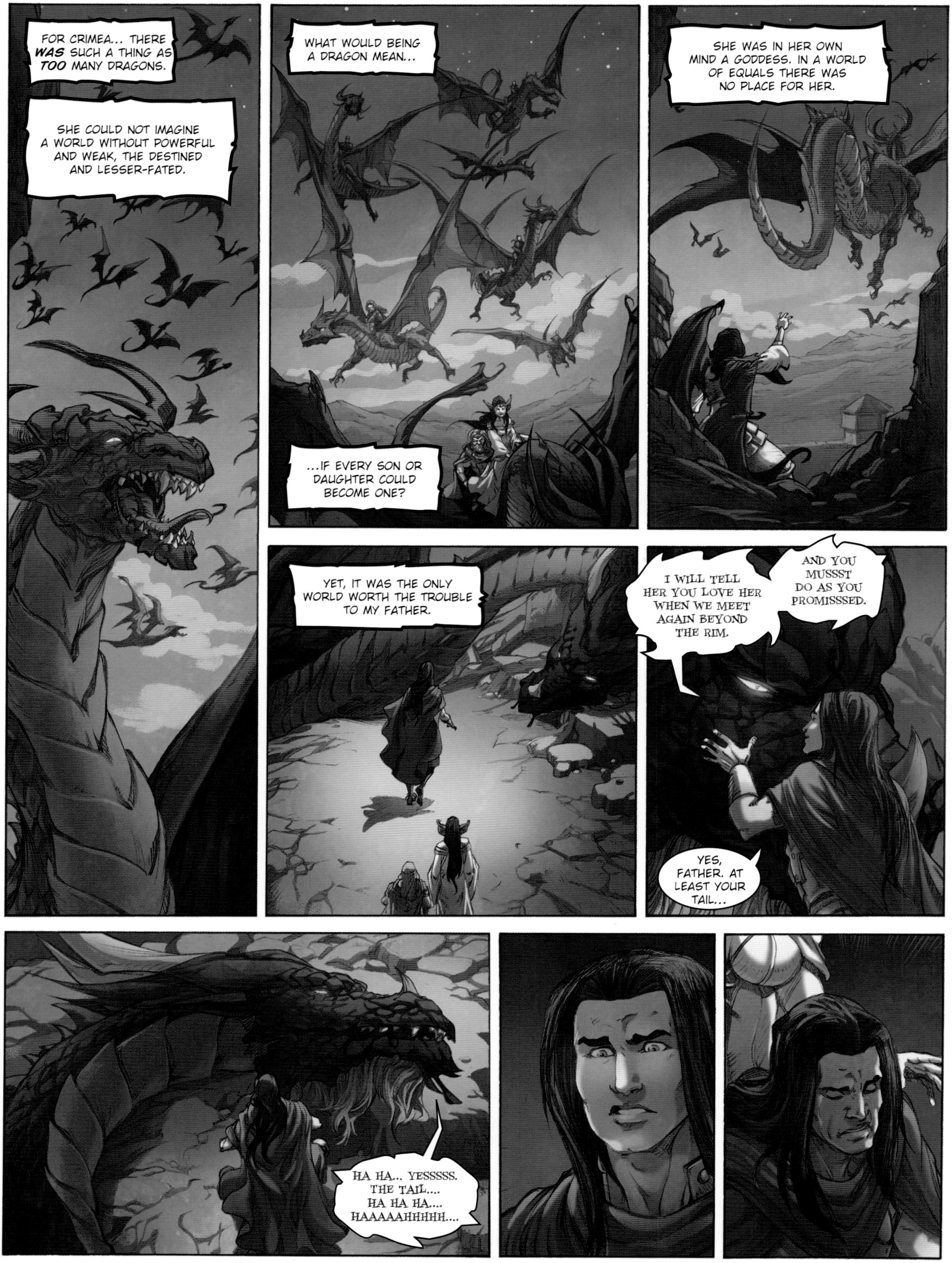
FOR CRIMEA... THERE WAS SUCH A THING AS TOO MANY DRAGONS.
SHE COULD NOT IMAGINE A WORLD WITHOUT POWERFUL AND WEAK, THE DESTINED AND LESSER-FATED.
WHAT WOULD BEING A DRAGON MEAN...
...IF EVERY SON OR DAUGHTER COULD BECOME ONE?
SHE WAS IN HER OWN MIND A GODDESS. IN A WORLD OF EQUALS THERE WAS NO PLACE FOR HER.
YET, IT WAS THE ONLY WORLD WORTH THE TROUBLE TO MY FATHER.
I WILL TELL HER YOU LOVE HER WHEN WE MEET AGAIN BEYOND THE RIM.
AND YOU MUSSST DO AS YOU PROMISSSED.
YES, FATHER. AT LEAST YOUR TAIL...
HA HA... YESSSSS. THE TAIL.... HA HA HA.... HAAAAAHHHHH....

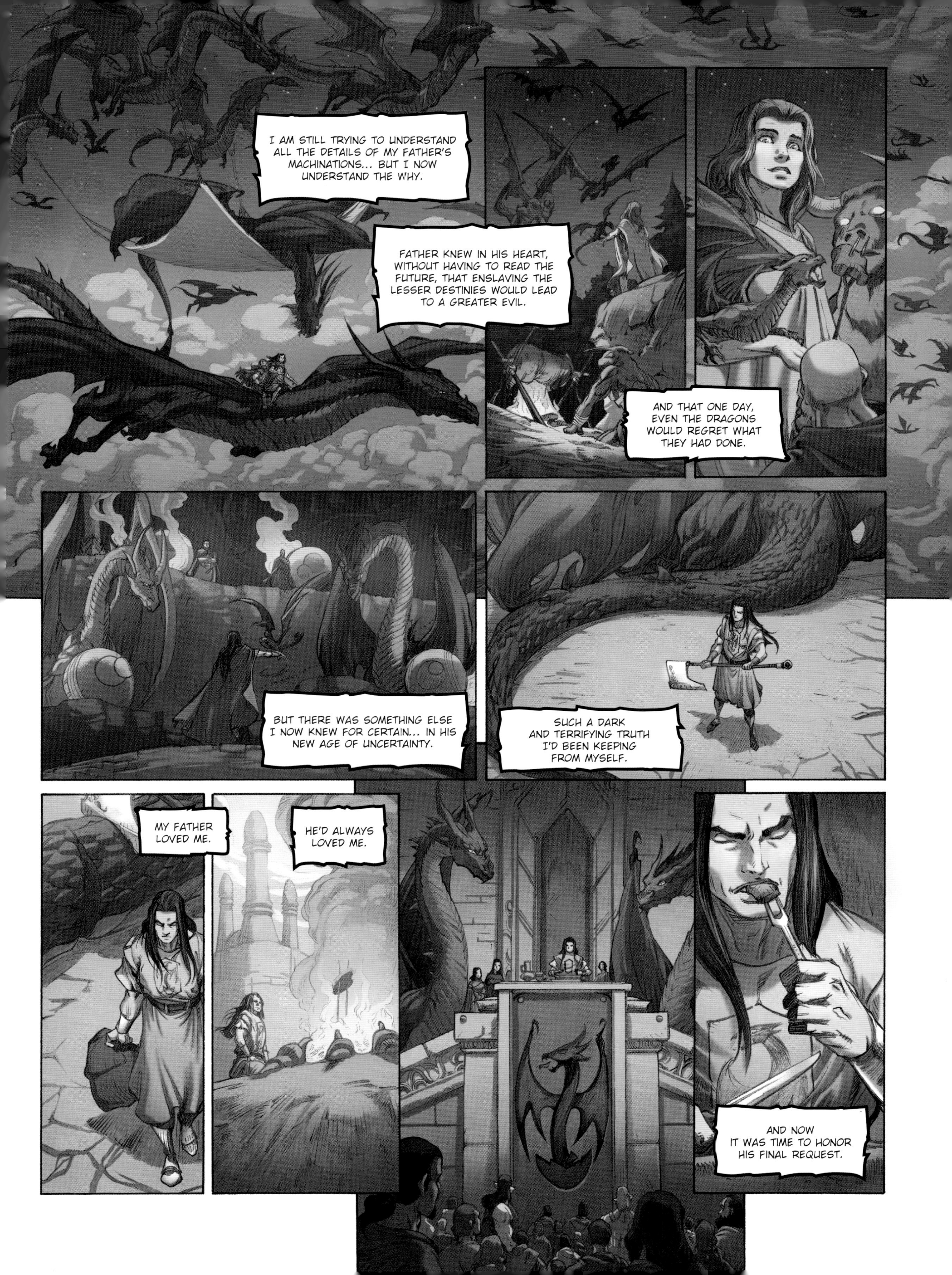
I AM STILL TRYING TO UNDERSTAND ALL THE DETAILS OF MY FATHER'S MACHINATIONS... BUT I NOW UNDERSTAND THE WHY.
FATHER KNEW IN HIS HEART, WITHOUT HAVING TO READ THE FUTURE, THAT ENSLAVING THE LESSER DESTINIES WOULD LEAD TO A GREATER EVIL.
AND THAT ONE DAY, EVEN THE DRAGONS WOULD REGRET WHAT THEY HAD DONE.
BUT THERE WAS SOMETHING ELSE I NOW KNEW FOR CERTAIN... IN HIS NEW AGE OF UNCERTAINTY.
SUCH A DARK AND TERRIFYING TRUTH I'D BEEN KEEPING FROM MYSELF.
MY FATHER LOVED ME.
HE'D ALWAYS LOVED ME.
AND NOW IT WAS TIME TO HONOR HIS FINAL REQUEST.

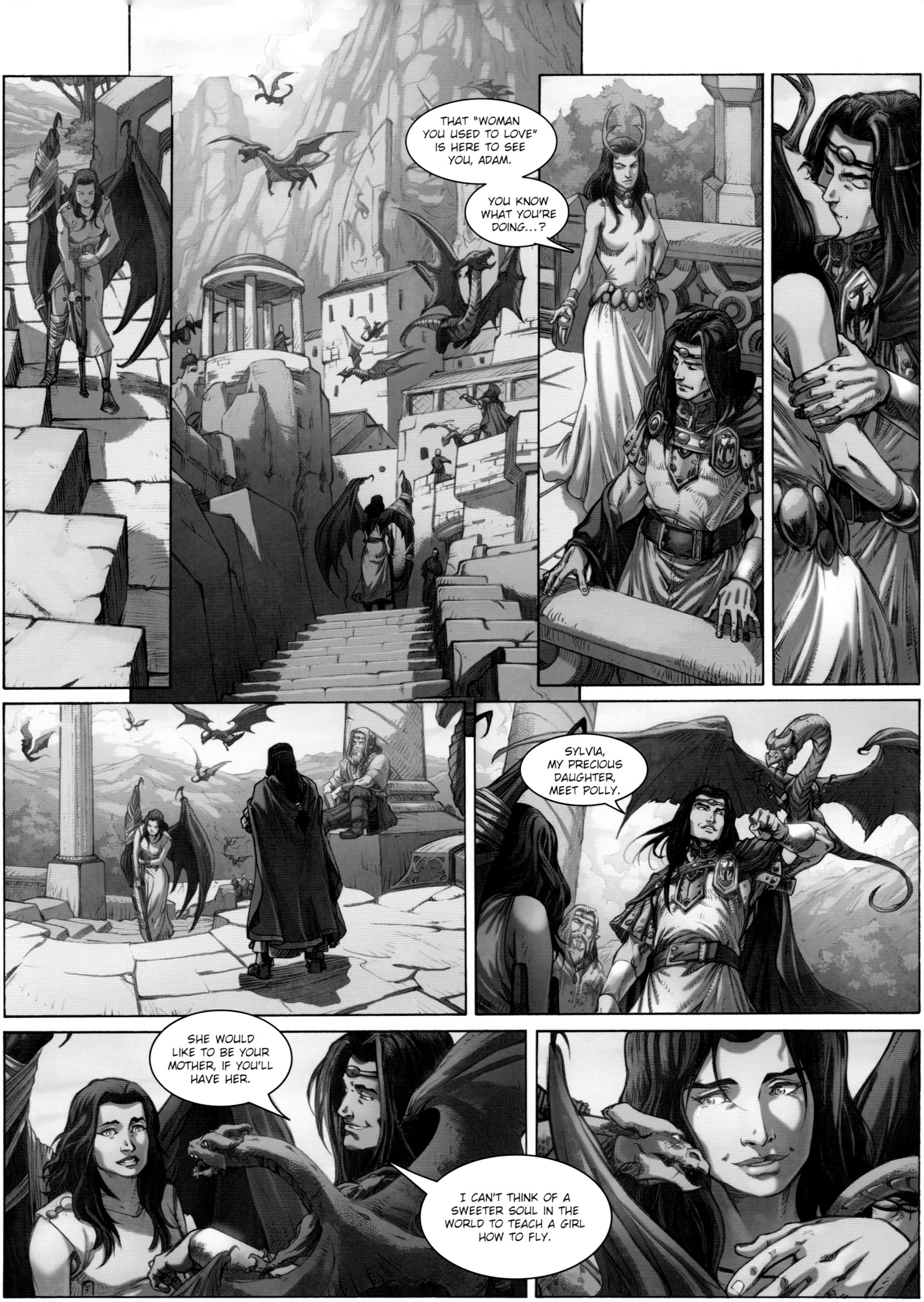
THAT "WOMAN YOU USED TO LOVE" IS HERE TO SEE YOU, ADAM.
YOU KNOW WHAT YOU'RE DOING...?
SYLVIA, MY PRECIOUS DAUGHTER, MEET POLLY.
SHE WOULD LIKE TO BE YOUR MOTHER, IF YOU'LL HAVE HER.
I CAN'T THINK OF A SWEETER SOUL IN THE WORLD TO TEACH A GIRL HOW TO FLY.

THE END.

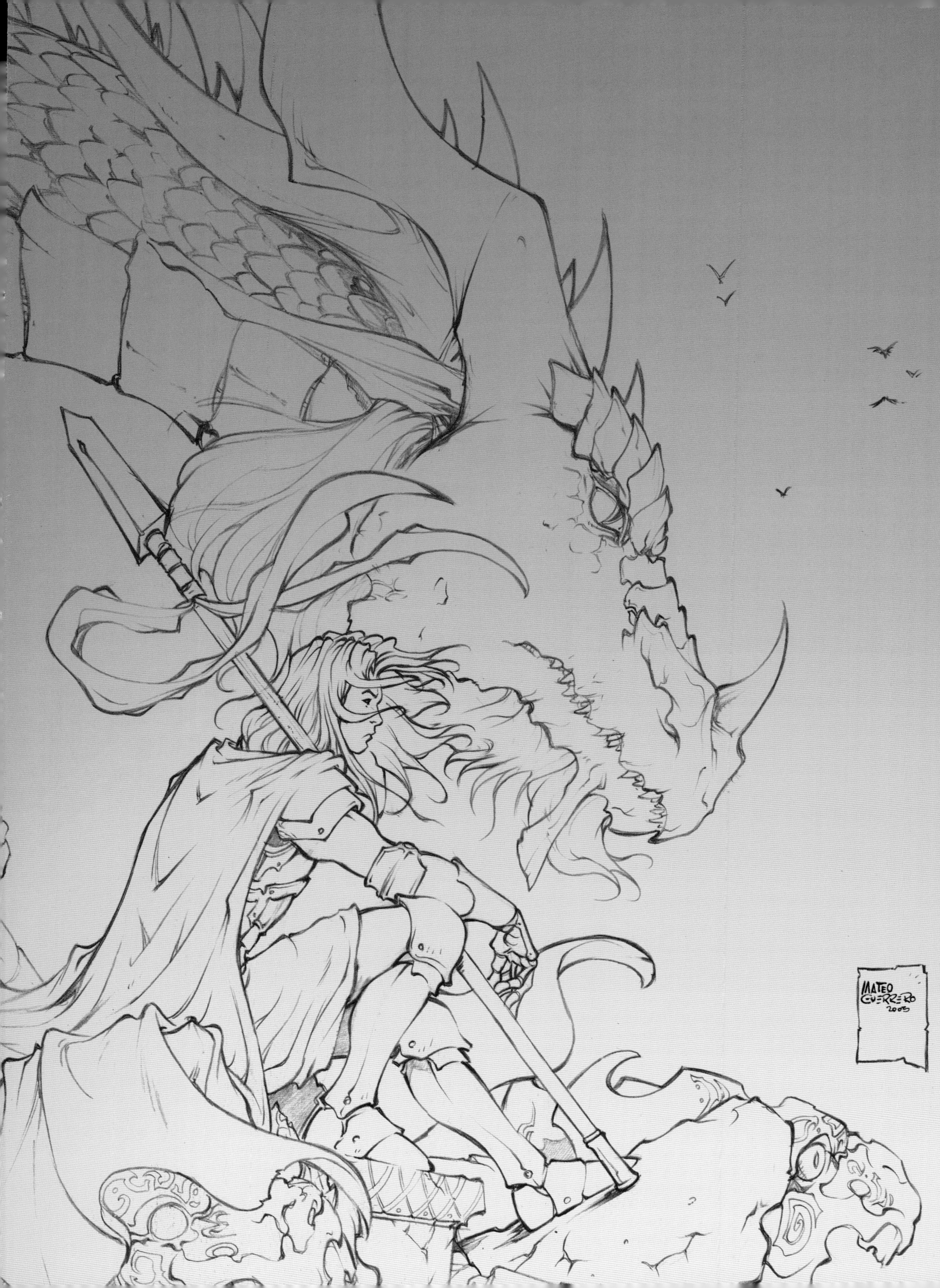
MATEO GUERRERO 2005

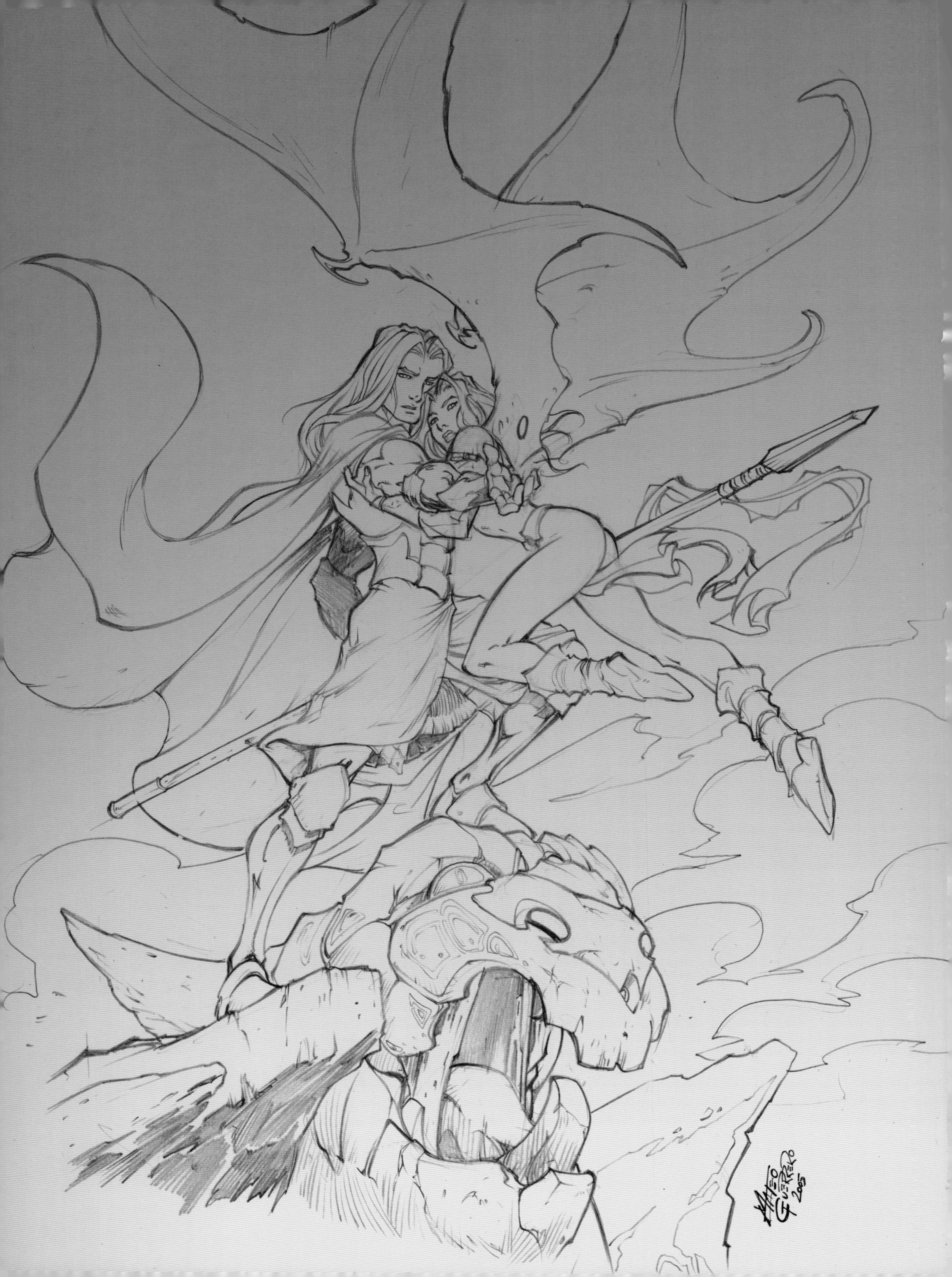

THE SEASONS OF KRATH

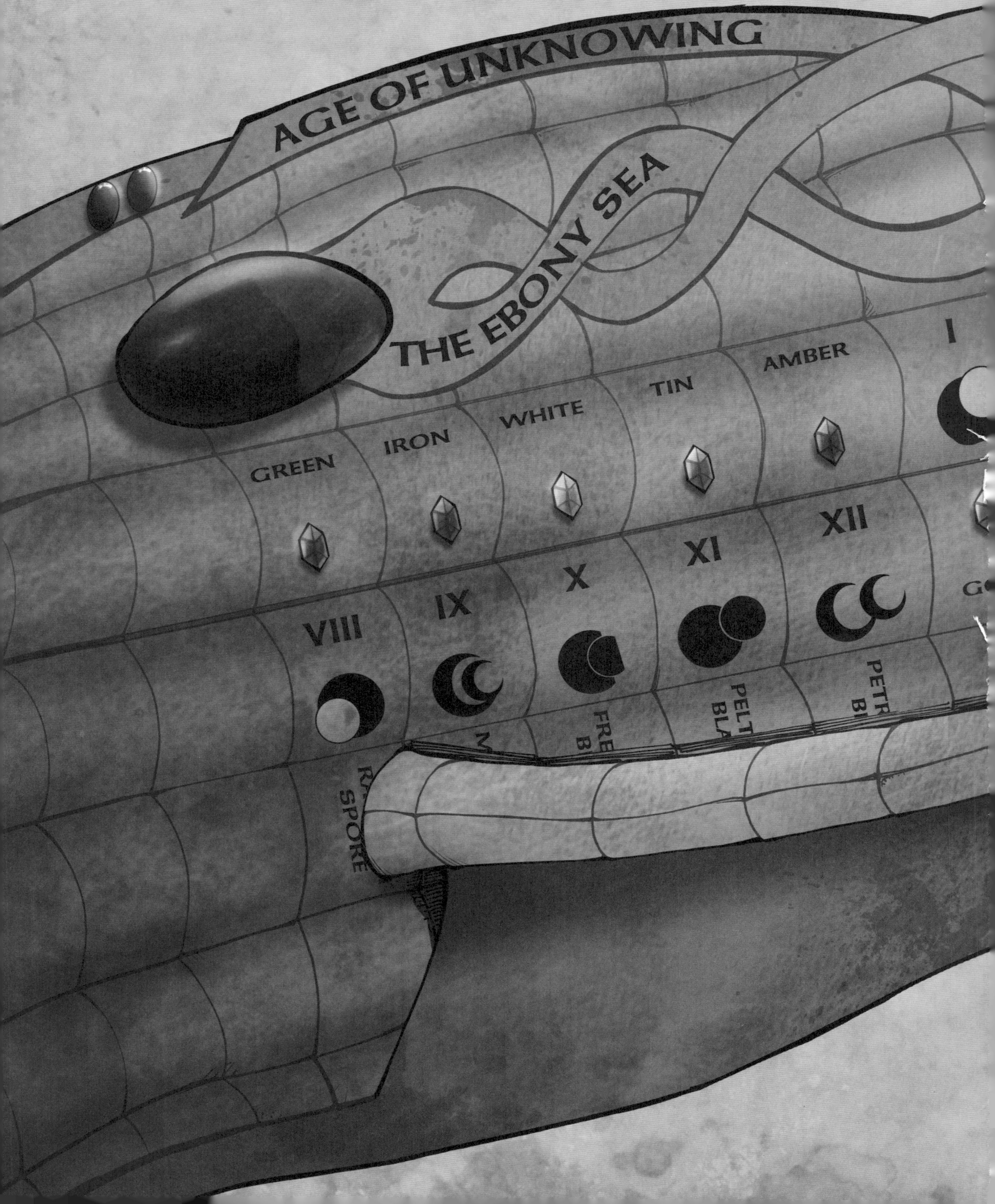
AGE OF UNKNOWING
THE EBONY SEA
GREEN
IRON
WHITE
TIN
AMBER
I
VIII
IX
X
XI
XII
SPORE